Truth According to Michael

Also by Stevan V. Nikolic
Weekend In Faro

TRUTH
According to Michael

A Novel

STEVAN V. NIKOLIC

Istina Group DBA
New York

TRUTH ACCORDING TO MICHAEL
A Novel
By Stevan V. Nikolic

Copyright © 2016 by Stevan V. Nikolic
www.svnikolic.com

Published by Istina Group DBA, New York
www.istinagroup.com

This is a work of fiction. Space and time have been rearranged to suit the convenience of the book, and with the exception of public figures, names of places and institutions, any resemblance to events, or persons living or dead is coincidental. The opinions expressed in this novel are those of the characters and should not be confused with the author's.

For information, please address Istina Group DBA
at istinadba@gmail.com

ISBN13: 978-0989696265
ISBN10: 098969626X

Printed in the United States of America

For Adelaide

Contents

"I was going after a woman believing that the key is in being with her. But the key is in writing about her. The key is in words and words are in me. Longing for her is just an impulse for words to come out. And the whole purpose is for words to come out. Words are important. Words about love. About life."

The Arrival

1

Michael arrived in New York around seven o'clock in the evening on Wednesday. He walked out of the International Arrivals at JFK. Waiting for him was cold, wet, and dark evening in early March. Rain was drizzling on the sidewalk in front of the airport terminal, filled with people pulling and carrying their luggage and walking in different directions.

Michael stopped under the glass canopy in front of the building entrance and lit a cigarette. He hadn't smoked for over twelve hours on the plane from Bucharest to Paris and from Paris to New York, and he needed a smoke.

He didn't want to admit to himself, but he was nervous. When he left New York three years ago, he was fifty years old, still married, had an apartment in Brooklyn, a functioning business, and lots of friends. And now upon his return, he was divorced and didn't have a place to stay. His ex-wife, already grown-up daughters, and many friends didn't want to talk to him. He had no source of income and only two hundred and thirty dollars in his pocket.

But, he was glad to be back. He made unsolvable and dangerous mess in Bucharest. And the only way out was to run away back to New York. 'I need to put myself back in order and try to fix problems from here,' Michael thought.

He still didn't know what he would do or how he would go ahead, but he had three days to find a solution. A room in the YMCA Hostel in Flushing, Queens was sixty dollars per night. He had enough for three nights, and that is where he planned to stay until he figured out his next move. If he didn't come up with anything, he would find himself out on the street. He didn't want that.

But at that moment, he was just tired and wanted to find the fastest and cheapest way to get to Flushing. He took the Air train to Jamaica Station, and from there he took a bus to Flushing. It was a long ride, and he arrived in Flushing a bit before nine. He walked two blocks from the bus station to the YMCA and checked into the Hostel.

Small, but warm room had a twin size bed, a table, dresser with a mirror and TV. The bathroom was outside at the end of the hallway. Michael unpacked his backpack. He had only two shirts, one sweater, two pairs of underwear, two pairs of socks, and his laptop in there. Besides the clothing he was wearing – a black suit, black dress shirt, black shoes, socks, underwear, leather spring jacket and silk scarf, those were all the belongings he had.

He walked out to buy food and toiletries at the pharmacy on Main Street. The rain was still drizzling, but it didn't bother him. He looked at the people walking around.

They were Korean. Flushing was a Korean neighborhood with lots of ethnic stores and restaurants. Michael knew this area well. He lived there for two years with his wife and kids. It was before they moved to Brooklyn.

Walking down the street brought memories back to him. He looked at the familiar storefronts, buildings, the bakery on the corner of Main Street and Roosevelt Avenue. He passed by the building where they used to live and could almost hear the voices of his daughters from the past talking to him. Melancholy took over him for a moment, but it was the past that couldn't come back. He should snap out of it and focus on his present situation. Three days will pass fast and he had to find a way of surviving in New York.

He stopped by the subway station and bought a weekly train pass. He would have to move around a lot in those days and that was the best way of transportation in the city.

In the pharmacy, he bought a toothbrush, toothpaste, soap, deodorant, shaving cream and razor, and a large bag of potato chips. He was left with fifteen dollars after these purchases, so he decided to buy a small bottle of wine for five dollars to celebrate his return to New York. The rest he would keep for food for the following days. He had two packs of cigarettes already, so he was set. As long as he manages to find a solution in next couple of days.

Back in the hostel room, he took off his shoes, turned on the TV and sat on the bed. There was no cable, only basic channels, so he turned on the local ten-o'clock news. It had been a long time since he had watched NY local news, but he really couldn't concentrate on the news. The sound of the TV was just an audio reminder of the fact of where he was. Like background noise.

He was back in New York with no money and nobody to turn to for help. In his mind, it was still better than remaining back in Bucharest. Back there it was just a matter of time until he ended up in the jail or dead. He was too deep in trouble, and the only solution was to run away. But now he had to act fast if he didn't want to find himself on the street. He had to find a place to stay and a source of income.

Michael opened the wine bottle. He was lucky that it was a screw top. If it had been a cork he would have had a hard time opening it. He poured wine into the small plastic cup that he had found on the desk in the room. He looked into his image in the mirror on the dresser across the bed, raised the cup up, and said to himself:

"Salute Michael. Welcome back to New York."

He wasn't happy with what he was seeing in the mirror. His hair and beard were grayer than before. He was seeing wrinkles on his face that were not there just a year ago. He looked older and troubled. The once constant glitter in his brown eyes that was almost his trademark for many years, was now completely gone. He was a tired and defeated man. In the past few months he lost quite a bit of weight, and for a normally six-foot-tall slim man, he now looked like a shadow of himself.

Michael took a small black Moleskine notebook from his backpack and started looking through it. In there were written his contacts for the last few years – all his former friends, business associates, and relatives. He went slowly from one name to another down the list. To most of the people on the list he owed something, a favor or money, so he couldn't call them to ask for anything. The rest were still close friends of his ex-wife and those he couldn't call either.

He was thinking about his past and the many people he met while living in New York. He never knew how to maintain and nourish friendships. Most of his friends he would call only when he needed something, and then he would not call them again until the next time he needed a favor. People were noticing that and often commented to him about his bad habit. He knew the importance of always keeping doors open behind him in any type of relationship. Somehow, he always managed to shut the doors and lose any opportunity to renew or come back to a given association or friendship. So, after twenty years of life in New York, the list of people that he could potentially turn to for help was very short.

He selected a couple of names of people with whom he might have chance and copied their phone numbers on a piece of paper. 'I will call them tomorrow,' he thought. Michael was tired but he couldn't sleep. After he finished the bottle of wine, sleep finally took over him.

He was awakened by the noise of the garbage truck early in the morning. He went to the bathroom and took a long shower. He got dressed, put his laptop in the backpack, and walked out onto the street. It was a wet and cloudy Thursday morning, cold, with no sun. Michael stopped by McDonald's and bought coffee to drink on the train.

He decided to go to the Barnes and Noble bookstore on Union Square. They had free Wi-Fi there and he needed to check his mail and look on Craigslist for potential employment opportunities. He didn't know if he would find anything. The last time he worked for somebody else, was fifteen years ago. Since then he was always self-employed. And he wasn't a young man anymore. For most of the positions that he could potentially apply for he would be either overqualified or too old.

It was around eight when Michael arrived to Union Square. It was then when he realized that Barnes and Noble opened at ten and that he would have to walk around till then. He could go to Starbucks, but that would mean spending an extra two dollars for the coffee. So he decided to walk.

He walked uptown Broadway to 23rd street, then crossed to Park Avenue, and back to Union square. In two hours he had made several circles already. He was looking at busy people passing by him. They were all going somewhere. Rushing to get to work or to school, or back home from work. It seemed to him that he was the only one walking aimlessly, slowly, waiting for time to pass. He felt like everybody passing by him knew that.

Up until three years ago, he was one of those busy people rushing around New York with a purpose. 'Now everything changed,' he thought. He was a homeless man with a few bucks in his pocket and with no visible perspective. Only God knew how he would get out of this position.

He stopped in front of Barnes and Noble ten minutes before ten. Several people were there waiting for the doors to open. Most of them were early customers who wanted to buy a book or a magazine or just have a cup of coffee in the cozy bookstore café.   Others were homeless people, unshaven and smelly. They wanted to use the facilities or hide in the corner trying to rest and warm up while pretending they were looking for a book.

Michael knew that the only thing making him different than these homeless men were two more paid nights in the YMCA Hostel and a few dollars in his pocket.

Michael entered the store and went to the third-floor café. He was one of the first people arriving, so he was able to pick a table next to the window overlooking Union Square. It was a good spot to spend the next few hours. He could organize himself, make some kind of plan, do research online, and figure out his options.

Just brewed dark roast coffee smelled inviting. He bought a small coffee and a glazed donut. This would be his only food for the whole day, he thought. He couldn't afford more if he was to eat something the next two days.

He logged into Craigslist but couldn't find any jobs there that looked promising. But that wasn't the only problem. Being self-employed for so many years didn't give him many employment references. Even if he did find a position to apply for, he didn't know who he would put as a reference.

Michael looked at his Google email account. There were several unpleasant emails from his, now former, business associates in Bucharest. By now, they realized that something went wrong and that he disappeared. He was sure that they were in the panic and looking for him in his apartment and office. If nothing else, he was at least saved from their wrath. He knew that he was in a tight corner when they brought that nasty looking loan-shark to his Bucharest apartment two days ago.

"Michael, everything you owed us, you now owe to him, and he wants it back in forty-eight hours," they told him. One look at this man was enough for Michael to realize that the line was crossed. If he didn't want to end up in the gutter on the outskirts of Bucharest, he had to run.

It wasn't an easy decision to make. Three years ago, when he left New York and went to Bucharest, he intended to stay there and never return. He had a small apartment in downtown Bucharest, a cat, a twenty-four-year-old girl-friend, and friends he liked to hang out with in neighborhood café bars. If not for the disastrous book publishing business he started there, the source of all his troubles, life in Bucharest would have been pleasant.

And now he was sitting in the Barnes and Noble café trying to figure out what to do next. He looked one more time through his Moleskine notebook, but besides two names he picked last night he couldn't call anybody else.

One of them was Jack Rothstein. He was a banker, working in the New York office of the Deutsche Bank on Park Avenue. Michael knew him and his partner, Mark, from the Grolier Club, where Michael was a member for many years. Michael thought they both still liked him. He used to borrow small sums of money from Jack, but he would always return it, so he thought, if nothing else, he was in good standing with them. Also, he showed no any prejudice towards two gay people living together, as many other members of the club had. Michael always thought that both of them respected that.

The other one was David Elliot. He was a marketing executive living in Greenwich, Connecticut. Michael knew him from the Masonic Lodge. For almost twenty years they were both members of the Lafayette Lodge No. 30 in the Grand Lodge of New York. Michael left Freemasonry in 2008, but he thought that David still liked him and that he would help. Years back, David lost a lot of money in the stock market, and Michael was one of many friends who helped him get back on his feet and restart his business. He hoped that David remembered that.

Michael wrote an email to Jack explaining his situation instead of calling him. He wasn't sure if Jack's old number still worked.

In the email he was telling Jack that he had been in Romania for three years, where he lost all of his money in a failed business venture; came back to New York; and was looking for a place to stay for a while; a job; and maybe a small loan to put himself back together. Michael didn't want to go too much into details. He wasn't sure if Jack and Mark were still in touch with his ex-wife, and she was the last person in the world he would want to share his troubles with now.

As he was sending email, he was thinking how sad his

situation was. In his Gmail contact list, he had over seven thousand addresses of family members, friends, business associates, acquaintances, and many others, that he had come across or gotten to know over many years of living in New York. And now, out of all these people, he could only ask two for help. He was asking himself what kind of person was he that went through life like the elephant through the china shop, leaving just damage behind. How was it possible he could maintain none of his relationships with the people around him?

Michael walked out of Barnes and Noble around one o'clock in the afternoon. He lit up a cigarette while looking for a phone booth to call David.

"Hello David," he said. "This is Michael. How are you?"

"Michael! Hi, my friend. What a surprise! I haven't heard from you in a long time. How are you doing?"

"Not well…That's why I'm calling."

"Why? What happened?"

"I'm back in New York and not in good shape. I'm not sure how much you know about my ventures?"

"Last I heard was that you got divorced."

"I spent the last three years in Romania, trying to do a publishing business there, and lost all my money in those investments. Now back in New York, I am looking for a job and for a place to stay. Also, I'm out of money and would ask you for a small loan of a few hundred dollars. Just to help me until I put myself back together. I'm in bad shape, my friend, and there are not too many people I can turn to for a help."

"I'm sorry to hear this Michael. Wish I could help you. But lately, things are not good for me. Business is slow; my wife hasn't been working for a year; and I myself keep borrowing money, left and right to pay my bills. It is difficult. My monthly expenses are high. So, tough luck for money. But a friend of mine is opening a new marketing company, and he may need writers. I can give you his phone number. You can call him and mention my name. This is as much as I can do. Sorry, bro."

"David, I'm embarrassed to say this, but anything would help." Michael kept insisting, "I'm down to my last ten bucks and have two more nights in the YMCA paid. If I don't do something, I'll be on the street next. I need immediate help, if you know what I mean."

"Sorry Michael, but I can't do anything. I could ask some of the other Brothers from our Lodge, but you didn't leave on good terms. I will ask anyway. Did you talk to your ex-wife?

"No, David, don't spread this. I don't want others to know about my situation. Not my ex-wife. Can you give me your friend's number, please?"

David gave him a phone number, and said, "I am sorry Michael. I have to take another call now. Good luck to you." He hung up.

Michael spent the rest of the afternoon walking around. He went all the way up Park Avenue to 96th street, then across to Central Park, through it to the West side, and down Broadway back to Union Square. He wasn't tired, but his backpack felt heavier after a while. Its weight made him feel uncomfortable.

In the evening he went to McDonald's to take a break and check his email. He ordered coffee. It was 99 cents, half price of the coffee at Barnes and Noble. Barnes and Noble's café was a much cozier and comfortable place, but McDonald's had Wi-Fi, too.

There was no answer from Jack. This wasn't good. Michael knew Jack well enough to know that he was very diligent when with correspondence. He never left his mail unanswered, regardless of how frivolous or unimportant they were. Was it possible that Jack would ignore him and his plea for help? Not even answer it with a yes or no; just ignore it?

When Michael walked out of McDonald's, it was already nine in the evening. It was chilly for March but still pleasant. Union Square was all lit up by the lights from the surrounding stores. People were walking in all directions across Union Square. There were so many beautiful young women passing by. Michael could not help but notice them. He was standing in the middle of the plateau on the square, smoking a cigarette, and watching girls walking by.

A thought came to his mind about times when he was the one walking across Union Square to the clubs and restaurants. He was wondering if days like that will ever return.

Michael returned to Flushing to his hostel room. The first day back in New York wasn't very successful. He felt like he wanted to drink something, to forget the situation he was in, but he didn't have enough money. If he bought wine again, he would be left with no money, and he couldn't do that.

He was looking at the TV screen without watching the program. Michael wanted to find a solution, but couldn't think of anything. Yes, so far it worked out. He was able to escape from Bucharest, but what now? Nothing was coming to his mind. It was making him nervous. What if, he doesn't figure out anything? What would he do next?

He couldn't sit in the room. Needed a smoke. So he walked around Flushing trying to come up with an idea.

His Romanian prepaid mobile phone rang. He had money on it, so it was still working. It was his girlfriend from Bucharest calling. He answered.

"Hi, Eliza, my love, how are you?"

"Hi, baby. I'm not good, Michael. Miss you…Miss you a lot. You didn't call. Made me worried. I couldn't sleep. Are you already in New York?"

"Yes, I'm in New York. I wasn't sure how much money I had on my phone. That is why I didn't call. I would write you a long email tonight."

"Mickey, Baby, here is a real chaos. A panic. Everybody is looking for you. When I came back from work last night, Volodya was in front of my building with two other scary looking men sitting in a car and waiting. They put me in the back seat and they drove to your place. They were parked there for two hours waiting for you. He was asking about your whereabouts and threatening me. I told him you went to New York and that you are coming back in a week, but he didn't believe me. He said you would travel nowhere without me. The man sitting next to me in the back smacked me in the face with his fist and told me that if I didn't tell them where you were that they would rape me and then slash me with a knife. It was only when I cried that Volodya opened the side door and they kicked me out. I still have a black eye and my cheek is swollen. I am afraid, Michael. My father was furious when he saw me and I couldn't tell him the truth about what happened and why. These men are dangerous, Michael. I am afraid that they will show up again."

"Please, don't worry Eliza. I will call Volodya and talk to him. They will not show up anymore. And have patience, my love. As soon as I settle here, I will send you a ticket to come and be with me. It will be before the end of the month. I promise you that. I love you so much and I miss you too baby."

"Oh, Michael, I need you next to me. I am used to sleeping in your bed with you. Please, rush with whatever you have to do. I want to be next to you; need your arms around me; love you, Michael."

"Love you, too, Eliza. Everything will be ok. You will see. Don't worry. I have to stop now. I think that I am running out of money. Good night my love and sleep well. Kisses."

"Love you. Kisses, Mickey."

Michael pressed the stop button on his phone. Upset that Volodya got to Eliza, he felt guilty for what had happened. His hands were shaking. He wanted to scream. But all he did was light up another cigarette. Michael felt helpless. He loved Eliza, yet he left her there, knowing full well that Volodya would try to get to him through her. It was not like he had a choice. He had no money. Even the money that helped him to run away to New York, he took from Volodya under false pretenses. That made Volodya even angrier realizing that his money enabled Michael to disappear. He must have felt stupid. And the story about settling in New York and sending her an airplane ticket soon was a lie. There was no way he could settle down by the end of the month and have enough money to get her a ticket. It could only happen by some miracle or if he robbed a bank – and didn't get caught.

It wasn't like Michael was lying on purpose like he wanted to deceive her. He wanted to bring Eliza to New York. But he never told her that there was nothing waiting for him in New York anymore. That he would have to start from the beginning, just as he did twenty-five years ago, when he first came to New York. Even worse. Then he had a place to stay, and he had a job right away. Now he had neither.

He was lying about calling Volodya too. He knew it would not be good. By calling him and asking him to leave Eliza alone, it would just show he cared about her, and they would go after her even more. The only chance was to ignore Volodya. They would calm down after a while, he knew that.

On the N Train

2

The following two days went fast. It was the same daily routine for Michael as the first day. Coffee at Barnes and Noble, long walks around Manhattan, another coffee in the evening, searching Craigslist, calling and writing to people he would never call, asking for help. But it was all in vain. In the next two days – besides coffees –Michael only had one egg on a roll from the corner deli and one cheese-burger at McDonald's.

On the third evening, he was sitting in the McDonald's at St. Marks Place thinking of what to do. Where was he going to spend the night? And what would happen the next day?

He walked out of the restaurant and walked down Third Avenue. It was a cold evening. He remembered March nights in New York being much warmer. But that night it was in the low thirties and windy. Almost a real winter day in New York, just without snow.

He wasn't sure where was he going. At this point it didn't

make a difference. Michael knew that he would end up sleeping on the subway, but didn't want to go there too early. He was already thinking that the N line would be good to spend the night. It was about an hour and a half ride from Astoria in Queens to Coney Island in Brooklyn. Four rides from one end to another would take him through the night. If nothing changed the next day, he could spend the next night on the F line.

But even that could not help him for long. He had no money in his pocket for food and his weekly subway card would be valid for just two more days. He had to find the solution.

Third Avenue merged into Bowery Street. Michael kept walking. Bowery Street changed since the last time he was there. It used to be a row of restaurant supply stores with a few homeless shelters. Most of the stores closed down, replaced by bars and restaurants and fancy residential condo buildings.

Michael passed by the Bowery Mission. It was one of the oldest homeless shelters in New York City still sitting in the same location for over a hundred years. In front of the building, there was a long line of homeless people waiting to enter a soup kitchen for a free dinner. He was hungry, but he didn't want to get in line.

Maybe he was homeless, but he still didn't want to admit that to himself. Nor to others. He kept walking.

Around midnight he walked back to Union Square, entered the subway and got on the N train towards Astoria. The train was still crowded with people going home from the city. Everybody on the train looked happy to Michael.

'They didn't know how fortunate they were,' Michael thought. Everybody had a destination. Everybody but Michael.

Around one thirty in the morning, the train cleared out. There were only a few late riders and several homeless people dozing off on the corner seats. Michael was sitting in the middle of the train car next to the door. He knew that if he took a seat in the corner, it would be warmer and safer, but he didn't want to appear like a homeless man. And the cold air that came from outside into the train car, once the train doors opened at the station, was keeping him awake. He kept his backpack on his chest with his arms crossed over it.

Michael didn't want to sleep, but he knew he had to rest. He was trying to keep his eyes open whenever the train was entering into a station and he would open his eyes at the smallest sound. The light napping is what he was trying to do. But once in a while upon opening his eyes, he would notice that more than one station had passed, which meant that he had fallen asleep and hadn't noticed.

He couldn't wait for morning to come to get out of the subway. With the first light, around six thirty, he walked out onto the Lexington Avenue and 59th Street station.

The fresh morning air on his face felt good. This was the first morning he didn't shave, take a shower or change his clothing. He felt dirty. He wanted to find a place to at least wash his face and brush his teeth. But it was too early for something like that. Several McDonald's that were already open were still not crowded and everybody there would notice if he went to the restroom. He didn't want to feel embarrassed.

Michael walked down Lexington Avenue, then he switched to Park Avenue, and after a while found himself again on Union Square. He needed to go to a restroom, so he entered a Starbucks that was getting busy. There was nobody in the restroom, so after using the toilet, Michael washed his face and brushed his teeth.

He spent the next few hours walking up and down Manhattan avenues without any destination. By noon he already felt tired, so he went to Barnes and Noble to get rest. On the top floor of the Barnes and Noble store on Union Square was a sitting area used for book promotion events in the evening hours. During the day, customers were sitting there reading books and magazines. Quite a few of them were homeless people resting and spending their time in the warm and safe environment.

Michael took the escalator up to the fifth floor. He walked down the history aisle, looking at the books. But all he was thinking was that he needed to sit down. He picked a book on Knights Templars from the shelf and walked to the sitting area. There were not too many people sitting there. Michael took a corner chair, far from the others.

He took out his laptop to check mail. There was only one mail from Eliza. "I love you and I miss you a lot. I can't wait to be with you again. It is so strange and so empty without you, my love. I hope you are taking care of your business in New York and that I'll see you soon. Be careful and don't forget to eat! When I come, you will need a lot of strength, because I won't let you out of bed for a week. And call me or write me! I know that you must be busy now, but

I want to hear from you. Much love and many kisses!!!"

Michael looked at Eliza's mail with a sad expression in his eyes. If she only knew what was happening to him. If she only knew the depth of the misery, he put himself in. He didn't have the heart to tell Eliza the whole truth about the trouble he was in. She knew about his debt to Volodya and she knew that getting involved with loan sharks in post-communist Romania was a dangerous thing. But he never told her he lost everything in New York and there is nothing and nobody to return to.

Michael was hoping that once in New York, he could get to some money and send for Eliza. Years before, when he was an established and respected entrepreneur with many business associates and friends, it was easy for him to get any amount of money needed. He was proud of his ability to convince people to lend him money. So he believed that he would still be able to do so. But he didn't realize that times like that passed away. He was absent from New York for three years and his divorce and the disarray in which he left his business, earned him a bad reputation with people who knew him then. For them, he wasn't the same Michael they knew.

Michael didn't know how to answer Eliza. He didn't want to lie to her anymore, but he couldn't tell her he was a homeless man sleeping on the subway. No, he couldn't.

He closed his laptop and then a thought came to him. Maybe he could sell his laptop in the pawnshop and get money for food if nothing else. Michael remembered passing by the pawn shop on 14th Street and Seventh Avenue." I will go there," he thought.

But he needed to rest first. His legs and back were hurting.

That afternoon Michael sold his Toshiba laptop to the pawn shop for eighty dollars. He bought another weekly subway pass and went to McDonald's to eat.

He was relieved because he had money in his pocket and his backpack was lighter without the laptop. But he worried too. That laptop was his last link to the world. Nobody could reach him now, nor could he reach anybody. He could not look for a job online. He could do nothing.

The next eight days Michael spent sleeping in the subway cars on the N, F, and Q lines at night and walking up and down Manhattan during the day. He limited his daily expenditure to six dollars: coffee in the morning and evening, two 99 cents cheeseburgers at McDonald's, buttered bagel from the deli and two loose cigarettes. Finding a place to wash and use the toilet was the biggest problem. But he found Starbucks on Astor Place and Barnes and Noble on Union Square to be very tolerant towards homeless people using their facilities, so he followed the examples of other homeless guys browsing through that part of Manhattan.

Michael didn't think anymore about finding a job or about calling anybody to ask for help. All he was thinking about was surviving. He knew that his subway card would expire and that he would run out of money again, but all that mattered to him was getting through the day. It was only about s urviving till the next day. However, without a change of clothing for almost ten days, everybody who could see him realized that he was homeless. He could not pretend anymore to be a late night subway rider or a customer browsing through books in a bookstore.

Eight days passed. His metro card stopped working, and he spent his last dollar on a cup of coffee. He knew that if he tried to sleep on the bench in the park, he would be arrested. The only solution was to go to some shelter. He remembered the Bowery Mission he had passed by a few times in the last several days. 'Maybe I could go there,' he thought.

It was March 14th at four o'clock in the afternoon when Michael entered the Bowery Mission. He would always remember that day. It was his birthday. He was fifty-three.

"Hi," – Michael said to the big black guy sitting behind the counter in the entrance hall. "I heard that here homeless people can get a bed to sleep and food. I am homeless and need a place to stay."

"Do you want to join the program?" the man behind the counter asked.

Michael didn't know what it meant, 'joining the program', but he didn't want to ask. He said, "Yes."

"Okay, go here to the chapel," the man pointed to the doors on the side. "Sit there and wait. I will call our admission counselor and somebody will take you to him."

Michael went through the side door and stood in the long and dark chapel with a high wooden cathedral ceiling and walls painted to resemble Romanesque-style stone walls. Rows of long wooden pews were lined up on both sides of the chapel, sitting on red brick tiles. In the back of the chapel was a large red door serving as a main entrance to the chapel. In the front was a stage with a few chairs and doors in the middle. Right below the stage in the center was a pulpit, concert piano on the left and organs on the right.

Michael sat in the last row. Two other men were sitting in the pew in front of him. One of them was a black man in his forties with an afro and a dark leather jacket ripped under the left arm. The other one was a young baby-faced light skin Hispanic man, not older than twenty with short curly hair wearing a brown t-shirt.

"Guys, are you waiting for a counselor?" somebody asked behind Michael's back. Michael turned. A short stocky man with a crew cut in jeans and white t-shirt entered through a side door and was standing behind him.

"Yes," Michael and the other two men answered almost in unison.

"Come with me."

The three of them followed this man back to the reception hall and up the flight of stairs to the second floor to a room in front of the admission counselor's office.

"Sit here and wait. The counselor will call you one by one," stocky man said and went back down the stairs.

All three of them sat around the large conference table in the middle of the room. Each one with his own thoughts. They didn't talk or introduce themselves. They didn't even look at each other. The doors of the counselor's office were open, and they could hear his voice. He was talking on the phone to somebody. Then doors opened wide. A white middle-aged man with blonde short hair was standing at the doorway. He was five feet tall and skinny, in gray worn out pants and cream dress shirt, with golden framed glasses over light blue, almost gray eyes.

"Who came first?" he asked.

Michael and the other two men, looked at each other for a moment, not sure what they should say. After a short hesitation, the young Hispanic man said, "I think I did."

"Okay, come in," the man at the door said and moved aside to let the young man into the office. He closed the door behind him.

It took around half an hour before the young man walked out of the counselor's office. He had a smile on his face. "I got the bed," he said and sat back at the table. "Counselor wants the next one to enter".

Man with the afro stood up and entered the counselor's office. The young Hispanic man turned his face to Michael and asked, "Do you know what time dinner is?"

"No, I don't know. I've never been here before," Michael said.

"Hope we don't miss it. I am really hungry. Haven't eaten in two days."

Michael didn't answer. He made a face as a sign of understanding. They said nothing after that. They both just looked at the table surface in front of them.

The stocky man who brought them there walked into the room.

"Who is Joel?"

"It's me," the young Hispanic man answered.

"Come with me. I'll show you your room. Do you have any luggage with you?"

"No, man. I don't even have a coat."

They left. Michael was now by himself. He didn't know what to expect. But all he had in his mind was surviving. He needed a bed to rest and food to eat.

The office door opened, and the other man, walking out, said to Michael, "It is your turn." And he sat back at the table.

Michael stood up, took his backpack in his left hand and walked into the office.

The counselor's office was a small room, maybe eight by eight feet, with a tiny window facing the building next door, which allowed for just a fraction of daylight to get into the room. One wall was covered with filing cabinets and bookshelves. The counselor's desk was facing the wall with several framed pictures and diplomas hanging on it. On one side of the desk was a stand with a printer. On the other side was an empty chair.

The counselor was looking at the screen of the computer in front of him and typing. "Have a seat, please," he pointed to the empty chair without even looking at Michael.

Michael sat in the chair and placed his backpack next to his feet. The counselor stopped typing, raised his head towards Michael and said, "Hi. My name is Allan Schapiro. I am the admission counselor here. What is your name?"

"My name is Michael Nicolau."

"What brings you here today, Michael?"

"I am homeless, have no place to stay anymore, have no

money or job. I've been sleeping for the last ten days on the subway. Don't know what to do next."

"Can you tell me how that happened?" the counselor asked.

"Three years ago, I left my wife and went to Romania. I started a business in Bucharest, but it didn't work out. Lost all of my money in the failed enterprise and came back to New York two weeks ago. I was trying to find a job or a place to stay, but nothing happened. After I ran out of the little money I had on me, I stayed on the subway."

"Did you try to go back to your wife?"

"No, our marriage is over. She is still hurt and angry. She would not help."

"Did you cheat on her?"

"Well, I left her for another woman in Romania. But it was not that simple. It was not just about being with another woman."

"It never is! What happened with that woman?"

"She left me a year ago when my business in Romania went downhill."

"Was she young?"

"She was thirty-three years old."

"And how old are you, Michael?"

"I am fifty-three."

"Why Romania? Are you from Romania?"

"Yes. I was born in Bucharest. I moved to New York in 1987."

"Do you drink or take drugs, Michael?" The counselor asked and started typed again. It seemed to Michael like he was filling out some kind a form.

"Well, when I was in Romania, I used to drink, but mostly wine. I don't drink beer, and hard liquor I drink occasionally. I took no drugs."

"How much wine did you drink?"

"Well, depends on… Usually, it was four to five glasses or one bottle a day."

"How's your health? Do you have any health problems? High blood pressure, diabetes…?"

"So far, nothing, thank God," Michael answered.

"Do you smoke?"

"Yes, I do."

"How much a day?"

"About a pack a day."

"Do you have children, Michael?"

"Yes, three daughters. Two with the first wife and one with the second."

"Oh, so, you were married twice, then?" The counselor asked.

"Yeah," Michael answered with melancholy in his voice.

"How old are your daughters and what are their names?"

"Hmm…twenty-nine the oldest – Sofia, Jenny is twenty -eight, and the youngest, Blanca is nineteen."

"Do you keep in touch with them? Do they know about your present situation?"

"No, I don't talk to them."

"Why not?"

"I don't know.I guess; I was never too good as a father"

Michael said and lowered his head.

"What is your profession, Michael? Also, the level of education?"

"I am a writer and publisher with BA in journalism."

"What do you write?" Counselor asked and turned his head towards Michael looking straight into his eyes.

"Well, history…mostly. I wrote and published sixteen books so far."

"It is difficult to live from writing. Is it?" Counselor asked.

"Yes, difficult. Last year, my total annual royalties were eighty-seven dollars and fifty cents. But I still believe that one day I'll be able to live from writing."

The counselor just smiled and kept typing. "How did you hear about us?"

"I have passed by your Mission many times. There are always homeless people in front waiting for the soup kitchen."

"Okay, let me tell you something about the Bowery Mission. The Bowery Mission has existed since 1876. We are a Christian-based recovery program for men. In another location, we have the same program for women. We deal with homeless men who are homeless because of their addiction, be that alcohol, drugs, pornography, or something else. We offer a six-month recovery program which helps men get back on their feet, cleaned out, get a job, and be able to live independently. After completing the program, our 'students,' as we call them, look for a job. When they find one, they may stay here another six months until they save enough money to move away and live on their own. During the program, our students have free lodging, food, and clothing. But there are conditions. The first one is to stay sober and clean of drugs. Anybody caught drinking or using drugs is kicked out. If you leave the program before its completion, you cannot come back. Also, you cannot have a cellular phone, computer, music player or any electronic device that would keep you in touch with the outside world or entertain you. During the six months, everybody in the program has to be focused on his recovery, so the best thing is to be separated from the outside world. Two times a week, students can go out for two hours for a walk or exercise in the park around the corner. After four months they are allowed to go to the Sunday service of a church outside. We have a nurse on staff, and we have a doctor seeing students once a week. Also, before meals, services are in the chapel every day for an hour and all students are required to attend. In the morning hours, we have Bible classes, time for prayer, and computer classes. In the afternoon are tutorial sessions, for those who want to improve or complete their education while they are here. If this sounds too restrictive for you, you can always come here, hear the service in the chapel, and have a meal. We serve breakfast, lunch, and dinner to homeless people every day. Also, twice a week, on Tuesdays and Fridays, homeless people can take a shower here and get a free change of clothing. In the winter, when the temperature is below 40 degrees, we allow homeless people to sleep in our chapel on sleeping mats. But it's on a first come first serve basis, and it fills fast. We cannot accommodate more than a hundred people. You are not the typical student we usually have. Most of them are lifelong alcoholics or drug addicts. But somehow, I sense that drinking and women had something to do with your troubles. So, what do you think, Michael, are you interested in joining our program?"

"Yes. I don't think I have another choice. I need to put myself back together. This seems to be the only way." Michael answered.

"Good. I will start the paperwork for you. These are the forms you have to fill out. Do you have a phone or any other electronic device with you?"

"I have my phone from Romania. But it doesn't work anymore. It's prepaid and it run out of minutes. I had a laptop, but I sold it to a pawnshop to get money for food, a few days ago."

"You will have to leave your phone with me. After four months, we will give it back to you. Do you have any ID's on you?"

"I have my passport and my Social Security card. Also, I have my New York drivers' license, but it expired over two years ago."

"Wow, that is more than most of the people who come here have. It is good. We need to make copies of it if you don't mind. I don't have any more beds available today. Just gave the last one to Joel, the young man who came before you. You and Victor will have to sleep for one or two nights in the chapel until I get beds free. I will call somebody to take you downstairs to the bathroom to take a shower and get clean clothing. Then, you can go eat with the rest of the students. It is almost dinner time."

The counselor picked up the office phone and dialed.

"Mike, we have two more new guys here. Their names are Victor and Michael. They will stay in the Chapel for now until we free beds. Could you please come and escort them to take a shower and change their clothing? Then you can show them around a bit and take them to dinner."

The counselor turned to Michael.

"One student will come and take you to the showers. If you need anything, come and ask. In a couple days, you will be assigned a counselor and you will go from there. Okay?" the counselor said to Michael.

"Yes, thank you."

"Welcome to the program, Michael. I wish you all the best. You can go now."

As they both stood up the counselor shook Michael's hand. Michael walked out of the office and sat back at the table.

The Bowery Mission

3

He was relieved that after so many days, he was going to take a shower, have something to eat and have a safe place to sleep. But six months looked very long for him to be cut off from the outside world. He promised Eliza that he will bring her to New York by the end of the month.

"What will I say to her? he was thinking. He didn't have the means now to contact her anyway. And for six months he wouldn't be able to look for a job or a way out of his situation. It seemed like such a long time. But he knew that he had to go one day at a time.

"For now, I am safe. Mid-March and the weather in New York is like winter in full swing. It is so cold. It is good to be here for now," he thought. "Gives me time to think about what to do next."

The stocky man in the t- shirt came back.

"Hi guys, my name is Mike. You are Victor and Michael, right?"

"I am Victor." The man with the big afro said.

"And you are Michael, like me?"

Michael just nodded his head.

"You are now the fourth Michael in the program. There are two more here. I will take you guys down to the clothing room to find something clean to wear, and then to the showers. I understand that you will be staying in the chapel for a couple of nights. It is not that bad of a deal. It is better than outside. I heard that two students are leaving today from my floor. Maybe, you'll get lucky and sleep in a bed tomorrow."

They went down the narrow staircase from the second floor back to the reception hall, and from there through the Chapel, they continued to the basement of the Mission.

On the left side of the long basement hall, with walls and ceiling painted in gray, was the clothing room door. Further down the hall were shower rooms. All three of them, led by Mike, entered the clothing room.

The clothing room was a large basement space lit with neon lights and painted white. Alongside one longer wall were metal shelves filled with folded clothing up to the high ceiling. On another side, were clothing racks with coats, suits, and shirts. Lined in the middle were long folding tables covered with piles of unfolded clothing.

"Rick, these are new students. They are going to take showers, so they need a change of clothing. Can you help them?"

"Do they have clothing requisition slips?" the skinny old man, hardly five feet tall, with gray hair, and a strong West Indian accent, asked.

"No, Rick. They are not assigned beds yet, so they will come with slips later. They just need one change of clothing for now."

"Okay. Here are underwear and socks." Rick started pointing with his hand around the room. "Here are pants and t- shirts. On other side are dress shirts and jackets. Over there are sweaters. Over here are towels and toiletries. Take one of each for now and when you get a clothing requisition slip, come back and I'll give you more. If you need shoes or sneakers, they are here, on the shelves. Try to find your size. Toiletry sets are on that table. Each contains razor, toothpaste and toothbrush, and a soap."

Once they got clean clothing, Mike showed them where the showers were. Michael threw his worn underwear, socks, and shoes in the garbage.

"Hey man, this really stinks. How long you went without a shower?" Mike asked.

"Almost two weeks. I spent the last ten days sleeping on the subway." Michael answered.

"No wonder it stinks."

Michael couldn't remember the last time he enjoyed a shower that much. He kept rubbing himself with soap, trying to remove the stench that got into his skin and his nostrils.

After the shower, Mike took them to the Manager's Office to introduce them to the Manager on duty, showed them the dining hall, and returned them to the chapel.

"Dinner will be in an hour and a half after the evening service here in the chapel. When service is finished, you just go to the dining hall and get in line with the other students. For now, you can stay here."

"Mike, can I go out and have a smoke?" Victor asked.

"Well, maybe, this is your last chance. You are not assigned a bed, so you are not technically in the program yet. If you have a cigarette, smoke it now because later you won't be able to. And go around the corner, not in front of the building. Students are not allowed to smoke."

Victor turned and looked at Michael. "Do you want to go out too?"

"I don't have a cigarette. Can you spare one?"

"I have two last ones. May as well smoke them. Come."

They walked out of the Chapel through the main red door. In front of the Chapel, along the building wall, all the way to the corner, a line of homeless people waiting to enter the Chapel had already formed. Victor and Michael went around the corner to the end of the line, stood on the side under the street light pole, and lit up cigarettes.

"This feels good," Michael was thinking. "I am clean, in clean clothing, have a place to sleep tonight, and soon I will eat."

"Can you spare a cigarette?" Michael heard behind his back.

A chubby girl, not more than twenty years old, with curly blond hair, a pale face with red cheeks from the cold, and smudged bright red lipstick approached Michael from the back of the soup kitchen line. "So, can you give me a smoke?" she repeated.

"This is my last cigarette," Michael answered.

"Listen, bro, don't be stingy. I'll suck your dick for a smoke."

"Sorry, I really don't have another cigarette," Michael said and turned towards Victor and away from the girl.

"Oh, what a faggot," the girl said and went back in the line.

Victor started laughing. "You see, man, if I didn't give you my last cigarette, she'd be sucking my dick now."

Michael couldn't believe what he just heard from this homeless girl. How desperate she was, that she would perform oral sex to a complete stranger for one single cigarette. "How tragic is the world I just entered," Michael thought.

That night Michael was sleeping on the mat on the tiled floor of the Bowery Chapel. Besides him and Victor, the only other person there was a homeless guy named Francis. He wasn't in the program, but he was almost a regular guest at the Bowery Mission. Everybody there knew his story and felt bad for him, so sometimes they allowed him to sleep in the Chapel even if it wasn't very cold outside.

Until five years ago, Francis was a young and ambitious adjunct professor of American History at Baruch College. His colleagues were predicting a bright future in higher education for this upbeat and very talented black man. He managed to rise up and out from his poor childhood in the Bronx projects to become a respected educator. Francis was married and had a two-year-old son. Then one day, in a freak hit and run accident, on Queens Boulevard, his wife and son were struck down and killed. Francis had a nervous breakdown, got hooked on drugs and alcohol and soon after ended up on the streets of Manhattan, wandering around all year around, year after year, sometimes almost naked, covered in his own feces, and refusing any help. The only place he would come for an occasional meal or shower was the Bowery Mission.

Michael was lying down, covered with a blanket, and looking at Francis walking up and down the aisles of the Chapel, mumbling to himself in some strange tongue that Michael could not understand. The light in the Chapel was dimmed and Francis, with his tall and very skinny body, looked almost surreal to Michael. He was barefoot, with ripped Docker pants and no shirt at all. His short black hair looked like strong thick brush coming out of his skull. His feet were sliding over the red Chapel tiles silently, and it appeared to Michael like he was not walking but floating.

"Don't worry about him, he is crazy, but he will not harm you," Victor, who was lying on the mat a few feet away, said to Michael. "I've seen him before. He is a lost case. Only God knows how he is still alive."

Soon after, Michael fell asleep. He was really tired after so many nights on the subway trains. Finally, he felt safe. He knew that he needed a break, a place to renew his strength and time to figure out what to do next. The Bowery Mission was his only choice, and it looked to him like the right one as well.

Michael didn't know what time it was when he was awakened by something very light falling on his face. He opened his eyes and saw Francis standing over him with a rose stem in one hand. With the other hand, he was picking petals from the half dry red rose bud and tossing them at Michael. While wiggling back and forth with his upper body, he was chanting with a screechy voice,

"Wake up, wake up, the end of times is coming,

Wake up, wake up, Santa Maria is waiting,

Wake up, wake up, soldier of Christ Almighty,

Wake up, wake up, Mother of God is crying."

Michael looked around. All over his blanket and around the mat were dry rose petals. He jumped into a sitting position and said, "What the fuck is wrong with you, man?"

Francis turned around fast and ran to the back of the Chapel while screeching: "He is awake! He is awake! He is awake!" He ran out of the Chapel through the side doors leading to the entrance of the Mission.

A few minutes later, a man dressed in a neatly ironed white shirt with tie and black dress pants entered the Chapel.

"Let's go, guys," He said. "It is time to get up. The Chapel will be open soon for morning service. You can go downstairs to the bathroom to shave and wash and then come back here for the service. After that is breakfast. And take your mats and blankets downstairs with you. Leave them behind the stairs. You may need them tonight again if you don't get beds assigned to you today."

Michael looked at this man. It was the same manager that he was introduced to by Mike last night. The light-skinned black man, with a completely shaved head, glasses with golden metal frame. With a large shiny watch on his wrist, and his medium build, a bit overweight, and a limp, he looked more like a Bronx pawnshop owner than a manager of the homeless shelter.

Victor and Michael went back to the same bathroom they took their showers in the night before. Michael took a shower again. He still felt the stench on his skin from his days on the subway.

Victor was running a pick through his hair.

"So Michael, what brought you here? You don't look to me like an addict, he asked.

"I left my wife, made a few bad business decisions and lost money, fooled around with women, drank more than I should, pretty much messed up my life and one day found myself on the N train without money, friends, or a place to go."

"Yeah, that would do it...," Victor said. "Sometimes I think that guys like you have it worse than guys like me. God gave you something and then he took it away. So it hurts badly. I grew up in the projects, never knew my father. My mother was constantly high and disappeared when I was twelve. I grew up with my aunt. Never finished high school. Been using drugs since I was fourteen. In and out of jails and shelters forever. This is my third time here. Never had a wife to leave; never had a business to lose. And I always say to God – better don't give me anything if you gonna take it away from me."

Then he stopped fixing his hair, turned towards Michael and said with a broken voice: "But he always finds a way. Always... Two days ago, my only baby sister overdosed in front of my eyes, with the needle I gave her. I still see her lying there, her eyes wide open. That is why I came here. I need to break this circle. There must be a better life out there. I need to clean out. I am tired of this."

Michael didn't say anything. He just looked at Victor. He never met anybody like him. Never knew anybody from the projects. The closest, he came to stories like this one was on the local evening news. And now he will spend the next six months with people with similar stories.

They went back to the chapel. It was already full of homeless people who came to have breakfast at the Bowery. The way it worked was that everybody would enter the Chapel, listen for an hour to a sermon by the Pastor or a guest preacher, testimonials by the students who completed the recovery program, and then they would, in an orderly fashion, go to the large dining room where the meal was served. It was the same routine for all meals: breakfast at six in the morning, lunch at noon, and dinner at six in the evening. Students in the program were sitting on the chapel balcony during the service, and had their meals before the homeless people from outside.

Michael and Victor climbed up a narrow wooden staircase to the chapel balcony. There were about eighty other men there already. They were all different ages and of different origins. From twenty to over sixty years of age, most of them were black or Latino, with a dozen white and a couple of Asian men. "The real New York in small." Michael was thinking.

The Pentecostal preacher who spoke that morning was a novelty for Michael as well. Before in his life, he attended many different Christian Churches, but they were all mainstream traditional denominations: Orthodox Christian, Catholic, Anglican, Presbyterian, and Lutheran. But he was never in a Baptist or Pentecostal Church, and never met any of newborn Christians. He couldn't hear everything the preacher was saying because of the bad sound system, but he heard a Bible verse that the preacher repeated several times: *"For I know the thoughts that I think toward you, says the Lord, thoughts of peace and not of evil, to give you a future and a hope."* It was Jeremiah 29:11.

After the service, the students went to the dining hall. It was a large room with fifteen round tables each seating ten, and with the serving line and kitchen in the back. Breakfast that morning was simple, oatmeal and fresh bananas. Michael took his plate with oatmeal and looked around the hall to find Victor and sit next to him.

Victor appeared with a cup of milk from somewhere.

"Do you want some milk in your oatmeal? It will cool it down. It's too hot."

"Sure," Michael replied.

"So, you guys are new here?" A chubby young man with thick glasses sitting across from Michael asked. Michael looked at him. He couldn't figure out if this kid was Latino or white, but he couldn't be more than twenty years old, Michael thought. His thick greasy hair was dark brown, almost black, but his eyes were blue and he had red chicks and pale white face.

"Yes, we came last night," Michael said.

"Do you have beds yet?" The kid asked.

"No, we slept in the chapel last night. They say maybe something will be available today." Michael answered.

"Oh, by the way, my name is Jeremiah."

"Michael," Michael responded and nodded his head.

"I'm Victor," Victor mumbled trying to swallow a mouthful of oatmeal.

"There are two guys going from the second floor to the fourth or fifth floor today, I think," Jeremiah continued, "All new guys are given a room on the second floor the first month. After that, they move to either the fourth or fifth floor. Those rooms are bigger and they have seating areas. I am still on the second floor. I came two weeks ago."

"Good morning." Rick, the old man from the clothing room came and sat at their table. "How's your first night at Bowery?" he asked Victor and Michael.

"We were with Francis in the Chapel. He was walking up and down the aisle all night," Victor answered.

"That lunatic, I don't know why they allow him to spend nights here. I think the Mission director has a soft spot for him. He is allowed to do many things that nobody else can do," Rick said. "The other day I gave him pants before a shower, and he threw them back into my face while yelling 'bad man, bad man.' I don't know why he called me a bad man, I didn't do anything, just gave him pants."

"Oh, he lives in his own world. Who knows what is in his head," Jeremiah said.

"Hello, gents,"A tall and well-built Hispanic man in a dark gray suit and blue shirt without tie, cup of coffee in hand, came and sat at the table. "We have newcomers, I see."

"Welcome, guys," he continued while looking curiously into Michael and Victor. "I know you," he said to Victor. "Were you here before?"

"Yes. Twice, but I haven't completed the program. The first time, I was kicked out for leaving without permission and getting high; the second time, I just left before the end of the program."

"The third time's a charm. How about you, young man?" he said with a bit of irony in his voice while looking at Michael.

"It is my first time here, or in any place like this, for that matter," Michael answered.

"I hope it will work out for you. It did for many. I am Pastor Lee Quinones. I have been a counselor here for the past twenty years. Twenty-four years ago, I came here the same way you did, as a homeless man."

"And they kicked you out three times," Rick said with a smile.

"Yes, I am not ashamed to admit it. I was a wild kid, hooked on everything that was available on the streets. It took me four times to complete the program. But I did. Anyway, you two probably don't know who will be your counselor yet, but if you need anything ever, my office is on the third floor. Also, I am the only counselor who lives in the Mission, so pretty much, I am available twenty-four-seven."

"Thank you," Michael said.

Michael finished his oatmeal. He didn't know what to do next. As students were finishing their breakfast, they were leaving the dining room and going to get ready for morning Bible classes. But since Michael wasn't assigned to any room yet, he didn't receive his schedule either. All he knew was that he could not leave the Mission anymore without permission. And he didn't have the desire to leave anyway. Still tired from sleepless nights on the subway, all he was thinking of were rest, food, and peace.

He stood up and took his tray with the empty plate to the station for dirty dishes at the corner of the dining room. He looked around. Homeless people were already taking the chairs of the students who were leaving. There was a big contrast between them. All of those in the program were in clean and often brand new clothing, shaven and clean, while most of the homeless from the outside were in ripped and smelly clothing, unshaven, and they all looked very stressed.

There were quite a few women with small children among the homeless. It was a sad picture to look at. It was the world Michael didn't know anything about. But for the last ten days, he was a part of it. He knew that for some of these people being homeless was the only way of life they knew. He couldn't understand how they could cope with it.

The last ten days had been like being in hell. And it seemed to him that he had escaped by a thread yet again. The more he looked at the students around him, the more he was convinced that he got lucky by joining this program. They all looked well nourished, well dressed, and content. The program would give him time to recuperate, recharge his batteries in peace and in a safe place. That is exactly what he needed.

That afternoon Michael got his bed in a room on the second floor. The admission counselor gave him a slip for clothing and he went to Rick in the clothing room to pick everything he needed. He got four pairs of jeans, four t-shirts, four dress shirts, four pairs of underwear, four pairs of socks, two new sweaters, a leather jacket, sneakers, brown dress shoes, and slippers for the bathroom. He also got four towels, shampoo, and more toiletries. Most of the things he got were brand new. Nothing one would expect to get in a homeless shelter.

"This is crazy. Like in a candy store where everything is free," Michael said.

"We call it "Blessing-dales" department store, you know, like Bloomingdales," Rick answered. "Most of the students come here without any clothing and by the end of the program, they have so much clothing that they don't have to buy anything for at least the next two years. The Bowery is one of the oldest and best-known Missions in the city and has many big donors. Some of the best fashion houses, like Brooks Brothers and Ralph Lauren, donate clothing directly to the Bowery. So you have a homeless guy just coming from the streets into the program suddenly wearing a three-hundred-dollar shirt and a suit worth over a thousand."

"This would be a good place to work," Michael said.

"It is good, but it is not easy at the same time. Twice a week we have a crowd of about two hundred homeless men from outside taking showers down here and we are providing them with a change of the clothing. It is like a mad house. Half of them are crazy, the other half wants only brand new clothing, so they can sell it after they walk out of here, and then after two days they are back in their old rags; and again demanding brand new stuff. Some of them are really nasty; like it is their right, not a privilege."

"But if you want, you can ask your counselor to send you here to work," Rick continued "Just so you know – I am the boss here, and there is a lot of work every day. We receive bags and bags of donated clothing and all of that needs to be sorted out, folded, and placed where it belongs. The good part of working here is that you get to pick the best pieces for yourself; of course, carefully, nothing in excess. Otherwise, other students will complain."

It took Michael only a few days to adapt to the new situation. He was assigned to a counselor, Pastor Charles Jourdan. He was a Haitian man in his fifties, always with a smile on his face, and always starting every conversation with a quote from the Scriptures. Every Monday morning, at 9:00a.m., Michael had to go for a session with the counselor to discuss the progress of his recovery, his plans for the future, and anything else that may help him get on the right path after the completion of the program.

Most of the working days in the Mission were the same. All students had to work one of many jobs within the Mission. Some were working in the kitchen, some as ushers in the Chapel, others in the clothing room or any other duties needed in running and maintaining of the Mission.

The lights would go out at ten in the evening and by that time everybody had to be in bed.

On Wednesdays and Saturdays from ten in the morning until noon, students had the right to go out to the nearby park, to walk around or play sports. Michael used that time to walk to Barnes and Noble on Union Square, look through the new magazines, and check out new book titles. After a while, he started feeling normal again. He started thinking about the future. He still didn't know what he would do after the Bowery Mission, but he was gaining his confidence back.

He managed to be assigned to work in the clothing room. It was a good place for him. He was good at organizing things, and he also liked good clothing. After just one month of working there, he had quite a nice wardrobe that would have cost a lot of money, if he had bought it in the store.

The only thing that bothered him was that he was completely cut off from the outside world. Yes, he could walk around the city twice a week, but there was no way for him to get in touch with anybody if he wanted. He didn't even have a quarter for the phone. And the use of internet in the computer room was limited and supervised.

The Magic of the Craft

4

Michael walked into Pastor Charles' office. The pastor was sitting at his desk and eating a slice of pizza.

"Pizza in the morning?" Michael said, "All that tomato sauce and melted mozzarella will give you a heartburn Pastor."

"Good morning to you too, Michael," Pastor answered smiling. "Don't worry. I don't get heartburn from pizza but from my students. Every Monday morning when I come, some new weekend story awaits me."

"What happened now?" Michael asked as he was taking a seat next to Pastor's desk.

"Apparently, one of my students snuck out Saturday night and got drunk. He was caught by the night manager on his way back."

"That was Jeremiah, right?"

"I shouldn't be telling you this, but it seems you already know. That boy really worries me. If we kicked him out, he won't have anywhere to go."

"Maybe it has to do something with his father's visit. I saw Jeremiah talking to his father in front of the Mission Saturday morning."

"I don't know. His father is not the best example. He is an alcoholic, a drifter with no permanent job or address. I'll talk to Jeremiah later. Please, keep quiet about it," Pastor said as he was cleaning his hands and mouth with a paper napkin. "Anyway, how are you doing Michael? I hear only good things about your work and progress with Bible classes. I also see that you gained some weight. Your face is not as pale as before when you first came. Those are all good things. But those are also the results of you being here. What I want to find out is how are you doing on the inside? How are you dealing with the things that brought you to us? We have to figure out those things and resolve them together. Otherwise, you will leave here in a few months and soon after, find yourself in the same situation. If you were a drug addict or an alcoholic or addicted to pornography, I would know how to help you to overcome those issues. But you are none of these. Still, I feel from what I see in your file that there is a big imbalance in your psyche, and we have to find the root cause of it and you have to learn to control it. You also have to learn to trust God, Michael. Surrender your will to God's will and live according to his word and miracles will happen in your life."

"I don't know, Pastor. I keep thinking about my life and the things that brought me here. I analyze every single act and every situation that I've been through and keep asking myself if I could or would do it differently now that I know what the end result is. But somehow I cannot find anything wrong with any of my actions nor do I think that I would do it differently. I'm not saying that whatever bad happened to me or whatever bad I did to others was somebody else's fault. I see all, as circumstances of life, the way things just happen beyond our intentions or our will. Almost like destiny. Like the hand of God. You say to me to surrender my will to God's will. Sometimes I think that is exactly what I was doing all my life. Maybe I'm wrong. Maybe that is just the way to calm my conscience about all the wrongdoings that I've done. I don't know…It is what it is…"

"Michael, we have to start here from the beginning, step by step and find out what is the seed of your troubles. I see here," Pastor continued as he was scrolling over Michael's file on the computer screen, "You came to this country in 1987, right?"

"Yes," Michael answered.

"How old were you then?"

"I was twenty-nine."

"Were you married at that time?"

"No, I was already divorced from my first wife back in Romania."

"You had two kids with her, right?"

"Yes, two girls."

"So, you must have gotten married very young. Why did you divorce?"

"I don't know. In hindsight, I think we were just too young to handle marriage. When we got married, we were very young and didn't have anything. Just two kids blindly in love. For me, everything started with my sincere desire to prove that I was able to provide for my family. I was rushing into trying to make a good living for my wife and my kids and unfortunately got involved with the wrong people. Within a year, everything went downhill. I saw that I was getting into trouble, but I didn't want to share that with anybody, not even my wife. There was always so much pride in me preventing me to admit when I made a mistake. I started drinking heavily. I was flirting with other women and spending time away from my family, ashamed of the things I've done. Finally, my wrong associations caught up with me. I ended up in the jail for a year. That is when my wife divorced me and took the kids to live with her parents."

"What happened after?"

"When I got out, I couldn't find a job. I was freelancing for a while for several newspapers and magazines as a journalist and photo-reporter, but nobody was offering me a full-time steady position. The amount of money I was making was small and the income wasn't consistent. I felt bad for not being able to support my kids. I was watching other journalism graduates much younger and less talented than I getting good full-time positions, but nobody was hiring me."

"Why you think that was happening?"

"The answer to that is easy. My father was a well-known anti-communist who spent many years in jail for his beliefs. Living as an enemy of the dictatorship in communist Romania wasn't an easy thing. We were all marked as enemies. Nobody in the media would dare give a job to somebody who was not loyal to the communist regime."

"So after a while," Michael continued, "I decided that there was nothing for me to look forward to in Romania and I left. I came to New York."

"How did you do that?" Pastor Charles asked.

"Adrian, a friend of mine from high school, moved to New York a couple years earlier, and he was a manager at a bakery on the Upper East Side. It was called Jacob's Bread, and it was famous at the time for its artisan French bread and pastries. My friend asked me if I want to come and work in the bakery. I told him, yes, and I sat on a plane with a tourist visa. And that was it."

"So, continue, continue," Pastor was insisting, "How did that worked out for you, a journalist and photographer suddenly working in a bakery?"

"It wasn't sudden. When Adrian told me about that work opportunity, I spent three months in a bakery in Bucharest learning the trade. So before I came here I knew the basics."

"I arrived here in the evening around 5:00 p.m.," Michael continued, "I don't remember the exact date or what day it was, but it was in April of '87. Adrian was waiting for me at JFK with the company van. He had changed a lot since I saw him last. He was now heavy, with a big belly and a curly black beard. As we drove from the airport towards the city, he asked me if I wanted to go to his home to unpack and rest or if I did want to stop by the bakery to see where I was going to work. I told him it was okay if we stopped by the bakery. We got there around 7:00p.m., and as we were walking into the store, the owner,

Jacob, came out of his office to greet us. My friend introduced me, and Jacob asked jokingly, 'So, Michael, are you ready for work? The night shift is starting right now. If you want, you can change into whites and start working right away.' Of course, I answered yes, and went to change my clothing."

"You landed at five at JFK and started working at seven the same night. That is very unique. I never heard such a story," Pastor said.

"Maybe, but since that day it feels like I have never stopped working. In the past twenty-five years, excluding the last three years I spent in Romania, I took maybe two or three vacations, a week or two each, and that was it. Everything else was work and work. And for what? To end up here as a homeless man talking to you. What a success. What glory."

"Michael, we cannot predict our lives. Only God Almighty knows and sees it all. We can only do our best and follow the path that He places under our feet. Things don't always turn out the way we want, even if we do everything right. Even if we live by the word of God, He will not always answer our prayers the way we expect. And it is not our place to question God's reasoning behind it, but only to have faith in His wisdom. And with you, I am not sure that you were obeying God always. Even now, I sense a particular pride and self-righteousness. You have to subdue that. God wants you to be truthful and humble to yourself and others. He made you good and industrious, but you can't benefit from it if you always stumble on pride. Do you truly believe in God Michael? Are you with God?"

"I don't know, Pastor. For some reason that I can't explain, I know that God has always been with me, even in the darkest hours. But I know that I haven't always been with Him. I never denied Him, but I wasn't always with Him…"

Michael put down his head. His voice turned hoarse and broken like something was in his throat.

"Okay, Michael, let's go back to the bakery. Tell me more about it."

"Oh, it was really good," Michael's voice returned to normal, "I discovered a whole new world that I instantly fell in love with. You know Pastor, baking is a real art. Especially bread baking. There is something so divine about it. It is a pure alchemy. And all alchemical elements are there: flour that comes from the earth and represents material, water that you mix with flour to make the dough, air released by the yeast fermentation that makes dough rise, fire that bakes the bread. It is fantastic. And the aroma of hot bread released during baking is the most pleasant fragrance for our senses. Think about that for a moment, Pastor. Any food aroma that we like, no matter how much we like it, gets overwhelming after a while, and we open the kitchen windows and close kitchen doors so the smell doesn't get into the living room. Any smell, but the smell of freshly baked bread. Did you ever hear anybody complain about the smell of baked bread? Nobody, Pastor! Nobody. You hear people complaining about their neighbors frying fish, roasting pork, barbecuing sausages, but nobody ever complains about the smell of baked bread. And you know why? Because it is divine. It is magic – the magic of the craft."

"But for me," Michael continued, "The best part was working with my hands. I love making things with my hands. Kneading the dough and forming it into the right shape is so powerful and calming at the same time."

"How many people worked in that bakery?" Pastor asked.

"Oh, it was sixteen of us in the production. Fifteen of them were from West Africa. They were all very experienced French bread bakers. And they spoke bad English. Among themselves they mostly used French. I was the only white guy there. The bakery was in the basement of a fancy gourmet store and restaurant on Madison Avenue and 91st street."

"How about your friend? He was a white guy too."

"Yes, but Adrian was managing the bakery and selling the bread wholesale. He wasn't involved in the production."

"Were you happy working there?"

"Yes, I think I was. But, it was hard work six days a week. I used to start at two o'clock in the morning and finish by two in the afternoon. I also learned a lot about bread baking and American and French pastries."

"You learned from West African bakers?" Pastor asked.

"Not as much from them. I certainly observed their work and followed their basic recipes, but those guys were not willing to share their trade. Like me, all of them were illegal. Their trade was for them, the only job security."

"Sharing it with somebody would mean that they may lose their jobs. So, they were trying to hide their recipes and ways of mixing the dough as much as they could. On another hand, the owner, Jacob, wanted to have all recipes and procedures written down and in his hands. So, he asked me to observe carefully and write down everything. It worked. In a few months, we had everything recorded and Jacob made me the bakery production supervisor. The Africans hated me for that, but they kept quiet. They were watching every one of my moves trying to catch a mistake and blame me for it."

"But I didn't stop there. I wanted to learn. So, I bought a bunch of books on bread baking and pastry making. I was experimenting every day after working hours and constantly making new things. Jacob loved it. He actually thought that I had a rich experience from Romania. He didn't know that everything was very new to me. Whenever I would make something that he didn't like, he would say, "Michael, I understand that maybe this is the traditional flavor and texture in Romania, but over here people have different tastes. Then he would explain to me what he would like. He had a great palate, and I carefully followed his suggestions. And it worked again. He was happy with my work, and I was happy with his guidance. And every day I was learning more and more."

"How much money did you make there?"

"Jacob was paying me four hundred dollars a week, in cash. It was good money then, especially for somebody who was illegal."

"Where did you live? Were you able to save some money?"

"At the beginning, for about three months, I lived in Adrian's apartment until I saved some money. Then I shared an apartment with the girl that worked at the counter in Jacob's store."

"Oh, a girl," Pastor said with a smile.

"No, it wasn't like that," Michael continued, "We were just roommates. She was a nice girl and in a serious relationship. For me, it was good because the apartment was only two blocks from work. It made a difference when I had to start at two in the morning.

"So, how long did you work at Jacob's place?"

"About a year and a half."

"What did you do then?"

"I started working in another gourmet store as Head Baker."

"Why did you quit Jacob's? You said you liked it there. Did these other guys offer you more money?"

"Yes, I was making more money at Fratelli's. That was the name of the store in the West Village. But that wasn't the main reason I left Jacob's."

"What was it?" Pastor asked.

"Well, it is a bit complicated. I don't think we have enough time to talk about it now. Bible class will start in five minutes. I'll be late," Michael said as he was looking at his watch.

"It is about the woman, isn't it?" The pastor asked as his face opened in a wide smile.

"Maybe, I don't know. We'll talk more about it next week," Michael said and stood up.

"Don't go, I'll excuse you with Pastor Quinones. We're just getting somewhere in this conversation."

"No, no, next time, Pastor. I have to go," Michael replied and rushed out of the office.

The First American Woman

5

Michael was standing at the entrance of the Bowery Mission and looking at people passing by. It was almost eight o'clock Monday morning in late May, and it was a bright and sunny day. Everybody was in a rush to get to work. There were quite a few good-looking women walking up and down the street that morning, and Michael enjoyed looking at them. They were not dirty looks associated with erotic thoughts. He just enjoyed looking at the beauty of their bodies and elegance of their moves as they were making their way through the crowd. He loved women who knew how to carry themselves. Of course, none of those women were looking back at him. Standing in front the Bowery Mission meant only one thing – that you were homeless. In New York, people avoided looking at the homeless.

"Hey, you are going to lose your eyes like this," Pastor Charles said as he was getting out of his car.

"Well, if I do, I want to be sure I'm looking at something

beautiful when that happens," Michael answered. "Good morning, Pastor."

"Good morning, Michael. How was your weekend?"

"Busy. We had many donations, and there was lots of clothing to sort out. But that is good. Tomorrow is shower day, and we need as much stuff as possible. We are still short on all sizes of shoes."

"I am sure something will come today. If not, you can ask the Director tomorrow morning. I know that we have extra shoes in storage," Pastor Charles said, "Would you mind going around the corner and getting coffee for you and me?"

"No problem Pastor, I'll do it. Just make sure to mention at the front desk that you sent me. I don't want anybody to think that I left the Mission without permission."

"Sure. Here is the money. One sugar and milk for me, please. Thank you."

Michael brought the coffees back to Pastor's office. Pastor Charles was looking at the computer monitor and reading the weekend report.

"What happened?" He asked as he was reading, "You found forty bucks in a donated jacket and turned in to the manager's office?"

"Yes," Michael answered.

"That was nice of you," Pastor said.

"It was the normal thing to do, but it wasn't that nice," Michael said with a smile.

"Why not?"

"Well," Michael started after he took a sip of coffee, "I turned in forty dollars. Everybody heard about it. The next moment, everybody was asking me for money. They didn't believe that there were only forty dollars. They couldn't believe that I would turn in everything. One guy even told me, 'You can't fool me. I see what you are doing. You are trying to make an image of the honest guy by turning in peanuts. Who knows what you got in there."

"You have to understand that people in the program are not like you. Most of them are addicts with troubling pasts. There are always valuables among the donated items – jewelry, watches, phones, and computers. Some of the guys who worked in the clothing room before you would take them and sell them out on the street and keep the money. And if they found money, they would just keep it. We know all of that but it is just hard to control it. The Director is thinking of putting cameras down there, but I doubt that it will work out. Sometimes things disappear even before they get to the clothing room."

"Yes, I heard of it and I really think that those guys are stupid. At least Blessing-dale is a place where one can get everything for free. So far anything that came to the clothing room as a donation that I liked, I was able to get with permission from the Director. Yes, it is kind of taking advantage working there, but it is not stealing. I would simply put a thing aside and go to the Director to ask if I could have it. So far, he hasn't refused once. I got the new watch. I got great leather boots and a leather jacket. So stealing something that you could have for free is really stupid."

"Yes, you are right. But not everybody thinks like that."

"I know. The other day I saw a guy from the program selling jeans, which he got in the clothing room, to a homeless guy for three dollars. I was really disgusted. And the very same guy was giving testimony during morning service of how the program did great things for him, how he gave himself to Christ, and other B.S. that people usually say when they get to the pulpit to give testimony."

"Who was that student?"

"It is not important. I will not tell you. I am not a snitch. I just wanted to say that it is often hard for people to change their ways."

"How about you, Michael? Do you think you can change your ways?"

"I guess I don't have a choice. Do I? Isn't that why I am here. If my ways were right, I wouldn't be here. Would I?"

"That is something we have to find out. It is the reason we have these sessions."

"The only problem is that I don't really know what is exactly wrong with the ways I do things and what I have to correct."

"Usually, it is not one thing. It is often things that we carry in ourselves, sometimes from childhood, that affect our behavior in such subtle ways that we don't even notice. And before we realize what is happening, we derail from the tracks and make mistakes. That is why we have the word of God, to guide us in all our actions. Applying Biblical teachings to our decision-making is one of the best ways to avoid making mistakes. That is what submitting yourself to God really means."

"That being said," Pastor continued, "You owe me a story from the last session."

"What story?"

"Last Monday, when you jumped and ran out of here like crazy, you were gonna tell me why you quit working in Jacob's Bakery, remember?"

"I told you. I got better pay at Fratelli's. And they put me in charge of the bakery department."

"Michael, don't play stupid with me. Let's not lose time. You told me there was a woman that was part of the reason. I want to hear about that. What happened?"

"It was nothing, Pastor. I really don't know why I mentioned this woman. Maybe because she influenced me to accept the position at Fratelli's. I don't know."

"Who was this woman?"

"Her name was Rachel. She was Jewish. She was a few years older than me at the time. Maybe thirty-four, thirty-five, I don't remember. She was hired by Jacob as a catering manager about the same time I was promoted to production supervisor. Jacob thought that she would be able to expand his catering operation. The first moment I saw her, I liked her. And she knew how to deal with men and made them like her. Of course, she was nice to me and wanted to learn as much as possible about the bakery operation. We started hanging out. Then we started going out. Everybody around us thought I was doing her already. But the truth was that I was very shy with her. To this day I don't know why. I wasn't like that with women before her. I wasn't like that after her. I kissed her just once. I never held her hand. We talked a lot. Sometimes we would spend all night at her apartment talking, but I never touched her. I was hoping that she would approach me, and I desired her so much, but I never had the courage to make the first move.

"On another hand," Michael continued, "I was spending money on her like crazy. I wanted to impress her. So I showered her with expensive presents, dinners in fancy restaurants, weekend get-a-ways, picnics in Central Park, and red roses at her desk at work every morning. She accepted everything, never told me to stop spending like crazy, and never kissed me."

"Wow, Michael, you don't look to me like a sucker, but she really did a number on you," Pastor said while smiling with wonder.

"Yes, she did. Then one day she took me downtown to the West Village to see a new gourmet store similar to Jacob's that was soon to open. It was Fratelli's place. She introduced me to the owners, three Italian brothers from Brooklyn, as Jacob's head baker. They were really impressed and immediately asked me how much it would cost them to have me run their bakery department. I was shocked by the question. I'd never thought of quitting Jacob's. He was good to me. But then Rachel started working me. It took her a few hours to convince me. At first, I was unmoved. But she was persistent. Finally, she told me that she was quitting Jacob's and that she was gonna work for Fratelli's. And then she kissed me. Our first and last kiss. That did it. Next day, I told Jacob I was leaving, without notice. He was surprised and mad. My friend, Adrian was furious. But I didn't care. I was already thinking how Rachel wanted me next to her and nothing else was important to me. All I was thinking was the next kiss. But it never happened."

"And?"

"And nothing. That was the story."

"But what happened with you two next? You worked together at Fratelli's, right?"

"Yes, we worked together for a few months. And then she was fired. I stayed there for the next two years until I opened up my own bakery."

"Why was she fired? Did you continue your relationship or whatever that was with her?" Pastor asked.

"Well, she was fired for the same reason Jacob fired her before."

"Jacob fired her? You didn't mention that" Pastor asked surprised.

"Yes, that was something I learned from Adrian years after. At the time she took me to Fratelli's, Jacob had already told her that he was not happy with her performance and to look for a new job. Of course, she didn't tell me that. What I realized later, was that she was a really good salesperson. Unfortunately, the only thing she knew how to sell was herself. So, she was popping from one job to another, always selling herself as an expert in whatever job she was applying for, just to be fired after her employer would realize that she was not what she claimed to be. Of course, when we started working at Fratelli's, she suddenly didn't have any more time for me and she was all over Fratelli's general manager."

"How did you feel about that?"

"At first, I was depressed. I thought that I made a mistake by being passive, by not making a move. Maybe, she thought that something was wrong with me. I was blaming myself. But then I realized that she was playing me the whole time. Even if I made the move, even if we slept together, nothing would be different. She was a calculating person. Knew exactly what she wanted. She was one of those people whose life philosophy was to get as much as possible with the least possible effort. If I jumped her, she probably wouldn't mind, but she didn't care one way or another."

"What bothers me about that experience was that I betrayed my good employer and good friend who brought me to this country for one lousy kiss. Whenever I think about it, I feel bad."

"Did you ever tell that to Jacob or Adrian?"

"I continued my friendship with Adrian, but it was never the same. Anytime somebody would mention me, he would say half-jokingly, "Who? Michael? You can't trust that man. I love him like a brother, but he would sell his brother for a pussy."

"And when it comes to Jacob," Michael continued, "He remained mad for years. For him, I was nothing but a common thief who took his baking secrets and gave them to his competition. In part, he was right. Working for him, I learned a lot and I gained a lot of respect in the profession. In New York, at that time, it was a great reference to have on your resume; to be able to say – Head Baker at Jacob's. It meant a lot. And it helped me a lot later.

"You told me how you felt then. How do you feel about

that episode of your life now?"

"I am trying to be philosophical about it. If I stayed at Jacob's, who knows what direction my life would have taken? Maybe I would still be there. Adrian is still the general manager at Jacob's. Of course, now it is a big operation with a central bakery and a chain of stores and restaurants. My life took a different path. Maybe it was for the best. Maybe not. One never knows. But what stayed with me was a realization that I wronged people who helped me and who were good to me. There was no need for it. I allowed myself to be deceived by my passions, for a woman; that was deception in itself."

"I have a feeling, Michael, that this wasn't the only time something like this happened to you. Was it?"

"Something like what?"

"Making decisions in life, based on your passions for a woman."

"Maybe. I don't know," Michael said and exhaled deeply, "I feel tired, Pastor. Maybe we should stop here."

"Yes. I agree. We can continue next Monday or if you feel like talking before that you can stop by my office whenever you have time."

Michael stood up and walked out without saying a word. Pastor Charles exhaled deeply, turned to the monitor and started typing. Finally, there was something to work on. But it wouldn't be easy, he thought. Michael had a long way to go.

Fratelli and Barbetta's

6

Michael knocked on the Director's office door. He worried. He didn't know why the Director asked to see him. Maybe somebody saw him smoking on the street while he was on one of his two-hour walks. But that was so rare. He didn't have money to buy cigarettes and once in a while, one of the students that were already working outside the Mission would give him a pack. Michael knew that it was kind of a bribe for letting them get anything they wanted from the clothing room without a requisition slip, but he didn't feel bad about it. He would let them anyway. He didn't ask for it; those cigarettes were a kind of appreciation for being nice to them. And he loved to smoke cigarettes. He kept saying he could quit anytime he wanted. When he didn't have cigarettes, it didn't bother him much. But he enjoyed smoking.

However, it was against the rules of the Bowery Mission for students to smoke while in the program. Smoking was understood as a form of addiction, equal to any other, and it was banned. Students caught smoking were subject to disciplinary measures as in the case of any other addiction.

"Come in," Michael heard the Director's voice.

"Good morning."

"Good morning, Michael. Sit down," the Director said.

The Director Keith Johnson was a man in his early forties, but he had a boyish face and looked like he was in his late twenties. With thick blonde hair, vibrant blue eyes, and a wide smile, he was always dressed in jeans and slim-fit shirts, which also enhanced his youthful look. He was Irish-American, and like many others on the Bowery staff, he was a former student with a troubling past, who managed to overcome his addictions, graduate school, and rise over the years to the position of Mission director. He was very strict as a manager, but at the same time very compassionate and understanding with students and the homeless. Many homeless people on the Lower East Side perceived the Director as their personal friend because of the way he treated them.

"How are you doing today, Michael?" the Director asked and turned his chair towards Michael.

"I am okay. Just the beginning of another week...," Michael answered, still wondering what was going to happen next.

"Do you know why I called you in today?"

"No," Michael answered. He knew that was a trick question counselors used just in case somebody felt guilty about anything and started talking before he was even accused. But he wasn't that stupid.

"Well, I spoke with your counselor, Pastor Charles, last week and I thought he had already spoken to you. But, in any case, let me get to the point. You've already been here for two months, right?"

"Yes, Director, almost. This Friday will be two months."

"And you are now on the fifth floor. How do you like being on the fifth floor? Do you get along with the rest of the guys?"

"Yes, more or less. Everybody there is okay. It is quiet in the evening, and everybody minds their own business."

"Do you know Manuel, the Floor Captain?"

"Yes, he is a decent guy. Very active in the Bible classes," Michael answered trying to figure out where the Director was going with this conversation.

"Well, Manuel will be graduating soon from the program, and it is time to appoint a new Captain for the fifth floor. We were thinking that you might be a good choice."

"Me?" Michael asked surprised.

"Yes. We've been observing you. You seem to be a serious man. All your duties here you are performing satisfactory. Your work in the clothing room is exceptional. It was never so well organized before you arrived. And you know how to deal with people, which is most important for the position of the Floor Captain. Do you know what the duties of the Floor Captain are?"

"Not exactly. I know that he wakes up students in the morning, turns off the lights in the evening and assigns floor cleaning duties to students."

"Right. Besides, the Captain has to see that no students

are in the room during classes or chapel service unless they are on sick leave. And, of course, the Captain has to make sure nothing illegal is going on in the room at any time. No smoking, drinking, getting high, or whatnot. Also, he is to make sure that there are no conflicts among students on the floor, and if there are any, to report them to the manager or counselors on duty right away. That's about it. However, there are perks to being a Floor Captain too. The Captain gets an extra hour walk time outside every day and Captains are freed from garbage or cleaning duties. So, what do you say, would you like that position?"

"Yes. But can I still work in the clothing room?" Michael asked.

"If you think you can manage both, it is up to you. I don't mind," the Director said.

"Okay, then. I accept. Thank you. I'll try to do my best."

"Then, on Wednesday, at the regular House Meeting, I will announce to all the students that you are the new Fifth Floor Captain. In the meantime, you can talk to Manuel, and he will fill you in on your particular duties and show you how to do things."

"Thank you, Director," Michael said. He was happy that he was going to be a Floor Captain. Having one hour outside every day was something he really liked. And not having to take out garbage two times a week with other students was good too. He hated those garbage duties. There was always so much garbage to bring out to the sidewalk. It was heavy and smelly. Each time he took out the garbage, he had to take a shower and change his clothing.

"That will be it, Michael. You can go now. Thank you for accepting this duty. I think it will be good for you," the Director said and turned his chair back towards his desk.

Michael walked out of Director's office and went down the hall to Pastor Charles' office. He didn't know if he was happier for becoming a Floor Captain or for not being caught smoking outside. Now that he had the right to go out for an hour every day, he would be able to have a cigarette or two each time, he was thinking.

The doors of the Pastor Charles' office were open.

"Good morning, Pastor," Michael said cheerfully.

"Good morning, Michael. You are late this morning. What happened, you were stuck in the bathroom?" The pastor asked and started laughing.

"No, I had to go see the Director this morning about the Floor Captain's job."

"Oh, did he offer you the position?" Pastor asked.

"Yes, he did, and I accepted."

"Hmm, the Director was fast this morning. I was hoping to talk to you before he called you." The pastor said with the worrisome expression on his face.

"Why? What is wrong?"

"Nothing now. You accepted, so it is done. The Director asked me about that last Friday. I couldn't tell him no because he was so optimistic about giving you that job. But I wanted to tell you to decline it because of your work in the clothing room," Pastor said.

"But why? I can do both. The Captain's duties are mostly in the morning and in the evening. They don't collide with my duties in the clothing room or with Bible classes."

"I know Michael. But I don't think that the Captain's position is for you. You are different than most of the students here. You come from a different world. These guys are not used to authority. They are allergic to it. It reminds them of jails or orphanages. It reminds them of cops. You don't want to deal with the guys on the floor as somebody who is in charge. You don't need that. You have to concentrate on yourself. I know it is easier for you to work and not think about things that you will face once you are out of here, but that is just an escape from yourself. You have to face yourself and fix whatever is broken, Michael. I looked at your grades in the Bible classes. You have all A's. Of course, you have studied the Scriptures before and you are knowledgeable, but that is not the point of the Bible classes. The point is to apply teachings to your situation, Michael. You have to accept Christ into your life, not only to know about him. So, I was hoping to get to you before the Director, but now we have to deal with this new thing. You have to be very careful in relating to other students as a Captain. Be firm but don't get into conflicts with them. If you have a problem with any of the students on the floor, come to me first, remember that."

"I think I'll be able to handle them. While working in the clothing room, I got to know most of the students. They like me," Michael was trying to prove a point. He disagreed with Pastor's opinion. Pastor really didn't know that Michael had a lot of experience dealing with different people and about his unique ability to bring himself to any level, in order to connect with them.

"Yes, they like you because you give them access to a free and good wardrobe. Wait. When you start bossing them around, we'll see if they are going to like you."

"Anyway, Michael, let's go back to our discussion from last Monday. We stopped…." The pastor looked at the screen to find his notes. "Yes, we stopped at you starting work at Fratelli's in the Village. Is that correct?"

"Whatever you say, Pastor," Michael said.

"Don't be a wise guy with me, Michael. If you don't want to do this, you don't have to. It is for your own good. Don't be upset with me for telling you my opinion. I'm not going to lie to you. I don't think that it is a good idea for you to be a Floor Captain. But what's done, is done. Let's talk about important stuff."

"So, what happened at Fratelli's?" Pastor asked.

"Working at Fratelli's was actually very good for me. They gave me the authority to organize the bakery department from scratch. I hired my help; I made menus – both for bread production and cakes and pastries production. I was doing the ordering of supplies and tools. They bought me fancy chef's uniforms with my name embroidered on the jackets. They encouraged me to walk around the store and talk to the customers. Kind of gave the place a personal touch. Everybody loved my strong Romanian accent. For them, it wasn't only about good bread and pastries, it was also about the show. I had to be a real culinary showman. And I enjoyed it. Then they brought a journalist from Food Magazine, who did an article on me and my bread. Almost overnight, I was known to everybody in New York interested in gourmet food."

"Adrian was joking after reading the article," Michael continued, 'Look at this prick! If these people only knew that two years ago, he didn't have a clue what bread baking was.' He would say, 'A journalist pretending to be a baker. And now look, he is a real star. I can't believe it. How did you do this, Michael? Did you write this article yourself?'

"But I didn't care about his teasing," Michael said, "I was really good. And I enjoyed what was I doing. It was fulfilling. A real art. I enjoyed that my customers and bosses appreciated my work. I continued experimenting with new items. I started learning cake decorating and with every cake, I got better and better."

"Okay. How was your private life at that time?" Pastor interrupted Michael in his story.

"I didn't have one. Technically, I was working from six in the morning till two in the afternoon, Monday through Saturday. But in reality, I was there seven days a week from dawn until late in the afternoon, often till closing at nine in the evening. I didn't care about the working hours. And the bosses liked that too. I think I was their favorite worker."

"It was like that," Michael continued, "until I moved to 46th Street, between 8th and 9th Avenues."

"Why did you move?"

"My roommate's sister was coming from Europe, and she needed a room for her, so she asked me if I could find a new place. I found another apartment on 46th Street. I shared a two-bedroom garden apartment in a brownstone with a gay black actor."

"Did it bother you that he was gay?"

"No. He was nice to me. And I didn't see him much anyway. When his boyfriend would come they would be in his room with closed doors, and I didn't care. He was very private about his life. I used to bring him fresh sourdough bread from work every day, sometimes pastries, and he appreciated it a lot. In return, he took over doing my laundry, since, he said, I never had time always being at work. That was at least what he said. But I think that the true reason was that my dirty, stinky laundry in the bathroom bothered him, and it was easier for him to wash it than to wait for me."

"Also, I was bringing bread and pastries to my landlord, who lived in the apartment below ours, and to the Puerto Rican chef who lived next door. They all liked my bread. And by being nice to them I managed to get a job in Barbetta's restaurant and ultimately, I was able to open my own bakery."

"Hold on, slow down! What was that? Another job? At the same time?" Pastor asked.

"Yes. Soon after I moved into that apartment, I met my next-door neighbor, Pedro. He was the pasta chef at Barbetta's, a famous Italian restaurant, just down the street from where I lived, on the same block. Barbetta's was looking for a pastry chef and he took me there. The owner liked my resume and gave me a job. I took it as a challenge. It was different than working in the bakery. I discovered that the rush of the restaurant kitchen was very exciting for me. Making desserts was one thing, but plating them and serving them, was an experience I couldn't have in a bakery, so I started working there as well."

"How did you manage to work at two places at the same time?" Pastor asked.

"Easy. I was at Fratelli's from six to two, and from three till midnight I was at Barbetta's. I had two days off there, so some days I could stay longer at Fratelli's, and everybody was happy."

"That's crazy. You must have been making a lot of money?" Pastor asked.

"Yes. I was making over fourteen hundred a week, and all my monthly expenses were only five hundred for rent and about a hundred for phone and electricity. I ate at work all the time, and once in a while I would buy new shoes or a piece of clothing, and that was it. In a year and a half working like that, I saved over sixty thousand dollars."

"That was great. So all that time you just worked. No going out, no dating girls, nothing like that – is that right?"

"Yeah, you can say that," Michael was hesitating.

"I can say that or it was like that? Which one is it? Are you not telling me something?"

"Well, there was a short fling with this Irish girl that worked at Fratelli's. But that was just an episode. Nothing serious."

"Oh, oh, I suspect that this will be interesting. Let's hear it."

"Let's leave it for next time. How about that?" Michael said.

"You always break when it is the most interesting. If you

think that next Monday will be easier for you, you are wrong. The sooner you spill out all your adventures, the sooner we will be able to find the cause of your troubles and hopefully find the right remedy. Of course, we know the remedy. You have to accept Jesus Christ, Michael. No more hiding. You can't hide from your Savior. He is everywhere and sees everything."

"I am with Christ, Pastor, since I was born and baptized."

"No, you are not. He is with you, but you are not with him. You know about Him, sometimes you pray to Him when you are down, but you are not with Him. You have so much pride in yourself, Michael, that it is spilling from your eyes and from the way you talk and act. It is so obvious. To accept Jesus, you have to get rid of all of that pride. That is why I didn't want you to be Floor Captain. You are stubborn, and you will get into conflicts with some of the students on the floor. I guarantee you that."

"I'll prove you wrong, Pastor. I'll prove you wrong. I am going now," Michael said and stood up.

"Go. You are sometimes too much, you know. And buy mint candy or chewing gum, okay," Pastor said as Michael was leaving.

"Why?" Michael stopped at the door. His face got red.

"I can smell the nicotine, Michael. It is your life, I don't care; you know it is bad for you, but don't let the Manager on Duty catch you. You know it is against the rules. I don't want to have to discipline you. I hope you are not smoking in the building," Pastor said and turned towards computer screen.

"I don't smoke," Michael said.

"Yeah. Yeah. Keep lying to yourself if it makes you feel good. You can't lie to me. Close the door behind you. And if you see Jeremiah, tell him to come. I need to talk to him."

The Second American Woman

7

That Wednesday at the regular House Meeting attended by all students and staff, the Director announced that Michael was the new fifth floor Captain.

Many students who had been there longer than Michael were surprised. Usually, floor captains were students who had already been at the Bowery for three, four months. Michael was fairly new. Also, he didn't have that appearance of street roughness that was so necessary to gain authority among those who grew up in the projects and the poor neighborhoods of New York, as most of the men in the Bowery did.

After the meeting, a few of the fifth-floor students were, making loud comments that they would not follow Michael's instructions. Michael didn't react. He knew they said that so he would hear them, but he ignored them. His plan was simple. There were thirty-eight guys on his floor. Those who were going to listen he would engage. Those who were not going to listen, he would ignore for now.

But the best part of being a Floor Captain was the ability to go out for an hour every day. It became Michael's routine till the end of his stay in the Bowery. Every evening after dinner, he would walk west on Prince, make a left on Mercer Street, and sit on the back stairs of the Boss Clothing Store, light up a cigarette and watch people rushing by. It was his secret spot. It was far enough from the Bowery that nobody could see him smoking and close enough he could walk back in minutes.

He would sit there and watch the large windows of the lofts in the buildings across the street. Those were luxurious SoHo apartments. He was thinking whether or not he would ever be able to afford any of them. If he had money, he would definitely live in SoHo. But he was so far from something like that. He still didn't know how he would make a living once he was out of the Bowery. Time goes fast and soon he would graduate the program and have to look for a job. If he didn't find one soon enough, they would not keep him in the Bowery forever. They would kick him out. So not finding a job was not an option.

He still couldn't understand how he could mess up his life like that. Twenty-something years in New York, so many good things that he had done, children he had raised with so much care and hard work, so many friends he had helped, and he could not turn anywhere for help. And he didn't blame his family or his former friends for it. He knew that the fault lay with him. But again, if he put himself in their shoes and tried to look at himself from their perspective he would never have ostracized himself the way they did. He rejected nobody in his life like that.

Most of the evenings on Mercer Street, Michael would spend thinking about his life and years that had passed. He knew that the biggest break in his life was when he left the culinary profession and went back to writing. It was at the same time he had his strange dream he often referred to as his "vision." It was five years before he got to the Bowery and it seemed that since that time, everything was going downhill for Michael. He got divorced, lost his business in New York, and lost his business in Romania. Yet, he was determined to find his purpose as he saw it in his vision. He knew that it was possible only through writing. But the real inspiration hadn't come yet. He knew what it was that he wanted to say, but it couldn't come out. His mind was blocked. He was convinced that soon things would turn around for him. But he had to write, he thought, because the success and prosperity that he wanted to gain back could come only from writing.

Michael's duties as a Floor Captain started without much stress. He thought most of the students on the floor didn't mind who the Captain was and they followed his instructions, including the cleaning schedule he made weekly. Those who ignored him, he ignored back. But he didn't want to report them to the Director. At least, not yet.

The following Monday, Michael was on time to Pastor Charles' office. The pastor was on the phone with somebody, and he pointed to Michael towards the chair next to him.

Michael sat down and looked at the computer screen over Pastor's shoulder. He wanted to see some of the Pastor's notes, but he couldn't. It was too far for him to see it without glasses.

Pastor hung up and turned towards Michael.

"Good morning, Michael."

"Good morning, Pastor. How was your weekend?" Michael asked.

"Oh, very busy. We had a guest speaker both Saturday and Sunday in my church. It was good, but it made me tired. By the way, in a couple of months, you will be able to go on Sundays to a church outside. I would like if you could come to my church. We have a bilingual service in English and French."

"Sure. I wouldn't mind. I like to visit different churches and temples." Michael answered.

"So Michael, how is it working in the new Captain's position? Any problems yet?"

"None, Pastor. Everything is cool. I enjoy it."

"Okay, let's get to our conversation from last Monday. I have to rush today. I have a meeting uptown in an hour. So, what happened with the woman you said you had "a fling" with? Let's hear it."

"Yes, that was an interesting story. I certainly never – before or after – had experienced anything like that. She was two years younger than me and worked in the accounting department at Fratelli's. She was Irish. Her name was Fiona. She was tall with short red hair and green eyes. She had a beautiful body, and she knew how to carry it. Every couple of days, she would come to me to pick up the invoices from bakery suppliers. She liked to chat, and each time she came, we would talk about something. After a while, our chats turned into open flirting that we both enjoyed. I was waiting for the right moment to ask her out."

"But then, one day she surprised me with the question, 'Okay, Michael, how long I will have to wait before you ask me out? Is there anything wrong with me?'

"I got embarrassed for a moment, feeling stupid, but I reacted immediately, 'How about tonight, Fiona?' I asked. She accepted."

"It was good timing. I was off at Barbetta's that day. So I took her to an Italian restaurant in the Theater District, one block from my home. The executive chef in that place was a friend of mine, and he ordered the whole dinner to be on the house. They treated us like royalties. After all, I was already a well-known pastry chef and my friend chef liked that I picked his place for dinner. He was eager to hear my opinion about his desserts, which were very good, by the way.

"Fiona was impressed with the way we were treated. Halfway through dinner, we were already tipsy from the good Italian wine. Fiona was in a silk white shirt that was almost see-through with nothing under it and a short black skirt. We groped each other while still in the restaurant, like some teenagers. Then she said, 'Let's finish this dinner fast and go to your place.' It was a good idea."

"What happened at my place that night I will never forget. I don't think I ever had a similar experience in my life. She was really hot, man. We just couldn't hold it. We first had intercourse while we were still on the stairs, in front of the apartment. Thank God nobody passed by. It was an earthquake all night. I was young and much stronger then, but I still don't know where I found all that energy. And Fiona just didn't want to stop. Who knows how long it would have lasted if I didn't have to go to work in the morning. Needless to say, that was my first sexual experience in New York since I got here. It had been almost three years since I'd touched a woman when Fiona showed up."

"She stayed at my place to sleep and came to work much later. Of course, I was already in love and red roses were waiting on her desk in the office."

"She came to work around noon and went to her office, just to run out of it all red in the face and came to my work station. 'Michael!' She yelled, 'What is wrong with you? Do you want to get me in trouble?' I was confused. I didn't know what I did wrong? 'What is wrong Fiona?' I asked. 'Roses, Michael! Roses! I am engaged. What if my fiancé shows up and sees these roses or somebody tells him about it? I'm marrying him in three months. I don't want any problems. We had a good time and that was it. There is nothing between us except good sex. And I hope you won't be talking about it around Fratelli's.' 'Of course, I won't Fiona.' I told her. She ran from my station, slammed the door, and went back to her office. I was stunned. I didn't know that she had a boyfriend. She never mentioned that before. And, I couldn't understand how she could make love to me when she loved somebody else."

"She didn't make love to you, Michael. She just had sex with you. It is completely different," Pastor said.

"But I never understood that. I could never enter into

sexual intercourse with anybody if I didn't feel something for that woman."

"Are you serious Michael?" The pastor asked, "You never had sex just for the sake of pleasure? Without feelings? Have you heard of prostitutes? Have you ever been with a prostitute?"

"Prostitute!?" Michael asked with surprise in his voice, "Never. And I don't think that I ever could. It is a degrading thing for both a woman and a man. Not only that, I never went to a topless bar or strip club and never watched porn. Those are all things for sick people. I feel bad for any woman that has to work as a prostitute. And all those pimps that make them sell their bodies should be raped and then killed like wild beasts."

"Oh, oh, wait, Michael. Don't get radical here. Only God has the right to judge people. That is not our job. So, how did you feel after? Did you go out with Fiona again?" Pastor asked.

"Only once. Her boyfriend was on a business trip and we went to her place. I still couldn't believe there was nothing between us. The sex was great, again. But two weeks after that, she got married. I was at the wedding. I also made the wedding cake for them. It was my gift. It took me a while to get over her. Even today, whenever I see a red-haired woman, my heart jumps."

"So, you like red haired women, right?" Pastor asked.

"Not necessarily. I don't know if there is a particular type of woman I like. Every woman I was ever in a relationship with, had something particular about them, some detail I liked – something that attracted me to them. I think of it as a remembrance."

"Remembrance? Of what Michael?

"I don't know, Pastor. The closest I can come to explaining it, is that there is some type of ideal woman deep in my soul. I cannot perceive it completely, but whenever a woman comes across my path that has something that reminds me of that ideal, I feel it, and I usually fall in love."

"Can you describe this ideal woman?" Pastor asked.

"I can't Pastor. It comes to me in flashes. Or better yet, through the women I've been with. My biggest problem with women was that I never loved any of them completely. In my mind, they all had something of that ideal that I was looking for, but they were never complete."

"You are too harsh on yourself. As much as I understand, throughout your life, all the women you were with, left you. You didn't leave them, except for your last relationship."

"Yes, that is true," Michael said.

"So, taking that into account you were for the most part always in love and faithful, why do you think you didn't love them completely?"

"I know I didn't. Now I know I didn't. And you are right, if things hadn't happened with my first wife the way they did, or if things hadn't happened with my second wife the way they did, I would probably still be in one of those marriages. I would never leave them for another woman. But since I got aware of this ideal woman, deep in my soul I don't have peace, Pastor. It is haunting me."

"What is haunting you Michael, or who is haunting you?"

"The idea that I have to find this woman. That is what is haunting me. The feeling we've been together already and we have to be together again."

"And if I understand correctly, you don't even know what this woman looks like, except for the details that you have recognized in different women throughout your life," Pastor was trying to summarize.

"That is correct," Michael said.

"Well, all I can tell you is that you are lucky that you are a writer. It will make for a nice romance novel. I think you are just confused and oversensitive. Are you too sensitive, Michael? What do you think?" Pastor Charles said.

"Maybe... I don't know."

"Not maybe. Definitely! We have an expression back home in Haiti, which says something like 'a man who is thinking with his penis.' That is what you are Michael. That doesn't mean that you are addicted to sex or pornography. You are not a pervert of any kind. Contrary! You are just too sensitive with women. You fall in love at the blink of an eye and all your decisions are based on your passions towards a particular woman. Your mind gets blurry because not enough blood goes to your brain. And your heart pumps all the blood back to your penis and that is why you are a man who thinks with his penis."

"Thank you for your vulgar explanation. Theologically it is very deep, you know," Michael said ironically, visibly upset with Pastor's comment.

"It is true, Michael. You have to learn to control your passions, especially your passions towards women. Why do you think throughout the Bible, the favorite tool of the devil to subdue man was a woman? That is where our weakness lies. From Adam to any man today, that is our weakest spot. And it seems to me you keep surrendering to it over and over again. You are too sensitive - weak towards women. You have to bind your passions, Michael. And you have to pray about it, a lot. Oh, yes, a lot!" Pastor Charles was almost shouting.

Michael saw the direction this discussion was going and he didn't like it. There was much he could say to Pastor about his vision and about the ideal woman from his soul. But Pastor wouldn't understand, Michael was sure. Also, Michael didn't want to tell him. He couldn't trust anybody with his secret. It was just his.

"So, what do you propose I should do?" Michael asked.

"For now all you can do is pray. Pray to God Almighty to bind your carnal passions and give you strength to control them. You have to find a way to re-wire your heart so you don't fall for any skirt that passes your way."

"I don't fall for any skirt that passes my way. That is simply not true." Michael said.

"Yes. And my name is not Charles. Please, Michael, don't deny the obvious things. I am not trying to be hard on you. I am not telling you this as a counselor. And I am not being cocky. I am telling you this as a friend who cares about you. I just think this image of the ideal woman from your soul you have, is just a way for your conscience to excuse your behaviors. You made this image in your imagination to make it easy on yourself. It is normal. Otherwise, you would blow up or jump from a bridge. Anyway, I have to rush to my meeting. We'll continue next Monday. Don't be upset. This was good today. We are getting somewhere. With God's help and blessings, you will be able to conquer your weaknesses. Remember what Scriptures says, 'I can do all things through Christ My Lord who strengthens me."

The American Dream

8

Days were passing by in the Bowery Mission. Michael was getting used to living there. Together with Rick, Michael was in charge of the clothing room. Pastor Paul, the senior pastor of the Bowery Chapel, was nominally the supervisor of the clothing room and shower program for the homeless, but he didn't have the time to be bothered with it so much. The appearance of Michael and his proactive approach to his duties in the clothing room gave Pastor Paul a break from watching over the clothing room, at least during the time Michael was there.

Within weeks Michael gained Pastor Paul's full confidence in running the clothing room. Pastor Paul was tall, blonde man with goat beard, from Amish Country, who gave up his idyllic way of life in Lancaster, Pennsylvania for his work with homeless. "I will give you your own set of keys to the clothing room and inform managers on duty that you are in charge of the operations and you can be there any time you want. Okay Michael," Pastor Paul said.

There were many benefits for Michael in working in the clothing room. The most important, he had space where he could be alone with himself and his thoughts. Spending time with other students in the program was very depressing. Most of them were from the world that was strange to him. Almost all of them were recovering drug addicts or alcoholics trying for who knows how long, to break their addictions. The majority of them grew up in poor neighborhoods, in broken families, never finished school, have had run-ins with the law, spent time in jail, and had a life attitude of survivors in a jungle that Michael liked to call "the bottom of the New York barrel."

Michael didn't judge them or look down on them. He had seen them as the victims of a system that was cruel and didn't forgive those who did not learn how to fit in. After all, he spent time in jail when he was young too. He spent nights on New York subways. But he knew that his experience was nothing compared to theirs. Some of them spent, not days, not months, but years on the streets of New York as homeless people. Others grew up on government handouts living from one welfare check to another, moving from one shelter to another.

Victor told Michael once, that he started dealing drugs on the street when he was twelve and that he started using drugs himself when he was fourteen. When Michael asked him why he started dealing drugs so young, Victor answered, "I never saw my mother buy food in the supermarket with anything else but food-stamps. I never had any new clothing or shoes until I made my second hundred bucks on crack."

"Your second hundred bucks?" Michael repeated in surprise. "What happened with the first hundred bucks you made on the sale?"

"I gave it to my mother. I wanted her to buy food with money instead of with food stamps, just once. Instead, she got drugs from her dealer and got high. I never gave her any of my money again. Soon after she left me and my sister and disappeared."

Michael knew that these men with whom he shared his life in the Bowery Mission lived in the vicious circle of poverty, drugs, crime, and addiction. It was a sad side to the American way of living, one that tourists couldn't see on their visits to New York. Those guys with their presence around Michael reminded him every day, not only how low he had fallen, but also how much deeper he could fall if he didn't get his act together. For Michael, listening to the life stories of other students in the program was like looking into a deep and dark abyss. "Hell," Michael thought, "We don't need to read sacred texts for a description of hell. The lives of these people are a living hell – hell on earth."

So Michael appreciated his time in the clothing room, away from most of the students and their realities. Rick was a recovering alcoholic who survived a stroke and a heart attack and was thrown out on the street by his wife who couldn't handle his drunkenness anymore. He was often going through cycles of depression; he would take medication and sleep for days. Rick welcomed Michael's presence in the clothing room because he spent many days in bed feeling sorry for himself. Michael didn't mind that. He liked to be alone.

There was yet another reason Michael liked working in the clothing room. He always liked to dress well. The last couple of years he spent in Romania before coming back to New York, he ran out of all of his good wardrobe and couldn't afford to buy anything.

According to the rules of the Mission, students enrolled in the recovery program, had a right to get all the clothing they needed for free; not only while in the program but also once they left the program. There were no set quotas on how much of a wardrobe one student could have. And of course, students were using and abusing the opportunity to get free clothing. Suddenly these poor men, who never had decent clothing in their lives, had dozens of jeans, pants, dozens of suits, shirts, leather jackets, and shoes. And most of the stuff that the students were getting, was brand new designer clothing donated directly by the fashion companies to the Bowery Mission.

Michael enjoyed looking at these men wearing Brooks Brothers suits, Ralph Lauren shirts, Cole-Haan shoes, Boss leather jackets, and Nike sneakers. There was something ironic in the fact that people on the outside had to pay a small fortune for the same clothing, yet these men were getting it for free.

Michael knew what a good wardrobe was because many years back he could afford it, and he wore it. But now he wasn't different than any other student. He was like a kid in a candy store, piling loads and loads of the expensive clothing into his locker. When he couldn't fit any more items in his locker, he put the items in big black garbage bags and placed them in the storage room on the fifth floor. And of course, being that he was working in the clothing room, all the best pieces of clothing that would come in, he would have the first pick.

He had mentioned to Pastor Paul how fortunate they all were for being able to get all of this clothing for free, and Pastor would just answer, "Michael, this is just one small sign from our Lord Christ, telling us that these are just small gifts from Him, foretelling the gift of eternal life to all of those who come to Him. This may be donated by different people and companies to the Bowery Mission, but it really comes from God. And we should be grateful to Him for all these gifts."

So, one Monday morning, Michael entered Pastor Charles office, dressed all in white. He had white Levi's pants, a white cotton shirt, and white Converse sneakers.

"Good morning, Pastor," Michael said.

"Good morning, Michael. Look at you! What is it today? A Blessing-dale fashion show?" The Pastor asked and started laughing, "Oh, life is good at the Bowery Mission."

"I'm not complaining right now," Michael said, "Do you like this outfit? I can get something for you, too. We have all sizes and brands. And the price is just right, ha, ha."

"Thank you, Michael. I'll stick to 34th Street sales. If I start shopping at Blessing-dale I am afraid that I would get used to it, ha, ha."

"It feels good to look rich. What do you say, Pastor?"

"Yes. It is even better to be rich, Michael, – rich in Christ. Are you rich, Michael?" The pastor asked as his face turned serious.

"I think I am." Michael answered, "I know I am."

"Hmm, let's see…where did we stop last time?" The Pastor said and scrolled through his notes on the computer. "Ok, we stopped at you working at Fratelli's and Barbetta's and living on 46th Street. What happened next?"

"I opened up my first bakery on 53rd Street and 9th Avenue," Michael answered.

"How did you manage that?"

"You remember, I mentioned my landlord at 46th street to whom I used to bring fresh bread every day?"

"Yes?" Pastor asked.

"Well, he kept telling me that I should open my own bakery. I would tell him that opening a bakery cost lots of money and that it would take time for me to save that much. So one day he asked me if I would open a bakery, in partnership with him. He didn't have much money, but he owned that brownstone on 46th Street, and he wanted to use it as collateral for a bank loan. I agreed, and soon after, we found a perfect location. It was a store between 52nd and 53rd Street on 9th Avenue that had been vacant for twenty years. But best of all, it was originally a bakery and still had a built in brick oven in the basement. That neighborhood was just coming back and recovering. It was in the time when Giuliani became Mayor and started cleaning Times Square and the surrounding neighborhoods. It was a perfect time to invest there. We negotiated a ten-year lease with good rent and three months free for construction."

"So your landlord put down his building as collateral for a loan for your bakery? That was a brave thing to do." Pastor said.

"Yes, it was. I would never do it myself for somebody else. But Timothy - his name was Timothy - he really believed in the success of my bread. And he didn't need that risk. At the time, he was sixty-five, a retired playwright, who wrote one hit play for Broadway back in the sixties, made money from it, and bought his brownstone. He hadn't done anything big after that, but thanks to the rentals, he was able to live decently. Most of his building, he converted into a rooming house for people working in the theater district, and there were two full apartments. I lived in the garden apartment with my roommate.

So, we got money from the bank and started construction with a contractor from the Bronx. Instead of three months, it took us six months to complete everything. All that time, I was working at Fratelli's and Barbetta's.

Finally, we completed all the work and opened our bakery in April of '90. It was exactly three years after I arrived in New York. I didn't have papers yet, but I had my bakery."

"What was the name of it?" Pastor asked.

"We named it, Famous Bread. And soon after, it became really famous. I still don't know if my bread and pastries were that good or we were just plain lucky, but without any advertising, business was booming from the very first day. Then Florence Fabricant, a food critic from the New York Times, showed up one day in the store. I knew of her but never met her before. She bought several pieces of bread and pastries and went on her way. The girl working at the counter came to me and told me of the woman that bought almost one of everything that we had in the store. I didn't think much of it. Many customers liked to sample new stuff. But the next day, Florence called me, introduced herself and told me to look for an article about my bakery on Wednesday in the Food Section of the New York Times."

"That Wednesday, the line of customers was out the store and around the corner of 53rd Street. I was baking all day like crazy. In the evening, when we closed, there was not a single piece of bread or pastry left in the store. Timothy was joking that if we wanted to sell an empty shelf, we could sell it. After that, reviews from the Daily News and Post followed. Business was great. Soon after, we opened up another store on the Upper East Side on Second Avenue."

"I started doing wholesale. All major gourmet stores, restaurants, and supermarkets were buying from us. I was on the top of the hill, or as Florence Fabricant put in her article, 'my American dream came true.'"

"But it was at the price. When I was at Fratelli's and Barbetta's, I was working long hours. But it was nothing compared to the hours I spent working in my bakery. Many days, I would work twenty-four hours straight, go to sleep for four hours and come back for another twenty-four-hour shift. Once, when my delivery driver was off, I was delivering bread to stores on the Upper West Side. It was 4:30 in the morning. On my way back, I fell asleep at the wheel, and my van ended up on the stairs before the Metropolitan Opera plateau. Thank God I didn't hit anybody.

"I had seven people working in the bakery, plus four

girls at the counter, and a delivery guy. Two of my assistants had worked with me before, at Fratelli's. They knew everything I knew and they were reliable. But somehow, I wanted to be there all the time and run the show. I felt strange if they were all working and I was just walking around."

"Timothy would come in the late afternoon to work at the counter until closing. He would always say to me, 'Go home and rest. I am here now. I will watch and close the store tonight.' But I couldn't. There was a special pleasure for me to close the store, close the cash register, count the money, write orders for the next day, and then go. It wasn't about being in control. It was about marveling over my own success."

"So, you really didn't have a private life then. Everything was about the bakery and work, right? How about your kids and ex-wife in Romania, did you keep in touch with them?"

"When I opened my bakery, I was thinking about the possibility to renew the relationship with my ex-wife and bring them all to New York. I spoke about that to my mother who lived in Bucharest. I asked her for her opinion. At first, she didn't want to tell me anything. But then, as I was pressing her, she finally told me that my ex-wife remarried and lived with her new husband and our kids in another town in Romania and that I should forget about them. I was broken. I wasn't sure if I felt anything anymore for my ex-wife, but the idea that my kids call another man 'father' was very hurtful to me."

"So, how did you meet your second wife and when?" Pastor asked.

"Oh, my second wife just walked in my bakery one day and two weeks after we were married," Michael said and smiled.

"What? After two weeks. How that happened?" Pastor asked.

"Oh, it is the funniest story ever," Michael said.

At that moment doors of the Pastor Charles' office opened. It was Pastor Paul.

"Sorry to interrupt, Pastor, but I need Michael in the clothing room now if you don't mind. Today is a shower day and he has to go downstairs to prepare everything. It is hot and muggy outside. I am sure we will have a lot of homeless in today for showers," Pastor Paul said.

"Sure, Pastor Paul, sure. Go, Michael. We will continue next Monday." Pastor Charles said and stood up to stretch his legs.

The Third American Woman

9

All his life Michael felt like the hand of God was involved in his life in a strange way. And no matter what he thought, decided to do and did, and regardless of circumstances, he felt that his life was predestined to go a certain way. The only problem was that he didn't know where that life path would lead him. But somehow, he knew he couldn't control it.

There were numerous examples from his life, of things that happened to him that Michael perceived as the hand of God at work, and he could not find any rational explanation, regardless of how hard he would try.

Again, the same thing was happening at the Bowery Mission. And to Michael, it was more obvious than ever before, that God was at work. On the fifth floor, there were five students who had been hostile to Michael. Hardcore criminals, recharging their 'batteries', after time spent in jail, under the cover of addiction. They wanted nobody to disturb them. Their jail mentality and behavior were keeping everybody at a distance. While with the counselors, however, they were playing troubled men who needed help with their addictions and wanted to turn their lives around.

For them, Michael represented everything they hated: well spoken, well dressed, educated, and in a charge of the floor. He was the symbol of the authority they despised from the bottom of their hearts. Everything Michael would tell them, they ignored. If Michael would ask them to do something, they would curse and threatened him. One of their favorite threat was, "You know, Michael, at some point you'll have to sleep. Do you ever think what may happen to you while you are sleeping?" The other favorite threat was, "Michael, there are four showers in the bathroom. What do you think would happen, if one day while you were taking a shower, three other guys share the shower with you?"

Michael tried to ignore them, but their threats were affecting him. He didn't know how to handle it. Until one day. That day, one of those five guys was caught getting high on the roof of the Bowery Mission. The offense was serious, and after discussion, counselors decided to kick him out of the program. Michael was happy. One less guy to worry about. The next morning, after Michael turned on the lights on the floor and started walking around to wake up the students, one of other four guys threw a shoe at him, yelling, "Stop talking, you son of a bitch. This is not a jail. I want to sleep!"

"If you want to sleep, I'll make sure you get kicked out of the Bowery like your buddy yesterday, so you can sleep in the subway as much as you want," Michael answered. He didn't know why he said that. He had nothing to do with other guy being caught on the roof or being kicked out. He just felt he needed to say that.

Three days later, the student who throw a shoe at him, was kicked out for having sex with a homeless man in the basement of the Bowery Mission. Again, Michael had nothing to do with what happened, but one of the fifth-floor students commented at the lunch time, "Hmm. Maybe it is not a very good idea to be aggressive with Michael."

Within the next month, the remaining three students were dismissed from the program for various offenses. Everybody in the Mission was convinced that Michael had something to do with their dismissals. He didn't, of course. But Michael thought of it as the hand of God and used that to his advantage. At the monthly floor meeting, while discussing the daily duties of the students, he said to them, "You don't have to listen to my instructions. I don't mind. But if you don't, make sure you have your bags packed. You already know what happens to those who oppose me."

By this time, nobody on the floor wanted to take a chance. But then, rumors went around the Bowery Mission about the Captain on the fifth floor acting like a dictator.

Pastor Charles was scratching his head. He couldn't connect the Michael he spoke to every Monday with the Michael students from the fifth floor were describing. The Director was happy. The fifth floor was spotless and there were no incidents of any kind there.

"Michael, what did you do to those guys on the fifth floor? Everybody is afraid of you. I don't understand,"

Pastor Charles said as Michael entered his office.

"Good morning to you too, Pastor," Michael said smiling. "What happened? Was somebody complaining about me?"

"No, not exactly. But word gets around that you are arrogant. That I understand, I can see you as arrogant! Also, some guys are saying that there is something scary in your eyes, like the voodoo look. And if you get angry with somebody, bad things happen to them," Pastor said.

"Do you believe that, Pastor?" Michael asked and started laughing.

"No, Michael. But I was born in Haiti, and I know of many things that can't be explained. These guys, who are talking about you, have been through everything in their lives. They are not easily scared. Yet, they are scared of you."

"That is nonsense, Pastor. I treat everybody with respect and I am fair in assigning the floor cleaning duties. In everything else, I am following the rules. Most of the guys from the fifth floor are actually privileged."

"How so?" Pastor asked.

"Well, I've never denied any of them from going to the clothing room and taking anything they wanted without a requisition form. All the other guys have to have a requisition slip from their counselor."

"Do you think that is right, Michael?" Pastor asked.

"Maybe not. But I had to do something to have those guys on my side. To make them feel privileged. My authority over the clothing room was the only leverage I had."

"Well, Michael, just try not to be too arrogant and bossy. You know that most of our students have issues with authority. So, try to turn down your enthusiasm, if you know what I mean, ok?"

"I understand, Pastor. I will pay attention to the way I act with others. Maybe you are right. Sometimes I get bossy. Without bad intentions... it just comes out of me."

"Okay. Good. Now let's go back to your story. You were gonna tell me about your second marriage if I am not mistaken? The pastor asked while turning his chair towards Michael.

"Yes, that was an interesting story. Certainly, messed up my life big time," Michael whispered with sadness in his voice and then continued, "One Monday morning I was with my partner Timothy in the store working at the counter. The girls were off that day, and sometimes we liked to be there to greet and talk to the customers. It gave the kind of a personal touch to our business. Customers appreciated that."

"Then she walked in. She bought a bunch of croissants and muffins for the carpenters renovating her apartment. She was tall, slim and blond, with short hair and big blue eyes. But what I liked the most were her lips. She had such sexy lips that would open into a beautiful smile. I was spellbound."

"Which is otherwise unusual for you." The Pastor said sarcastically and laughed. "I am sorry for the interruption, Michael. I couldn't hold it in. You are really an amorous person. Continue, please."

"I started flirting with her. Her name was Sarah. She was originally from California and worked on Wall Street as an accountant for a major financial firm. Sarah told me that her father was Romanian and her last name was Romanian. But she didn't speak the language. Her mother was a Russian Jew, and Sarah had a bunch of brothers and sisters."

"She left after chatting with me for half an hour and promised to come back to the store. Timothy looked at me with a funny expression on his face. I told him, 'Good-looking girl, Timmy. What do you think?'"

'Yes, she is definitely good looking, but I don't think you have any chance with her,' Timothy answered.

'Why not?' I asked.

'I think she is out of your league. She is a Wall Street gal and you are a baker, who smells like bread and yeast. Besides, there is something about her that doesn't seem right.'

'Like what? I asked. He just shrugged his shoulders and said, 'don't know, but in any case, you don't have a chance with this girl.'

'You want to bet?' I asked him. He agreed. So we made a bet for one hundred dollars she would go out with me. I was going to ask her out the next time she came."

"We didn't have to wait for a long time. Same day, she came back in the afternoon to buy sandwiches for the workers in her apartment. We spoke again. Timothy was pretending that he couldn't hear. I didn't waste time. I told her straight out, 'you know Sarah, I would like to ask you out, maybe for a drink or dinner, and if you decline, I will lose one hundred dollars.'"

'How so?' She asked.

'I made a bet for hundred dollars with my partner you would go out with me if I asked you,' I said. She started laughing and looked at Timothy who was serving other customers.   'Okay.' She said, 'I will go out with you, but under one condition.'

'What is the condition? I will be a perfect gentleman if that is what you ask,' I said.

'No, it is not that. I know you will be. But I want your winnings of a hundred dollars to be spent on our dinner. It is the only fair thing to do. By revealing to me your bet, you got an unfair advantage, so you shouldn't profit from it. And because I enabled you to win, you should spend it on me,' Sarah said and smiled.

"Wow, a woman with a sharp mind," Pastor Charles commented.

"Yes, Pastor. She had a sharp mind. Always. She also had a very good business sense. She was a no-nonsense person in every way," Michael said and continued, "So, we went out for dinner to Panarella Restaurant on Columbus Avenue and 85th. She told me that she was quitting her job and moving back to California. The only reason she was renovating her apartment, was because she wanted to rent it out for more money. I was kind of disappointed. I just met a girl I liked, and she was moving away. I asked her what would have to happen in order for her not to move back. She answered, 'Only if somebody asks me to marry him,' and started laughing. After dinner, we walked back to her apartment. It was a wonderful spring evening in Manhattan.

Everything was blooming and there was a smell of renewal of life in the air. We couldn't stop talking. But once in her apartment, we didn't speak anymore. We went straight to the bedroom. She was as sharp in bed as she was in appearance. She knew exactly what she wanted and how to get it. I enjoyed it."

"I had to get up at four to be in my bakery on time. Sarah promised she would join me for breakfast. She showed up around noon. I gave her a tour of the bakery, introduced her to my staff, and we went to a Diner next door for a late breakfast. She told me she was going to California in three days. I asked her again if there was any way she could change her mind. She lowered her head looking down at the table in front of her and answered, "I don't think so, Michael. There is nothing for me in New York anymore." I smiled and asked jokingly, "What if I ask you to marry me?" She raised her head, looked at me with those big blue eyes like she couldn't believe what I was saying, paused for a moment and then said, 'So, ask me.' Now I was caught by surprise. I didn't expect such a direct answer. But then I said 'Will you marry me, Sarah?' She said yes without hesitation and almost without emotion like she was agreeing to a business proposal or to some common everyday suggestion. I was so much into my own exhilaration I was going to marry a beautiful and smart American girl that I didn't notice the particular way in which she said yes. I simply didn't pay attention to it.

"Then she stood up and said, 'Okay, we have a lot to discuss and plan. Let's go. I will come to the bakery after closing, so we can talk about everything.' I stood up and wanted to kiss her, but she stepped back. 'Michael, I don't like to show affection in public. Our love is our private stuff. We don't have to show off. We are not kids.'"

"That evening I told Timothy that I had proposed to Sarah and she accepted. Astonished, he looked at me in disbelief for a few moments and then he said, 'But you just met her yesterday, Michael. What do you know about this girl? What does she know about you? You are both out of your minds!'"

"I told him that there is nothing he could say to change my mind. Just before closing, Sarah came. I introduced her to Timothy. He was trying to act nice to Sarah, and Sarah to him, but I could sense coldness between them and didn't know why."

"Two weeks later, we went to City Hall and got married. Her sister that lives in New York, and my friend Adrian were witnesses and the only two people present at our wedding besides us. We had a nice dinner in a restaurant downtown, and then Sarah and I got a room at the Plaza Hotel to spend our wedding night there."

"As she had planned before meeting me, Sarah rented out the apartment she lived at to somebody and quit her job at Wall Street. Soon after, we rented a penthouse on 52nd Street, between Eight and Ninth Avenue, just around the corner from my bakery. I bought new furniture and we were working on fixing up the penthouse. I was spending less and less time at the bakery and more and more at home. Timothy didn't mind. He thought I deserved time for myself. Things were going smooth anyway."

"Then Sarah got involved in my business. At first, she was just curious, but then she proposed that I should fire the accountant, who was doing our books, and let her do it. Then she said that it would be a good idea to hire her as a bakery manager. I saw nothing wrong with it. I thought that paying my wife was like paying me. It goes into the same house. But Timothy was furious. He didn't like involving the family in our business. 'Michael, you are the manager of your bakery. Why do you need to pay a manager, even if it is your wife?' He said. I didn't listen to him. According to our partnership agreement, I was the majority partner and my decision was final. So I did it. The moment, Sarah started working in the Bakery, Timothy stopped showing up in the evenings. Once in a while, he would stop by to see if all the bills were paid."

"Once again, because of a woman, I hurt and neglected the man who helped me start my business and put his property as collateral for my success. But at that time, I didn't see things like that. I was in love. I would do anything for Sarah. She was talking about having a chain of bakeries from the East Coast to the West Coast, about franchising my brand, about making millions, and I was talking about having kids and a nice house upstate."

"At night, she would often find an excuse not to make love. I didn't mind. Now, since Timothy was not in the store in the evenings, I was spending, even more, time there, so I was tired. In reality, Sarah was the real owner, coming in at noon for a few hours and then in the evening to count the money. Again, I didn't mind. She was my wife."

"Then, she started going back to Los Angeles to visit her parents and family. Those visits became more frequent. After a while, she would spend a week in California almost every month. Again, I didn't mind. I felt guilty that I was working so much. She needed time for herself."

"Two years passed very fast. I was happy. I was a successful business owner who worked hard, made lots of money and had a beautiful and intelligent wife. I was really proud of her appearance, wherever we were. Everywhere we went, she was ruling the space."

"Then, one day I came home after a long night at the bakery. Sarah had just gone somewhere. As I was getting ready to take a shower, I saw the red light on the answering machine blinking. I pressed the button to hear the message. It was the voice of Pamela, Sarah's friend from Los Angeles. She was crying and talking, 'Sarah, I can't live like this anymore. This is not a life. It is torture. I miss you, my love. I miss your touch. I miss your body next to mine. You have to make a decision. I love you, Sarah.' I couldn't believe what I was hearing!! I listened to the message over and over again, I still couldn't believe it. I met Pamela when I was on a trip to Los Angeles with Sarah. She was introduced to me as Sarah's high school friend. But this wasn't the message of a high school friend. It was the message of a lover, of a woman that was in love with my wife."

"I was furious; I didn't know what to think. Then Sarah came back. I played the message for her. 'Do you care to explain what this means, Sarah?' I asked her. 'No, Michael.

I don't want to explain anything. I am leaving you. I am going to California to be with Pamela," she said and walked to the bedroom almost like nothing happened. I was frozen. My whole world was collapsing in front of my eyes. The woman, I loved so much was leaving me for a woman. I walked to the bedroom. She was packing her clothing. 'When are you leaving?' I asked. 'As soon as I rent a U-haul truck and pack my things. Maybe in a day or two. I want to drive cross-country. I've never driven cross-country. I am going to ask Pamela to fly to New York, help me pack and drive with me if you don't mind.'"

'If I don't mind. That is an ironic thing to say. I guess, I will go stay with Timothy until you leave. I don't want to watch you pack. Before you go, just drop off your keys at the store. If you don't mind, I don't want to see you again. Also, you can take anything that you want from our apartment' I said and went out of the bedroom. Then I left."

"Three days later, she dropped off the penthouse keys at the store. I went home. The only things she left were our bed and TV stand. She took everything else. I went to the fridge and took a bottle of vodka from the freezer and went to our roof terrace. I used to be so proud of that roof terrace. We had a view of all of Manhattan from there. It felt like we were on top of the world. I spent all night drinking there until I finished the bottle. If I didn't jump from the roof then, I never would. I was completely broken and seriously thinking of just jumping over the ledge."

"From that point on, everything in my life started going downhill. I lost all pleasure in running the bakery. Bills were piling up, not because there was no money to pay them, but because I wasn't opening the mail anymore. I was drinking heavily every night. Everybody was noticing that something was wrong with me. I started being late with the loan payments. Timothy, who had left the running of the bakery in my hands, was getting very nervous. Then, one day he came to me with our lawyer. He said 'Michael, we are very concerned about the way you are running our business. We understand that you are going through a tough period, but I can't afford to lose my building. We need to put some control mechanism in the way things are going here.'"

"Timothy really didn't mean anything bad by what he was saying. He was concerned with reason. But he made me very upset. I tossed my store keys in his face and said, 'Here, it is all yours. I don't care about this bakery anymore. I don't care about you anymore! Have our lawyer draw up papers and pay me what you think is mine. I don't care. I took off my apron and went home."

"A week later our lawyer brought me papers to sign and a check for thirty-five thousand dollars. When we started I invested sixty-five. But I didn't mind. It didn't mean anything to me."

"Soon after I moved out of the penthouse to a one-bedroom apartment on the 43rd Street."

"Wait a minute, Michael. I am looking at your file here," Pastor said after turning to the computer screen, "It says here that you have three children, two daughters from the first marriage, and one from the second. But you didn't mention a child. How did you have a child with Sarah, if she left you?"

"Well, Pastor, that is the second part of the story," Michael answered.

"Michael, your life is really like a novel. I am going to need time to digest all of this. You are a real sucker Michael. Big time. But we will turn that around. God is on your side. You know that. He has always been on your side," Pastor said.

*The Fourth American
Woman*

10

That weekend in mid-June marked three full months in the Bowery Mission. Both physically and mentally, Michael was getting stronger. He still didn't know exactly how he would manage his life once he was done with the program, but slowly his self-confidence was returning together with various ideas on how to make money.

The opportunity for making money showed up by itself one day – in the form of donated books. Many people were donating not only clothing, but also electronics, household items, and lots of used books. The list of allowed titles for the library of the Bowery was short, and space to put the books limited. Homeless people who were eating and taking showers at the Mission had little use for the books. Some of them who liked to read would once in a while take copies of pocket editions of various novels, but roaming the streets of New York for days and carrying books along for the ride wasn't anybody's favorite idea.

Usually, Michael would keep donated books on the bench in front of the clothing room for homeless people to pick up whatever they wanted, but as soon as the pile would get too big, Pastor Paul would instruct him to get rid of those books, particularly those that were not in line with the Christian view of life.

Frequently, a nineteen-year-old tall and skinny white homeless kid would show up with shopping carts asking if he could take books. Then he would fill up the shopping carts and leave. The first time Michael asked him why he needs all those books, he just told Michael that he liked to read. Michael didn't comment, but he knew that the kid was lying. The next time the same kid showed up, Michael told him, "Ok, I will give you as many books as you can take in your shopping cart, but I want to know how it works."

The kid just smiled and said, "I take them to the Strand bookstore. They buy used books. For a full cart, I usually get twenty bucks."

"How often do you go there?" Michael asked.

"Whenever I fill my carts. Usually, I pick out books from the paper recycling that people leave in front of their buildings. But it is always hard to find books. The Bowery is a good place to get books, but the guys before you were throwing books away rather than giving them to me."

"That is so stupid. You can come here anytime you want," Michael said.

The same day, Michael went to Pastor Paul.

"Pastor, I have a question for you," He said.

"Shoot, Michael. What is the problem? Pastor Paul answered.

"There is this kid who comes once in a while and takes a shopping cart full of donated books," Michael said.

"Yes, I know about him. He is probably taking them to Strand. It is okay. You can give books to him. He is a nice kid," Pastor said.

"How about if, once in a while, I take some books to Strand?" Michael asked.

The pastor smiled and looked at Michael's face.

"Michael, you know very well that something like that would be against the rules. And if you're asking if you can do that, my answer is no. But then again, if you do that on your own, without asking me, just to have a few bucks for coffee, there is no way I would ever know. I do appreciate that you are honest with me and ask. Somebody else would just do it. If you do, just make sure it is after four in the afternoon, after I am gone. And of course, you never asked me, and we never had this conversation. And, also, I will not tell Pastor Charles that you asked me something like that. Are we clear about this?"

"Crystal clear," Michael answered.

He walked out of Pastor's Paul office. His brain was working fast calculating how many books he had in the clothing room.

In the following weeks, Michael was able to make between twenty and thirty dollars a week from Strand. Still, there were enough books left for the kid and his shopping carts, and for the homeless people who liked to pick a book to read once in a while.

Michael had enough money for cigarettes and coffee at

the pastry shop on Prince Street. He liked that store. It reminded him of the times when he had a bakery.

He also bought a prepaid Track flip-phone. He knew that he wasn't allowed to have a phone until he completed four months in the program, and there was nobody he could call anyway, but it felt good to have a phone. It just felt good.

"Pastor Charles, good morning," Michael said upon entering Pastor's office.

"Good morning, Michael." The pastor said and continued typing. He seemed preoccupied with his work at the computer.

Michael sat down. He was looking around the office and waiting for Pastor to finish. He didn't feel like talking much today, but Monday sessions with a counselor were a required part of the program. The idea of these sessions was to get to the essence of the troubling issues weighing on the students and to find a way for them to face and overcome those issues, whatever they may be. Being a Christian-based program, it was heavily based on the Biblical teachings in fighting issues and addictions.

The other part of the program was directed towards enabling students to get a high school degree if needed and various skills to be able to get a job and live independently.

Unfortunately, the success rate of the program wasn't too high, and there were many who were coming back to the program for the third or fourth time in order to break with their addictions.

Michael didn't think that he had any particular problem

with his character, which he should fight against. He still perceived his life as a number of unfortunate circumstances, which he had to go through. He saw it as destiny. And he didn't lament over it. He still felt that things in his life will turn around for good and that he will again be on the top of the hill.

"Sorry, Michael, I had to finish this report," Pastor said and turned his chair towards Michael, "How are we feeling today? You look prosperous."

"What do you mean – prosperous?" Michael asked.

"Well, managers on duty are telling me that you often go and buy coffee at that fancy shop on Prince Street. That money must have been coming from somewhere. I hope you are not doing something illegal."

"Oh, that. No, Pastor. I just got some small royalties from Amazon on my PayPal. Nothing much. But it is enough for coffee."

"So, it is from book sales. You are not lying to me Michael, are you?"

"Pastor, I swear to God it is from book sales," Michael said hoping that Pastor wouldn't ask him to show him his PayPal account.

"Good then. We have to be careful here about how our students are handling money until you are eligible to go and work outside. Even then, you will have to give us half of your paycheck for safe keeping as long as you are in Bowery. When you are ready to move out, we will give you all your savings back."

"Yes Pastor, I understand that. But you know that even

if I had money, I would not be spending it on drugs or liquor or anything like that." Michael said.

"I know. I know, Michael. But rules are rules. Our managers are trained to observe students and their habits and actions. So, they noticed that you are often coming back from your walks with coffee. That coffee is two bucks. The coffee in the bodega around the corner is fifty cents. So, it pokes their eyes. They are wondering where you are getting money to buy it. The only other person that buys coffee in that shop is our Director, as far as I know."

"Yes, I have seen him there a few times. I can't help it, Pastor, I like good coffee. They have good coffee."

"Yes, it seems to me that you like good things and good looking women. And so far, it seems that you have paid a hefty price to enjoy it, ha, ha." The Pastor said while laughing.

"So, Michael, what happened after you broke your partnership and left the bakery? What did you do next?"

"For a while, I was down and depressed. I felt defeated. Not as much for losing a good business as much as for losing Sarah. I couldn't get it. Why did she get into a relationship with me at all if she was a lesbian? What was she thinking? What was she expecting? I didn't know."

"Michael, some people are just confused about their sexuality, trying to come to terms with it. There are others who are bisexual too; it doesn't mean she was trying to deceive you. She must have just been very confused." Pastor said.

"Maybe, but her confusion ruined my life, and now,

years after, in the eyes of our daughter and people who knew us, I was the bad guy; I was the culprit. You know Pastor, that I told nobody why she left me. I was simply ashamed to say it."

"Why Michael? This is the twenty-first century. You and I may not agree with it, but this society is opening to everything. Soon gay marriages will be legal in all states; the media are promoting gender changes as normal. There is no shame in anything. Everything goes. Everything is normal, except being normal. So, you shouldn't be ashamed. You should forgive her and leave that behind. God is the one who shall deal with her sins as well as yours. You should be in peace. So, what happened next?"

"Well, after I got back to myself, my friends convinced me to go out with them to bars and meet people. They thought my biggest mistake was in not socializing, but just working. I listened to them and started going out, but it was just a waste of time. The type of woman that I would like to be with, would definitely not be one that would go to a bar or a night club by herself."

"Then one day, I met a girl in the hallway of the building I lived in. She lived two flights above me. She needed help with her bike, to bring it up a few stairs to the elevator and I helped her. We introduced ourselves and started talking. She remembered my bakery because she had shopped there a few times and liked my bread. One word led to another, and I asked her to have coffee with me. She agreed. She left her bike in her apartment and we went to Starbucks for coffee."

"Her name was Audrey. She was fashion designer working for some Jewish people in the Fashion District. She was Jewish too. I don't remember meeting a more decent person ever in my life. She wasn't a beauty like Sarah, but she was pretty, with dark curly hair and gray eyes. We started seeing each other regularly. She wanted to get to know me. And I wanted to get her to bed. But she wasn't giving it up easily. The furthest she would let me go was a friendly kiss."

"I told her about my separation from Sarah and the broken partnership with Timothy without mentioning the true reason for the separation. She felt sorry for me and thought I was taken for a ride. Audrey encouraged me to start my bakery business again. She would scout different locations and come back to me with ideas. She picked the name for the new business. She called it 'Cuisine d'Art'. She thought that it was appropriate. 'You are an artist Michael,' Audrey would often say."

"I was becoming more and more fond of her. But she wasn't giving it up. I couldn't get her to bed. Finally, I asked her, 'Audrey, what is the problem? I really like you, and I think I am falling in love with you, but you avoid being intimate with me. Tell me what am I missing here?'"

'Michael, you are falling in love with me, you say? I am already in love with you. But I still officially have a boyfriend, actually fiancé. He lives in France. He expects me to go there and be with him. And I am getting ready to call him and break off our engagement. Even if I am in love with you, I don't want to be unfaithful to him. Once I break that relationship, you will be first to know. Just give me some time.'

"I said nothing. But I liked her reasoning. In my mind, it reflected an honest person. And she was just that. She was also very caring, kind and compassionate. As I said already, I never met a person like that."

"Sure enough, one evening, a couple of weeks after our conversation, she called me to come up to her apartment. When I walked in, she didn't say anything, just took me by the hand and led me to her bedroom. Then she undressed and lied down. I knew it was time. When we were done, she said, 'I broke off the engagement. Now I am your girl… That is if you want me.'"

'Of course, I want you,' I told her.

"And we had a really good time. She was a perfect woman and perfect partner in everything. It seemed like we complimented each other. Very down to earth, very rational, good with money but not stingy, respectful of all my needs, she was a dream come true. I still had a wound from Sarah, but each day with Audrey was making that wound heal more and more."

"After a few months, her lease expired and she moved in with me. She insisted on paying half of the rent. Sarah never mentioned anything like that in all the time we were together. Of course, I refused, and we had our first argument over it. Audrey also insisted on sharing all other expenses. 'I don't want to be on your back, Michael. I make money, too. And you need to open a new bakery, so you should not be spending money on me. It is just not right,' Audrey would often say."

The Second Bakery

11

Michael was walking down Bowery Street towards the Mission. He was half a block away, when he noticed a police van parked in front of the Mission, and two cops standing next to the open side door of the van.

Michael wondered what that might be about. Didn't like the sight of cops. He didn't think that they were after him, but he owed so much money to different people, had so many unpaid tickets for traffic violations, and owed back taxes, that he was always scared that somebody was going to bring criminal charges against him.

He walked passed the cops without looking at them and walked into the Mission. Then he noticed another two cops standing at the door of the manager's office.

Michael turned toward the student sitting at the front desk and asked, "What is happening?" while pointing at the cops in front of the manager's office.

"Oh, it is a warrant squad. Every couple of months they come to check the list of students, to see if there is a warrant out for any of us. If there is a warrant for you, you better disappear. They already picked up two guys," the student at the front desk answered.

"Who did they picked up?" Michael asked.

"One of the ushers, the guy from the fourth floor, I don't know his name, and your buddy, Rick."

"Rick?" Michael asked surprised, "For what?"

"I don't know. I saw Rick go into the manager's office, and then a cop took him to the van in handcuffs."

Michael ran to Pastor Paul's office and opened the door without knocking. Pastor, who was sitting at his desk, looked at Michael and said, "Michael, if doors are closed, it means you should knock first, don't you know that?"

"Yes, Pastor, I am sorry, but it is kind of emergency."

"What is happening? Any problems in the clothing room?"

"No, Pastor. The cops just picked up Rick. It seems like there was a warrant out for his arrest!!" Michael said all excited.

Pastor Paul looked out the window. His office was right above the main entrance of the Mission.

"Oh, the warrant squad, I see..., well, he had something outstanding. Hopefully, it is nothing serious. In Rick's case, I would think, it could be only disorderly conduct or drinking in public. We could find out from the manager on duty after the cops are gone. Is everything okay in the clothing room? Are we ready for shower day tomorrow?"

"Yes, everything is fine. But if Rick is not back by tomorrow, I will need extra help. I may ask Jeremiah to come down and help me," Michael answered and continued, "I hope that everything will be all right with Rick. I will ask the manager later. And sorry for entering without knocking."

"Not to worry, Michael, not to worry," Pastor Paul said and turned back to his computer.

Michael walked out of his office but he wasn't sure where he would go. The presence of these cops made him nervous. He went down to the clothing room and started folding t-shirts. Michael listened to the sounds outside of the clothing room and worried that the doors would open any second, and cops would come in to pick him up. He couldn't explain to himself why was he so scared. He did nothing criminal. It was true that he had borrowed a lot of money from many people without ever repaying them. But it was never on purpose. It was always in good faith that he would be able to pay it back. If he had any money, he would pay back whatever he could. But circumstances were working against him. Bad luck and risky business decisions brought him to this point. And it is not like he was borrowing for a lavish life, gambling, or easy women; it was always for business. Every penny he ever took from anybody went directly to outstanding bills and new investments; nothing else. He hoped that one day he would make enough money, to repay all of his debts, and surprise all of those who claimed that he was nothing but a con-man and a crook.

One hour passed. Michael went upstairs to the entrance of the Mission. The police van was gone. "Good," Michael thought. He went to the manager's office, but nobody was there. Then he heard a voice, "Michael!" He turned fast. It was Pastor Charles standing behind him.

"Oh, Pastor, it's you. Good morning," Michael said.

"Did I scare you, Michael?" Pastor asked.

"A bit. I didn't see you coming."

"Why are you not in my office? It is 9:15 already. You are fifteen minutes late. Did you forget about our session?" Pastor asked.

"No, Pastor. I was just about to go upstairs. I was stuck in the clothing room. Did you know that the cops just picked up Rick and one more guy?" Michael asked.

"No, I didn't know that. But I saw a warrant squad van in front of the building. They come regularly. Many of our students have outstanding warrants, so they check our files."

Well, if nothing else, Michael was thinking, now he knew that there wasn't a warrant out for him. If there had been, they would have certainly picked him up. But he still didn't know why he was so scared; why he even thought that something like that was possible. He should relax, he thought, and delete those bad ideas from his mind. Thinking about that was like asking for something bad to happen, like a bad omen. He didn't need that. He should delete such thoughts immediately.

"Michael!" Pastor Charles shouted, "Where are you? I am talking to you, but you are somewhere else?"

"Sorry, Pastor, I was just thinking about Rick."

"Okay, go get our coffees around the corner and come to my office. Here is the money," Pastor said and went up the stairs to the third floor.

Michael walked into Pastor Charles' office with a tray,

holding two coffees in his left hand and sat down next to the Pastor who was reading his notes from the computer screen.

"This is yours. Pastor. One sugar and milk."

"Thank you, Michael."

The pastor took a sip of coffee and then said, "We were talking last about your life with this girl Audrey, and about your ideas to open a bakery again. So, let's continue there."

"Yes, that was a good time. Audrey was a great inspiration for me. She gave me the will to work and to live again. She also suggested that I should look for a location outside the city limits."

'You know, Michael,' she would say, 'if you go to Rockland County, there are many small towns where people appreciate good food, but they don't have many options. Commercial rents are lower than in the city, and there is less competition. You should consider it.'

"She was right. So, we drove together in her car, looking for the right location. After two months, we found a store in Nyack on Main Street that was for rent. It was not a big place, some sixteen hundred square feet, but it was enough for what I wanted. I didn't think about wholesale and chain stores. I wanted to have a small boutique bakery, with high-end products at the right price; and the appropriate name – "Cuisine D'Art."

"I rented the place, and did all the construction myself with the help of my friends. Audrey was there every day working side by side with me. The only things we couldn't do ourselves, and had to call licensed contractors for were the plumbing and electrical work. Within a month the bakery was completely built and equipped, ready for the grand opening. Being a designer by trade, Audrey did the complete interior design of the store. It looked like it was from the pages of a magazine. When you entered, you didn't know if you are in a bakery, art gallery, or antique shop. It was beautiful."

"For the grand opening, I invited all my friends. Audrey invited her parents and friends. I designed the best menu ever, and filled the store shelves with bread, pastries, and cakes. Many Nyack residents, who heard about the new bakery on Main Street, came for the grand opening. There were so many people there. Since most of the people couldn't fit in the tiny store, it turned into a street party. Breads and pastries were flying off the shelves. Audrey was at the cash register."

"That day, I bought an engagement ring and proposed to Audrey in front of everybody. She accepted. For me, it was a new beginning. I was happy again."

"And again, the bakery was working almost on its own. With no advertising or anything like that, within weeks, we built up a decent number of customers. It was nothing like in the city, but the income was enough for a good living. I had one assistant, who worked for me on Mondays and Tuesdays, and two girls at the counter. I was working every day from five in the morning till eight in the evening. Soon after, good reviews in the Rockland Journal News and New York Times brought more customers. Florence Fabricant wrote about me again."

"I have to admit, I was very inventive, too. Not only did

I come out with new and original products, but I was always thinking of new ways to bring attention to the bakery. One of our regular customers was a young guy who played the violin and studied at Julliard. He liked the choice of music I had in the store. I learned from him that he played in the school chamber quartet. So, I thought it would be a good idea to have the Julliard Chamber quartet play in my store on Sundays. We made a deal, and after that, every Sunday, I had live chamber music in the store. It was a real hit. I bought two benches and placed them in front of the bakery. People would come, buy muffins and coffee and sit in front of the bakery listening to the music. My bakery became a gathering place for locals. Everybody was talking about the Romanian baker and his sweet fiancé and their bakery on Main Street. We were kind of local celebrities. Many customers had to double-park to come and shop in the bakery, but police never ticketed anybody. The chief of police was a customer too. Once, he told me, 'Not to worry, Michael. What is good for business, is good for the village. I told my guys not to ticket your customers until we figure out a solution for additional parking around your store. Not to worry.'

"It was a real pleasure to run the business in Nyack. Everybody was friendly, and everybody knew each other. There was something so relaxing about everyday routines. After a while, business stabilized, and it was much the same on the same days. More or less, every day, I knew which customer would come at which time and what it was that he or she would buy. Sometimes, I would put things aside for regular customers even without them asking me to do so.It was still hard work with long hours, but there was no pressure and no tension of any kind. Audrey was coming to the store every day after she was done with her work in the city, and stayed with me until closing. She liked to dance, so often, after closing, we would drive to the city to some of the many dance clubs. I wasn't big on dancing, but she was teaching me, and soon we had some good moves together."

"Once in a while, we would go and visit her family in Princeton. They were nice people, and they accepted me as their son-in-law. Her father was especially nice to me. Audrey and I were talking about the wedding after my divorce went through, and about buying a house in Rockland County."

"She didn't want to rush anything. She was down to earth, pragmatic girl. 'Michael, it would take a year to save money for a wedding. Then probably another two years to save for the down payment for the house. We should watch every penny.' Audrey would say."

"It was a good time. And I was happy... but I already said that, didn't I?"

"Yes, you did, Michael," Pastor said and smiled.

"Even my mother from Bucharest noticed that I was happy. She could always tell from my voice, when we spoke on the phone, if something was wrong, or if something was bothering me. I could never hide anything from her. But, during those times, whenever we spoke, I was upbeat and cheerful. One day, out of the blue, she said to me, 'Michael, please, treat that woman well. She is good for you.' I asked her, 'Why are you telling me that mom? Of course, I treat her well, and I will continue to treat her well.' 'I am just saying, Michael. I know you. You are sometimes impulsive. Just be careful not to mess this up. She is the right woman for you.'"

"Your mother was a smart woman. So, did you mess this up, Michael?" Pastor asked.

"Yeah, Pastor, I did…I broke the heart of a precious girl…"

A Child

12

Michael was doing the inventory of the underwear and socks when Victor walked into the clothing room.

"Hi, Mike! How's your kingdom today?

"Hey, Vic! My kingdom is just fine. Blessing-dale is open today for happy customers. What brings you this early?" Michael answered. Victor was assigned to the fourth floor, and he was working in the kitchen, but he and Michael stayed close buddies since the first day they came to the Bowery Mission.

"I have a favor to ask, Mike."

"So, ask. If I can help you, I will."

"You guys have women's clothing too, right?" Victor asked.

"Yes, over there in the corner. We have a limited selection of women's clothing only for emergencies if homeless women show up in the Bowery and need help. But otherwise, you know that we don't do any regular clothing services for women," Michael answered and continued with a laugh, "You aren't thinking of wearing women's clothing, are you?"

"No, no. It is for my girlfriend," Victor answered.

"Your girlfriend? You mean to say, the woman you sit next to every day during the service in the chapel, is your girlfriend?" Michael asked surprised.

"Yes. I met her here. She and her son have been homeless for six months. They sleep in the shelter on St. John's Place in Brooklyn, but the food is better here. So, every day they come here to eat.

"My God, Vic. Couldn't you find a girlfriend with an apartment or job or both? Instead, you got hooked on a homeless girl with a kid?"

"Don't say that…she is a good girl, Mike. Good mother too. Never been on drugs. Just fell in love with a son of a bitch in Newark, who beat her up every day and forced her into prostitution. But she ran away to New York and wants to start a new life here." Victor said.

"So, how can I help you? Do you need clothing for her?" Michael asked.

"Yes. Her birthday is coming up soon, and I want to get her something nice, something really lady-like…and something that looks new… you know what I am talking about… do you have anything like that?

"What is her size?"

"Oh, I don't know… you saw her. She is almost my height and little bit hefty… I don't know women's sizes…I don't even know mine," Victor answered with embarrassment in his voice.

Michael walked to the rack on the far end of the clothing room where the women's clothing was held. He looked through the items on the hangers and picked a nice beige two-piece set comprising of a jacket and a skirt. It was a brand new Liz Claiborne design.

"Maybe this will do. It is size fourteen. I can find a matching white shirt," Michael said while raising a hanger and showing it to Victor.

"Great, Mike! She will go crazy when she sees this. Thank you. You are a pal." Victor said.

"No problem, Vic. Just tell nobody that I gave you this. And don't let anybody see you giving it to her."

"Oh, yes, Mike, speaking of giving it to her…I have one more favor to ask," Victor said with a smile on his face.

Michael looked at Victor with the understanding of what Victor was going to ask. "No, Vic. No! The clothing room is not a hotel. I will get in a trouble."

"Mike, Mike, listen to me, buddy. Let me just tell you. My girl is upstairs in the chapel waiting for me right now. Breakfast just finished. I only need fifteen minutes here. Give me just fifteen minutes, please Mike, please…"

"What if Pastor Paul comes down, Vic?"

"If anybody catches me, I will tell them I came down on my own; that the doors were unlocked, and that you had nothing to do with it."

"Yeah, like somebody is gonna believe you," Michael said and walked to the door. He knew he would not refuse this favor to his friend, but he didn't want to make this a habit of Victor's. "I will be back in twenty minutes, Vic.

When I come back, I don't want to see you here! And lock doors behind, once you are done. And don't leave any stains anywhere, or I'll kill you! Is that clear?"

"Clear as skies, Mike."

Victor ran past Michael up the stairs towards the Chapel.

Michael went to the third floor to see Pastor Charles. He knew that what he did could cause him to be kicked out of the Bowery along with Victor, but he couldn't say no. If he had a girlfriend there, he would most likely do her in the clothing room. So, why would he prevent his buddy from being happy, at least for a few minutes? He smiled thinking of Victor with that woman. She had a big ass, and Victor probably liked that.

The doors of Pastor Charles' office were locked. The light inside was on, but Pastor wasn't there. He looked left and right, confused for a moment, not knowing what to do. Maybe, Pastor was in the bathroom, he thought; he would wait.

"Good morning, Michael," the Director said coming down the hall.

"Good morning, Sir. Do you know where Pastor Charles is? I'm supposed to have a counseling session with him now," Michael said.

"Oh, counselors have their quarterly meeting today. He probably forgot to tell you. I am on my way to the meeting room. Do you want me to tell him you are here?" the Director asked.

"If you don't mind, Director, so I know what to do."

The Director walked down the hall to the staff meeting room and closed the door behind him. A few minutes later, Pastor Charles walked out and came to Michael.

"Sorry, Michael. I forgot to tell you about our meeting. But it worked out for me. It gave me an excuse to leave those guys for a while. I can't listen to them anymore. Every meeting we go over the same questions like we haven't discussed them before. It gets frustrating after a while." The Pastor said while unlocking his office door.

"Come in, Michael, sit down. We will do a fast session, maybe thirty minutes," Pastor said while looking on the computer for Michael's file.

"Okay, Michael, how did you break Audrey's heart? What did this rascal do to break the heart of his fiancé?" The pastor asked with a smile and looked at Michael with expectation.

"It was nothing funny," Michael said seeing the expression on Pastor's face.

"I didn't say that anything was funny, I just smiled. Trying to be nice. You don't like that, Michael?"

"No, no… it is just whenever I think of this girl, I get depressed. She was such a nice girl…I feel bad I lost her… But I guess, it is for the best. If what happened, hadn't, I wouldn't have a beautiful daughter today," Michael said and smiled with sadness.

"How so? Pastor asked.

"Well, this is what happened. It was in December, just before Christmas, when Sarah called me from Los Angeles. Audrey was on a business trip for a week in Paris. I thought

Sarah called to discuss the terms of our divorce. I was looking forward to completing that process. But she said, 'Michael, I am coming to New York for two days on business. I would like to see you and talk.' 'When are you coming?' I asked. She said she was arriving the next day in the afternoon and leaving the following day in the evening after her business meeting. So, she asked me if I wanted to have dinner with her after her arrival. I thought, okay, why not? It would be easier to discuss divorce with dinner. So I said yes."

"The next evening we met at the corner of my street and Ninth Avenue. She came straight from the airport and still had her carry-on bag with her. 'Can I leave this bag at your place until after dinner, so I don't have to carry it with me to the restaurant?' She asked. I said yes again. I looked at her. She looked even more beautiful than when I met her at first. Something tightened around my heart. At that moment, I knew I wasn't over Sarah yet. I knew I was in love with Audrey and adored her loving kindness and care for me, but Sarah's appearance had opened a wound that had just healed."

"We walked to my apartment. Upon entering, I asked her if she wanted something to drink. She asked for white wine. I opened a bottle of chilled Pinot Grigio. She commented on the apartment, how it was cozy and decorated with taste. She didn't comment on any of the woman's stuff that was lying around. She was sitting on the sofa and drinking wine. Suddenly, she dropped the glass on the floor and burst into tears. I never saw her crying before. I was surprised and confused. Didn't know what to say or do. I was just sitting next to her and staring at her beautiful body shaking from all that grief. I didn't understand what was happening. Then she quieted down and started talking, 'Michael, I am so sorry for what I have done to you. I still love you. It was a big mistake to leave you. I want to renew our marriage. I don't want a divorce. Night after night I dream about you holding me in your arms. I love you, Michael.' She said that, wiped her tears and came closer to me. Her face was so close to mine, that I felt her breath on my lips. My heart jumped. I wasn't sure if I was hearing all this right. Then we kissed."

"Of course, we didn't go to dinner. We went straight to the bedroom. Around midnight, we ordered Chinese take out to be delivered. We ate and continued making love. I still don't know to this day if I knew what I was thinking then. I don't think I was thinking about anything, but her magical body. I certainly didn't think about Audrey, and what she would think."

"In the morning, after only two hours of sleep, Sarah took a shower, commented ironically that my girlfriend had a bad taste in perfumes, and dressed in her business dress for a meeting. And poof! She was back to the Sarah I knew from before, the no-nonsense businesswoman. 'Michael, thank you for a great evening. I am flying back to L.A. tonight after my meeting. I'll call you sometime tomorrow. 'Do you want me to drive you to the airport tonight, Sarah,' I asked. 'No, I already have a ride,' she said, kissed me on the cheek and walked out of the apartment."

"The next day she didn't call me. I tried to call her. She didn't pick up the phone. I left her a message on the machine to call me. She didn't. I realized that she had a moment of weakness. So, I wanted to forget that evening. I did a big cleaning of the apartment before Audrey's return. Didn't want her to find out about Sarah's visit. The more I was thinking about it, the angrier I felt with myself for being weak. Felt like I betrayed Audrey's love."

"When she came back, I was extra nice to her. She even noticed that I cleaned up the apartment. 'I didn't expect you to do a big cleaning before my return. I was just thinking on the plane flying back, how messy our apartment would be after my man was alone for a week. I was wrong. I am impressed.' I smiled at her comment thinking if she only knew what motivated me to clean."

"Things went back to normal. Christmas past. Our holiday business in the bakery was great. We were thinking of taking a week off in the middle of March, for my birthday, and going somewhere on a short vacation. Audrey suggested the Caribbean Islands. Then in the middle of February, the phone rang in the bakery. It was evening, just before close. Audrey was up front at the counter. I was in the back in the workshop. I picked up the phone."

'Hi, Michael, this is Sarah, how are you?'

'I am good, how about you?' I answered. I didn't want to ask her why she didn't call or anything else. I was afraid that Audrey would hear something that I didn't want her to hear.'

'I am good. The reason I am calling is that I have news for you. Good news.'

'What is the news?' I asked.

'Michael, we are pregnant. We are going to have a baby. Isn't that great?'

"I froze. Didn't know what to say. I was shocked at what I heard. Then I mumbled, 'We… what do you mean with – we?' 'You and me, Michael,' she said. You remember that night in December? Well, we did it.' I was just able to say, 'I'll call you later after I close,' and I hung up. Audrey walked in the workshop just at that moment. She looked at me and asked, 'Michael, what happened? Your face is so pale. Who called you? Is everything okay?' 'It is nothing, Audrey. I think somebody was making a prank… breathing deep into the phone. Some weirdo.'"

"I didn't sleep all night thinking about what Sarah told me. If she was telling the truth, what would that mean? Did she want to get back with me? What was I going to tell to Audrey? How would I explain having the baby with Sarah when I was supposed to be with her? What was I going to do about that baby? Was it really mine? I had so many questions, but no answers. Next day, when I came to the bakery, I couldn't wait to call Sarah. Finally, I got her on the phone around noon."

'Sarah, were you serious about what you told me last night?'

'Of course, I was. I wouldn't joke about it,' she answered calmly.

'And what do you propose we do now?' I asked.

'Nothing. I hope you won't forget you have a child in L.A. and that you will be a good father who is around and who fulfills his parental obligations.' Sarah said.

'Do you want to get back together?' I asked.

'No,' she said, 'We will proceed with divorce as planned. I am with Pamela, and we are happy. She is excited about the baby. But if you want to be close to our child, I think it may be a good idea that you relocate your business to Los Angeles. People here like good bread, too. You would have great success.'

'Just like that?' I asked. I was getting angry.

'Yes, just like that. You should be happy about our baby.'

'You mean to say your baby and Pamela's?' I was almost ready to explode.

'No, Michael, yours and mine. It is our child!' Sarah raised her voice.

'And it just happened. In one single night of weakness when you didn't have anything else to do but come and cry on my shoulder, right?'

'Michael, it wasn't that simple. I wanted to have a child. You are still my husband. Maybe I had calculated when I would be ovulating, so what! I wanted a baby, and that is it!' Sarah said and hung up on me."

"I wasn't sure what to do next. A child is not something you can hide. It would be mentioned in the divorce papers. I would have to pay child support. Eventually, Audrey would find out. I had to tell her. I just didn't know how to bring it up. I didn't know how she would react. Couldn't just say, oh you know, Sarah was here while you were away, we had sex, and now we have a child."

"Of course, I didn't bring up my secret. Seven more months passed. In August, I received a letter from Sarah. Inside was just a picture of a baby, with words written on the back – 'This is your daughter. Her name is Blanca Nicolau.'"

"I was sitting on the same sofa where I kissed Sarah that night, holding the picture in my hand when Audrey entered. 'What's happening, Michael? You look awful. What is wrong my sweetie?' Audrey asked me."

"I showed her the picture and told her the whole story to the last detail trying to point out that I was tricked into something I didn't want. But it didn't work. She didn't accept my excuse. She kept saying, 'How could you? How could you, in our bed? Michael, how could you?'"

"She cried without making a sound for a whole hour. Then she took off her engagement ring, left it on the table, went to the bedroom and packed all her stuff. She left the same night. I never saw her again."

*The Fifth American
Woman*

13

It was six o'clock Monday morning. Michael was standing outside the arrival terminal of the La Guardia Airport waiting for a plane from Atlanta, Georgia. Pastor Charles had asked him to come to the airport and pick up a young Latino man sent by a church. This man was a heroin addict and alcoholic and they couldn't help him there in regular programs, so they wanted to try the Christian-based program that the Bowery Mission provided.

Michael liked that Pastor gave him this assignment. It was an opportunity to have extra time outside of the Mission. He could feel normal for a while. He could also smoke without fear that somebody would see him.

He was watching the early morning travelers and thinking about the many travels he had made over the years. In good times, as he liked to say, he used to travel a lot, particularly to Europe. But his last trip, back to New York, was not so happy an event. It was the desperate move of a defeated man to save his skin. If he hadn't left, he would be rotting in a grave at Bucharest cemetery.

The sudden crowd of passengers exiting the terminal, made Michael return from his thoughts to reality. He was looking for a twenty-year-old kid, five-foot-tall, dark skin Latino, with short black hair, in a Yankee's jacket and jeans, with a red Marlboro backpack.

After just a few minutes, he noticed the kid in the crowd walking from the terminal.

"Hi, are you Jose Andrade?" Michael stopped a kid with his hand and asked.

"Yes. You must be Michael. Pastor Charles Jourdan told me you would be waiting for me," the kid answered.

"Yes. I am. Is this all the luggage you have?" Michael asked while pointing to the kid's backpack.

"Yes, that is all…"

"Okay. Let's go. First, we will take the bus to the subway station, and then the train to Spring Street. From there it is only a couple of blocks to Bowery."

They walked out of the terminal toward the direction of the bus station.

"Are you a counselor too?" The kid asked.

"No. I am the student in the program, just like you."

"Oh, sorry. You look like a counselor," the kid said.

"Why do I look like a counselor?" Michael asked with a smile.

"I don't know… maybe it's the way you are dressed, or just the way you look. You don't look like an alcoholic or drug addict to me. Why are you in the program?"

"Women and booze, I guess…" Michael answered as they continued walking.

They stopped at the bus station.

"Jose, do you smoke?" Michael asked.

"Yes, but I don't have any cigarettes on me," the kid answered.

"Do you know that during the program, you will not be allowed to smoke?" Michael asked.

"Yes, I was told that."

Michael took a pack of cigarettes out of his pocket, took one out and lit up. He offered the cigarettes to Jose, "Do you want one?"

Jose hesitated for a moment, but then he took a cigarette. "Thanks," he said.

"And of course, if somebody asks, we didn't smoke, right, kid?"

"I got you, bro. You don't have to worry about me," the kid answered smiling and lit up his cigarette.

After they finished smoking, they took the bus to the Roosevelt Avenue Subway Station, then the R train to Union Square, where they changed to the 6 train to Spring Street.

When they walked out of the subway, Michael said, "From here we have just two blocks to Bowery Street where the Mission is located."

"Do you think we could have one more cigarette before we get there?" the kid asked.

"Sure," Michael said and smiled.

They stopped for a shade under a Linden tree on the corner of Spring Street and Mulberry, right next to a playground.

"Here is good. If somebody comes, we would be able to notice them before they noticed us,"   Michael said and took out a pack of cigarettes.

They arrived at the Mission by 8:30 a.m. Michael took Jose straight to Pastor Charles' office.

"Pastor, good morning, here is your kid, in one piece," Michael said upon entering the office.

The pastor stood up and shook Jose's hand. "Welcome, Jose. How was your flight?"

"I slept on the flight all the way to New York," the kid said.

"Okay, sit over here, Jose," Pastor said pointing to the chair next to his desk, "Michael, gives us half an hour. I need to talk to Jose. When I am done with him, I'll call you."

"Not a problem, Pastor," Michael said and left.

Michael went to the clothing room. After about forty-five minutes, Jeremiah walked in.   "Michael, Pastor Charles wants to see you upstairs in his office."

Michael looked at his watch. It was fifteen minutes passed time for his session with Pastor. He walked to the third floor and entered Pastor's office without knocking.

"Michael, I need one more favor from you, in connection to Jose," Pastor said.

"Yes, Pastor, tell me, how I can help?"

"We need to send Jose to detox in Beth Israel for a week before we place him in the program. I called them and they have a place for him. You just have to walk with him to the front desk of the detox center. They are on First Avenue and

16th Street. Could you do that?" Pastor asked.

"Now?"

"Yes. It will take you fifteen minutes. And when you come back, we can do our session."

"Okay, let's go, kid," Michael said to Jose and started walking out of the office.

They went to Beth Israel. On their way there, they had one more cigarette. Jose was talking about his life in Georgia. He was one of five children of illegal immigrants from Guatemala. His parents worked hard to put them through school, but at thirteen he dropped out of school and joined a gang. After that, everything was a nightmare, eight years of nightmares. In and out of jail, in and out of recovery programs, nothing worked. He hit rock bottom at the age of seventeen when his parents kicked him out of the house. He had almost everything on his rap sheet, except for murder and rape. A month ago, he overdosed. They saved his life by a thread. His grandmother asked her priest for help, and he called the Bowery Mission. They convinced him to come to New York to join the program, and the church from Atlanta paid for his plane ticket. And now he was here. Before he left Atlanta, he was drinking for four days straight, so Pastor didn't want to take any chances in getting him into the program without detox first.

Michael left Jose in the reception room of the detox program in Beth Israel. "Okay, kid, good luck. I'll see you in a week," Michael said and walked out.

It was a busy Monday morning for Michael. He enjoyed all these activities out of the Bowery Mission. He liked to walk. It gave him an opportunity to think without distractions.

"Your order is fulfilled, Sir," Michael said with a smile, upon returning to Pastor Charles' office, "Jose Andrade was delivered to the detox center."

"Thank you, Michael. Now it is your turn to talk. We stopped at when Audrey left you for cheating on her with your wife, ha, ha - that sounds funny. You really knew how to mess up your life. You actually had a fiancé while you were technically still married."

"I was already separated for almost a year, Pastor," Michael said, "when I got engaged. I wasn't planning to get married before I divorced, of course."

"Of course, you didn't, but I wouldn't be surprised if you did get married before you got divorced, ha, ha. Continue, Michael," Pastor said while laughing. "I am sorry Michael, but your life story is so unusual. Did you ever think about writing memoirs? You are a writer, and it may be interesting for people to read your story."

"I hate memoirs. But I am sure I will write a book about the Bowery Mission," Michael said.

"Anyway, do you want to hear this or not?" He asked the pastor impatiently.

"Sure, sure, I will not interrupt you anymore. Sorry."

"When Audrey left, I was angry. Angry at Sarah for using me in the worst possible way, for what she wanted. Angry at Audrey for not accepting my story and my apology. I loved that girl. All that happened was a moment of weakness. Why couldn't she understand that? There was a great confusion in my heart. I didn't know if I should cry or rejoice for having one more daughter. For me, it came at such a high price, yet I knew, that it was just an innocent beautiful human being brought into this world by the will of a self-centered and selfish woman. Regardless of everything, I knew that she was going to need a father in her life. One day, whenever that day came, she was going to need me."

"Nevertheless, life kept going. My bakery wasn't the same happy place anymore without Audrey, but things were rolling. I was pretty much spending all day long in the bakery, with occasional breaks, like going fishing with friends in Long Island Sound. Then, my assistant quit. I couldn't find the right person to fill his position right away. I had to work seven days a week."

"Then, one day, with no specific intentions, I started flirting with one of my regular customers. She was the wife of a famous movie director and worked in the entertainment industry herself. She had two teenage kids. Her name was Alice. She was about ten years older than me, in her mid-forties, but in tip-top shape; slim, with beautiful curves, vibrant blue eyes, and long blonde hair coming over her shoulders. I forget how it all started, but I remember that she had just separated from her husband, who left her for another woman and moved out of the house. I don't know if she was trying to prove herself, get revenge, or what, but one day, we just ended up fucking on the working bench in my workshop still covered with flour from kneading bread, while her kids were waiting for her in the car in front of the store."

"Michael, please, watch your language," Pastor said while raising his eyebrows.

"Sorry, Pastor," Michael said and continued.

"After that, we were hooking up every day, while trying to hide our relationship from everybody. It lasted like that for about a month. She was hot and never had enough. I was horny and enjoyed her desire for me. Finally, she invited me to her home to stay overnight. After that night, all of Nyack, including her husband, knew about our relationship. Her children were not that thrilled I was sleeping with their mother, but they kept quiet, at least in front of me. One day, the local priest came to talk to me about Alice and her marriage. He was counseling them, trying to mediate between Alice and her husband, to save their marriage. According to him, I was the stumbling block in that process. In a very nice way, he was asking me to stop seeing Alice. Of course, I kicked him out of my bakery. Soon after, I realized that was a bad move. He started bad-mouthing me around Nyack. And as the result, a number of my regular customers stopped coming to the store."

"Then Alice filed divorce papers and took a restraining order out against her husband. Since I was spending almost every night in her house, one day she asked me to move in. I knew that the kids would not be happy with it, but she was persistent. So, I broke my lease of the apartment in the city and I moved into her house. It was a beautiful old Victorian, with a large yard in the back."

"We were the talk of the town. Everybody knew her and her husband and everybody remembered my sweet fiancé, Audrey. They were appalled by our appearance together, especially when we were with her kids. And Alice, in turn, didn't hide her affection for me in public. Whenever she would see somebody giving us a look, she would turn to me and give me a deep passionate kiss and say, 'They want something to talk about? Here it is!'"

"The bakery was doing okay, but Alice's style of living was way over what I could afford. I wasn't paying her bills or anything like that, but I think she had her husband by the balls when it came to finances and paying the expenses of the children. Being with her was becoming too expensive for me, even if I was paying just for my share."

"And I noticed that she didn't like it when I was hesitant to go somewhere just because it was too expensive. She was born to and raised in a rich family, married a rich guy, and never knew what it meant to be without money or not being able to afford something."

The phone in Pastor's office rang. The pastor picked up the phone.

"Hello…yes, this is Pastor Jourdan…yes?" Then he was listening for a while, "But, we just dropped him off like an hour ago… Really? Oh, that is not good…I will call you back."

The pastor turned towards Michael.

"Michael, tell me one more time, where did you leave Jose? In detail." The pastor asked Michael. His voice sounded serious.

"I went with Jose to the detox center, went to the reception desk, Jose gave the nurse his ID and his social security card, she told him to sit and wait, and she told me that I could go. So I left. Why are you asking?"

"They just called me from the detox center at Beth Israel. While the nurse went to talk to a doctor, Jose walked out of the reception room, and they could not find him." The pastor said, "Now I have to call Atlanta…I really didn't need this…I hope he'll be all right."

Losing Everything

14

It was dark and rainy Monday morning in July. Michael hadn't slept well. The Saturday before, two detectives from the homicide division were at the Bowery Mission, talking to Michael, about Jose Andrade, who walked out of the Beth Israel detox center the previous Monday. And then they spoke to Pastor Charles, who came in that Saturday to work. Jose's body was found in the projects, on the Lower East Side of Manhattan. He was shot in the head, execution style. Nobody knows how or why it happened, but some of the police informants were telling cops they heard that on the same day the kid left the detox center, a young Latino man tried to mug a drug dealer on the corner of Willet and Grand Street. The drug dealer apparently caught him. But the informants didn't know what had happened to him next.

The detectives wanted to know all the details about Jose Andrade's arrival to New York, and especially about the events that preceded his disappearance from Beth Israel.

Both Michael and Pastor Charles were very disturbed by the tragic events. Michael blamed himself for not staying with Jose until he was checked in; the Pastor blamed himself for not escorting Jose to Beth Israel Hospital. The Director was upset that Pastor Charles had asked Michael to go to the airport in the first place and then later to escort that young man to the detox center. His principle was that something like that should always be handled by an employee of the Mission, preferably a counselor. But what was done, was done. The mitigating circumstances for both Michael and Pastor were that at the moment of his disappearance from the detox center, Jose was, technically, already under the detox center care. Thereby, his disappearance was the hospital's responsibility.

Michael felt terrible and spent all weekend thinking about the kid he met at La Guardia Airport just a week ago. Jose didn't appear to be a bad kid at all; just a lost soul that needed help. Their destinies touched for a brief time. They spoke, they had a few cigarettes together, and now he was gone forever. The curtain went down on the tragedy called 'Jose Andrade's Life.'

Sometimes the life stories of people in the Bowery Mission were just too overwhelming for Michael. Compared to others, he had a good life and was blessed with many things. Other students in the Mission probably never had anything good to remember from their pasts. He felt compassion for them, but he wanted to shut himself out from their life stories; like bad dreams, he never wanted to have. But, at every turn, he would hear yet another story, more tragic than the last. Where was the end, he was asking himself? Where was the end to human suffering and calamity? Those who made it to the Bowery Mission program were actually the lucky ones. There were much more who died on the streets of New York, abandoned from people and from God.

He revered the counselors and staff working in the Bowery Mission. Their dedication to helping homeless people was admirable. They didn't get big salaries or have fancy offices. They didn't get paid overtime or holidays. Yet, they worked hard for the benefit of those poor, sick, and homeless men and women who were desperately in need of their assistance. They didn't have a separate cafeteria. They ate at the same tables with homeless people, and they treated them and talk to them with the utmost respect.

As Michael was standing at the entrance of the Mission, he saw Pastor Charles crossing the street holding a large black umbrella in one hand and a tray with two coffee cups in the other. As he was approaching, Pastor said to Michael, "Good morning, Michael. How do you feel today?"

"Good morning, Pastor. I feel lousy. I haven't slept well since Saturday."

"Yes, I know what you mean. I feel the same. That is why I bought these coffees at your fancy bakery on Prince, to cheer us up, and to find out what is so special about this coffee."

"It is not my bakery, Pastor. I wish! They do such good business," Michael said and smiled, "It is my favorite in this area."

"Maybe one day you will have a bakery again," Pastor said as they were walking up the stairs towards the office.

"Oh, no. No, Pastor. That chapter of my life was over years ago. I am a writer and that is what I'll be till the end of my life," Michael answered.

"Why not, Michael!? You could open bookstore – bakery, similar to what Barnes and Noble has. Your books and your bread."

They walked in the office. Michael sat down, while Pastor was putting away the umbrella. Then Pastor sat, took a sip of coffee, and said, "You know, the Director may take disciplinary action against me for what happened to that poor kid, and for the way I handled the whole thing. I may lose my position. If that happens, you will have a new counselor. And I would still like if you could come to my church when you are allowed to go to an outside church on Sundays."

"Don't worry, Pastor. You will not lose your position."

"How do you know that, Michael?" The pastor asked with a sad expression on his face.

"I know because God is good and merciful, and He is on our side," Michael responded.

"Now you are being my counselor, right?"

"I don't see anything wrong with it. We are the same age. We can counsel each other. I will not charge you for it. In Blessing-dale everything is free," Michael said, and they both laughed.

"Well, it is time to get back to work. Let's continue with your story. What happened with your relationship with that older woman, Alice…her name was Alice if I am not wrong?"

"Yes, Alice was her name. So, this is what happened. We lived together for a few months. I was trying to keep up with her way of living – buying expensive clothing, going to expensive restaurants, buying front row tickets to Metropolitan Opera, and buying her Tiffany jewelry. Every day it was getting harder and harder to keep up. I was making less and less, and spending more and more. Of course, that money had to come from somewhere, and it was; I was defaulting on my bakery bills left and right. Before I knew it, my main supplier stopped delivering to me until I paid my debt to him. I had to go to bakery supply warehouses to buy supplies for cash every day. I was getting tired and couldn't do it anymore. Then the landlord sued to evict me. I owed him rent for six months. And with all those problems in my head, I felt pressure building between Alice and me.

"Then one day, a court order came, ordering me to vacate the store premises in three days. I continued working while trying to reach some kind of agreement with the landlord. It didn't work. He already had somebody who wanted to rent the store. On the morning of the fourth day, the Marshal showed up, put a sticker on the front door of the bakery, and asked me for the keys. I cleaned out the cash register, took my papers, and left."

"When I got to Alice's house and broke the news to her, she lost it. We had our first fight that day. She was out of control, yelling and cursing. 'You lost your bakery!? You didn't have twelve thousand dollars for back rents? Are you telling me you are broke? How are you going to live? Do you think I'm gonna carry you on my back? I can't believe you didn't have just twelve thousand dollars like it is some big amount of money? And now the whole of Nyack will laugh at me. And that rat of ex-husband will have the time of his life. Alice got hooked up with a loser!? Like I really need that right now?'"

"I told her I would get out of the tight situation quick, and get back in business. But she wasn't impressed with my rhetoric. The truth of the matter was I had actually lost everything. I was completely broke except for the few hundred dollars I took from the cash register when the Marshal came to the store."

"And the worst was yet to come. Soon after, my van got repossessed by the bank because I defaulted on the car payments. So, I lost an important tool to move around and look for business opportunities."

"I knew that the only way out was to get a job. Fast! So, I spoke with some friends, and they told me about a Greek guy on the Upper East Side, who was opening a bakery café but didn't have a clue about the bakery business and was looking for a baker who would bake and run the place for him. I went to see this man, and it worked out immediately between us. It was a very nice Greek family; this guy, his name was Peter, his wife, daughter, his mother, and father, all working together. I was the only one there who wasn't a member of the family. We agreed that he would be paying me a hundred dollars a day, cash, seven days a week until the business was up and running, and after that, we would agree on a weekly paycheck. So, I started working there. Unfortunately, Alice wasn't happy, again. 'What? You will be working all night and half of the day in somebody else's bakery, for a hundred dollars a day. You are a real loser. I was completely wrong about you! What about me? Do you expect me to wash your dirty laundry when you come back home tired from work? Like a real peasant girl! Do you think just because you fuck like a horse, I will lower myself to be your maid?'"

"After just one week at my new job, she called me at work and told me she wanted to break up with me, to find a new place to live, that my stuff was outside on the porch, and that I should pick it up, or she would throw it in the garbage in the morning."

"My boss, Peter, was next to me when I spoke to her, and he heard everything. I was very distressed and upset, so he told me to stay and work, and he went to pick up my stuff. He came back with a cardboard box with my dirty laundry. That was all she left on the porch. She kept my furniture and paintings that I brought with me from my old apartment. She even kept my personal jewelry that I left on the nightstand next to bed. And when I called her and told her I was coming the next day to collect all my stuff, she used that as a threat and took out a restraining order against me. As a matter of fact, she had a local Sheriff call me to tell me that if I showed up anywhere close to her house in Nyack that he would have me arrested."

"So, she really did a good one on me. And again, exactly

like in the case with Sarah, I felt used and robbed. And I knew that it was all my fault."

"Yes, exactly! The pastor said, "Now we come to the same conclusion as before. You were not thinking with this head," he pointed to Michael's head, "but with that head." He pointed to Michael's crotch.

"I lost everything. At that time, I was in New York for eight years already, and after all the hard work, and all the money I had made and all the bakeries I had, I was back to the beginning. I felt awful."

"Thank God that I had a job. Those people were really nice to me. They accepted me like their family. Peter allowed me to sleep in the bakery's office on the sofa after I was done with the night baking. In the morning, when they would come and open the store, he would give me his house keys, and I would go there to take a shower, get another couple hours of sleep, and come back to work. I lived like that for three months until I had enough money to rent a one-bedroom apartment on 81st Street and First Avenue."

A Signing Pen

15

Michael had already been in the Bowery Mission for four full months. He was finally allowed to have a cell phone and use the internet in the computer room. He didn't have to hide his phone anymore.

Because of his dedicated work in the clothing room, the Director and Pastor Paul agreed to give Michael a laptop computer for personal use.

"You are a writer, Michael, and we know that you need a computer not only as a means of communication but as a necessary tool for your work," Pastor Paul told him while giving him the IBM 15-inch laptop.

Michael was so happy. It was a used laptop, a few years old, but he didn't mind. After four months, he could write again. He had so much in his head he wanted to put on paper, and now he would be able to. He was also able to get online every day, do research and look for business opportunities.

His self-confidence was coming back strong. He wasn't

looking on Craigslist for a job anymore. He was looking for ways to get freelance work for writing and publishing services. Being in the Bowery Mission, he saw it as a good break to organize his freelance work. He had two more months left in the program, and up to another six months, if he found a job. But nobody said that he had to work for somebody. He could be self-employed, as long as he was making a decent income so he could live independently, once he left the Bowery. So, practically, he had at least three months to develop his freelance work to a level that the counselors would accept as legitimately livable income and approve his stay in the Bowery for the remainder of second six months.

It was an opportunity, and Michael wanted to take full advantage of it. Michael spoke with Pastor Charles, Pastor Paul, and the Director about his plans. They were skeptical. Usually, most of the students were looking for jobs with regular paychecks. And once they found them, it was easy to help them to organize themselves for independent living. What Michael was talking about was a plan they had never encountered before. However, they knew that Michael was a published author, a professional with experience in the publishing industry, an entrepreneur, and therefore, they were approaching his plan differently. Finally, they told him he could pursue his course and that they would help him if he needed any help in organizing his freelance work.

Sure enough, he needed help. To publicize his writing and publishing services online, he needed a website. The Bowery Mission Director approved the domain name michaelnicolau.com and hosting for the website for a year to be paid by the Mission. Michael, once again, was so happy. He designed and developed a beautiful website for himself. The Director and Pastor Charles were impressed. They were showing Michael's website to everybody on the staff. This brought the first freelance project to Michael. When Pastor Lee Quinones saw the website, he ran to Michael.

"Michael, I didn't know that you knew how to make websites. The Director showed me the site you made for yourself. It looks great, man. I need a website for my church. Do you think you could make it, and how much would something like that cost?" Pastor Lee asked Michael.

"Yes, Pastor, I'd be happy to make a website for your church. Depending on what you want, how many pages, static or interactive – there are many things that affect the price, but maybe it would be better if you told me how much you are willing to spend on it, and I will tell you what I can do for that price. Or I have an even better idea; how about we look at different church websites online; you tell me which one you like and I'll tell you how much something like that would cost you," Michael answered.

It took Michael about two weeks to make Pastor Lee's church website. The Pastor and everybody in his church liked how it looked. They paid Michael five hundred dollars for it. This was the first money Michael had made since returning to New York. Pastor Charles was happy that Michael started making money even before the completion of the six-month program.

"Do you know how many churches are out there without websites, Michael? Maybe that is a good opportunity for you to look into," Pastor Charles told Michael.

Michael listened to Pastor's advice and in the following month, he built two more websites for another two churches. The Director was very proud of Michael since he was the one who initiated giving a laptop to Michael and paying for his website. Nobody had any more doubts that Michael would do well.

But Pastor Charles was still concerned about Michael's emotional issues. By now, he already knew well that Michael was a man able to earn money and live independently, but he saw in him many emotional weaknesses, which had to be taken care of. He had to help Michael finds a way to control his emotions, especially those towards women. In Pastor's mind, all of Michael's problems would be solved, if he sincerely gave himself to Christ and lived by the words of the Scripture. That would be so easy for Michael. He knew the Bible in and out. He was well versed in theology and philosophy. Pastor sometimes felt intimidated by Michael's knowledge, that was far greater than his own, but Michel had so much pride and passions in himself, which was preventing him from using that knowledge as a rule and guide for his life.

The pastor knew that Michael was a person who needed to be in a relationship, needed to have a family, needed to love and be loved. He felt bad about all the unhappy circumstances in Michael's life, but ultimately, it was his own pride and passions that brought him down, and he needed to learn how to prevent that from happening again.

On Monday morning, Michael walked into Pastor Charles' office with two cups of coffee from the bakery on Prince Street.

"Good morning, Pastor," Michael said, "I bought some coffee for us."

"Thank you, Michael. Oh, fancy coffee… business is going well, I see. Any new projects that you have?" Pastor asked.

"Somebody just hired me to do a book cover and format his book for publishing. It will be around four hundred dollars, so it is not bad."

"Not bad at all! You have another month in the program, and then you will be released from all duties in the Bowery Mission and be able to concentrate completely on your work. If you continue like this, I think you'll do well. The key is to save money. Use this time while you are living in the Bowery to save as much as you can; especially since you don't have any living expenses. It will be much harder later."

"Yes, I agree, Pastor," Michael answered.

"Michael, we need to get deeper into your issues and try to find solutions for everything that is preventing you from being continuously successful in everything you do. And you can be successful. You already proved that many times. But you need to learn how to maintain your success in life, both in relationships and in business. So, you have to complete your life story as soon as possible, so we can spend some time discussing the issues themselves. Do you think that is a good idea?" Pastor asked.

"You are the counselor, Pastor. It is not for me to say,"

Michael said while smiling, "but yes, it sounds good."

"Okay, so, what happened while you were working in that Greek bakery on the Upper East Side?" Pastor asked.

"As I said, they were treating me well, and I was doing my best to make them happy. I really didn't pay attention to the number of hours I was working."

"When I finally rented an apartment, Peter gave me a futon bed and some extra furniture they had. His wife gave me extra bed linens they had, and his mother and father gave me a set of china for four as a moving in present."

"How about your private life? Did you have one? Were you seeing somebody? I want to know that part. This is where your problems are usually coming from," Pastor said impatiently.

Michael looked at Pastor with disapproval over what Pastor just said. He still didn't accept that his relationships and his passions towards women were the cause of all of his problems.

"Well, I am not sure if you are right, but anyway, during my work at Peter's place, I had a kind of relationship, with one Jewish girl."

"Another Jewish woman? What is it about you and your affinity for Jewish women, Michael?" Pastor asked.

"I don't know…I think it is just a coincidence. And with this girl it was more of a friendship. We never got into any intimacy. We were going out and talking a lot, enjoying each other's company, but she wanted things to go slow. She was very serious about everything she did, and she understood our relationship as a process. I was very attracted to her. If she hadn't held back, I would have done her the first time we went out, but she wasn't that kind of a girl. She was letting me know that she was attracted to me, but she didn't want to rush. So I respected that and went with the flow.

"Her name was Miriam. She was short, hardly five feet, slim, with beautiful light brown curly hair, grayish eyes. Her nose was a bit bigger than it should have been, a real Jewish nose, but it looked cute and gave a special character to her face. She wore glasses at all times, and I used to joke with her that she looked like a 'naughty librarian'."

"How did you meet this Miriam?" Pastor asked.

"We met at Peter's bakery. She was a customer and liked my baking. I liked her," Michael said and smiled, "With her, I, again, had that strange feeling like I had known her forever. Everything about her reminded me of something that I already knew, already experienced, but I didn't know what. It was a strange feeling. I was able to talk to her about everything openly and without any hesitations. In her company, I always felt complete, like we were two parts of one entity. I knew that meant I was in love, but it was more than being in love."

"She had much respect for who I was. She didn't see me as just a baker, but a talented writer and journalist. I translated for her some poems of mine I wrote when I was young. She memorized them and recited them to me. She loved them, and she told me I should forget baking and go into writing."

"Before Miriam, I never thought of being a writer. I

graduated with a degree in journalism, worked as a journalist in Romania, but except for the poems I wrote as a young man, and then news articles and essays, I never wrote anything else. But she told me she enjoyed my narrations, regardless of what was I talking about. 'Michael, storytelling is a rare talent which you have. You should be writing your stories. You would have great success as a writer. I would be your number one fan,' Miriam often used to say."

"Then, for my birthday she gave me a beautiful silver fountain pen. 'Michael, this pen is to sign your books, for when you publish your first book and become a famous writer.' 'Why do you think I will ever write a book?' I asked her. 'I don't know. But I am sure you will. Whenever you are telling me your stories, I feel like I am turning the pages of a book. It is a funny feeling.'"

"She never learned how right she was. It took another ten years until I started writing, and I've never stopped since. I wrote sixteen books and numerous papers and articles. For my first book signing – and all that came after – I used the fountain pen Miriam gave me. I still have it. I never became a famous writer…still working on it."

"So, what happened with Miriam and you? If you loved her so much why it didn't last?" Pastor Charles asked.

"Oh, my stupid cursed life. Whenever I would find a woman perfect for me, something had to happen," Michael said with sadness in his voice.

"And what happened this time?"

"One day, just as I was finishing my working day in the bakery, the phone rang. It was my ex-wife from Romania.

She had never called me since I left Romania. I was surprised and perplexed how she got my phone number. She told me that my sister from Bucharest gave it to her."

"To make a long story short, she ran away just a day before she called me, together with our daughters from Romania, from her second husband, who was abusive to her and the kids. They came to St. Louis, in Missouri, where her brother had already lived for years. She asked me if I could take care of the papers for our daughters, so they could continue going to school here in the United States. At that time, I already had my green card, and was in the process of getting citizenship."

"Yes, you never told me that. I knew that when you opened up your first bakery, you were still in this country illegally. When did you get your papers?" Pastor asked.

"Oh, that was one good thing, besides our daughter, that came out of my marriage to Sarah. Through marriage with Sarah, I got my green card," Michael replied.

"Yes, that makes sense," Pastor said, "continue, Michael, please."

"Anyway, I called a lawyer, and he told me that to get papers for my children, they would have to live with me. I didn't know what to do for a while. I knew I didn't have any feelings for my first wife anymore. Eight years had passed. I have married again. She has married again. But those were my children. I couldn't just leave them in St. Louis. So, I called my ex-wife and told her the kids should be with me, in order to get papers for them. Of course, for her, it was out of the question to let me have the girls. 'Where my daughters go, I go. Where I go, they go. I didn't give birth to them to send them away,' she told me. I thought for a while, and then I asked her to come with the kids. 'You want us to live together again, Mr. Nicolau?' she asked me. 'No, only to raise the children together. Isn't that what you want?' I answered. And she accepted."

"The next day, I told Miriam that my children were coming to New York and that they would live with me. I didn't mention that their mother was coming with them. But I didn't have to. Miriam felt that. She said, 'Oh, Michael, I am so happy for you, that you will reunite with your daughters.' But I noticed the sadness in her voice."

For the rest of the day, she was quiet, and she didn't smile. That evening, when I walked her home and asked her to meet me the next day, she answered, 'No, Michael, your kids will need you now more than I do. I don't want to take your time away from them.' And that was it. She never answered my phone calls again and never came by the bakery again.

Return to Beginnings

16

Another privilege of students who had been in the program for four months was being able to go to Sunday services to an outside church. The idea behind this was that students would gradually incorporate themselves back into society by interacting with people on the outside who would not judge them for their failings and addictions. An outside church seemed the perfect place for it. Counselors had a list of churches willing to accept Bowery students, but students were not limited only to those from the list. They could pick any other church as long as their counselors knew and approved their choice.

Most of the students were using this privilege because it meant being out of the Bowery Mission for most of Sunday. While for some of them, it was about hearing the word of God, praying and praising the Lord, for others it was just about being outside and eventually meeting a woman.

According to Bowery students, the outside churches were a perfect place to meet women. Churches were full of single and lonely women of all ages. By default, being faithful women, they were usually full of compassion for the troubled men trying to get on the right track and recover from their addictions. Well dressed and well fed, thanks to Blessing-dale and wholesome meals from the dining hall, Bowery guys were often very attractive.

People in the Bowery Mission were telling each other stories of the students who met women in the outside churches, hooked up, got married, and started new lives. Those were happy stories. There were also stories about some church women who were targeting Bowery students just for sexual pleasures on Sundays. Information about these women, and in which churches they could be found, were carefully passed from one generation of students to another.

Victor, who liked Michael, wanted to hook him up with a woman in a Baptist Church on the Upper West Side.

"Mike, man, listen. Last two times I was in the Bowery program, I used to go to this church. Both times, I was with this Jamaican woman. She was a real barracuda, man. She is in her early fifties and very well maintained. I don't understand why she is single. But regardless, she likes dick more than white bread, and fucks like it is the end of the world. The church service was from eleven to one. She lives close to the church. She would take me home and we would spend all afternoon in bed smooching like dogs. Then she would even drive me back to the Bowery. Best of all, I think she prefers white guys. If you want, we can go there together one Sunday, and I'll introduce you to her. If I were not with my girlfriend now, I would definitely go after her again," Victor said.

"Thanks, Victor. But if I need a woman, I will find one on my own. I am not that desperate to become a free male prostitute," Michael answered.

Michael decided to go to Pastor Charles' church. Months before, Pastor had mentioned that he would like to see Michael come visit, and Michael promised he would. It was in the Bronx, on White Plains Road. Built as a Catholic church, it was bought by Pastor Charles' congregation years ago and converted into a Pentecostal church under the name - The Pentecostal Church of God. Michael liked that all the interior furniture and decorations were kept intact. He liked the appearance of the traditional church.

Pastor Charles was the Senior Pastor of the large mixed congregation. Although mostly Haitian, there were French, Canadian, African-American, Latino, Chinese, and White members. The service was both in English and French.

Going to a Pentecostal church in the Bronx was an enjoyable experience. He never before went to a Pentecostal church, and it was interesting to analyze how it differed from the services in traditional churches. Parishioners from Pastor Charles' church were all pleasant with Michael, but except for the cordial conversations, Michael didn't interact much with them. He thought he would not be going there after he left the Bowery Mission, and he didn't want to get too close to anybody.

But going out on Sundays from eight o'clock in the morning till late afternoon felt good. The church service was from 9:00 a.m. till 11:00 a.m., and the rest of the time, Michael would spend roaming the city. Often, on his way back, he would get off the number four train on 86th Street and Lexington Avenue and walk all away down to the Bowery Street.

Sometimes, he would stop by St. Stephan, the Catholic Church on 31st Street and Lexington, just in time for communion at the end of the service. He liked that church, and he liked taking communion as often as he could. The communion in Pastor Charles' Pentecostal Church was only on the first Sunday of the month. Also, instead of wine, they were using grape juice. Michael preferred real wine.

After returning to the Mission, Michael would change from his church clothing into something casual and run to the clothing room to unpack and sort out the Sunday donations. Sunday was a big day for donations because many people would clean out their closets on the weekends and drop off donations on Sunday.

In the evening, he would take his regular walk to Mercer Street after dinner. And the last thing in his schedule on Sundays, before going to bed, was organizing the fifth-floor guys to take the garbage out. It was a dirty and hard job for most of them, and they hated it, but it had to be done, twice a week, on Wednesdays and Sundays. For Michael, it was like playing a game of cat and mouse with them. Somehow, whenever the garbage needed to be taken out, everybody would disappear, and Michael would run up and down the Mission trying to catch them. Often, some of them would avoid their duties, but Michael didn't mind. He knew that he would act the same if he were in their shoes.

The day would end with those who carried the bigger

loads of garbage complaining to Michael about those who avoided their duties. He would always say that he would take care of the cheaters, but once he turned off the light in the room, everything would be forgotten by the next morning.

"Good morning, Pastor," Michael said upon the entering Pastor Charles' office.

"Good morning to you, Michael," Pastor said smiling, "I see after more than four months of being here, you still haven't learned how to knock on the office door before entering."

"Pastor. Your office doors are glass. I can see through them and know if you are busy or not. What is the point of knocking? You see me on the other side of the door. Don't you?"

"Yeah, yeah, yeah, Mr. Philosopher. Let's get into your story. Do some work! I just looked at my notes. Do you know that already I have over a hundred pages of notes on you? Maybe I'll write a book about you one day," Pastor said and turned towards Michael, "I am listening."

"Okay. We stopped with my daughters and my first wife coming to New York. So, this is how it went. I remember that it was in late March when they came. The winter was still going strong in New York, and that day it was snowing. Peter gave me his minivan, and I drove to LaGuardia to pick up my daughters and their mother."

"I don't remember if you ever told me the name of your first wife. Did you?" Pastor interrupted Michael.

"No, I don't think I did. Her name is Natasha. Russian

name. Her father was a communist, and he liked Russian names," Michael answered and continued, "Anyway, the moment I saw Natasha coming out of the terminal with the kids, I knew I had made a mistake. But it was too late."

"Why do you say that?" The pastor asked him and raised his eyebrows.

"I don't know, Pastor. Something came over me and all I was thinking was how I had made a terrible mistake. Natasha just looked different. Not that she was older. She just didn't look like the person I fell in love with, married, had kids with. She looked like somebody I'd never met. Like a complete stranger. The girls were, of course, bigger. After all, eight years had passed. When I left, one was two, and the other one was a year old."

"Yet, I repressed those thoughts, opened my arms, and knelt down to hug my daughters. I took them to the apartment, and the very next day, I enrolled my daughters in the public school on 82nd Street and Second Avenue, just around the corner from where we lived."

"The following ten years my private life was all about raising my daughters. I don't know if I was a good father or not, but I worked hard to give them the best I could."

"What about your daughter from the second marriage?" Pastor asked.

"Blanca would come with her mother to New York from L.A. regularly, a few times a year. Usually for the holidays. Sarah would let her stay for a few days at my place. Over time, the girls got to know and like each other. That made me really happy."

"And how about Natasha?"

"I don't know. I guess she was trying. I didn't ask her for anything but to take care of the kids. She didn't work. And legally she couldn't because she didn't have papers. Because of the kids, to the outside world, we were pretending to be married, but I never wanted to get married to her again. So, she was waiting and hoping for another amnesty to get a green card. But years were passing by."

"Why didn't you want to get married to her again?" Pastor asked.

"I think I never got over my anger. And I was angry about many things. First, I never forgave her for divorcing me the first time. Yes, it was true, I messed up. But the reason I messed up was because I wanted to make a better life for us. She should have known that and stuck with me, not divorce me. Then, when I opened my first bakery and was thinking of bringing her and kids over from Romania and reuniting with them under better circumstances, she was already smooching with that crazy wife-abuser that she later married. And each time I would look at her, I would think of Miriam. Miriam was such a sweet girl. And I would think about Audrey. Both of these women were so perfect for me, and both of them left me because of my ex-wives. I could not forget that. I was a very angry man. It was one thing to raise kids. They were my responsibility as much as hers. But marrying her would have been a completely different story. It would have been an acceptance of defeat."

"But, Michael, most of everything that happened in your life, except for a few things, happened as a result of your decisions. I am not saying that Natasha or Sarah or any of those other women were right or wrong, but it seems, that more often than not, you were making choices for yourself. If you had made different choices, things would be different probably." Pastor said.

"I think you got me wrong. I am not blaming Natasha or Sarah for anything. I see everything as a hand of God, as destiny, as something that had to happen. If anything, I am blaming myself. I was angry at myself, and I am still angry at myself. I feel like twice God sent me two angelic beings to take care of me, and I pushed them aside with my actions. I was just too weak of a man. When I slept with Sarah and got her pregnant, it wasn't because I wanted to bang my estranged wife one more time. It was because she fooled me with her crying on my shoulder. And Audrey left. When I told Natasha to come to New York with the kids, it wasn't because I wanted to rekindle an old flame. There was nothing there. It was because of the children. And then Miriam left."

"Michael, it was a good thing to do. Having children means being responsible for them. You took it upon yourself, your responsibility. Sometimes in life we have to sacrifice other things for the benefit of our children. We love them as our Father loves us. Our Father sent his own Son to shed his blood and die on the Cross, for our salvation. He sacrificed himself for us sinners. It is something that all of us who are parents should think about and learn from. God doesn't ask us to die on the cross for our children, but to love them and care for them, as He loves and takes care of us. So, I think that you made the right choice, regardless of your feelings. You showed that, if anything, at least, you were not selfish," Pastor said and added, "You had a new beginning in life."

"To me, it felt more like a return to the beginning, than a new beginning," Michael said with sadness, "Anyway, life kept going on."

The Waldorf Days

17

By the end of the fifth month, Michael was one of the most liked students. Everybody knew him and everybody had something good to say about him. The Director liked him for keeping the fifth floor in order as the Floor Captain. Pastor Paul liked him for managing the clothing room and shower program with enthusiasm and commitment to service. Students in the program liked him for always supplying each of them with just the right clothing, even without the clothing slips from their counselors. Homeless people liked him for always being available to assist them with anything they needed; be it a shower out of schedule, new shoes, a warm coat, a blanket, or most often a spare cigarette. They all knew he would never refuse them when they asked for a cigarette.

He was always ready to give good advice to fellow students and to tutor those who were preparing for the high school equivalency test. He was writing resumes for students looking for jobs and often filling out their job applications.

Counselors were noticing his positive influence on others, and they respected him for that. Once, Pastor Lee Quinones told him he should consider staying at the Bowery Mission, become a Mission trainee, and work as a counselor or a Manager on Duty.

"Michael, if you stay here and work with us, it would be beneficial for you in many ways. The salary is not too big. You cannot get rich on it. But you could live here rent free, have your own room like I do, eat for free in the dining hall, work with the students, and in your free time, you could write and not worry about anything," Pastor Lee told him, "plus, with all of these life stories we hear from our students and homeless people, you would have an inexhaustible supply of inspiration for writing. A prefect environment for a writer."

But Michael couldn't wait for the day when he would move out of the Bowery. Regardless of all the benefits of being in the Bowery Mission, this place was still very depressing for him, and a constant reminder of the ultimate failure in his life; of being on the street, with no place to go and not a friend to ask for help. He was very grateful to the staff for accepting him in the worst moment of his life and for their help in bringing back his strength, self-confidence, and dignity. He respected them for the work they had been doing. Dedication to their ministry for the homeless and needy was obvious at every step. It was the noblest thing one could do for another human being. But still, Michael didn't want to be a part of it.

He liked Pastor Charles, but he didn't see any purpose

in the sessions he had with him. If they were not a mandatory part of the program, he would never have them. Of course, he had never been in any type of therapy or counseling, so he didn't know how it worked or what the aims of it were. But in his mind, all he had been doing was telling his life story to his counselor for five months. Maybe just telling his story to somebody was giving him an opportunity to look at his own life, from a different perspective; something that eventually could be beneficial. But he didn't feel any different.

Michael was convinced that everything in his life was destiny; something that had to happen, just the way it did; something that wouldn't be different even if he wanted. Yes, he felt a deep longing for dear people and times he lost, but ultimately, he believed that everything happened for purpose. When the right time come, he will be rewarded for all his suffering.

That Monday morning, before going to Pastor Charles' office, Michael bought two coffees, a slice of cheese pizza, and a toasted bagel with cream cheese.

"Good morning, Pastor. I brought goodies for breakfast. I hope you didn't eat yet. This is yours," Michael said upon entering Pastor's office.

"No, you know I never eat before coming to the office. What do we have to thank for this treat? Did you get a new freelance job?" The pastor asked while taking the coffee and the paper bag with the pizza from Michael's hand.

"No, but today is exactly five months since I came to the Bowery. It is kind of a small anniversary. But the best part, I only have one more month to go."

"Yes, but you will stay another six months after you complete the program in order to save money, right?" Pastor asked.

"Not necessarily six months. As soon as I feel I have enough saved and I am able to rent an apartment, I will go."

"You don't have to rush, Michael, you know that. You have to be sure you can live on your own. I don't want to see you back here again in a few months."

"No, Pastor, this will never happen again. Never!" Michael said.

"Okay, just so you know, nobody is pushing you out. Use this free time to save more money and strengthen your business. It is an opportunity," Pastor said before starting to eat his slice of pizza, "Hmm, this is good...I like this thin crust."

"I used to make great pizzas while I was at Fratelli's. Everybody loved them. People were buying my pizzas and taking them all the way to Texas," Michael said.

"Really? You should come to my home one day, and we could cook dinner together. My wife likes Italian food, and of course, my children are crazy about pizza. They could live on pizza, burgers, and Coke."

They finished their breakfast and coffee. Michael enjoyed his toasted sesame bagel with cream cheese. He loved bagels. That was one type of bread he never completely mastered. But one day he would, he thought. He always dreamt of having a house with a yard and a small brick oven outside, so he could make fresh homemade bread daily.

"So, Michael, I would like to hear about your professional life during the time you lived with your two daughters and your first ex-wife. How long did you stay with Peter in his bakery and what did you do next?" Pastor asked.

"I was with Peter for another year. It was a good place to work. The business was steady, but it wasn't growing. Whatever we would do, the average income would stay the same. I wouldn't have minded that if I had been alone. But I needed to make more money. The apartment on the Upper East Side wasn't cheap. The girls were at the age when they wanted everything, and they could not understand when there wasn't money for something. And not only that. I wanted to give them as much as I could."

"Peter knew that after a while he wouldn't be able to afford me anymore. And I was trying to be fair with him. I had an assistant, an illegal Mexican kid. His name was Chicco. He was young, in his early twenties, but very smart. I trained him well. After a while, he was able to work on his own. I also trained Peter's father in bread baking. I just didn't want to leave that place or burn any bridges."

"Soon after, an opportunity for a good position came up. The Waldorf Astoria Hotel was looking for an Assistant Pastry Chef. Not only was it a well-paid position in the famed hotel, but it was also a very secure position; taking into account it was a union job that came with all the union benefits and perks."

"So, I applied and went on several interviews: with Executive Chef John Doherty, with the Food and Beverage Manager, and with the Director of Human Resources. I'd never worked for a big company before, and all those interviews were a novelty for me."

"Finally, Chef John Doherty asked me to do a sample presentation of my work in their Pastry shop. I went there one morning, worked all day, made several samples of the best desserts I had, and got the job."

"I was thrilled. Working in the Waldorf Astoria for any Chef meant being at the top of his profession. And again, I felt like being on top of the hill. The first time I felt like that, was when I opened up my first bakery and had a write up in the New York Times."

"It was also the very first time that I had a normal work schedule. I worked from 7:00a.m. till 3:00p.m. with paid overtime. Also, holidays and weekends were paid at a higher rate."

"Regardless of my vast culinary experience, after working for eight years in bakeries and restaurants, the Waldorf Astoria was a completely different ball game. The volume of high-end desserts and pastries we were making there on a daily basis was just unbelievable. The Executive Pastry Chef was in charge of the Pastry Shop, and he had two assistants. One of them was me. Under us, we had sixteen experienced pastry cooks."

"Also, for the first time in my culinary career, I was working for celebrity customers. Guests of the Waldorf Astoria were some of the most powerful, wealthiest, and most famous people in politics, business, and entertainment, from all over the world. At one point, during the Annual Session of the UN, I was making desserts for over hundred presidents and prime ministers from all over the world, including the President of the United States."

"After a while, I became First Assistant Pastry Chef. Part of my duties was to make special cakes for birthdays, anniversaries, and weddings. I brought my cake decorating skills up to perfection. I remember the birthday cake I made for Cardinal O'Connor. It was a five-tier cake with baked meringue all around. It was a real masterpiece."

"People in the hotel and restaurant industry noticed my work again. The celebrity status I once had, as a master baker, which died after I lost my bakery in Nyack, came back in full force."

"And my girls enjoyed the benefits of my job too. Almost every Sunday, they would come to the Waldorf Astoria for brunch. Of course this, one of the most expensive brunch deals in New York, was free for them. It was one of many perks I had as a Chef in the Waldorf."

"They liked that their father worked there. Every day, when I came home, they would ask me which famous person I cooked for that day."

"What was your private life like during that time?" Pastor Charles interrupted Michael's narration.

"It was stable and regular. The girls were going to school, Natasha was taking care of the house, doing all the house duties, and helping the girls with homework. Every day I came home, I had my cooked dinner ready and an ironed shirt for the next day. On Friday nights, I would take them all out for dinner in one of the nearby restaurants. I bought a nice Pontiac minivan, and on weekends I would often take them to upstate New York or to the Poconos for day trips. The girls loved those drives out of the city."

"Sometimes I would just drive out of the city and have them pick the turn on the road and then see where it would lead us. It was a good time...or at least I thought it was."

"Why do you say that, Michael? Were you happy with the girls and Natasha?" Pastor asked.

"Yes and no. I don't know how to say it. I was happy to see my girls growing up into beautiful young ladies. I was proud of their intelligence and their appearance. I was proud of their achievements in school. And they were good girls. Never had any major problems with them, like some parents had."

"But there was something inside me that was eating away at me. I can't explain it. I knew that I was doing everything right. But I felt like I was out of place. Almost like I didn't belong there."

"After a while, I started sharing the bed with Natasha. I think she liked that. I think she was seeing me as her husband again. But I knew that I didn't love her. For me, it was more the convenience of having a woman's body in my bed to satisfy my needs, than commitment coming out of loving somebody. All those years, I couldn't stop looking around at women. I was flirting with every skirt coming my way, but I never took it further than that. Probably the only reason I didn't have an affair was out of concern that I might hurt my children. Believe me, Pastor, it wasn't easy. At work, I was surrounded by beautiful and available women, and I looked awfully handsome in the white chef's uniform."

"I hated myself for pretending that everything was normal with Natasha. But once I accepted her into my bed, I couldn't go back. Again, I was afraid of hurting the children. So, this is why I said that I was happy and I wasn't happy. Deep within myself, I thought and I felt that my place was somewhere else. On the other hand, I felt a strong guilt for having such thoughts. My soul was like a ticking bomb. I just didn't know when it would explode."

Culinary Art

18

Rick walked into the clothing room. He looked grumpy that morning. The day before he came back from the Brooklyn County Jail on Atlantic Avenue, where he spent thirty days on an old warrant for disorderly conduct.

He completed the program in the Bowery Mission a month ago, got his disability benefits approved, and it was time for him to leave soon. He was just waiting for the approval of his Section 8 apartment application.

Jeremiah and Michael were already there folding the clothing that arrived as donations over the weekend.

"What's up, Ricky, you don't look happy this morning?" Jeremiah asked.

"You wouldn't look good if you spent thirty days in the lockup. If the warrant squad hadn't found me, I would already be out of the Bowery Mission and in my new apartment. My bitch wife refused to pay the fine for me, so I had to spend thirty days in the slammer. Can you imagine that? After all, I did for her. I spoke to that bitch yesterday.

She won't let my daughter visit me in my apartment. I told her I am moving out of the Bowery and I am getting a nice studio apartment in the Bronx. She doesn't want to hear it. So if I want to see my daughter, I have to go to Brooklyn. She won't let me be alone with my daughter. I don't know how I could have married such a bitch," Rick said with much anger in his voice.

"Ha, ha, you didn't complain when you were fucking her," Jeremiah said laughing.

"Yeah, that whore took me to the cleaners. If I were paying professional whores, I would have gotten a better deal. This one was too expensive. I bought a house and put her name on it. I bought a car in her name. She never worked a minute while we were married. I was treating her like a queen." Rick said.

"Com'on Ricky, you told me yourself that when you would get drunk, you would beat her up like shit. She had to be stitched in the emergency room several times and had to lie about somebody attacking her on the street so you wouldn't get arrested. That is not treating somebody like a queen." Michael said.

"Yes, but that was after I really got into drinking. I would lose it. I wasn't myself anymore. And my heavy drinking started when she started refusing me. She would always find a reason not to sleep with me. Then she moved to our daughter's room. When I asked her why she told me my snoring was bothering her. It hadn't bothered her for ten years, ha." Rick answered.

"Well, you should have thought about that when you

married her. She was twenty-seven years younger than you," Jeremiah said, "Now you are sixty-two and she is thirty-five. She doesn't need an old, sick fart; she needs a dick that can keep her busy all night, ha, ha."

"You watch your mouth, kid, or I'll keep you busy all night, okay!? My dick works just fine. But a whore is a whore. She takes you, gives you a pussy, takes all your money, and throws you out on the street, like a piece of useless garbage."

"You know," Rick continued, "When I had my heart attack and then my stroke, she never visited me in the hospital, nor brought my daughter to see me. I could have died, and my daughter wouldn't have seen her father for the last time. How evil was that? And when I asked her why she told me, 'I didn't want our daughter to get depressed seeing her loser father like that.' What a bitch. She came to me with one small suitcase, with 99 cent flip flops on her feet. I bought her everything. She was illegal. I got her papers. She never worked. Even now, she is not working. She is renting out rooms in our house. We have seven extra rooms. Do you know how much money that is weekly? And she still wants one-third of my disability benefit check for child support. She is even complaining that it is not enough. Like I make some money! From where?"

"Ok, Ricky, forget that. It is water under the bridge. It can't be undone," Michael interrupted Rick, "Tell me another thing; did you get everything you needed for your apartment yet?"

"Well, the Director told me to pick one of the TV's

donated to the Bowery that is sitting in the basement. I got all my linen, comforters, and pillows from here. It is already packed. I also got china from Pastor Paul. As soon as I hear from the Housing Department, and have the address of my apartment, I will buy a sofa bed, table, and chairs. So, I'll be set," Rick answered.

"What about moving? Did you talk to the Director about a van?" Jeremiah asked.

"Yes. He told me to tell him a day before, and he will have the Bowery Mission van transport all my stuff from here to the Bronx."

"And then, after you move in, we will come and visit, ha, ha, and bring girls," Jeremiah said, "and some booze."

"Oh, no booze… don't even joke about that. I want to see my daughter grow up. No more drinking for me. If I continue, it'll kill me. If the fourteen medications I am taking daily don't kill me first. But girls you can bring, yes," Rick said and smiled.

"You are taking fourteen medications every day? Michael asked surprised, "For what, man?"

"For everything – diabetes, cholesterol, heart issues, bipolar disorder. You name it, I got it." Rick answered.

Michael looked at his watch. It was time for him to go see Pastor Charles.

"Okay, guys, I got to go see Pastor Charles. Finish this without me. I'll be back in an hour," Michael said to Jeremiah and Rick and left.

As he was walking up the stairs, he was thinking about Rick and his new beginning in life. Hopefully, he won't drink, watch his health, and have a peaceful remainder of his life. It was yet another life tragedy that Michael didn't want to hear or know about, but it touched him. It disturbed him. There were eighty students in the Bowery Mission program. And all of their stories were worse or similar to Rick's.

"Hey, Pastor, how are you this morning?" Michael said upon entering Pastor Charles' office. He sat with a slam on the chair next to Pastor's desk.

"Good morning, Michael. You look cheerful and upbeat this morning."

"Oh, Pastor, I have to be. After listening to the guys in the program talk about their life stories, I get to think that I didn't have it that bad. It could be worse." Michael said and smiled.

"Why? What did you hear now?" Pastor asked.

"I was just downstairs in the clothing room with Rick. He came back from lockup yesterday. As usual, he was complaining about his wife. I don't defend him, but I really don't understand why she wouldn't pay the fine for him but instead let him sit in jail. After all, she is his wife."

"Michael, Rick wasn't a nice guy for many years. I am surprised he didn't end up in jail for domestic violence. There were also stories about him molesting his daughter when she was just eight, but that didn't go anywhere. It seems his wife didn't want to put their daughter through more psychological torture and scar her for life. She didn't want to cooperate with investigators. But it was at this time she kicked Rick out of the house and took out a restraining order against him. So there are many sides of the same story. When you look at Rick, the one you call, 'my Ricky', he looks like a sweet old harmless man. He finds compassion in everybody. But he is a big deceiver with a rotten soul. I am happy that he is leaving soon. Our program didn't help him much. He has a long way to go with facing himself and facing our Lord God. But of course, I didn't tell you any of this, please. I shouldn't be talking like this. I hope Lord will forgive me," Pastor said and lowered his head and his voice.

"Not to worry, Pastor. I will keep this to myself. By the way, I liked your sermon yesterday at Church." Michael said.

"Really? What did you like about it? What did you take away from it?" Pastor raised his head and asked.

Michael felt like he was caught in an unnecessary lie at that moment. He didn't remember much of Pastor's Sunday sermon. He just wanted to say something to change the subject and cheer up the Pastor.

"Well, each time I hear you speak," Michael started, desperately trying to find the words that would cover up his little lie, "I feel like I want to jump, come to the pulpit, and give my testimony. Your words are always so uplifting and inspiring, Pastor."

Pastor smiled. "Thank you, Michael. That is a nice thing to say. Maybe, it is not a bad idea that you give your testimony one of these Sundays. As a matter of fact, I will talk to our secretary about putting you on the schedule for next Sunday. What do you think?"

Michael felt trapped, but there was no way back. He put himself in this situation with his big mouth. He hated testimonies. Standing in front of a bunch of unknown people and talking about his spiritual experience, and how God did good things in his life, just didn't sit right with him.

"Sure, Pastor. I would like that," Michael said.

"Good. I will call our secretary, and you will have a week to think about what you will say. Now, let's go back to our discussion. You were telling me last Monday about the Waldorf days and your life with the kids and Natasha. Let's continue with that story. I am listening," Pastor said and leaned back in his chair trying to get into a more comfortable position.

"Yes, I remember where we stopped. Well, I was at the Waldorf Astoria for almost four years. While I was there, the Executive Pastry Chef left, and everybody thought that the position would be offered to me. However, Chef Doherty thought differently and brought a new Pastry Chef from outside to run the Pastry shop. I didn't mind much. It didn't hurt me. But that is when I started thinking that I could be an Executive Pastry Chef."

"I didn't have to wait long for the opportunity. I was offered the position of Executive Pastry Chef at the Peninsula Hotel on 5th Avenue and 55th Street. Pay was much better than at the Waldorf, so, I accepted it."

"The Peninsula was a boutique hotel for the rich and famous. Upon getting the job, I had to sign a confidentiality agreement stating that I would never reveal the names of the guests or talk about them. Everything about that hotel was top notch and high end. The general manager of the hotel expected nothing less."

"This is where I brought my culinary art to perfection. And, I was again noticed by food critics. Ruth Rachel from the New York Times wrote a beautiful review about my deserts. Quickly, I became part of the New York City culinary establishment. I was being invited to cook at charity events at the James Beard House with other celebrity chefs, and many other places, like the Metropolitan Museum and Lincoln Center. No charity event would occur without desserts by the Pastry Chef from the Peninsula Hotel."

"My friends were suggesting that I should go into the food show business. That I would be a real attraction with my accent and my strong appearance, but I just couldn't imagine myself doing that. I liked cooking, but I wasn't an entertainer."

"While at Peninsula, I accepted side jobs with kosher caterers who were often renting banquet facilities in New York hotels. Each day after work, I would go and work on one of the banquets as a pastry chef till late in the evening. Some weeks I was booked for seven days straight. It was good money. Kosher caterers were paying chefs two hundred dollars cash at the end of each party for a few hours of work. It was a great gig for me. Also, I enjoyed learning about kosher cooking."

"At the same time, it was the welcome influx of money we needed as a family. In spite of the fact, that the Peninsula paycheck was good, it was never enough. The girls were growing and their needs were bigger. Natasha still didn't work. And each year living expenses in New York were higher than the previous year."

"For me, working long hours again felt good. I enjoyed what I was doing. On another hand, it was kind of escape for me. Sometimes, I felt bad I wasn't spending more time with the girls like when I was at the Waldorf Astoria. But on the other hand, I was excusing myself by providing more for them."

"Once in a while, Natasha would start a conversation about her papers, and how it would be good if I married her, so she could work, but I ignored those discussions. Sometimes I would just tell her, 'There are twelve million illegal immigrants working in this country. If you really wanted to work, you would have already."

"Finally, after so many years, I broke down. I couldn't listen to her anymore. I thought she would really get a job if we get married. It would be easier for everybody. So one day we went to Brooklyn County Office and got married again."

A Better Life

19

Since my birth, God Almighty and Merciful was always with me, but I wasn't always with him," – was the pitch line of Michael's testimony the following Sunday in the Pastor Charles' Church. He repeated this several times while talking in front of the large congregation about misfortunes that brought him to the Bowery Mission. He didn't know if this was true or a false feeling, but it sounded nice and it was something believers liked to hear. On the contrary, he often thought he was sidelined by God more than once in his life. And again, he wasn't sure about this thought either. After all, he had so many good opportunities in his life. In most cases, it was by his own choice he didn't take advantage of them. He was a head-baker at Jacob's Bread; he left. He was a partner in the successful bakery; he walked away from it. He was a pastry chef in Waldorf Astoria; he left. He was an executive pastry chef in Peninsula Hotel; he left. His life was full of examples of opportunities he walked away from.

And in each of his abrupt departures from the opportunities given to him, there was a story about yet another woman. And in each case, he would leave a mess behind him.

"You know, Michael," Pastor Charles would often tell him, "some men get high on drugs and make a mess while they are high; others get drunk and behave like animals while under the influence of alcohol; and you Michael, you fall in love and lose any sense of reality. It is the same like getting high. You are an addict too. You are addicted to women. But not in the perverted pornographic or sexual way. Sex is just a part of it. Your addiction is more about love. You are addicted to falling in love. And the only remedy for your addiction is the ultimate love; love of God and love for God. Turn to God Michael. He loves you. Show your love for him and you will be healed."

Michael didn't agree with Pastor Charles' conclusions about his condition. He wasn't an addict. Yes, he loved women. He admitted that much. But which man doesn't? He loved God too. But in his own way. He didn't need to show off his love for God. It was his intimate relationship with the Divine and not for public eyes, he thought. And more than anything else, sense of Divine mission and pre-destination was always present in his life. He always had that strange feeling that everything in his life was predestined and that he was on the mission from God. He just didn't exactly know what that mission was and where his destiny would take him.

It was four o'clock, Monday morning when Michael woke up to Victor shaking his shoulder and whispering, "Mike, Mike, wake up."

Michael opened his eyes, not sure if he was dreaming or if this was happening. It was still dark in the room. He recognized Victor's voice, but all he could see was a shadow standing over his bed.

Michael looked at his watch.

"Victor, what is wrong with you? It is four o'clock. Why are you not in your bed sleeping?" Michael asked, "If the Manager catches you walking around you'll be in the shit.

"Michael, I need your help. I need twenty bucks. Please, Mike."

"What? Why?" Michael asked surprised, "I don't have any money right now. But what is happening? Are you in some kind of trouble?"

"My girlfriend is outside, across the street. She needs money to get to Albany. It is some kind of family emergency. I want to help her. She is desperate. Please, Mike. I'll pay you back as soon as I can," Victor said.

Michael knew that something was wrong. Victor didn't sound coherent. And rule number one with guys like Victor was never to give them money. Not only because he didn't have the means to pay it back, but most likely that money would end up being spent on drugs.

"Sorry, Vic, I can't help you. Ask Jeremiah. Today I am completely out. With the money I had I bought a pack of Marlboro last night. Why don't you wait a couple of hours until breakfast, and we can figure out what we can do?"

Michael wanted Victor to stick around till daybreak. He had a strange feeling that Victor was up to no good.

Victor turned and walked out of the room fast without

saying a word. Michael just sighed and turned over on his bed. He had one more hour before wake-up time. Usually, he would wake up at five o'clock, shave, take a shower, and dress, and then it would be time to turn on the lights and wake up the other guys in the room. The official wake up time was 5:30 a.m.

At breakfast, Michael looked around and didn't see Victor in the dining hall. Then he saw Jeremiah coming towards his table with his food tray.

"Jeremiah, did you see Victor this morning?" Michael asked.

Jeremiah placed his tray on the table and sat next to Michael. He took off his glasses and wiped them off with the paper napkin.

"Well…?" Michael asked impatiently.

"Victor? Let me see…You mean the guy who woke me up this morning at four o'clock and hustled me into giving him forty dollars I may never see again… Yes, I think I saw him, or at least his silhouette. It was still dark in the room."

"And you gave him forty bucks? Are you crazy?" Michael asked surprised.

"He was persistent! What could I do!? He wouldn't go away until I gave him money! You know the way Victor is when he wants something. Gave me some story about his girlfriend, some emergency, I couldn't understand half of it. It was only when I woke up this morning I realized I'd been hustled. That was forty bucks out of sixty that my grandma gave me for my birthday. It was supposed to last me the whole month." Jeremiah answered.

"And you didn't see him after that, did you?" Michael asked again.

"No. And I don't think he was in his bed last night. He is in the bunk bed across from me, and last night when the lights were turned off, he was definitely not there," Jeremiah said.

"I hope he doesn't do something stupid. We came to the Mission on the same day and have one more month to complete the program. And this is his third time here. That would be a real shame if he were to relapse again," Michael said and continued with his breakfast.

At that moment Pastor Lee Quinones walked to their table and stood between their chairs.

"Good morning, gentlemen," he said and continued without waiting for greetings in return, "Did any of you, by some chance, see your buddy Victor last night or this morning?"

Michael and Jeremiah looked at each other for a long moment. Then Michael raised his head and looked at Pastor Lee.

"Why do you ask?" Michael asked.

"No, that is not the correct answer, Michael. You should not answer my question with a question. Makes me think that you are hiding something. But if you really want to know, it seems that your buddy never came back from church yesterday. He didn't sign in, and the Manager on duty reported that. All I want to find out is if maybe he forgot to sign in when he came back, or if he went AWOL." Pastor said.

"Sorry Pastor, but I didn't see him. I hope he is around." Michael said and looked at Jeremiah.

"I didn't see him either. He must be around with his girlfriend. She comes over here for meals every day," Jeremiah said while looking at Michael.

"Hmm, you two got your stories straight. Okay, I can see that. Just so you know, I spoke with some other guys from the fourth and fifth floors and learned that Victor woke up some of them in the middle of last night hustling them for money. He took about a hundred bucks from different guys. If you two gave him some money, you won't see it again. Anyway, thank you for your cooperation," Pastor said and walked away.

Michael and Jeremiah kept looking at each other.

"Shit, he relapsed," Jeremiah said, "I don't care about the forty bucks, but I feel sorry for him. He was doing well. We both passed the GED last month, he was getting ready to apply for porter's jobs in a few hotels. He seemed determined to defeat his addiction this time around."

"It happens, Jeremiah. It could happen to anybody. You remember when you were caught drinking. If not for Pastor Charles, you would already be kicked out. Who knows where you would be now, in which gutter. We all have moments of weakness. They usually come in the worst of times," Michael said and smiled with sadness.

As he was walking up the stairs to the Pastor Charles' office, Michael was thinking about Jeremiah and the other guys that gave Victor money. How stupid they were, he thought. Not only because they unintentionally hurt Victor, but also because they could be disciplined for doing that. Borrowing or any kind of money transaction between students was strictly forbidden. Technically, none of them, except those who already completed the program and were working, should have any money on them.

But in reality, many students would find a way to get to the money. Some of them, being homeless, would apply for food stamps, without their counselors' knowledge. Then, in one of the nearby bodegas, they would exchange food stamps for cash. They would get seventy dollars in cash for a hundred dollars in food stamps. Others would sell their new clothing, acquired in Blessing-dale, out on the street. The most sought items were fancy sneakers. They were the easiest to sell.

Michael could make a lot of money through the sale of donated watches, phones, laptop computers, and sometimes jewelry. He could take anything. But he never did. Whenever the electronics, watches, or jewelry would come in as a donation, he would take them to the Director. It wasn't like he wasn't tempted. A few times he thought of keeping certain items or selling them. But he just couldn't do it. He was happy with selling donated books to Strand. And it seemed like after a while everybody knew about his secret small business. But nobody ever told him anything.

Pastor Charles, walking fast up the stairs behind Michael, interrupted Michael in his thoughts. "Good morning, Michael."

Michael looked behind. "Oh, good morning, Pastor. I didn't hear you coming."

"Yes, you were in your thoughts. Look, this time, I bought coffee for us. It is from the bodega around the corner. I hope you won't mind," Pastor said.

"Of course not," Michael said.

They entered Pastor's office and sat down. The pastor turned on his computer and started looking through the weekend report. Then he raised his eyebrows and looked at Michael.

"What happened to Victor? The manager on duty reported him absent."

"I think he relapsed. He didn't come back from church yesterday, but it seems that he snuck in early this morning, hustled a few guys for cash, and left again. By now, he is probably already high somewhere in East New York or the Bronx," Michael said with disappointment.

"Well, I was surprised that he lasted this long. Maybe he'll make it next time if he ever gets to that. The problem is, he never had enough strength to get better. He doesn't believe in God and doesn't believe that a better life exists. Once, when I asked him if he believes in God he told me, 'No, Pastor, I don't. If you come and live in my neighborhood for as long as I have, you wouldn't either. "

The pastor took a sip of coffee and continued, "So, enough about Victor. Let's talk about you. Do you believe that a better life exists? It seems to me that you had a good life when you were with your daughters and Natasha. Didn't you?"

"Yeah, that is a good question. I don't know. Now looking back, I could say yes. But then again, I was never completely happy. Deep in my soul, I felt a longing for something or somebody. I don't know what it was or who it was, nor where I could find it. It was just like some unexplainable sadness."

"On another hand, each year that passed, I worked more and more. I was making more and more money, but it didn't feel like I was achieving anything. It felt just like basic living. I could not say that it was like just surviving because my girls never missed out on anything, but in essence, we lived almost from one paycheck to another. I could never save any money. No matter how much I would make, it was always going to the bills, food, clothing, and other living expenses. That also made me upset. I was watching people around me, who were making the same or less money than me. They were buying houses, new cars, boats, summer cottages, and fancy watches. And it wasn't like they didn't have families to support! You could see them gaining wealth, being prosperous. The only time I experienced something like that was when I had my first bakery. Never again, after that. And by all standards, it should have been different. I was more experienced, had a good position, good paycheck, cash income on the side, but it just wasn't happening."

"Regardless of how hard I worked, I felt stuck. No, I wasn't blaming Natasha or girls for that. I took it upon myself to raise them, and I never regretted that. So, did I have a better life with them? I don't know, Pastor. I don't know."

"Did you go to church, Michael? Did you pray?" Pastor asked.

"Church? Yes, we would go to church almost every Sunday. But I wasn't big on prayer, I have to admit that."

"Did you ever think that a better life is not all about accumulating wealth and having a comfortable living? For me, a better life started when I accepted Christ and committed my life to spreading His word. Up to that time, I had a similar experience to yours. I was a car salesman for years, a good one. I had a good paycheck and good commission. But like you, I felt stuck. I felt empty as if there was something more out there. Once I accepted Christ I discovered I could have a one-on-one relationship with an almighty God. A God that loved me and filled that void I didn't know I had. I gave myself to God, and he gave me back a better life." Pastor said.

He looked straight into Michael's eyes for a while, and then he continued, "Maybe that thing that you were longing for and you couldn't explain, was Christ himself. I guarantee you, Michael; give yourself to Christ, and you will have a better life. Your soul will not wander confused anymore."

Michael looked back into Pastor and smiled. He admired Pastor's faith. But he didn't trust him enough to tell him everything about Christ…the way he felt.

Freemasons

20

Michael woke up with a headache. It must have been from the very strong air conditioner they had in the fifth floor room, he thought. It was on all night. Michael preferred open windows and natural airflow versus air conditioners, but most of the students in the room complained about it, especially in the warm and muggy New York summer nights. So, he had to keep the A.C. on.

He didn't need this headache. That morning they were going to have a test in Bible class that required the memorization of verses. He was lazy during the weekend and thought he could memorize them on Monday morning.

Bible classes were from 10:00 a.m. till noon. They would start with a half hour of communal prayers. All students were invited to pray out loud, with the others supporting them in their prayers. Counselors believed that it was very important for students to learn how to pray, and how to pray regularly. It was an important part of their inner healing and strengthening. If one was to believe in the power and omnipresence of God, he had to learn how to communicate with Him through prayer.

However, there were those who were praying all the time and those who never prayed. If silence would occur during prayer time, the counselor who was running the Bible class that day would jump in with his prayer, until another student would take over. Michael wasn't big on the communal prayer. He prayed every day, in the morning and evening regularly, and often during the day, but always silently. Michael believed that the God Almighty would hear our prayers and our requests even if we didn't say them out loud. He understood the purpose of the communal prayer which required out loud statements of somebody's request to God if one is to expect from others to support him in his prayer, but he just wasn't used to it. In all the months he spent in the Bible classes in the Bowery Mission, he prayed out loud during prayer time once or twice.

Other than that, Michael was active in the Bible classes. He liked to discuss the Biblical subjects they were studying. Some counselors presiding over the class would feel intimidated with Michael's constant comments, and they would avoid letting him speak often. Others enjoyed Michael's initiative, and they would let him take over the discussion. Michael had a great ability to challenge others to voice their opinion. Sometimes, thanks to him, Bible classes looked like a debate club. Guys who would never speak felt compelled to express their thoughts.

For Michael, it was interesting to listen to other students speak about God. The majority of them had little of a traditional schooling. They grew up in the projects or poor neighborhoods, and most of their education came from the school of hard knocks. Yet sometimes their thoughts about God, faith, truth, and life, were surprisingly wise. Michael knew that natural wisdom was a gift from God and had nothing to do with the level of education or amount of academic knowledge one possessed. However, he was still amazed by the spiritual depth some of those students expressed.

That Monday they had a written test about Proverbs. They had to memorize the seven verses from the Book of Proverbs they liked the most, write them on the test paper, and comment on what they had learned from them. Michael chose the following verses from Proverb 22:

1. *A good name is more desirable than great riches;*
to be esteemed is better than silver or gold.
2. *Rich and poor have this in common:*
The Lord is the Maker of them all.
3. *The prudent see danger and take refuge,*
but the simple keep going and pay the penalty.
4. *Humility is the fear of the Lord;*
its wages are riches and honor and life.
5. *In the paths of the wicked are snares and pitfalls,*
but those who would preserve their life stay far from them.
6. *Start children off on the way they should go,*
and even when they are old they will not turn from it.
7. *The rich rule over the poor,*
and the borrower is a slave to the lender.

He didn't know why he picked those verses. 'Maybe

because they were clear and easy to explain,' he thought. But that Monday, with his headache, nothing looked easy.

He wrote the verses on a small piece of paper, and tried to memorize them during the morning service in the Chapel, and while he was eating his breakfast.

That worked well because it seemed he wasn't the only one who left memorization of the verses for the last minute. At the breakfast table, most of the students had their Bibles open on the Proverbs, trying to memorize their parts. Nobody was distracted with small morning chat.

Then Michael heard whispering coming from the left.

"Can I sit next to you during the test? Would you mind?"

He turned his head to the left and smiled when he noticed Jeremiah's nervous face expression.

"Sure, as long as you don't copy everything from my paper verbatim," Michael said.

"What does it means ver...ba...tim?" Jeremiah asked, confused concerning the expression he didn't know.

"It means exact. I don't want you to copy word by word everything I write. We both could get in trouble for it."

"Oh, no. I just wanted to copy your verses, and then I would write my comments on it. I was never good at memorizing, so I wasn't able to memorize any."

"You were just lazy, Jeremiah," Michael said and continued reading his verses while munching on a blueberry muffin.

Michael entered Pastor Charles' office while mumbling the verses he was supposed to have memorized and sat in the chair.

"Good morning to you too, Michael," Pastor said with a smile.

"Sorry, Pastor. Good morning. I was just reciting the verses from Proverbs that I had to memorize for today. We have a test today," Michael said.

"Hmm, memorization. As I am getting older, it is harder and harder for me to memorize anything. How about you, Michael? Do you memorize things easily?" Pastor Charles asked.

"Yes. Memorization is something you can train your brain to do. It is an acquired mental skill. The more you memorize, the better you are in it. Also, memorization is an excellent prevention tool against many illnesses that cause a decrease in brain functions. It was proven that people who study later in life live longer," Michael said.

"I didn't expect a dissertation on memorization, but it seems that you know quite a bit on the subject?" The pastor asked with and smiled again.

"I guess so. I never thought about how much I know about the subject, but when I was involved with Freemasonry, I used to memorize a lot of rituals. At one point, I knew more than a hundred and twenty pages of ritual work by heart, and I could recite ritual text at any time of the day with no prompting," Michael said proudly.

"You were a Freemason? I didn't know that," Pastor said surprised, "Are you still with the Freemasons?"

"No, I am not a member of any Masonic Grand Lodge now, if that is what you're asking. But for me, Freemasonry is more a point of view about life, than belonging to a particular organization. Understanding it that way, one can be a Freemason regardless of his standing with an institution."

"Well, that is true about any institution that represents any set of beliefs or any ideology. Just belonging to a church doesn't make one a Christian. One has to hold to, and practice Christian values, and give oneself to Christ in order to be true Christian. However, God gave us the church for a very important reason," Pastor said and paused for a moment. Then he asked, "So, Michael, do you still feel you are a Freemason?"

"Yes, I do," Michael answered, "I believe that one is born a Freemason and dies a Freemason," Michael answered.

"How did you get involved in that?" Pastor Charles asked. His facial expression was revealing his dissatisfaction with Michael's statement. He obviously didn't have a nice opinion about Freemasonry. That was not a surprise for Michael. He knew that many Baptists and new born Christians had great misconceptions about Freemasonry.

"It runs in my family. My father was a Freemason back in Romania, and his father before him. One day, when I was thirty-three years old, a man approached me on the street, here in New York, and introduced himself as my father's old friend. He told me a story about my father I had never heard before, neither from my father nor from my mother. It was a story about Freemasonry. It impressed me. I asked him if I could become a Freemason, and he said, 'Yes, all you have to do is to ask.' So, I asked him. He told me he would put me in touch with the members of the Lodge, which he thought I should join. A few months passed, nothing happened. Then we met again. I asked him again. He told me not to worry, that he was working on it. A few more months passed again. I stopped thinking about him. I thought that probably nothing would come out of it. Then, I met him again. I told him, 'Listen, you don't have to worry if you can't do anything about it. And I don't want to bother you whenever I see you. So, I will ask you one more time.' He smiled and said, 'That is what I was waiting for.' He put his hand in the pocket of his jacket and pulled out an application for membership and handed it over to me. 'You see,' he said, 'your father was an old-fashioned Freemason. I am too. We believe that a man should ask three times to join before he is handed an application. Your father should be proud of you now."

"He gave me all the instructions – where to go, who to meet, what to do – and within six months I was initiated into Freemasonry and became an Entered Apprentice in one of the oldest New York State Lodges. I think that joining Freemasonry was the biggest turning point in my life and ultimately affected the direction in which my life was going."

"What makes you think that way, Michael?" Pastor Charles asked. He was listening to Michael's story with much more attention than usual. He knew little about Freemasonry, but from what he knew, he seemed to perceive it as a false religion, manifesting a satanic attitude toward the Bible, the deity of Jesus Christ, and the blood atonement of Jesus Christ.

"Before I joined Freemasonry, I lived a superficial life, based on temporary material values. I thought of myself as a spiritual man who believed in God, who was baptized and raised Christian, but I never thought what all those things really meant. I never had time to stop and reflect on where I was coming from, where I was, and where I was going in my life. Freemasonry gave me tools to get into my inner world, into my soul, and understand myself. It gave me practical tools to work on the abstract subjects within my heart, my soul, and my mind. At the same time, it strengthened my faith in God."

"So, for how long were you a member of Freemasons?"

"For almost twenty years," Michael answered.

"Wow, you must be very experienced. Recently I saw online a book on Freemasonry that you wrote. I thought you wrote about it as a journalist and historian and didn't pay attention. But now I realize that you were an insider. Hmm, how interesting. Please, tell me more." Pastor said and leaned back into his chair like a man waiting for a good story.

"Well, Freemasonry was a big part of my life. I was an active member of the organization from the beginning. I took on all my masonic duties with much dedication and responsibility. It was noticed, and I was advanced through the degrees and ranks relatively fast. More I was working; I was given more responsibilities. Soon enough, Masonry took over my life. I was in the Masonic Temple almost every night either doing Ritual or at the different meetings. I became one of the most active members of the Grand

Lodge. Everybody was predicting for me dazzling future in Masonry."

"What do you mean by 'doing Ritual.?' What kind of ritual you are talking about?"

"Masonic Ritual," Michael answered, not quite sure what is that Pastor wanted to know.

"Yes, but what is that ritual comprising of?" The pastor said impatiently, "Sorry for my ignorance, but I know very little about Masonry. A bit I learned about it is negative. And I never spoke to a mason about Freemasonry. So I am curious what you will say."

"It's difficult to explain in a few words. Masonry uses symbols and allegorical stories to teach its members important moral lessons, thereby making good men better and more useful members of the society. These moral lessons are communicated in the ritualistic setting symbolically representing building of King Solomon's Temple. Tools and grades of the operative masons were used to rationalize philosophical ethical teachings and implemented as teaching tools of Freemasonry and its most important symbols. I don't know if I'm clear so far?"

"Yes, yes, but tell me about rituals."

"Okay, that's next. In Masonry, everything is a symbol, and all symbols are communicated through Ritual. Masons meet in their Lodges symbolically representing Temple of King Solomon. Lodge Temple is furnished with the Altar on the top of which are placed open Holly Bible, Square, and Compasses. These are three most important symbols that Masons call 'three great lights.' Altar is placed in the East or in the center of the Temple. The Master of the Lodge and two Wardens preside over all lodge work. They open and close the Lodge and conduct most of the ritual work. Opening and closing of the Lodge is a ritual too, where present members are each time reminded of their duties and purposes. At opening and closing, prayers are said invoking the aid and blessings of the 'Great Architect of the Universe,' as Masons refer to God."

"Yes, I read that expression somewhere. But why "the great architect of the universe?""

"Because Freemasonry is universal and open to men of all religions. To make them all feel comfortable and equal, a non-dogmatic expression is used when referring to the God Almighty. Anyway, three most important Rituals in Masonry are Initiation into the degree of Entered Apprentice, passing into the degree of Fellowcraft, and raising to the degree of Master Mason. During the Initiation, a candidate is introduced to a new beginning in his life and given basic moral lessons of his degree. He is taken to the Altar, where he is caused to kneel, place a hand on the open Bible, Square, and Compasses, and give a solemn obligation of Apprentice. He is then thought a secret word, grip, and sign of Apprentice, to enable him to recognize another Apprentice out in the world."

"Tell me if you can, please, what is that about secret words, grips, and signs. I heard about that. Do Masons really use them?"

"In old times, those were used as modes of recognition between Masons. Today, they are just symbols. Anyway, most of these, together with contents of all rituals, could be found online. Of course, reading them online is not the same as experiencing it, but this is just to say that all those 'Masonic secrets' that conspiracy theorist are talking about are not really secrets. Everything is already available."

"And what about obligation? Is it true that Masons have severe punishments for those who break their obligations?"

"As I said already, everything has just symbolic meaning. Although, many Masons enjoy that lure of secrecy and mystic around them and purposely avoid answering any direct questions just in order to perpetuate that sentiment in the public. I am not sure if that is really good. Sometimes I think it is counter-productive, with all conspiracy theories and anti-masonic propaganda."

"Well, Michael, you present everything very benign, but you know how they say "where there is a smoke, must be a fire." Not that everything people say about Freemasonry is the truth, but there must be something about it that is not right. I am not a Catholic, care little about Popes, but several Popes over past three centuries condemned Freemasonry and forbidden all Catholics to join them. There must be some reason for it." Pastor said.

"Yes, the relationship between the Church and Freemasonry is a complicated and long story. But, you asked me about Rituals. I am trying to complete that first."

"I am sorry. I got carried away. Please, continue."

"After Initiation, Entered Apprentices learn about Masonry and take part in the Lodge work for about a year, before they are passed to the degree of Fellowcraft. As

Fellowcrafts, they learn about different arts and sciences, and their ethical and moral applications. Again, after about a year, they are raised to the degree of Master Mason. This is the highest degree in Masonry. It is also called philosophical degree because most important lessons about our existence are given here."

"Before you said 'passed' to the degree, and now you say 'raised' to the degree. Is there a difference?"

"Yes. Passed means he was given new knowledge and placed in a different position. 'Raised' refers to the manner in which the lessons of the third degree were given. In this degree, the candidate was symbolically killed and then "raised" to life again. Here lessons of the immortality of the soul were given to newly raised Master Mason. These are considered the most important lessons of Freemasonry."

"You said that the third degree is the highest in Masonry. But I heard about thirty-third degree, the degree of Knights Templar, Rosicrucians, and many others. What is the story with those?"

"Those are additional degrees. Some people call them higher degrees. But in their essence, they all just deepen the lessons of the third degree. In American Masonry, they are two main branches, or as some call them Rites. Scottish Rite, where the highest degree is thirty-third, and the York Rite, where the highest degree is Knight Templar."

"So, how far did you get in Masonic degrees?" Pastor asked.

"In Scottish Rite, I got to thirty-second degree, and in York Rite to the degree of Knight Templar. I was about to be proposed for the thirty-third degree, but before it happened, I left Freemasonry."

"So, what happened? Why did you leave?" Pastor asked.

"There were many reasons. On one side, I felt that American Freemasonry was too dogmatic and stagnating and that it should open to the ideas of European Freemasonry, that was more liberal. I wrote about it in Masonic publications and many Freemasons didn't like that, which made me very disappointed. On another side, I was involved in business dealings with some of the members of the Grand Lodge, and when the business went sour, they were blaming me. Yes, it was my fault. It was a bad investment. It could happen to anybody. But they jumped at me like I stole money like I swindled them. That was upsetting. And finally, all this was happening at the time I decided to go back to Romania and start publishing business in Bucharest. So, one day I got really fed up with all that pressure in my Masonic life, sat down and wrote a letter of resignation to all my Masonic duties to the Grand Secretary of the Grand Lodge. Soon after I left for Bucharest. I never heard again from them."

"Correct me if I am wrong, but didn't you go to Bucharest because of the woman?" The pastor asked with the smile on his face.

"No, I went to Bucharest to start my business and then I met a woman."

"So, this woman you met in Bucharest had nothing to do with you leaving Freemasonry. Right?"

"Yes. That is correct." Michael said.

Pastor Charles said nothing after Michael gave him this answer. He kept looking at Michael. Michael felt that Pastor didn't believe him. After all, it was with the reason. Michael was lying to Pastor. But he couldn't admit that yet. The reason he went to Bucharest and started the business there was because he met a woman. And he thought she was the one he was looking for. So, in reality, this woman had something to do with him leaving the Freemasonry.

"And what about publishing? You never told me how did you get from being baker and pastry chef to being published, author and publisher. I mean, I know that you graduated journalism, but that was back in Bucharest when you were still young."

"Pastor, I am still young," Michael said and smiled.

"Yeah, yeah, like me, ha, ha. So tell me, you wrote sixteen books, is that right?"

"Yes. Freemasonry has a lot to do with me going back to writing. Constant learning and study is required for all who practice Freemasonry. That was how I got back into writing. At first, I was doing mandatory research papers. Then I got hooked on writing about esoteric subjects. My papers appeared in Masonic publications around the world. Then one day I thought I should put my papers in the form of a book. I did, and that was my first book on Freemasonry. It received great reviews, and it was a big success. That was over fifteen years ago. More books followed; sixteen in total so far. When my girls grew up and moved away, I quit food business completely and devoted myself to writing and publishing. There wasn't much money in it. Nothing even comes close to what I was making in the bakery or in catering. But it was a real joy. Until I moved and started a business in Bucharest. That was when everything went down the hill."

"Hmm…This is an interesting story. I always admired people who can write a book," Pastor Charles said, "I always wanted to write one."

"Pastor, everybody should write one book. There is a book in each of us. It is just a matter of bringing it out. Some people are capable and willing to do that, some are not. I still remember the day when I decided to devote to writing completely. It was in the reading room of the Livingston Library in New York. I was working on a paper and using as a reference this old book written by somebody in early Eighteen Century, almost three hundred years ago. I looked across the room and there was this young guy sitting at the table in the corner. In front of him was my book. He was using it to write something. At first, I felt proud. My book was in the library and people were reading it. But then I looked back at the book in front of me and it came to me. The greatest thing about writing is that in three hundred years, somebody will be still reading my book in this or some other library as I was reading the book from the author that lived in the Eighteen century. Through his writings, he was talking to me, as I will talk to my readers in three hundred years from now. Leaving a book behind keeps your thoughts alive in this world forever. So, in some ways, your spirit never dies. It is the best way to achieve immortality."

The Inner World

21

Michael was looking through the window of the fifth floor room. It was a rainy and gloomy Monday morning. Nothing one would expect in August. But after a couple of weeks of a heat wave, it was good to cool down the overheated New York asphalt.

Across the street was a covered bus stop for the M103 bus. Michael could see Francis, who was laying on the bench on the bus stop and sleeping. As usual, he was shirtless, just in dirty and ripped gray dress pants. Those pants were brand new when Michael gave them to Francis after shower day, just five days ago. A few people were waiting for the bus under the cover but at a noticeable distance from Francis. Nobody liked to be close to a sleeping homeless man, Michael thought.

Michael heard steps behind him. It was Jeremiah coming with a slice of carrot pound cake in his hand.

"Here, this cake is for you," he said and gave the slice to Michael, "The guy from the kitchen told me to give it to you.

This came in last night's donation from Starbucks."

Michael had somewhat a standing order with students working in the kitchen. He was supplying them with good clothing, and they were supplying him with good food. Day old Starbucks' pastries, donated by neighborhood Starbucks stores to the Bowery Mission, were Michael's favorite snacks. Every night before he would go to sleep, one of the kitchen staff would bring him some of Starbucks pastries. If he would go to sleep before the donation arrived, they would give it to him in the morning.

"Hmm, I love carrot cake. It is so moist." Michael said while biting into the slice of pound cake.

"What are you looking at?" Jeremiah asked.

"Oh, I am looking at Francis. He slept all night on the bus stop bench across the street. Last night was chilly. I don't know how he can do that."

"He does the same in the middle of winter, why wouldn't he in the summer?" Jeremiah answered.

"Yes, but if I slept like that, I would freeze."

"Oh, no, you wouldn't. You would learn very fast. I was sleeping on the street for seven months. There is a trick to it." Jeremiah said.

"What do you mean a trick? I slept on the subway for ten days. It is not like I wasn't on the street. The only reason I would fall asleep was because I was so tired and hungry I couldn't keep myself up and my eyes open. But I still felt cold coming from outside whenever the train doors would open."

"That is in the beginning. Later you learn. You see, the

trick is to disassociate your mind from your body. Once you do that, you are able to withstand extreme colds and extreme heat. You just don't feel it. You may get frostbite, but you don't feel it. Because you are not there to feel it," Jeremiah said.

"And where are you if you are not in your body?"

"Oh, you are in your body, but you are not with it. In your mind, you go into the land of dreams, wherever you feel good, and slowly you start losing the reality you are in. And before you know, you don't feel cold, wind blowing, rain or snow, nothing. You are not immune to being frozen to death if it's cold, or dying of overheating if it is really hot, but you just don't feel it because you are somewhere else, in a world deep inside of you, where everything is just right and where you are not a homeless guy sleeping on the street. Something like that is happening to Francis now. I have seen homeless guys sleeping in the cardboard boxes, covered with a foot of snow, and if you look at their faces, they are smiling, dreaming of who knows what."

"So, you are saying that they are in some inner world of their own, where everything is a lullaby? According to you, it is so easy to be homeless sleeping on the street," Michael said ironically.

"No, I didn't say that. Don't twist my words. Why do you think so many homeless guys are mentally ill? They go through such horrendous circumstances living on the street that usually the only solution is to escape from and deny reality. It hurts less. And from denying your reality to being crazy is a very thin line," Jeremiah said agitated with Michael comments.

"So I would do well as a homeless man," Michael said through laughter, "I am a big day dreamer."

"Michael, if you spent longer on the street than your ten days, you wouldn't laugh about that now," Jeremiah said.

"You are right. I wasn't joking about it. Sometimes I laugh when I feel uncomfortable about something. Those ten days were the worst of my life. I will never forget them. I don't want to experience anything like that again," Michael said and continued, "And now I have to go to Pastor Charles for my Monday confessions."

"What do you have to talk about that takes so long? I don't tell him anything. Our sessions are like five minutes long. I think he gave up on me, ha, ha," Jeremiah answered as they were going out of the room.

"Jeremiah, could you do me a favor," Michael asked.

"Yes. What do you need?"

"Could you get a sweatshirt from the clothing room and take it across the street to Francis? Make sure it's gray. He is very specific about colors he wears. Goes crazy if you give him green or brown."

"Yeah, it is really hard for Francis to go crazy about something, ha, ha," Jeremiah commented, "But I'll do it right away. Don't worry."

Michael knocked on the door of the Pastor Charles' office and waited for an answer.

Pastor Charles looked at him through the glass doors.

"Who is it?" he asked with a big smile.

"Michael, your favorite student," Michael answered.

"You may enter," Pastor said still smiling.

"Wow, Michael," Pastor said when Michael entered and sat in the chair next to Pastor's desk, "This program really works for you. You finally learned some manners."

"What can I say, Pastor. I am a success story," Michael said and started laughing.

"We will see when you get out of here. But I hope you are. I think you really learned your lesson by now. So, how was your day so far? Did you learn something from this morning's preaching at the chapel?"

"I wasn't at the service this morning,"Michael answered.

"Why?" Pastor asked.

"I had to deal with the guys on the fifth floor who didn't feel like doing their cleaning duties. So I had to supervise them. But I had my morning lesson, nevertheless."

"How come?" Pastor asked.

"I looked out the window, and I saw Francis sleeping on the bench at the bus stop across the street. It inspired Jeremiah and me to have an enlightening conversation about our inner worlds."

"Jeremiah? What does Jeremiah know about the inner world? And what does Francis have to do with your conversation," Pastor asked with disbelief.

"Oh, Jeremiah may play stupid with you, but he is far from stupid. It seems that he knows quite a bit. I commented on Francis sleeping shirtless through the cold night, and Jeremiah's theory was that the reason he doesn't feel cold is because he disassociated his mind from his body, and he resides in his inner world of dreams, thereby not feeling any cold."

"Jeremiah told you that? I will have to talk to him differently. So, what do you think about it? What do you think your inner world is?" Pastor asked.

"I don't know how to put it, but, for me, my inner world is the 'real me'. It's the part of me that nobody knows and I always try to conceal from everybody. Those are my dreams, inspirations, thoughts, feelings, ideas, who I truly am, who I want to be."

"Does anybody know your inner world or have access to it except yourself?" Pastor asked.

"Every human being has two personalities, two different faces. The inward face that, besides me, only a couple of people may see; and the second personality is represented by the outward face, one that everyone sees. The outward personality is like a blurred image of the 'real me', but most people never know it from the outside unless they see glimpses of my inner world."

"So, what do you think is the role and the purpose of your inner world?"

"Through my inner world I interpret and measure everything around me, and how everything makes me feel. It's the way I answer questions like, 'How it makes me feel?' and 'Why?'"

"Very good, Michael." The pastor said, "This is a good conversation to have. Your ideas about what the inner world represents are close to my understanding. The inner world is a complex system of thoughts, beliefs, values, ideas, stereotypes, assumptions, memories, faith, ideologies, attitudes, goals, needs, desires, and pretty much everything we pick up through our life, experience, and store in our mind. Our inner world, in many ways, determines how we communicate with others. You see, no two people have exactly the same inner world because no two people have exactly the same experiences in life. When we talk about something, we are describing ideas, impressions, interactions, and conclusions that originated within our mind, or to say it differently, within our inner world. Many communication problems occur just because our inner experiences are different. Our perceptions of the very same issues and objects are often different."

"Michael," Pastor continued, "to accept our Savior Jesus Christ and to surrender to the will of God, it is very important to start this renewal process of being born again in your mind, or in your inner world. As Apostle Paul says in the Book of Romans, *'Do not conform to the pattern of this world, but be transformed by the renewing of your mind. Then you will be able to test and approve what God's will is — His good, pleasing and perfect will.'* Do you understand what I am trying to say?"

"I am not sure, Pastor," Michael said.

"What I want to say is this; God didn't give us our mind to lock ourselves in it. Our inner world doesn't exist so we can escape from reality. It is not a place to dream dreams that will never come to fruition and just to wake up to the cruel facts of our reality. Even the deepest and darkest abyss of our inner beings, where nothing awaits our soul but a certainty of death, is the right place to come not only to our true self but to come to Christ, to connect to God, to be born again. And that is exactly what you need to do, Michael."

Michael looked at Pastor Charles without words. Pastor's faith and his convictions were so strong, he thought. But he couldn't understand how Pastor didn't see that he was talking to somebody who was already with Christ, for a very long time.

The Path of the Pilgrim

22

Michael was sitting in the clothing room with his laptop. It was a lazy Monday morning. He folded all the donated clothing the night before, so there was nothing much to do. He didn't feel like going to the morning Chapel service. Although he hadn't completed the program yet and chapel services were mandatory, managers on duty would often excuse him because of his work in the clothing room. So sometimes he would just use that as an excuse and hide away in the corner of the clothing room.

He looked at his Google mail, but there was nothing there, besides junk mail. Nobody was writing to Michael. The last time Eliza wrote to him from Bucharest was four months ago. It was a short mail telling him that she was breaking up with him, and not to write or call her anymore. Michael saw that mail only after he got his laptop, which was three months after it was written. Didn't answer it. He probably wouldn't even if he saw it earlier. Michael felt bad about it for a while, but he knew it was the best thing for both of them. It was just the way it had to be, a destiny. It was good while it lasted. He certainly enjoyed her young body very much. She had such a white and smooth skin. Sliding into her would always make her whole body tremble. She was so sensitive to touch. Michael knew that, and his hands were all over her all the time. He smiled while thinking about it.

Michael googled his name. He always liked to check if there was anything new online about him. There were about ten pages of references connected to his books and work. Not bad for a homeless guy, he was thinking. But there was almost nothing new. The only new reference was his new website.

The clothing room doors opened. Michael turned to see who it was. It was Rick.

"Good morning, Ricky-man," Michael said with a smile and turned back to his laptop.

"Hi, Mike. What are you doing? Watching porn?" Rick asked.

"No, Ricky. That is not my thing. I don't watch porn."

"Why not? What is wrong with a good porn?"

"I prefer to do it myself, rather than watch it," Michael said annoyed with this conversation.

"So, what is this?" Rick asked while looking over Michael's shoulder at the computer screen.

"Those are references on Google about me," Michael answered.

"What do you mean, references? Is somebody after you, so they put it online," Rick asked.

"No, Rick," Michael smiled, "Those are all articles and sites about the work I did over many years, my books, things I achieved, projects I did. Everything that was ever recorded about me through digital means, one can find on Google."

"Hmm, look at this…" Rick said and kept staring at the screen, "so you can't lie to anybody about anything. Everything is here!"

"Yes, pretty much. Even The Bowery Mission, ha, ha…" Michael giggled.

"The Bowery? You are kidding. How come?" Rick asked with surprise.

"You remember a couple months ago, there were guys from some TV station filming in the dining room during the dinner?" Michael asked.

"Yes, I remember."

"Well, I was in the line to get my dinner, and I told the guy with the camera he can't film without permission of those filmed. He looked at me with this expression like 'Who the fuck you think you are' and kept filming. So, the video they made, they sent to the Bowery Mission, and the Director put it on Bowery Mission website. So, anybody watching that video can see me in the line with other homeless people getting my dinner. I hope nobody ever sees it. It is so embarrassing."

"Ha, ha, so now you are not only a famous writer, you are a movie star as well?" Rick couldn't stop laughing.

"I see nothing funny in it," Michael commented.

"Ha, ha, of course, it's not funny, it is sad. But you were giggling too" Rick kept laughing, "Ha, ha. The life path of

Michael Nicolau, from Romania to rich and famous in New York to the Bowery Mission dinner line, ha, ha! Man, it's better to watch porn. With this, you only get depressed."

Jeremiah entered the room.

"What are you laughing about, guys? What did I miss?" Jeremiah asked.

"Oh, Michael is a movie star in the special feature about the Bowery Mission. Maybe, he'll be nominated for an Oscar, who knows."

"I saw that video. It was on the Channel Two News." Jeremiah said.

"What?! You are serious, Jeremiah?!" Michael asked in disbelief.

"Yes. But don't worry. It was only on the late night news, and you are on the screen just for a second or two." Jeremiah answered.

"But you recognized me?" Michael asked still in disbelief.

"Of course, I did. I look at you every day here. It was easy to recognize you."

"Shit," Michael said, "I hope nobody else saw it."

"Why not? Who cares, Michael? It is your life. It happens to many people. You should not be ashamed of it." Rick said. "Fuck them all. Whoever says anything bad about you being in the Bowery is not your friend."

"Ricky, it is not about that. Anyway, I don't have too many friends left. If I had friends, do you think I would have ended up in the Bowery? I don't care about that. It is just that I don't want my daughters to see this or some of their friends. I don't want them to feel ashamed of their father, to think that their father was some loser," Michael answered.

"Okay, Michael, tell me this," Jeremiah jumped like he was in a debate club, "How old are your daughters?"

"Two are almost thirty, and one is nineteen. Why?" Michael asked.

"Did they finish schools? Do they work?" Jeremiah continued with questions.

"Yes, two older daughters work. The youngest is still in the college."

"So, now tell me this: do they know that their father was homeless in New York and that he is in the Bowery Mission," Jeremiah asked again.

"They knew I was in New York penniless. I called them to ask for money..."

"And?" Jeremiah insisted on hearing the complete answer.

"They told me they could not help me," Michael answered quietly.

"So now, you are ashamed if they find out you were in the Bowery Mission? You are crazy! If I were you, I would write them on a Bowery Mission postcard, and tell them – Look, this is where your father is! The same one who made you and raised you, who worked hard all his life, so you could be what you are today! Be proud! That is what I would do. And not be ashamed!" While talking, Jeremiah was moving his hands through the air making gestures in support of his statement.

"Jeremiah, it is easy for you to say that. You are not a

father. Yes, I made them and raised them. But I wasn't a good father. There is a lot of anger and disappointment in my daughters. And I think not only for me leaving their mothers. I know I was trying to be a good father, but I don't think I gave them all they expected from me. They never told me why they were upset and angry with me, but I know that they don't think of me as a good father," Michael said.

"Good or bad father! It is all the same, Michael. A father is a father. Unfortunately, we cannot pick who is going to be our father. According to you, if our father becomes a failure, we should just abandon him and turn our backs to him. What should I say then, about my father? He is an alcoholic, a drifter who never had a permanent address. He never had time for me, never paid child support. The only time I would see him was when he would come to my mother to hustle her for couple of bucks or to drink gin together until the supply ran out. Even now, while I am in the program, he comes to see me only on the first of the month, when I receive food stamps, so he can get a twenty for a bottle of booze. I feel sorry for him. Sometimes he makes me angry. I want him to be different. But he is my father, and he always will be. I have to live with it." Jeremiah said and sat down.

"Jeremiah is right, Michael," Rick said, "Now when I think about it, all I remember about my father was his long and heavy leather belt he used to beat me up for the smallest mistakes I made. One of the reasons I ran away from home when I was sixteen was that belt. He left my mother, and he lived like a lone wolf, not talking to anybody in the village. Then he had a stroke. They found him two days later on the floor of the kitchen. After the hospital, they wanted to put him in some rundown retirement home. I never allowed that. I was sending money from New York for visiting nurse service and full-time home aid for ten more years until he died. He never said thank you. I don't know if he ever recognized me when I went to visit. But I don't mind. He was my father. It is what we are supposed to do as children."

"Well, I don't know. I just don't think that I was enough around for my kids when they were growing up. And I felt bad when I called them to ask for help. Even worse, when they refused me. But I don't blame them. I should have never called them in the first place. They feel like I betrayed them. I know if they knew all the circumstances of my life that they would feel different. But again, it was my fault. I never shared anything with anybody. I never knew how to communicate with my children." Michael said.

"Again, I am saying none of it is important." Jeremiah said, "Love between parents and children should be unconditional. And if parents don't give enough love to their child, that is not an excuse for a child not to love their parents, and vice versa."

"You see, Michael," Rick said, "You mentioned your life path. Maybe your life path was meant to be the way it turned out. Maybe there was nothing you could do about it. So, don't blame yourself for how your children act with you. One day, when they have children, they will learn. Unfortunately, most often, by the time kids learn what it means to be a parent, their parents are already gone."

The phone rang in the clothing room. Michael answered it. It was Pastor Charles on another side.

"Michael, did you forget about me? It is quarter past nine and you aren't here."

"Sorry, Pastor," Michael answered, "I was caught in conversation with Jeremiah and Rick. I'll be there right away."

Michael entered Pastor Charles' office after knocking, but without waiting for an answer.

"I am here. Sorry," he said.

"So what was so important that you forgot our session?" Pastor asked.

"Oh, nothing. We were just discussing our lives, and how somebody's life path may affect the way his children grow up and relate to him," Michael answered.

"That is nothing? That is a bundle. Maybe we can continue on the same subject. How do you perceive your life path so far?"

"It is hard to say. Or maybe, I am just afraid that you wouldn't understand. No disrespect intended, Pastor. You are Pastor and a counselor, but sometimes I feel that even people close to God don't understand what am I talking about when I try to explain my life path."

"So, try me, Michael. If you don't tell me, I certainly can't understand." The pastor said, annoyed with Michael's comment.

"My whole life was like the path of a pilgrim. Whatever I was doing, wherever I was going, something was missing inside my soul. Something was lost. And the only way to find it was by giving myself to God, to praise Him and honor Him constantly. But somehow, that very same God kept eluding me, like He was playing some kind of game with me, like He was testing my faith. I used to joke that when I was born, God was taking a nap, so He didn't even notice my birth. From early childhood, I had a deep reverence for the God Almighty. But somehow I felt like He was always paying more attention to everybody else, including those who never believed in him. But instead of giving up on Him, I kept searching, trying to find Him, to let Him know that I am here, to help me find whatever it was that I was missing within." Michael said, kept quiet for a while and then continued.

"That is why I joined Freemasonry. I thought that Freemasonry was going to give me some answers, some direction where to go and how to find that which I was missing. I enjoyed the mysteries of the Masonic rituals and the meanings of the Masonic symbols."

"And did you get the answers you were looking for, in Freemasonry?" Pastor asked.

"For a while, I thought I did, but I didn't. However, I learned a lot." Michael answered.

"What did you learn?" The pastor asked again.

"Many things. But the most important lesson was never to give up, never to stop searching for that which was lost. The key to the fulfillment in life is to never stop searching."

"And what do you think about how your life's pilgrimage affected your children and the way they relate to you?" Pastor asked.

"I think I was preoccupied with myself and with my inner search, and I never gave my children the full attention they deserved. Even when I was with them, I wasn't with them. I mean, I was fulfilling all my duties as a father, the best I could. They felt neglected by me. That everything else was more important to me than their welfare. They felt abandoned. And then they became angry."

"And were they right? What do you think?" Pastor interrupted Michael.

"Yes, they were right, up to a point," Michael answered and continued, "But I couldn't stop. There was something stronger than my will that was keeping me on that pilgrim's path. It felt like it was my obligation to continue. Like I gave my promise to somebody I would find that which was missing."

"When did you start feeling like that Michael? Do you remember what were your circumstances when you started feeling this way?" Pastor asked.

"In some ways Pastor, I always felt misplaced. The same place never kept me for a long. When I was a kid, I was a loner, very introvert. I preferred roaming the streets of the old city in Bucharest and exhibition halls of the National Museum for hours, then playing with my friends. Like I was always looking for something. I was a big daydreamer. I think I still am. Sometimes, people are talking to me, I look at them, but don't hear a fucking word because my brain is somewhere else, in some other world."

"Michael, please no "f" word over here. You should learn that by now. This is the House of God. Show respect, okay?"

"Sorry Pastor. It just gets out of my mouth. All these guys around me. Every second word is "f" word. It looks like I picked the habit."

"Instead of you picking up bad habits from them, they should pick something good from you. Anyway, what is that you are looking for in your life, Michael?"

"I don't know how to explain that to anybody Pastor. All my life I was like lost in the space. Never happy with what I had and always looking for something else, not knowing exactly what am I looking for. Then, five years ago, I had a strange dream that changed all that. And all my life turned upside down like it wasn't enough complicated already."

"A dream?" The pastor asked while raising his eyebrows.

"Yes, a dream, Pastor."

"What was the dream about?"

"In a dream I was visited by Archangel Michael who told me who I am and what I have to do." Michael said and looked straight into Pastor's eyes to see his reaction.

For ten seconds, Pastor said nothing. Then he asked: "Can you tell me what was said to you by Archangel?"

"I am sorry Pastor, but I am not sure if I should," Michael said.

"Okay, think about that for a while. I would like to discuss your dream with you. But it is up to you. Let's pray for a moment."

The pastor took Michael's right hand with his left and placed his right on the top of Michael's head. He closed his eyes and started praying out loud.

Free Will and Destiny

23

There was almost no place left to sit when Michael walked up to the balcony of the Bowery Mission chapel. The morning service was already halfway through. Pastor Paul was talking about free will and destiny. As a matter of fact, he was more reading from the notes than talking.

Michael sat on the windowsill at the back of the balcony. He smiled, thinking for a moment about Pastor's sermon. It sounded more like a theological paper fitted for seminary students than a morning preaching to a bunch of homeless people. But that was Pastor Paul's style. It seemed he enjoyed listening to his own rhetoric.

In the last two months, Michael was seldom in the chapel during the services. His duties as the Captain of the fifth floor and the clothing room attendant were always providing excuses for him not to attend service. But this morning, he felt he needed to come to the chapel and just be quiet. There was much on his mind.

The day before, on Sunday, Rick left Bowery Mission and moved out to his apartment in the Bronx. Michael and Jeremiah were helping him load the van with his belongings. The same evening, Victor, who now lived on the streets again, stopped by the Bowery to have a dinner and see if they would let him stay in the Chapel overnight. Unfortunately, all the spots were already taken, so he had to go back on the street. Michael gave him a four-dollar metro card, so he could get on the subway and doze off on the train. He never saw Victor again.

Michael was just two weeks away from the completion of the program. Soon he would have to leave the security of the Bowery Mission and go back to the uncertainty of independent living somewhere in New York. He was looking forward to it, but he was also very nervous. He still wasn't making enough money to rent an apartment on his own. Another problem was in the references any landlord would ask for. He simply didn't have any. His credit was a complete disaster. He lost his apartment in New York for not paying a mortgage while he was in Romania. The last time he was renting an apartment was ten years ago before he bought his apartment in Brooklyn. He didn't even know if he could find contact information for his last landlord. Everything was pointing towards having to get a room in a rooming house or become a roommate with somebody who already had an apartment. He didn't like either of these options. But that wasn't the worst of his worries.

He felt lonely. With his actions over the last few years he alienated everybody from his past, and isolated himself from his children, family, friends, business associates, and anybody he ever had any contact with. All his life behind him was like an empty notebook, with the barely visible marks of erased text, as illegible remnants of something that was written there a long time ago.

Strangely enough, he didn't feel any guilt for separating himself from his past. Five years ago, he clearly heard in his dream a message brought to him by Archangel Michael from the God Almighty, telling him he should get up and leave everything behind; that his place was not there; that it was time to go in search for his true self and for his true destiny.

Now, five years after, he was sitting in the Bowery chapel, a broken and homeless man, still trying to find that which he was looking for. But he didn't regret anything he had done in those five years. In his mind, it wasn't his doing. He sincerely believed that he surrendered his own will to the will of God and that everything that happened to him, good or bad, had to happen for some reason. It was God's doing. It was his destiny. He just had to figure out why.

He remembered the words the angel told him in his dream that night five years ago. The angel told him, 'She is waiting for you. Find her and fulfill your destiny. Your family is in your future, not here. Your happiness is in obeying your Lord. You owe him your allegiance. Go now. A rugged and dangerous road is ahead of you. Your enemies will be behind you every step of the way. But you should not be afraid. Don't ever turn back. From now on you have to trust your Lord God and follow your heart. Your heart will lead you to her.'

Michael didn't know what that dream meant, but ever since, everything in his life had changed. He wasn't the same man that went to sleep the night before the dream. He woke up a different person. And regardless of how unclear everything about that dream was, he was acting like he received some detailed instructions. Michael didn't have a clue who was he supposed to look for and where; who was waiting for him; why would his enemies be after him and who were they? All he knew was that he couldn't stand still.

The problem was that he didn't know where to start. Michael spent the next two years re-examining his life, trying to find a clue to where he should go and who he should look for. He was in a state of constant anxiety. He felt this terrible urge to go, and with the passing of time, it was becoming more and more painful to be still. Everybody around him noticed a change in his behavior. But he didn't care. To him, all the people around him, including his family, looked like strangers he never quite knew.

In the beginning, he felt remorse for having such thoughts. He was a father who spent years raising his children, and having these thoughts, feeling alienated from them, didn't seem normal. He loved his children. But, he couldn't help it.

Night after night, he would go to sleep thinking of her. Who was she and why was he supposed to find her? How old was she? How did she look? Then he would fall asleep, and the images of a young woman he never saw before, would flash in front of his eyes. They would not last for long. Each would appear for a second or two and then would fade away.

In the morning he wouldn't remember much. He didn't know who this woman was, but he felt some strange closeness to her. 'Was this woman the one he was supposed to find?' he was asking himself. After a while, he could form a picture of this woman in his mind. He couldn't exactly put a face to it because flashes were fast and often blurry, but he had an idea of her general look. She wasn't tall, maybe 160cm, pale white skin, a slim woman with nice curves and curly dark brown hair over her shoulders. Blue or greenish eyes. He wasn't sure. Sometimes she wore glasses, sometimes she didn't. Small lips. But he still couldn't see the whole face.

Five years later, these images were still appearing to him in his dreams. It was like an obsession of his. But he wasn't any closer to finding her than he was at the beginning. In the meantime, because of his obsession with his dreams, he messed up his life and lost everything, including his dignity. But somehow he didn't lose hope and the determination to complete his life endeavor. Yes, no matter how strange that would sound to anyone, he believed that odd encounter with the angel in his dream and words the angel spoke were directive he had to follow, no matter what.

Michael awakened from his thoughts just to realize that the morning service ended a long time ago and that he was sitting by himself on the chapel balcony. It was past breakfast time, so he must have been there for a good hour after everybody left. But it felt good to be in that place alone for a while. There was something so powerful about the interior of the Bowery chapel, some magical sacredness, the obvious presence of the spirit of God, Michael thought.

It was already time to go to the session with Pastor Charles. Michael enjoyed talking to Pastor, but sometimes, he had doubts about the concept of counseling sessions. He wasn't sure if they had done anything for him in all these months, and if they were necessary at all. By now, Pastor knew almost everything about Michael's life.

Michael walked from the chapel to the main entrance into the Mission and up two flights of stairs to the Pastor's office. While passing by the front desk, he noticed a homeless man inquiring about the program. In the past five and a half months in the Bowery Mission, he saw many men coming and going. Two weeks before the completion of the program, he was one of the senior students in the Bowery.

In two weeks, he would have to give up all of his duties in the Bowery Mission and concentrate completely on his work outside the Mission. He would be one step closer to the reality of the outside world.

He knew that he could always count on support from the Director and counselors in the Bowery. It was standard practice that students who moved away after successful completion of the program, and could financially support independent living, could still come back to the Mission for another year or two to get free pantry supplies, free clothing if needed and anything else that may help them in easing into their new life.

In spite of a great desire to leave and be on his own, he was afraid of the uncertainties of the outside world. The trauma of spending nights on the subway was still fresh in his mind, and the thought that something like that could happen again was devastating.

He came to the Pastor Charles' office just as another student was walking out. It was one of the new students assigned to Pastor for counseling. Michael didn't remember his name. But he remembered his face from the day this man came to the clothing room for the first time.

Michael looked at him as he was passing by. He had a very sad expression on his face, and his eyes were red and watery like he was crying. The man said to Michael, "Good morning," then turned his head away fast. "Good morning," Michael replied and looked after him as the man walked away down the hall.

"What happened to that guy?" Michael asked as he was entering Pastor Charles' office.

"Ah, just another Bowery story." The pastor answered while looking through his files on the computer screen.

"It must be very hard for you to sit over here all day long and listen to tragic stories students bring with themselves. It surely must affect you. How do you sleep at night?" Michael asked.

"It takes a lot of prayers. All of these men are in one way or another under attack from the devil who wants to destroy them and their hopes for better life. Doing this job is like facing other people's demons every day. But somebody has to do it. It is our mission to help people come back to the Lord. That is what God wants us to do. Yes, it takes a lot of prayers…"

"Did you ever think that you would end up as a Pastor and a counselor for homeless people?" Michael asked as he was taking his usual seat.

"To be a Pastor? That was the last thing on my mind when I was in my twenties and thirties. I dreamt of having my own BMW car dealership one day. And if I stayed in that business, I probably would. But then, I messed up my life. Like many students here, I hit the bottom. That is where our Lord Jesus Christ have found me, lifted me up, and showed me the way to a new life. I accepted Christ when I was thirty-five, and since then, all my life has been dedicated to this ministry."

"You never told me how you messed up your life. What happened?" Michael continued with his questions.

"I didn't? I thought I did. Usually, I tell my story to all students. Anyway, when I was in my mid-thirties, I was a talented car salesman working for the biggest dealership in the Bronx and Yonkers area and already been there for ten years. My boss loved me and made me an assistant manager. Everybody thought I had a bright future in the business. So, one summer, my boss left me in a charge of the company, and he took a long European vacation for his twentieth wedding anniversary. I was running the business for two months."

"At that time, some of my old high school friends came to me with the idea to forge papers for stolen luxury cars and sell them through my dealership. It was supposed to be a one-time deal with four vehicles. My cut of the profit was supposed to be really good. And I needed the money. I liked fancy cars, expensive clothing, dating nice women, and going to nightclubs. I thought it wouldn't hurt. Nobody would ever find out. Alas, in two months, we channeled fifty vehicles worth over one million dollars through my dealership. When my boss came back, I couldn't stop. And I couldn't think rationally. Soon after, the FBI knocked on my office door, and everything was over. I cooperated with them, told them everything I knew and got out easy with suspended sentence and a huge fine I am still paying in installments every month."

"Nevertheless, I lost my job and my reputation. Nobody would hire me again. There was no place to turn to for help. And worst of all, I had just gotten married and had a baby with my wife when all that happened. It was my wife who told me we should go to church and pray. Before that, I was a non-practicing Catholic, who would go to the church only for Christmas and Easter. But that first time I went with my wife to the Pentecostal Church in our neighborhood in the Bronx, something broke in me. I realized that I was wasting years. And only after the devil took me deep into his abyss, I woke up and cried out to the Lord. He answered my prayers."

"In a short while, I got a job again. And guess what, it was a job appropriate for a sinner like me. The same Pentecostal Church we went to pray hired me as a janitor. So, in a matter of months, I went from assistant manager in a prestigious car dealership to the janitor in a small church in the Bronx. However, in five years, I rose up to the position of the Associate Pastor. I also graduated with a degree in Theology from St. Joseph College. Following that, with the help of my Pastor, I got this job in the Bowery Mission."

"For my forty-third birthday, I was in church for Friday night prayers, when God Almighty called me to start my ministry. I spoke to my Pastor, and he encouraged me to turn to my Haitian people living here in New York and minister to them. Soon after, I had a group of about fifty followers. We rented a basement in another church in the Bronx and founded a church. And that was it."

"I often ask myself if I hadn't hit the bottom that hard, would I ever be here now talking with you." Pastor finished his story.

"Yes, I ask myself that same question often. Regardless of how hard it has been for me to sleep on the subway, and knock on the doors of the Bowery Mission, I can't stop thinking that maybe everything happened for a reason; that my life path had to go through this downfall," Michael said and then asked Pastor, "Do you think that things in our lives were predetermined, that we all are just following our destiny?"

"In Christian theology," the Pastor started, "God is described as all-knowing, all-powerful and ever-present, which means that not only has God always known what choices individuals will make tomorrow, but has actually determined those choices. That is, we believe, by virtue of his foreknowledge he knows what will influence individual choices, and by virtue of his omnipotence he controls those factors. Keeping this in mind, yes, we could say we are just following our destiny."

"So, what happened to our free will? Do we really choose circumstances in our lives by ourselves, or is it just an illusion we are the ones making the choices?" Michael asked.

"Yes, that is the question that many theologians can't agree on," Pastor continued, "I like to use the parable of a drowning man here. God sent him a boat from which sailors throw a rope to the drowning man. But it was the drowning man's choice if he was to hold onto the rope or not. In some ways, God's omnipotence works in synchronicity with human will."

"So, what you are saying is that there is such a concept like destiny, but it is connected somehow, and works in parallel with our free will. In other words, like in those stories written in the way that readers can pick by their own potential developments and the conclusion." Michael said.

"Yes, something like that. I think that both our lives and the potential directions our lives may go are predestined. By using our free will in making our life choices, we do nothing else but picking up one of many already predestined options. To us, it seems like we were making the decision, while in reality, we just selected one of many possibilities that were already a part of our destiny."

"Don't you think God is so powerful that he can make us believe that we made some choices, when in actuality, he had made a choice for us?" Michael asked.

"That is true too. You know, theological interpretations of the free will and destiny are not completely aligned and clear cut. Even within the Christian community, there are disagreements about the relation of these two concepts.

Anyway, how did you get started on this subject?" Pastor asked.

"I don't know. Maybe because Pastor Paul was talking about it this morning in his sermon. And I told you before, sometimes I think everything that happened in my life, happened because it had to. It was predestined. So, I am trying to understand myself," Michael answered.

"Don't go down that road, Michael. Even if it was so, that way of thinking is not helpful. It makes it easy on your conscience, gives you an excuse for your failings, but it doesn't help you overcome your issues. It is time for you, Michael, to make a line in your mind, and say to yourself, 'I messed up my life because I was like this, like this, and like that. My issues were those and those. I will stand up like a man, and face them responsibly, and overcome my demons. I can do all things through Christ, my Lord.' This is what you have to say. Saying that everything was just destiny, that everything happened because it had to happen, is just an easy way out. I wouldn't recommend that to you because you would stumble again, and that is the last thing you want, isn't it, Michael?" Pastor asked.

"We don't understand each other. I am not trying to ease my conscience. Just trying to understand why everything happened the way it did," Michael said.

Pastor and Michael continued their conversation about free will and destiny for another hour. Michael had a hard time accepting Pastor's views. The pastor insisted that Michael should forget any thoughts about destiny and concentrate on practical remedies to his problems. In some ways, he was right, Michael thought. But he couldn't give up his dreams just like that. He couldn't give up on his search. He believed in his dreams, and he was determined to continue wherever he left off, as soon as he was able to.

Giving and Receiving

24

Michael walked into the clothing room, turned on the lights, and looked at the folding table in the middle of the room. It was covered with a pile of bags full of donated clothing and household items. On the floor next to the table was another pile of bags that could not fit on the table. "Nice beginning to the week," Michael thought, "Over the weekend people were generous."

He often thought that maybe one day, when he got back to himself and became independently wealthy, he'd be the one bringing donations to the Bowery Mission. Now, together with other homeless people, he was on the receiving end of somebody's generosity and compassion. But he wanted to be on the giving end. He remembered reading a quote by St. Francis of Assisi, which said that by giving we actually receive the most. Michael liked this saying. He knew how much joy there was in giving. He gave a lot to others. But he never tried to make a point of it, or to remind others how much he gave them. He was always trying to be almost invisible in his generosity. 'It was the only right way to give – anonymously,' he thought.

And he was good at doing that, in giving to others without being noticed. Many people that Michael interacted with in his life, including his children and members of his family, never realized how much Michael gave them in many ways. He didn't mind that. In his understanding, getting and receiving from others was a way of making the living, but giving was a way of life.

Like in everything else in his life, he was going to extremes in this. In spite of it, often he would hear "Oh, you never gave my anything," from somebody he gave a lot, just because the same person never noticed Michael's many generosities for his or her wellbeing. Michel would just smile with sadness and say nothing. "Maybe one day they will realize how much I gave them," he would think.

Michael sorted out the contents of the bags. That was his favorite task in the clothing room. Sometimes it seemed like opening Christmas gifts. One never knew what he would find there. Sometimes, it was brand new clothing from the store with the price tags still attached. Other times it was clothing so old it would rip apart on the first try to refold it. Often, Michael would find money in the pockets of donated clothing. In most cases, they were small bills or pocket change that people forgot to take out before donating the item. But sometimes, it was obvious that money was placed there as a donation.

Michael was tempted many times to keep the money and keep quiet about it, like many students, who worked before him in the clothing room, were doing almost routinely.   But he never did.   He would always report any findings to the Manager on Duty.

He remembered the time he brought to the Manager on duty a one hundred-dollar bill he had found in the pocket of a donated lady's leather jacket.

"Hmm, you have found a one-hundred-dollar bill." The Manager said.

"Yes, I did. In the pocket of a leather jacket." Michael answered.

"Did you tell anybody about your find?"

"No. I came straight here as soon as I found it." Michael said.

"Well, three things you can do with it. Actually, only two things now. The first one you cannot do anymore," the Manager said with the smile and then continued, "We can split this hundred bucks fifty-fifty and keep quiet, or you can just put this bill into donation box here, and I'll give you a receipt saying you turned the money in."

"And what was the first thing I could do, that I cannot do anymore?" Michael asked.

"Oh, you could have kept the money and never said anything to anybody, but you were sucker enough not to do that." The Manager said and started laughing, "Now you will have to share with me or be an even bigger sucker and put in the donation box."

Michael looked at the manager on duty. The same man was in the recovery program a year ago. He completed the program, became Mission trainee, and now he was one of the Managers on duty. 'He must be the one who was going through the donation bags before they would be brought downstairs to the clothing room, looking for different valuables. What a shame, what a shame,' Michael thought.

"Okay, give me a receipt for the hundred bucks. I'll be a sucker all the way," Michael said and dropped the hundred-dollar bill into the slot of the metal donation box sitting at the corner of the Manager's desk with the smile.

The Manager looked at Michael with a strange expression on his face. It was a mix of anger, despise, and surprise. Then he said, "Well, Mr. Nicolau, if that is what you desire," He wrote a receipt, signed it and handed it over to Michael. "You understand that I was joking when I said that we could share it. I was testing you, you know."

"Sure. It never crossed my mind you would consider something like that." Michael said and walked out of the office.

Since that time, the same Manager was watching Michael constantly trying to find the smallest irregularity he could bring up against Michael to his counselor.

He wrote complaints against Michael to Pastor Charles twice on made up charges. Michael had a hard time explaining to Pastor Charles that he had done nothing wrong.

"Michael, why would the Manager on duty make up charges against you if you had done nothing?" The pastor would ask.

"I don't know, Pastor. For some reason he doesn't like me. But I don't know why."

Michael didn't want to bring up the event. He knew that the counselors would try to clear that up and that it would be his word against the Manager's word. And since the Manager already brought charges against Michael, it would seem like Michael was trying to get revenge. So Michael just kept quiet and avoided any interaction with that Manager.

This particular Monday morning, most of the donated clothing was almost new. There was also several of oversized dress shirts. In the Bowery Mission, they were always in a shortage of oversized shirts. Many of the Mission students, as well as many homeless men taking showers and changing clothing regularly in the Mission, were tall and large men.

Michael couldn't understand how ironic it was that so many homeless people were actually tall and oversized, two to three hundred pound men, who maintained their weight in spite of the fact that their nutrition was sporadic and poor, and their living conditions – spending nights and days on the street – atrocious.

He put aside six oversized dress shirts for two of his colleagues from the fifth floor. They would be happy to get new shirts, he thought. He would give three shirts to each of them. He enjoyed this "giving" part of his clothing room job. It wasn't quite according to Bowery Mission regulations, to give clothing to students without the proper requisition slips from the counselors, but Michael didn't pay much attention to that. He enjoyed making people happy.

After five months of working in the clothing room, he knew dress sizes of almost all eighty students in the Bowery

Mission program, and he knew what kind of clothing they liked.

So every single day he would find something that would fit one of the students, and he would just bring it to them. Many of the students were coming to Michael with special requests and Michael would fulfill them as the needed items came in.

Of course, he was taking care of himself as well. He had excellent taste in clothing and knew how to pick the best items. Jeremiah would often make a comment, "You know Michael, you are indisputably the best-dressed man among the forty thousand homeless people in New York City, ha, ha, ha."

For Michael, the fact he acquired so much expensive and quality clothing for free was the result of the divine intervention. He always liked to dress well, but in last two years he lost all his clothing, and he didn't have money to buy anything new. Getting into the Bowery Mission and working in the clothing room enabled him to have unlimited access to the same clothing he always loved and wore. He could not explain it in any other way than as divine intervention. God gave him back what He took from him. He was watching over Michael again. Michael thought of it as of a good sign.

Almost everything in his life Michael understood as the result of divine will. Not that he blindly believed in the power of destiny. But often, he would think for hours about specific events that influenced the direction in which his life was going. In each case, he would think about various choices he could have made, and how they would have influenced the outcome of the particular event and provide direction in his life.

But each time, he would come to the same conclusion. Regardless of his choices, the result would always be the same. He believed that for whatever reason, his life story was written long before he was born. He just didn't know why. That is until he dreamt of being visited by Archangel who spoke to him. From that day on, he was on a mission to fulfill God's will.

And with Bowery Mission and his position in the clothing room, he saw that as a double blessing. On one side, he could give to others according to their needs and desires. On the other side, he was given so much. Sometimes he felt like the prodigal son from the biblical parable who came back home to his father, who ordered servants to dress his lost son into best clothing and adorn him with expensive jewelry.

"So, Michael, how do you feel today?" Pastor Charles asked as Michael walked into his office, "In three days you will complete the program. Are you ready for the next step?"

"I guess I am. We will see. Right, Pastor?" Michael smiled while taking his usual place in the chair next to the Pastor's desk.

"Well, all left for you to do now is to work and save money while you are still here. Be smart and don't spend anything until you move out. Later you will need every penny." The pastor said, "Do you have any idea how long you will stay in the Mission? You know that you are allowed six months as long as you save money regularly?"

"Yes, I know, but I would like to be out in two months at the most if everything goes as planned," Michael answered.

"You don't have to rush. Nobody is chasing you. I know that you want to get out, but you should be wise. Free lodging and food mean more money in your pocket." Pastor said. "And your savings so far are not too big. You don't want to stay without money once you pay your first month's rent and security deposit for your place. You always need to have emergency backup fund.

"Yes, I agree. But, if possible, I want to spend Thanksgiving in my place. And with God's help, I will. Not that I have anybody to invite for a Thanksgiving dinner. It is just something I want to experience as a symbol of my return to a normal life if you know what I mean." Michael said. "I want to sit down in my place for Thanksgiving and thank God Almighty for deliverance."

"Yes, yes, that is what Thanksgiving is all about, anyway. A time to stop and give thanks to the Lord for all manifold blessings He has been giving to us over the year. A time to rejoice in the unity. You said that you have nobody to invite for Thanksgiving?" Pastor asked.

"No," Michael said while smiling with sadness, "I don't think I have anybody I could call."

"How about your daughters? Did you talk to them at all, since you got here?" Pastor asked.

"No, Pastor. I haven't spoken to them. Don't know if they would speak to me even if I called them. They are upset with me." Michael answered.

"But do you feel you would like to speak to them?"

"I am not sure, Pastor. It is a strange feeling I have. I would like to see them and talk to them. But somehow I feel they should reach out to me, not the other way around. I spent years raising them. I think I deserve that much. Even if I wasn't a good father; even if they feel disappointed or hurt; I am still their father; they should reach out." Michael answered.

"On one side of the coin, Michael, you are right. If you put it that way it seems like you are right. Your kids are grown-ups already. They have their lives, their own families, and professions. You brought them up. For what is worth, they should reach out to you. But on the other side of the coin, they are your children. They always will be. Even if they turn their back to you, you should never turn your back to them. You should reach out to them. Call them. Send them e-mails. If they don't answer, do it again and again. Call them for all holidays and all birthdays. Show them you care. And one day, they will come back to you. They will seek their father." Pastor said.

"It is not all that simple, Pastor. In relationship with my children, it is more complicated than just father and children not communicating." Michael said.

"Why you say that? Why is more complicated? Is there anything I don't know? Did you do something inappropriate?" Pastor raised his voice.

"Don't get excited, Pastor. Nothing like that. I think that I was always a caring father who worked hard for his family, as much as I could, of course. But there is something else. I am not sure if I mentioned this before…maybe I did…" Michael was trying to find the words with which to start, "but I felt all my life like I was misplaced. Like everything I did was the wrong thing to do, at the wrong time, with the wrong people. Like I didn't belong to this world."

"Yes, you mentioned that misplaced feeling. You are repeating yourself, Michael. And you mentioned your dream you never explained. But what do you mean, wrong things, wrong time, wrong people?" Pastor interrupted him.

"Well, I mean, I was doing things in life that people normally do. I finished school, got a job, got married, made children, divorced, got married again, got another job, made another kid, got divorced again; and in all that time I felt like I wasn't with the people I was supposed to be. I can't say I didn't love the women I was married to or had relationships with. I can't say I didn't love and care about my children. But in all of that, I felt alienated from myself. Like I was trapped in the body of another man who was doing all those things. Like I was wasting my time. Like I had to be somewhere else. And now, after all of that is over, I feel nothing about the women I was with, and I don't feel any attachment to my children. Almost like they are not my kids. And I feel a terrible guilt for feeling like that because it is not normal for a father to feel that cold about his children. And I would like if they reached out and helped me have a normal father-daughters' relationship with them."

"Why do you think you feel like that?" Pastor asked.

"I don't know. I just do. On the other hand, I want to

have a family, to have a wife, to have children, to care about them, and to share with them in the joys of family life. But I don't think I have found my true wife and my true children yet. It sounds crazy to say that, especially if you are my age, but that is exactly how I feel."

"So what you are saying is that you would get married and have kids again if you could?" The pastor looked at Michael with wonder.

"Yes, but not to anybody. It is not about getting married and having a wife and children. It is about a very particular woman. I feel that somewhere out there is a woman I belong to; a woman I always belonged to; she is looking for me as I am looking for her, and we have to find each other. It is my mission, Pastor, and I am obsessed with it. I know that it sounds crazy, but it is all I think about."

"Is this what was said to you in your dream Michael? Or this is just a feeling you have?"

Michael didn't answer. He just lowered his head.

"I don't know what to tell you, Michael. First, you are not a youngster anymore. Second, you have to get out of here and work on regaining your life again. I hope it happens fast for you, but usually, it takes some time and lots of work, especially in your situation. You are not getting a weekly paycheck that would guarantee financial stability. You have to fight every day for new work. It is difficult being a freelancer, but that is your choice, and we support you in it. You are good at what you are doing, but unfortunately, that is not always a guarantee of success. So, you have to tread lightly and carefully in your life. Starting a new relationship and a new family is always connected with expenses. For that, you need financial stability and security."

The pastor stopped here for a moment, like somebody thinking about what he was going to say next, then continued, "You should try to rebuild your relationship with your daughters, and maybe even with your ex-wife. There is a lot you could give to your children. Soon they will have their own children, and their children will need a grandfather. There is a great joy in it, and it is something you should look forward to."

"Grandfather?" Michael looked up and said with surprise, "I can't imagine myself as a grandfather."

"Why not?" The pastor asked, "You are of that age, and your daughters are of age to have children. Nothing wrong with it. Are you afraid of being a grandfather because it would mean that you are old already? I am a grandfather, and it is a much bigger joy than being a father, ha, ha." Pastor started laughed.

"Why?" Michael asked.

"Because you get to play and enjoy and spend quality time with your grandchild and then get up and leave him or her to the parents to deal with all the hard parental duties." Pastor said.

"Pastor, I am not an ordinary man in his fifties afraid of getting old and dying, and thereby thinking about a young woman and a new beginning. Nothing like that. It is about returning to myself, to who I really am. It is about gaining back my soul, Pastor. Giving up my will and submitting to the will of God. Completing a mission at any cost. Don't think for a moment that I am not aware of all difficulties and challenges. I wish I had it easy – getting out of here, stabilizing my life, working, writing, and living in peace. But it's not about what I want. It is about what I have to do."

"You said that you need to return to who you really are. Who are you Michael, what do you think?" Pastor asked.

"My name was written in the Book of Life next to hers. We were united by the will of God for a purpose only He knows."

The Book of Life

25

It was the first Monday in September, six and a half months since Michael entered the Bowery Mission recovery program. First Mondays of each month were reserved for a graduation ceremony.

At six o'clock that evening, Michael, Jeremiah, and four other guys, dressed in their best suits provided by the Blessing-dale, walked up the stairs to the stage behind the pulpit in the Bowery Chapel, to receive their Certificates of completion of the Bowery Mission Discipleship Program.

They sat on the chairs lined up on the right side of the stage. Their counselors were already sitting on the left. Pastor Paul and the Director were sitting in the middle of the stage, just behind the pulpit. The chapel was full of homeless people who came for the regular evening service before dinner. Pastor Paul approached the pulpit and gave opening prayer. Then Director stood up and gave a speech about Bowery Mission recovery program. Most of the home-less people in the chapel were regulars for the meals at the

Mission, and they've heard this speech many times. Some of them were even former students.

Michael looked around. In six months in the Bowery Mission, he got to know almost everybody in that room. Most of those homeless people were taking a shower and changing clothing twice a week in the Mission. Some of them Michael knew by name and even knew their clothing sizes. 'If nothing else, but once I walk out of here' Michael thought, 'I will never again look at the homeless people the way I did before entering Bowery Mission.'

He turned his eyes towards Jeremiah and students sitting next to him. Out of all students who entered the program in March, Jeremiah and Michael were the only two who completed it. Other four students came in April.

"Success rate for March wasn't that high. It was almost twenty of us who came in March, right?" Michael whispered to Jeremiah.

"Yeah… it's difficult… Remember Victor? I never thought he will drop out again." Jeremiah answered. Then after few second he continued: "And who says we are a success, Mike? What if we return in six months?"

"Oh, never again. Never." Michael answered.

Counselors were introducing their graduating students and presenting them Certificates. Each certificate contained a quote from the Scriptures that was chosen for a particular student by his counselor. After receiving Certificates, students would give their testimonials. Jeremiah's testimonial was the shortest one: "Hi everybody. Buy everybody. Hope never to see you again… Also…   Big thanks to God, Pastor

Charles, and the Bowery Mission."

Michael was the last one to receive his Certificate. Pastor Charles read his name from the certificate. Everybody was cheering and clapping when Michael stood up and came to the pulpit. "Hey Micky, I need Nike's, size eleven! New!" – Somebody in the public yelled. Everybody laughed.

Then Pastor Charles read the quote from the Certificate: *"He that dwelleth in the secret place of the most High shall abide under the shadow of the Almighty. I will say of the Lord, He is my refuge and my fortress: my God; in him will I trust."*

He presented Certificate to Michael and shook his hand. It was time for Michael to speak.

This was for Michael the first time to give a testimonial in the Chapel. Pastor Paul asked him many times before to give a testimony during regular service, but he would always find some excuse not to do so. He just never felt comfortable in sharing his most intimate thoughts about his faith, and his relationship with God. Now he had to speak.

"I was thinking all day long what should I say tonight. Never gave testimonial before. Always thought it's nobody business what's between me and my God and how I feel about it. In these past six months, I've heard many students talking from this pulpit about miracles God did in their lives. Then I would see them again two weeks later sitting as homeless people after dropping out from the program. So much about miracles. That doesn't mean I don't believe in miracles. I do. But for miracles to happen, God, need our cooperation. As Pastor Charles once told me, God can throw us a rope to save us, but we have to hold to it. As I already said, I was thinking all day long what smart should I say tonight here that would impress everybody? But then I realize: I don't think I could say anything smart. If I was smart, I would never end up in the Bowery Mission. But, even when we are not smart and not watching our actions, God is watching over us. So, instead of trying to be smart, we should try to trust to and be faithful to our God, and he will grant us wisdom in return. And by God's grace and through our trust and faith in Him, miracles will happen. On another hand, what is that I could say to a bunch of homeless people that would impress them? Well, we have a hot chicken soup, mashed potato and a meatloaf for a dinner. Let's go eat before it gets cold. Thank God Almighty for providing."

To make the occasion more festive, a separate buffet dinner was set up in the second-floor conference room for graduates, their guests, counselors, and other Bowery Mission staff. In reality, not many guests would come. Graduates were encouraged by their counselors to invite family and friends to their graduation. However, students in the program were in most cases troubled people with no friends and broken family ties.

This particular Monday, the only guest present was Jeremiah's father.

"So, Mike, Jeremiah told me you too will leave Bowery soon?" Jeremiah's father, holding a slice of pizza in one hand and a hot dog bun in another approached and said to Michael.

Michael looked at this short, skinny, and bold headed

fifty years old man with a pointed mustache. He smiled. "Well, it is better to leave than to be kicked out. Right?"

"Yeah. But you, Mike, are a smart dude. You should stick around here. This is a good place for you. I've been watching you. You could be a manager here, even counselor. Bullshitting to addicts all day long. Easy life. You know what I mean." Jeremiah's father said and slide the whole hot dog bun in his mouth.

"So, are you proud that Jeremiah graduated, and that he is getting a job in the UPS warehouse?" Michael tried to revert conversation to another subject.

"It's okay. Not what I wanted for him, but he is a knucklehead. Does what he wants. When he entered the program, I told him to play crazy and dumb as much as he can and apply for disability while he is here. I know many guys his age who tricked their way into disability benefits by playing dumb. For him, it would be easy. He was born dumb. But no. Mr. dumb wants to work for his money in stead of getting a free money from the Uncle Sam. How dumb is that?"

"I think you are wrong. It is great that he wants to work. Security guard in the warehouse is not that hard of a job. He can spend that time to study and graduate college." Michael said.

"Jeremiah? College? Ha, ha. That would be the first. Nobody in our family ever went to college."

"What are you talking about?" Jeremiah joined them and asked.

"I was telling your father you may study college while

working as a security guard," Michael answered.

"I have to start working first and make some money."

"You will. When is your first day?" Michael asked.

"Next Monday. This Friday I have to go to get my uniform and ID."

"Talking about money," Jeremiah's father interrupted, "Jeremiah, come here on a side. I need to discuss with you something in private. Sorry, Mike." He said and pulled Jeremiah towards the door of the room.

Michael looked after them. 'Hmm, he will hustle Jeremiah for money again,' he thought, 'What a father to have.'

"Michael!" Pastor Charles waived at Michael from another side of the room, "Come."

Michael walked to Pastor Charles. "What's up, Pastor?"

"What's up? I never heard you say that before. Ha, ha. Sounds funny when you say. Anyway, getting this certificate doesn't mean you are off the hook with me yet. You owe me two more sessions. We can do one tomorrow morning and one next Monday if it works for you."

"Sure Pastor," Michael said with a smile, "Then I can start counseling you. You know, like in that joke about the crazy guy in the asylum chasing a doctor down the hall with a big knife, ha, ha."

"And what happened?" Pastor asked.

"Doctor got to some dead-end and turned to face a crazy guy with the knife. A crazy guy approached screaming, then suddenly stopped, turned knife around and offered to a doctor while saying, 'I caught you. Now it's your turn to chase me.'

"Yes, Michael. After I am done with you, I'll be the one who will need a counselor."

Michael knocked on the Pastor Charles' office doors and entered without waiting for an answer. "Good morning Pastor. Here I am as promised."

Pastor shook his head as a sign of acknowledging Michael presence but didn't say anything. He was preoccupied with reading his notes on the computer screen.

Michael sat down and looked around the room. There was something different? Then he realized. All Pastor's diplomas and pictures that were hanging on the office walls were off the wall and lined up in the cardboard box in the office corner. 'Something is wrong with this picture.' Michael thought.

After couple of minutes Pastor stopped reading and turned to Michael.

"Sorry Michael, I just had to go through some of my notes. There was so much we discussed in these six months. At our last session, you mentioned something very interesting. The Book of Life. What do you know about the Book of Life, Michael? What do you think that is?"

"For both Christians and Jews, the Book of Life, or in Hebrew *Sefer HaChaim*, is the book in which God records the names of every person who is destined for eternal life in Heaven. It was mentioned in the Bible fourteen times. Out of that six times in Revelation."

"Yes, that is in general terms. But what is the Book of Life for you? How do you perceive it personally? Last time you told me that your name was written next to hers in the

Book of Life. What it means for you when you say something like that?"

"I see the Book of Life as the point in the Creation where we meet our Creator. A place where our destinies were pre-written before the beginning of time. Once we reach that point, our circles of material life are over and we are heading for the eternal life in the presence of our Creator."

"What about Jesus? Where do you see him in relation to the Book of Life?"

"He is there to enlighten our way with his teachings and to inspire us with his example to reach that point."

"Hmm, to inspire us? And what about his sacrifice, his blood spilled, his death on the Cross?"

"Jesus is my Lord, Pastor. So, don't misunderstand me when I say this, but sometimes I think that he spilled his blood in vain. We learned nothing from his sacrifice. Even worst, most of the Christians think that by his death on the Cross they have a blank card to sin, as long as they accept Christ at the end."

"You said that our destinies are pre-written. So, how you control sin if the sin is a part of our destiny?"

"Our actions and choices are not pre-destined, but only the end result, the consequences of our actions. For example, I may jump through the window. It's a bad action, bad choice. It's a sin trying to kill myself. But it is God's decision, or rather my destiny if I am going to die or survive. If I am going to be crippled or not. Often, I felt during my life, that no matter what I was doing, things were going the way they had to go, regardless of my actions or choices. The end result was always the one I didn't intent to have. Then I realized, it's a destiny."

"Yes, you told me something like that already. But before we go further, let me give you my take on the Book of Life. First, it is important to understand that we are all sinners. Let me read something to you. In Romans 3:23, it was written, '*For all have sinned and fall short of the glory for God.*' Sin means that we have missed the mark that God has set for us. The penalty for sin is death. Here we read in Romans 6:23, '*For the wages of sin is death, but the gift of God is eternal life in Christ Jesus our Lord.*' This verse says that death is the wage of our sin. It is what we earned. We deserve to die and live separated from God forever. But, this is not the end of the message. In Romans 5:8 we read, '*But God demonstrates his own love for us in this: While we were still sinners, Christ died for us.*' Jesus Christ died in our place, in your place, Michael. The good news is that you can be saved through faith in Christ, and as it says in Ephesians 2:8 to 9, '*For it is by grace you have been saved, through faith, and this not from yourselves, it is the gift of God, not by works, so that no one can boast.*' So, it is only through our Savior that your name can be written in the Book of Life. You say that Jesus Christ is your Master, but did you really receive him, Michael? Receiving Jesus is a matter of truly asking Him to come into your life, to forgive your sins, and to become your Lord and Savior. It's not merely an intellectual undertaking, but rather, an act of sincere faith and heartfelt will. This is not a ritual based on specific words, like you have in Freemasonry, but rather, a prayerful guideline for your sincere step of faith. The Book of Life was not made by human hands. It is eternal, made in Heaven, the Book of the Lamb of God."

"Pastor, you said the same thing I said, but in a different way."

"No, Michael. What you said sounded like you were talking about some magical, occult book. 'Meeting your Creator, circles of material life' that's what you're saying. What I am talking about is meeting your Savior, receiving Jesus. Forget circles of material life and that new age occult mumbo-jumbo. Receive Jesus!" Pastor yelled.

"Sometimes when we are discussing things, it feels like mute is talking to a blind. I tell you again. Jesus is my Master. I am already with Jesus. I don't need to receive him again."

"Why not? I can receive Jesus three times a day, every day. By saying words out loud you are not receiving Him again, you are just confirming your faith in Christ. It is a simple act. What are you afraid off?"

"I am not afraid of anything. We perceive things differently. For you receiving Jesus means shouting from the hill praises to the Lord. For me, it is a deep and intimate mystical experience. For you living by the Word of God means having leveled and measured life, not smoking, not drinking, and obeying to His Biblical commands as strict as possible. For me, living by the Word of God means trying to find my true path and destiny. Learning who I am, why I am here and what God wants me to do. To find that out, sometimes I have to dig deep into those magical and occult books, which you dismiss so easily."

"The only book you need Michael is the Holy Bible. Everything is written in there. All the answers you are searching for. But you have to read with your heart, not your mind. All those other books will just confuse you and blur your mind."

"I disagree. I can't believe I am hearing this from the Pastor of the church in the twenty-first century. Are you sure you didn't fly in with some time machine from the inquisition age." Michael said ironically.

"No, Michael. I am serious. All those occult books are no good. They have no magical powers or secret knowledge in them. They are work of devil who wants to confuse us. Devil is a liar."

Michael just looked at the Pastor for a while thinking what to say. He knew that there was of no use discussing this subject with Pastor Charles anymore. 'Pastor was so limited in his understandings,' Michael thought.

"What? Why are you not saying anything?" Pastor asked.

"I just don't know what to tell you. I spent many years studying Freemasonry and other esoteric teachings. Wrote several books about it. I had a great collection of very rare and old books on various esoteric subjects. I learned a great deal from them. For a while collecting old and rare occult books was my passion. I was even accepted to be a member of the New York Grolier Club."

"So what happened with your book collection?" Pastor asked.

"A year before I left for Bucharest, I sold my collection to a book collector in Iceland. I felt bad for doing it, but I had to. I needed money. In turn, the buyer donated my collection to the local library under the condition that all the books always stay together cataloged under the name 'Michael Nicolau Library.' The buyer was a man who respected my Masonic scholarship and works in the field of esoteric sciences and he wanted to honor me with his gesture. On another hand, I was pleased that my work would be remembered and preserved somewhere. That was the end of my rare book collecting career. I never went back to the Grolier Club."

"But you still didn't answer my question. What did you mean when you said 'my name was written next to hers in the Book of Life?' Who were you talking about?"

"I was talking about the woman I have to find."

"Who is this woman?" The pastor asked, "It this your Bucharest's girlfriend?"

"I thought it was, but it wasn't."

"What do you mean you thought it was? Explain to me."

"It was the woman from my dreams. The one I belong to. But I don't know where and how to find her."

"What made you think that Bucharest girl was the one?"

"The timing when she appeared in my life. I didn't think it was by accident. But I was wrong. I lost time, money, and energy."

"You never told me what exactly happened in Bucharest?"

"Yeah... Maybe it's better to leave that for our last session."

"If that's what you want Michael... fine with me." The pastor answered with hesitation.

"Pastor, now I have a question for you. What is the meaning of this box with your pictures and diplomas? Are you moving out of this office?"

"I don't know Michael. This morning I had a heated discussion with our Director. Apparently, they are not happy with my performance as a counselor... After twenty years...So suddenly. Could you imagine that? I am thinking of quitting before they fire me. I am so upset."

"Hang on Pastor. Don't do anything stupid. Think about your students. They need you. Director has to play games with the Executive Board. They are the one giving money. If things go bad he has to blame on somebody."

"Ha, you already started counseling me," Pastor said and smiled. "Please, don't share this with others. But there is a lot of pressure lately. Our success rate is not very high. And donors want results. Compared with other programs our numbers are not that great. Some are even talking about dropping Christian aspect of our program altogether. Bible doesn't work with addicts – they say. If they do that, it would be the end of the Bowery Mission as it is now."

The Bucharest Story

26

After graduation, days in the Bowery Mission were passing much faster for Michael. He didn't work anymore in the clothing room and wasn't the Captain on the fifth floor. Wasn't required to attend chapel services either. The only duty he still had was to work one shift a week at the front desk. Although he was freelancing and didn't have a set working schedule, he was going every working day at nine o'clock in the morning out of the Bowery with his laptop and doing his work at Barnes and Noble Café at Union Square or at Starbucks at Astor Place till five in the afternoon.

Freelancing with web design was very competitive considering a large number of young and talented web designers in New York, but Michael was doing better and better every day. Some of his main clients were local churches associated with the Bowery Mission. His savings were growing and he was looking at different options to get his own place.

At the beginning of October, an opportunity presented itself.

One of Michael's web design clients was a real estate company from Brooklyn. Michael worked on their new website for a month and did a very nice job. The owner and the agents in the real estate agency liked his work and his attitude. Michael knew that it was a long shot to ask them for an apartment considering his credit line that was a complete disaster, but he asked anyway.

He would never know if they turned the blind eye on his credit report and his lack of regular income or they didn't bother to check out, but one day they called him and told they have an apartment available for him. More than that, when he went to sign his lease, they asked him only for the first-month rent, dropping out the required deposit on the account of the bonus for the work he did for them. He was supposed to move in on November 1st. Michael was exalted. He would have again his own place. And before Thanksgiving. Just as he desired.

He had none of the furniture, but he was sure that something will come up till the time to move. He spoke with the Director who told him to keep an open eye for all incoming donations of furniture and home appliances.

"Son of a gun, you made it!" Pastor Charles said with the big smile on his face when Michael walked into his office, "Director told me about your apartment. That was a real surprise. So fast. Tell me more. I want to know details."

"Well, not much to say. It is one bedroom on the third floor of a big building in Midwood area of Brooklyn, one block from the Q train station. The rent is nine hundred and includes electricity, water, and heat. I signed a one-year lease and will move in by November 1st, as soon as they repaint the place."

"Nine hundred! Wow, that's a great deal. God has been good to you. Is there any furniture in the apartment?

"The kitchen has the gas stove with oven and a big fridge. There is a large built-in closet in the bedroom. That's about it. Also a laundry room in the basement. I will have to get some basic furniture."

"There must be something in our storage you could use. Also, I will talk with people in my church if somebody has something you may use. For now, you need just a bed with a good mattress, table, and chairs."

"True. Most of the small things I already got from donations. I have linen for bed, two lamps, basic china, silverware, toaster, microwave, radio, and TV. So I am almost set. I will definitely need a bookshelf, but that is always easy to find."

"Great. Great. Now you have to make sure you are always ahead of the game with your bills. Watch every penny. It is so easy to fall behind with rent payments and then you are in trouble."

"Yes, But I got lucky there also. The building is managed by the real estate company whose website I built and will have to update daily. So, we have a kind of ongoing business relationship. I am sure my income from them will help to keep things in order. On another subject - Pastor," Michael said and changed the tone of his voice to more serious, "Last few days I was thinking a lot about your conflict with the Director. Did things calm down? Are you okay now?"

"Don't worry about me and Director, Michael. You have more important things to think about now. Whatever happen here will be because God wants that way. I was praying a lot lately about this issue and now I am in peace. God told me to be calm and everything will work out for good. Let's go back to important stuff. You owe me one more story and I owe you my final evaluation. This is our last official session. So, why and how did you end up in Bucharest?"

"Okay," Michael said while touching his eyebrows, "I don't know how to start this one. It's complicated."

"Ha, I learned that about you already. You are a real artist to make things complicated when it comes to women. Like they are not enough complicated themselves already."

"No, it's not like that. Do you remember a dream I told you?"

"Yes. The one you had five years ago. With Archangel Michael. But you never told me what was the dream about. What did Archangel Michael tell you?

"I am not sure I should tell you."

"Why not?"

"Because you'll think I am crazy."

"Hmm. That is easy to overcome. I'll tell you right away you're crazy and you tell me the dream. You are crazy. This is the third time we are mentioning this dream. Spit it out."

"Not that easy Pastor. But one thing I can tell you. A

part of the message that Archangel gave me was about the woman. Very specific young woman. I had to find her, marry her, have a son with her and protect and care for her forever after."

"Oh, oh. Here we go. I knew you gonna make it complicated. That is why you told me before that you desire to marry and have a family again, right? So how would you find this woman? Who was she and why you had to have a son with her?"

"I told you already Pastor. I can't tell you everything."

"So tell me what you can." The pastor was becoming impatient.

"From the information Archangel gave me, I knew her age and about her looks and character. Archangel told me that this woman and me were together before, and that we will recognize each other?"

"Before? Like in another life – before?"

"Yes. Something like that."

"And? What happened?"

"Just a few months after I had that dream, one of my books was translated and published in Romania by a publishing company from Bucharest and they invited me for a Book Fair in Bucharest to promote my book. I accepted the invitation and that was the first time in over twenty years that I was going back to Romania. My book promotion was a big event with a lot of press attention. There I had an interview with a journalist. A woman. Very interesting woman. After I came back to New York we continued our correspondence. I thought that maybe she was the one I was supposed to find. She was the right age. But I wasn't sure. Then for her birthday she invited me to come. It was more like a tease. She didn't expect I would sit on the plane in New York and go to Bucharest just for her birthday. But I did. She was surprised and impressed. After birthday guests left she asked me to stay. We spent the night together. That is when I decided to move back to Bucharest.

"Ha, ha, truth is coming out. Do you remember when you told me you went to Romania because of business and just then you met a woman? I knew you were lying."

"I wasn't lying!" Michael raised his voice, "I moved to Romania because of business. As independent writer and publisher it wasn't easy making a living in New York anymore. I thought if I keep the same level of income it would be easier to manage life in Bucharest than in New York. Living expenses there was just a fraction of living expenses in New York."

"Okay, okay, continue, please." Pastor said.

"So, I went back to New York and told Natasha I am moving back to Bucharest."

"How she reacted?"

"She was shocked. But I told her it was something I had to do."

"Did you tell her why?"

"Not in as many words… I mentioned business part. But she felt it was more than that. Then I opened up and told her about my dream. She thought it was a middle age crisis. That I was after young chicks."

"Was she hurt?"

"She was. She also worried about her future. She was still not working."

"Did you worry about that? After all, you were together for so many years. You had some responsibilities there, even if you felt nothing for her anymore."

"No. I was just thinking how I'm going to get to Bucharest as soon as possible. I told her bunch of lies. Now when I think about that, I am ashamed. No matter what, she didn't deserve that. I acted like a real self-centered and selfish pig."

"Did you tell your children about your decision?"

"No. I never spoke to them."

"You didn't think that was important? I mean leaving their mother, moving to other country to be with another woman."

"As I said, all I was thinking was getting to Bucharest. And I knew that nobody would ever approve of my actions, so I didn't bother explaining myself to anybody. I packed two suitcases, fit in there what I could, and left for Romania a few days after."

"Just like that?" Pastor asked.

"Just like that."

"No planning, no preparation, not informing anybody? How about your New York business? You had responsibilities and obligations there, didn't you?"

"I left everything unfinished and let things collapsed. I stopped paying all my New York bills including the mortgage for the apartment. In a few months, Natasha had to move out because the bank was going to repossess apartment. Didn't care where she was going to live. I even didn't care about my things I left in our apartment. Many artworks, the large book library with over two thousand books, computers, electronics, furniture, clothing - I left everything and didn't care about any of it."

"All you cared was how to get between the legs of that young woman in Bucharest." The pastor said sarcastically.

"You see. Even you, a Pastor, think about my actions at the lowest possible and vulgar level. Even you can't accept that I had a mission to fulfill. It wasn't about lust and passions. It was calling from God."

"Whoa, whoa, slow down Michael. I am just saying how it appeared. If you believe Archangel or God told you to do these things, you can't expect everybody to approve of it, even if it's so. You said yourself that you acted like a pig with Natasha; let your business collapsed; the bank foreclosed on the apartment. You left everything and everybody. Come on, God would never ask anybody to do something like that."

"Never?" Michael asked.

"Never." The pastor said again.

"How about God telling Abraham '*Take your son, your only son, whom you love—Isaac—and go to the region of Moriah. Sacrifice him there as a burnt offering on a mountain I will show you,*' or when Peter told Jesus '*We have left everything to follow you,*' what Jesus answered, Pastor? The famous verse?"

"*"Truly I tell you," Jesus said to them, "no one who has left home or wife or brothers or sisters or parents or children for the sake of the kingdom of God will fail to receive many times as much in this age, and in the age to come eternal life."* The pastor said the verse.

"So, you see. You know it. Everybody knows this verse. It is acceptable and understandable if it was written in the Bible and if it happened thousands of years ago. But if it is happening to somebody today, it is not possible and it is for condemnation. Okay, so if by some chance, Jesus Christ shows up tomorrow in Vatican, saying he is the son of God, they would probably say he is crazy man believing to be Jesus and they would put him in lockup. Just as they did over two thousand years ago."

"Oh, so now you are comparing yourself to Jesus or Abraham?"

"No, I am just saying…"

"Michael, this discussion won't take us anywhere. Let's go back to your story. You packed up two suitcases and left New York. What happened in Bucharest?" The pastor asked impatiently. he seemed irritated by the direction in which this discussion was going.

"Okay. As soon as I arrived in Bucharest, I rented a furnished apartment in a very nice area of the city and filled papers with the Government Agency to start a company. I rented a space in the shopping mall in the center of Bucharest for a bookstore and office. I made a business plan, hired fifteen people to work in the publishing company and the store, and things were going in the right direction."

"What about this woman you were with? What was her name anyway?"

"Her name was Hanna. She was short, skinny, red hair

and blue eyes. Energetic. Like a lightning. And the excellent journalist."

"So what happened to her? Did you live together? Get married?"

"Well, she moved in my place after two months of dating. But she was against getting married and having kids."

"Why?"

"Her father was my age. Her mother was two years younger. She was telling me she loves me, but she could never go to her father and tell him she wanted to marry me."

"How did you feel about that?"

"I didn't like it, but I hoped that in time, she will get used to the idea. Also, I hoped that she would get pregnant. But it wasn't happening…"

"And?"

"It was like that for a year and a half. Unfortunately, my publishing business wasn't going as expected. I was pumping money into it from a couple investors I had back in New York, but there were no returns. Wasn't working. Whatever I tried, it wasn't giving results. Then, one day I woke up just to realize that I was completely broke. I used all of my backup funds and my investors from New York stopped investing into my venture. Bills were piling up, and the income wasn't enough to cover even basic expenses. I was doing everything I knew about publishing and marketing but with no significant effect. The tension was rising in my and Hanna's relationship and I started drinking too much. Then one day I came home from office and Hanna wasn't there. She moved out. I was devastated. Soon after, I was forced to close down my bookstore and publishing company. Several of my Bucharest friends came to my aid and arranged for me to get a job as a director of the local Library, so I could have some income to live from. That helped. I went back to writing. Also, I started working as an editor for a literary magazine. Things were getting back to normal. But I felt lonely. I was still thinking about Hanna."

"Did you try to get her back?"

"Yes. I tried. She even came two times for a dinner. But she told me she was not coming back. 'I'm not the one you are looking for, Michael. You made mistake.' She said to me."

"Were you thinking about coming back to New York?"

"No. I was thinking about starting publishing business again. Opening a new company. I still believed that it was possible. Then one day I met a new girl. She was waiting tables in the neighborhood pizza restaurant. At first, we were just flirting, as people often flirt with waitresses in the places they often go. But then it became serious. She was nothing like the woman I was looking for. Nothing like Hanna. She was much younger. She was twenty-four, blonde and tall, with big blue eyes. I don't know what was that she had found in me. I was more than twice her age and had little money. But it seemed that she was very committed to our relationship. Faithful and caring. Wasn't asking for much. I enjoyed being with her. My friends made jokes about me and her. They would often say: 'Okay, we could understand if he was a money man, why would a young chick stick to him. But he is an old fart with no money. He must be doing something right to her, ha, ha.' Or sometimes they would say: 'Oh, this is the right time for you to make a baby. Your woman can use the same pampers for a baby and for you, ha, ha.' Didn't mind these jokes. They were boosting my self-confidence, which I have lost after Hanna left. I was also becoming more and more impatient and ambitious in renewing my business. So, I approached some of my Bucharest friends to help me financially in restarting my publishing. Offered them good and fast returns. I had no basis to think that returns would be good and fast, but I wanted to make it happen. And I told them what they wanted to hear so they would help me."

"Hmm, that wasn't very smart." Pastor said.

"No. That wasn't smart. That was really dumb. Giving false hopes to your investors was the worst thing one can do. And again, I was doing everything I knew about business, publishing, marketing, and sales. And I think I was doing everything right. But again, nothing worked. Friends that gave me money were becoming nervous. I kept asking them for more. My girl, Eliza told me, 'Mike, why don't you give up this. You have your salary as the Library director. It is not much but it is enough to live on. You can do your work and have time for writing in peace. No tensions, no panic.'"

"She was giving you a good advice." Pastor said.

"Yes, but it was too late already. I was in debt over my head with no way to return it fast. Soon after, my creditors lost their patience and sold my debts to a very dangerous Bucharest loan shark. He came to my place and gave me forty-eight hours to come up with money or else. At that moment I knew that the line was crossed. That was at the beginning of March this year. In less than twenty-four hours I ran away and came to New York. The rest you know. So, this was my story."

"Michael, Michael…" The pastor said and smiled while trying to figure it out what to say. "I had in all these years many men passing through this chair; with different addictions, different habits and characters, different stories; but none of them were like you. Yes, I had students addicted to pornography, sex, and women. But I can't say that you fit into any of these categories. You're not into pornography. But women and sex are definitely the big part of your problem. The biggest part. I could even say you are addicted to women. However, you are not looking into women just as the objects of sexual desires and passions. Although, when it comes to sex, it seems to me that you are mentally at the level of a teenager. The moment a woman invites you between her legs, all your blood goes from your brain into your penis and you are absolutely incapable of thinking rationally. And there are numerous examples from your life experience to prove that. So, this is a serious problem you need to think about and work on. All I can suggest is to pray. Pray a lot to God Almighty to protect you from your own carnal desires. Furthermore, you are able of falling in love in the blink of an eye. Each time deeply, sincerely, and passionately. In that sense, I can say, you are also addicted to love. A part that is hard for me to understand is your dream and the length you were willing to go to fulfill it. There is something there you are not telling me, so I can't have an opinion about it. But you are in a certain way obsessed with it. Even now, I sense, all you think is how to go on with your dream."

The pastor turned toward computer screen to look at his notes and after a while, he continued: "I am not sure if I believe in your dream or not. Yes, it is possible that your dream is just the result of subconscious efforts to excuse your actions to yourself and to ease on pressure on your mind. So, you convinced yourself that you had a dream. But on another side, you are so persistent with it, that it makes me wonder. What if you really had that dream? What if Archangel Michael really came and spoke to you? Whatever it is, solution for you Michael is one and the same. Turn to our Savior Jesus Christ for guidance. With Him, all things are possible. You told me you have a mission to fulfill. If that is true, with Jesus by your side, you will triumph. So far, to fulfill your dreams, you were going like a bull, with your head through the wall; hurting yourself and others in the process. No need to do that. You were just causing others to be angry, disappointed, or to hate you. You are a good man. You have a lot to give – to God and to people around you. Place your trust in God and be in peace. And the rewards will come."

Pastor moved his chair closer to Michael, leaned forward and continued: "But first and the most important is to strengthen yourself and to stabilize your situation. You are still very stressed and your situation is shaky. As a freelancer, you need at least a six-month backup money. So far, your savings can cover only three more months of rent and living.

That is not enough. So, your priority now is your situation, and your health of course. Forget women for now. And if your dream is meant to be realized, God will find a way to fulfill it for you. Don't forget that you are not a youngster anymore. You can't afford to slip again. It will kill you. Personally, I think that you should reach to your children. They are grown-ups but I am sure they need their father. And you need them. There is much happiness in being a part of your children's life. You forgot how to love your children Michael. If you learn that again, it will only do good to you."

"And last," Pastor said while raising his voice, "You rented apartment already, so it is kind of late to say this, but you rushed into it. Yes, it was a good deal. I think that you should have stayed here as long as possible; saving more money and calming your spirit. But it was done, so we will go from here and see what will happen. Don't forget that my office is always open for you. Whenever you need to talk, I'm here. Also, everybody in my church likes you, Michael. You should continue coming regularly. Don't lose touch with people and think about joining our congregation. Of course, if you want."

This was the last counseling session Michael had with Pastor Charles. When Michael left Pastor Charles office, Pastor stayed for a while sitting and staring into Michael's files on the computer screen. He started praying.

Faith and the Action

27

On Wednesday, October 31st, it was seven and a half months since Michael entered the Bowery Mission. On that day, in the early afternoon, Michael was moving to his apartment in the Midwood section of Brooklyn. Pastor Charles arranged for his church van and a driver to help Michael move. A parishioner from the church donated a large sofa bed, a desk, and four chairs. Bowery Mission gave him an old TV and DVD player. With everything else Michael collected over time from donations to Bowery Mission, he obtained all basic furniture and appliances for his apartment.

When he came to Bowery Mission, back in March, Michael had just his backpack, old cellular phone from Romania, and almost no clothing. Now, upon moving out from the Bowery Mission, besides all stuff for the apartment, he had twelve large black plastic bags full of new clothing and shoes, a laptop computer, two cell phones, over hundred books, and three watches. He didn't have to think about buying any clothing or shoes for at least two to three years. Also, the Bowery Mission kitchen supervisor provided for Michael three big boxes of dry and canned goods for his pantry.

Michael wasn't the only student leaving the Mission like that. Bowery Mission was providing for their graduating students abundantly. Not only during the stay in the Bowery, but also after they leave. While working in the clothing store, Michael met many former students who came to get a new suit, or leather jacket, or shoes for free. They were also coming regularly to the Bowery kitchen to get free pantry supplies. The idea behind all of these was to enable graduating students to incorporate into outside independent living as painless as possible, by providing to their needs and help them save on expenses on clothing and food. It was very generous idea and thanks to large donations that Bowery was getting, it was possible to maintain.

And the most important, Bowery Mission doors were always open for the graduates to come back and talk to their counselors or to the Mission Pastor. In the case of a relapse, graduates could return to a program only after six months.

However, things were not perfect with this Bowery Mission strategy. Many students were misusing Bowery Mission generosity by excessively piling up clothing. Many of them, before entering the program, never had more than one pair of shoes or jeans. During the program, they would suddenly end up with twenty or thirty pairs of shoes and as many pants. Sometimes, counselors were shaking their heads while looking at the students moving out. The Director would threaten that he would introduce some type of control into it, but everything would end up with that. Michael had this theory that, actually, they all liked to see students going out with a lot of stuff. During Bible classes, counselors were often mentioning to students a parable of the prodigy son coming back to his father, where the father told to his servants: '*Bring forth the best robe, and put it on him; and put a ring on his hand, and shoes on his feet: And bring hither the fatted calf, and kill it; and let us eat, and be merry.*' For counselors, everything that students were getting into Bowery Mission was God's reward to them for coming back to Him. It was a cause to rejoice and celebrate, and not to complain.

Also, many former students were coming back to volunteer in the Mission during Holiday months or from time to time for many years after. Some of them were often bringing donations in clothing and food. For Michael, it was a nice thing to see, a former student bringing donations. Giving back was as important as receiving. He knew that and he often thought about the day when he could come back and bring a donation to the Bowery Mission.

It took Michael about one hour to say goodbye to everybody he wanted to greet on his departure. From Pastor Charles, the Director, Pastor Paul, to all other counselors and managers, nurse on staff, students that Michael got to know over the months, and quite a few of homeless men hanging around Bowery Mission, who liked Michael for his generosity and easy going attitude whenever they needed something. Pastor Charles walked out on the street to speak to the driver of his church van. When he saw van packed to the top, with almost no room for people to sit, he said to Michael:

"Michael! Oh, My God, it was very profitable for you to work in the Blessing-dale, ha, ha! God was good to you. You better rush. I don't want Director to come out and see this. He keeps complaining about students being excessive. You have over here enough clothing for an army, ha, ha."

Several students helped Michael load church van with his belongings. Two of them got permission from their counselors to go with Michael to his apartment and help him unload. Jeremiah wasn't there to help him. He was out working already. But he promised to come to visit on the weekend. He decided to stay in the Bowery till after Christmas, and then to move in with his maternal grandmother who lived alone in the Bronx and needed help around the house.

The apartment still smelled of fresh paint when Michael entered. It was nice off white ivory color. Kitchen and bathroom had ceramic tiles and the rest of the apartment had refurbished hardwood floors. The terrace in the living room was looking at the street. The apartment was on the East side of the building. Michael liked that. He liked to waken up by the warmth and light of the morning sun.

The sofa fitted perfectly on the longer wall of the living room. Michael decided to keep it there. Table and four chairs he placed right under the terrace window. He told students that were helping him unload, to put all bags in the middle of the bedroom. The bedroom had a large built-in closet and that's where Michael wanted to put most of his clothing.

After they unloaded his stuff, Michael gave ten bucks to each of the students, thanked the driver for his help and asked him to drop off students in front of the Bowery Mission on his way back to the Bronx. They left. Michael closed the apartment doors and turned. He lighted up a cigarette. For a while, he was standing like that, smoking and looking around. He was in his own place. Again.

What next? His head was full of different thoughts. He was thinking about his last days in Bucharest, about Eliza, his escape to New York, his days on the subway, and refuge in the Bowery Mission. Everything was still so fresh in his mind like it happened yesterday.

'After all, seven and a half months wasn't that long to recuperate,' he was thinking. 'Now he has his own place with a proper lease, about three thousand dollars in savings, and two web design projects still in work. Quite different from the first day he landed on JFK in March.'

"I could even buy a ticket for Eliza to come and be with me,' he thought. But he knew it was too late. She broke up with him after not hearing from him for a while, and had a new boyfriend already. After he got his phone back and the laptop from Director, he sent her a number of e-mails and messages, but she never responded. He knew it was over. It was time to go on with his life.

The most important thing was that he was writing again. He felt that there was so much he needed to say. Before, he was always struggling to find the right words whenever he was writing something. But now, words were spilling out of his mind like a waterfall. It was hard to control and record everything. But he knew that it was a part of his mission, anyway. Archangel told him in his dream that is very important for Michael to keep writing his thoughts. Through them, he will find a way to Her, the woman he was looking for, he was told. With them, he will inspire many people. By them, he will reach fame and the immortality.

Next few days Michael spent getting utility services and internet in order. His credit was so bad he couldn't get phone service, cable, and the internet on his name. Members of the Pastor Charles' church came to his aid again. The same woman that gave him sofa bed, table, and four chairs, got the phone, cable, and internet service on her name. Michael promised her to pay bills always on time, so she doesn't get in trouble. That was a great favor she did for a man she barely knew. "It takes a lot of fate to do something like that," Michael told her. He was really thankful. Internet was very important for his work. This woman's comment was only: *"You have faith and I have deeds. Show me your faith without deeds, and I will show you my faith by my deeds..."*

Michael knew this quote from James 2:18. It was saying that faith in itself without good deeds had no meaning and not a reason for existence. That was something Michael was struggling with for many years. He knew that was the problem of many people around the world. They were presenting themselves as religious and faithful, believing in God and subscribing to main religious tenets, whatever religion they may be. But in reality, they all lived profane, wicked, and selfish lives, justifying everything around them by the universal tolerance, freedom and equality, and liberty of conscience. 'How far we can go with our liberty of conscience, without offending God, and disturbing the natural order of things,' Michael was often asking himself.

Michael was admiring the Director and staff of the Bowery Mission for their dedication to helping addicts and homeless people of New York. Bowery Mission was the place of true faith. The front line of the fight against the evil within ourselves and around us. The place where faith and good deeds go hand in hand. The place where the only acceptable expression of faith is in the work for the benefit of the fellow men.

'Those counselors must have been testing their faith every single day they go to work. Yet, they stay steadfast in their dedication to helping those fallen in the abyss of addictions, and those stuck in the constant poverty and homelessness. If I didn't have my own calling from the Lord, I would definitely stay as a mission trainee and work with them,' Michael thought, 'The noblest work one can do.'

Those words from the Bible about faith and action for Michael had yet another meaning. For him, they were a justification of all of his actions in last several years, since he had that dream. In his mind, God was calling him to action. At the same time, God was testing Michael's faith. To achieve his goal and to fulfill his mission no price was too big. Michael knew that if he told this to Pastor Charles, his comment would probably be 'Oh, you are only trying to excuse your errors, to make easy on your conscience.' But everything wasn't that simple. Yes, maybe he felt bad about many things he had done. But he believed that everything that happened had to happen. He was sure that everything has its purpose as a part of a much bigger plan. He just couldn't see the whole picture yet. But he had to keep going.

In doing his web design work, Michael got associated with several Evangelical and Pentecostal Churches throughout New York City. By writing content for websites, he became a real expert for their teachings. He didn't agree with everything they subscribed to, but he knew how to write it to sound compelling. He was a good wordsmith although English was his second language. This quality of Michael's was noticed by Pastors of the Churches who asked him to write for them newsletter articles, blog posts, even sermons. He almost never charged them for this work. In return, Pastors were spreading the good word about his web design work and helping him get more clients.

As he desired, for Thanksgiving, Michael was in his place. During the day, he went to the Bowery Mission to help them serve lunch to the homeless. He cooked a nice Thanksgiving dinner at home and invited Jeremiah, Rick, and a woman from Pastor Charles' church who gave him furniture. Her name was Grace. She was a black American woman of Haitian descent in the late fifties.

They all came. Jeremiah was talking about his work, Rick was criticizing his wife and praising his daughter's achievements in school, Grace was complimenting Michael's cooking, and Michael ran between kitchen and living room, bringing more and more food and talking about the ways he prepared dishes. He wasn't in the culinary business for many years already, but he still enjoyed cooking good food and hosting people. When they left, Michael stayed up till late washing dishes, listening over and over again to Lucio Dalla singing Caruso, and drinking white wine. 'Last time I drank wine, was the day I came back to New York,' Michael thought.

Next several months Michael spent preoccupied with writing and with his web design work. He was writing a novel about the man obsessed with occult books. That subject was close to Michael. He himself was a collector of rare and occult books for a long time.

Web design work had a steady flow and his income and savings were growing. As soon as he would finish one project, another one would show up. His designs were original, clean, and fast. Besides that, he was always providing a full content writing service at no extra charge. His clients were happy. Michael kept reminding his customers to keep spreading the word about his work. He knew that was the key and best way of advertising.

In December Natasha called him to tell him she has his mail from the IRS that came to her address. It was forwarded from their old address in Brooklyn. She now lived in Queens and worked in the office of an insurance company. Michael knew nothing about how she survived after the bank foreclosed on their apartment and she had to move out, but it was obvious that she went on with her life and lived independently. Michael was happy for it. 'It is ironic,' he thought, 'that in order for Natasha to discover her own strength and abilities, he had to leave her hanging over an abyss. When they were together, she was always leaning on him for everything.'

They met for a coffee in Starbucks on Fourteen Street. She gave him his mail and told him she has some of his books and artwork from the old apartment if he was interested in having it back. He agreed and two days later Grace drove him to Queens to pick up his stuff. As he expected, Natasha didn't let him come into her apartment. She brought boxes outside of the building. Michael was happy to have his belongings back. While he was loading boxes in the trunk of the car, Natasha was looking at the Grace sitting in the driver's seat.

"Is this your new girlfriend?" She asked ironically, "She is a bit old for your taste, isn't she?

"No, Natasha, "Michael answered, "that is just my friend from the church I go to."

When they left, Grace turned to Michael while driving and said: "Your wife must be still very hurt with your breakup."

"She is not my wife. She is my former wife." Michael said.

"Oh, I am sorry." Grace said with a smile, "And she thinks that I am your girlfriend, doesn't she?"

"I guess so."

"How would you feel about me being your girlfriend, anyway? Would you like that?"

Michael looked at Grace. He knew that she liked him. Since they met in the Pastor Charles' church, she kept calling him in the evenings just to chat with him. She was always there to help him with anything he needed. The only social life that Michael had since he left Bowery were occasional coffees with Grace at Barnes and Noble Café. But she was older than him. And he didn't need another relationship right now. He liked her company, admired her faith, and appreciated her help and support, but he wasn't attracted to her.

"I am not sure if it would be a good idea for me right now to enter a new relationship."

"Why?" Grace asked.

"Sometimes I feel like I have a mission to fulfill and shouldn't commit to another person. That wouldn't be fair."

Grace said nothing else. She kept driving.

But now, Michael started thinking about Grace. 'She was good looking for her age. Well-kept and well preserved, it seems.' Michael thought. 'It would be a nice thing to bang her. I never before had a sex with a black woman. That would be an interesting experience.' On such thoughts, his penis went into erection. He didn't have a sex with anybody since he left Bucharest.

When they arrived in Brooklyn, Grace helped him with the boxes up to the apartment. They sat on the sofa to rest from carrying heavy boxes with books. They kept talking about the relationship. It was obvious that she was attracted to him. Michael was trying to be diplomatic. On one side, he didn't want to hurt this good woman. On another side, he was aroused and all he wanted right now was to indulge in her body. He hoped that she would find a reason to get up and leave, but she kept talking. Talking was the last thing on Michael's mind. It was getting dark in the room, but none of two of them got up to turn the lights on. Then, at one moment they kissed. By now, Michael wanted only one thing, and he knew how to get it. His kiss was long, passionate, and breathtaking. 'It always works.' Michael thought. His hands were going all over Grace's body. He placed his hand between her legs. Her breathing was heavy. She was very excited, "No, Michael, no," she said, "we shouldn't. God will punish us for this." Grace said and tried to move his hand.

"No, Grace, God doesn't punish those who are in love," Michael said and pulled down her panties. When he pushed his penis into her wet and warm pussy she just said, "Oh, Micky…" When they were done, she just smiled and asked him, "Do you want to do it again?" They did it again. And again. Then she dressed up, kissed him, and left.

Michael stayed sitting in the dark on the sofa and thinking. The pastor was right. He was addicted to women. He would say anything and do anything just to get to what he wanted. Grace was good and faithful church going woman, with sincere and honest feelings for him, and he used her passions just to get to her body. He lied to her. He felt bad. He was disappointed with himself. How was he going to fulfill his mission if he would jump every woman that comes his way and show any interest in him? And what would he do now with Grace? She would come back and expect more. She would want a serious relationship with serious objectives. All he could give her were lies.

And Grace kept coming back. She was always there for Michael whenever he needed anything. At first, Michael felt bad for letting her believe that there was future for them. But then, he convinced himself that God placed Grace in his life with a purpose. 'She would not be here if it wasn't meant to be this way. God is not stupid. He knows what he is doing.' Michael would often think.

Almost the whole year passed. It was October. On the outside, it seemed that everything was going in the right direction for Michael. His income was growing; his workflow was consistent; he was paying his bills on time; he was volunteering at the Bowery Mission once in a while; his writing was going well - he almost finished his book; he was a member of the Pastor Charles' Church and he was there every Sunday; he had next to him a good woman who cared about all his needs. But, Michael felt alone and often very depressed. Often, he was thinking about his dream and his need to fulfill the mission. He didn't know where to start. Where to look? How to find the woman from his dreams?

Maria

28

One day, while he was online, browsing through Goodreads book social network looking for interesting stuff, he came across the page of a young woman. Her name was Maria. She was Portuguese. The first thing he noticed was the list of books she posted as her favorite. Same books, and exactly in the same order, were his favorite. 'What a coincidence,' he thought. He was curious, so he sent her a friendship request. Maria accepted it. They exchanged several messages about books and writing. She wrote poetry. After only two weeks of online communi-cation, he felt some inexplicable closeness with this woman who was at that moment a complete stranger. He didn't know what drew him to her, but he kept communicating.

With every passing day, their conversations were becoming more and more personal. As they were talking online, they realized that both of them had similar issues with their everyday realities. They both felt like they didn't belong to this world like they were misplaced. They both dreamed of a different life that was more fulfilling than the one they lived. Maria told him about her dream. Yes, she had one too. He didn't know details of her dream, but he thought that maybe this woman was the one he was supposed to find. She was the right age. She was thirty-three. More he was thinking about Maria he was more convinced.

Two months of online communication passed quick. Maria and Michael were spending hours every day till late in the night, sometimes till five in the morning chatting online. At first, they were using gmail chat but then they switched to Skype video call. It was completely crazy. One day, they spent sixteen hours online without a brake. It seemed like they were mesmerized with each other. Like nothing else in the world exist except two of them and their conversations. And it seemed like they have so much to talk about.

Grace noticed a big change in Michael. For Christmas, she came to have a dinner with him. She brought him a nice present and was expecting to spend a pleasant night with Michael. But Maria called during dinner and the rest of the evening Michael spent in front of the computer talking to her. Grace couldn't hear their conversation because Michael took the laptop to the bedroom and closed the door behind him, but she knew that something was going on. More than anything, she was hurt. It was a special occasion, a Christmas Dinner, and he decided to share that time with another woman.

So, only after two months, Maria and Michael, two people who never met in person, fell in love with each other. It was strange and unbelievable long distance virtual relationship. If this was happening to teenage kids, one could understand. Maybe? But they were not kids. They were grown-ups who knew about each other only their online profiles. Nevertheless, they felt like they had known each other forever; like they were meant to be together. There was only one small problem. He was in New York and she was in Portugal.

More and more every day, Maria was expressing her longing for Michael's presence and her desire for a physical contact. Often she would send selfies of her naked body and start erotic conversations. They were driving Michael crazy, but he enjoyed them too. He never in his life had such experience. Sometimes, he would ask himself if all of that was real or just a virtual game of the young woman with an old and crazy man.

Michael was completely smitten with Maria's appearance. She was exactly like the woman from his dream. With light brown curly hair, gray eyes, and pale face, she was small, not more than 160cm tall, but with the proportional body and sexy curves.

"You are beautiful, Maria!" He would often say.

"No, I am not. I am simple. Just average. And you are blind and in love."

"No, I am not. I know well what I am talking about. I am objective. You are beautiful!" He would repeat.

Maria would just smile and say again: "No, I am not."

The same conversation would take place several times a day, every day. They would never get tired of it.

Maria was a teacher of English in the Middle school in

Portimao, a town in the district of Faro, in the Algarve region of southern Portugal. For last ten years, since graduating from the University of Lisbon, she was working for the Portuguese Department of Education as English teacher with annual contracts. Almost every year in different school and different place anywhere in Portugal. For some people that would be a burden, but Maria liked moving every year from town to town, from village to village, always meeting new people and making new friends. She enjoyed her solitary life and didn't like long-term commitments. So this style of living was just what she wanted.

Like Michael, she lived in her world of dreams. Maria was reading a lot, writing poetry, daydreaming, taking long walks, talking to animals and plants, and it that world there wasn't much space for anybody else. She was telling Michael that all her life she was dreaming of the man she could never find, and he only existed in her dreams. And she never believed that she would find this man in the real life. So she stayed with him forever in her dreams and never committed to any relationship with another man in the real life. Then Michael showed up, and she thought that maybe he was the man she was dreaming about. She wasn't sure yet, but she never felt about any man the same way.

It was almost unbelievable how her story was so strikingly similar to his story. 'What was the chance that this was only the coincidence?' Michael thought. He didn't believe in coincidences. He believed that he was the man she was longing for and that she was the woman he was supposed to find.

Maria was writing poetry in Portuguese and once in a while she would translate her poems, so Michael could read them. Michael loved to read her poetry. Of course, he was in love, and everybody would say he wasn't objective, but he thought he never read something so striking like her poetry.

"Maria, you don't realize how good these poems are. You should publish them and have the whole world enjoy in them. These are the words of an angel. You are not a poet. You are an angel."

"Oh, Michael. You don't know what are you saying. You are not objective. These are just scribbles I do for myself and now for you. Sometimes I share with one or two friends online and that's it. I don't want to share this with anybody. Do you know that my parents still don't know that I am writing poetry and I started when I was sixteen?"

"Why they don't know? Why don't you tell them?"

"They wouldn't understand. They are serious people. For them writing a poetry is a silly thing people do. I don't want them to think that I am silly. They already think I am strange because with thirty-three I am still not married. Whenever I go back home for a summer break, they bring local guys to introduce me to. Like having a husband is the only thing I am looking for, ha. And I have to go through this summer after summer. So, imagine if, on the top of that, they find out I am writing a poetry."

"So what if they find out? They should be happy. I think you should translate your best poems in English and I would publish them for you as a bilingual edition here in New York. I could do the cover and formatting of the book."

"Michael, you are crazy!"

"No, I am serious. I think that is something we should work on right away. And don't say no, because I will not accept no as an answer."

Maria was actually impressed with idea that Michael wanted to publish her poetry. She never before published any of her writings. Few of her friends, who read some of it, told her already before that she should consider publishing, but she was always too shy to offer her work to any magazine or publisher. And now Michael showed up with his crazy idea. So, after couple of days of nagging, she accepted Michael's offer, and they started working on her book of poetry.

The plan was that in three months, by Michael's birthday in March, they would already have enough translated poems to put the book together. Michael was thrilled that they are working on this project together. He thought that a published book could be a great opportunity for him to go to Portugal and bring copies to Maria.

"When the book is done, I will sit on the plane, and bring you author's copies."

"Are you serious Michael? You would come all away to Portugal?"

"Yes! I will come! I already decided."

"That is in three months, Michael. It will pass fast."

"I know."

"And where will you stay? You can't stay at my place. I live near the school and I don't think that woman I rent a room from would approve of me having guests. Especially not male. That would be embarrassing?"

"There must be a hotel in Portimao."

"Of course. But Portimao is a small place. Maybe it would be better if you stay in Faro. It's bigger and there are more things to see there."

"I am not coming to see things, Maria. I want to come to be with you."

"I know. But I have to work, Michael. I can't just take time off. Doesn't work like that. I could be with you on the weekend and maybe take Monday off if I ask a colleague to do classes for me. How long you would stay, anyway?"

"Forever."

"Michael, be serious. How many days would you stay?"

"I don't know. Everything depends on… Maybe a week or ten days."

"So if you come for a whole week we could have two weekends together. One could be a long weekend if I take Monday off and the second weekend just from Friday afternoon till Sunday. Would that work for you?"

"Yes. That would be great. I will research Faro online to see where I could stay."

It was the last week in December when Michael and Maria started counting down days until their first meeting in March. The prospect of meeting each other in person made erotic insinuations in their conversations even more intensive. What were they going to do to each other when they meet was the main subject.

The time difference between New York and Portugal was five hours. They would get online together as soon as Maria would return from work, around six o'clock in the afternoon which was around one pm in New York. Then they would stay together till late night on Skype, sometimes till five in the morning Portuguese time. Maria and Michael didn't want to leave each other. They were eating in front of computer screens at the same time; They were doing other work on the computer while their Skype was still on. They didn't want to quit. Sometimes, when it would get very late, Michael would ask Maria to get offline and go to sleep because she had to be at work at eight in the morning. He worried that she would be too tired next day. But she would always refuse, claiming that all she wanted was to be with him.

At the beginning of January, it was just a week in Michael's and Maria's countdown.

"Seventy more days Michael!"

"Did you count the day of my arrival?

"No."

"Then it is sixty-nine." Michael corrected her.

"Oh Michael, this goes so slow…"

"Yes." Michael answered, "I agree. On the second thought why we have to wait until March. I can come earlier?"

"But you said March because you wanted to bring my finished books."

"Yes, I can still come in March. But how if I come earlier just to see you?"

"Michael! Don't joke with me. You want me to have a heart attack?"

"No Maria. I am serious. I was thinking about that this morning. Nothing is holding me from coming to you earlier. If I stay like this, in front of the computer, looking at you for next sixty- nine days, I will go crazy. If I want, I could come tomorrow. All my work is online. Doing it from Faro or from here doesn't make a difference as long as I have the internet. So what do you say?" Michael asked.

"Michael, tell me you are not joking, please."

"No Maria, I am serious. What do you think?"

"If you can do, that would be great. But wouldn't be too expensive to come before March and in a March again? When would you come?"

"I don't know. I would have to look for a good flight. But it is already out of season so tickets must be cheap. I will check and let you know."

"Oh, Michael, that would be great. I can't believe that we will be together. I dream every night about you being next to me…our bodies touching…I can't wait."

Michael had found an available plane ticket for next Wednesday, which was in two days. He would be in Lisbon on Thursday morning, take the train to Faro and be there in the early afternoon. Maria said that she would come to Faro on Friday evening, right after her work, and stay with Michael till Monday. They were both very excited about their plans.

Michael researched on Faro. He was surprised to learn that the cost of living in Portugal is much lower than in New York. According to his calculations, for fifty percent of the smallest monthly income in the US, one could live quite decent in Portugal. Also, hotel prices were much lower. Michael discovered that the oldest still operating hotel in Faro was called Santa Maria. And the room in the hotel for one night was only thirty-nine dollars. 'It would be good and proper to stay there with Maria,' Michael thought. He went on the hotel website and booked a room for two for a week.

When Maria finally got offline and went to sleep, Michael stayed in front of the computer still for some time thinking about what he just did. It was a bold and crazy move to decide to go to Portugal so fast. Of course, Michael wouldn't be Michael if he wouldn't come up with bold and crazy ideas. He decided to travel to Portugal to be close to the woman he loved. This happened in less than three months after they had started communicating. But for Michael, that was normal behavior. Doing things fast, without much preparation, was the story of his life. Somehow, he was sure that Maria was the one he was supposed to find. For him, it was the explanation of all the restlessness and unhappiness he felt with anything and anybody throughout his life. He felt that destiny brought him to the point where he should be united with this woman. And everything she was telling him was fitting so perfectly in his line of thought. 'What were the odds that both of them feeling the same if it was not true?' Michael thought, 'It must be true.'

But then, Michael had another problem. What would he tell Grace?

"I am traveling tomorrow to Portugal," Michael said.

"What? I mean why?" Grace almost spilled her coffee when Michael told her this while having a coffee with her at Barnes and Noble Café.

"I am publishing a book for a Portuguese author. So I will meet this writer."

"Does this has to do anything with the woman you are talking online every day? Is she that writer?"

"Yes, she is."

"Michael, what do you have with this woman? Every day, whenever I come to your place you are online talking to her. Do you guys ever rest? Are you in love with her?"

"Grace, don't ask me things like that. I told you when we met that I feel I have a mission to fulfill and that I will never give up my dream. This trip is my mission. I don't know where I'm going, but I have to go. It is God's will, not mine. It's stronger than me."

"Don't put this on God Michael. You know better than that. This is your lust that's controlling you. She must be young, isn't she?"

"I don't want to talk about that. I have to go and I'm leaving tomorrow."

Grace said nothing for a while. She looked at the cup of coffee in front of her at the table. Then she asked:
"So how long are you going to be in Portugal?"

"For a week. I'll be back on Monday evening."

"Where are you going?"

"To Faro, in the south of Portugal. First I will fly to Lisbon and then take a train from there."

"What about your apartment?"

"I was thinking of asking Jeremiah of staying there for a week. But you can also check on it when you can."

"You were thinking? You are flying tomorrow and you didn't ask him yet. When are you going to ask him? From the airport?"

"C'mon. You know that I do everything in the last minute. I'll talk to him tonight. He is at work now."

"Do you need any money? Do you have enough for your trip? That must be expensive."

Michael didn't answer this question. He looked at Grace. He never met anybody like her. She knew that he was going to be with another woman, and yet she was still offering her help and support. She really loved him. He felt bad for her. But again, he thought she must be with him for a reason. A part of a bigger plan. God put her next to him to help him in his mission. The irony of the situation was that by helping him, she will lose him. Nevertheless, Michael thought he never belonged to her, or for that matter, to any other woman before. The only woman he belonged to and that he will ever belong was the one he was going to meet in Faro. Maria was his destiny. She was the Queen of his soul.

"So, do you need any money? It must be expensive going after a young girl in the foreign country?" Grace said ironically and with much bitterness in her voice.

January in Faro

29

Dressed in skinny Levi's jeans and slim fit Massimo Dutti white cotton shirt, Michael would look much younger than fifty-four if not for his short cut gray beard, mustache, and hair. He lost lots of hair in his early age and what was left, he kept short. For his age, his face was smooth with few wrinkles that would intensify only when he was tired. After his stay in the Bowery Mission, he was very agile and kept in shape with long walks. Almost two years passed since he left Bowery, and Michael was in a great physical shape. Nothing on him would ever suggest that less than two years ago he was exhausted, worn-out, and a troubled homeless man looking for a refuge in the Bowery Mission. With deep, dark brown eyes and a self-confident, mystic smile, he was a real charmer.

"Mister Nicolau, mister Nicolau—"

Michael opened his eyes. There was a stewardess touching gently his shoulder and saying, "Mister Nicolau, we are about to land in Lisbon. Please, fasten your seatbelt and put your seat in the upright position."

Michael looked at his watch. The plane was arriving in Lisbon earlier than he had expected. He hoped that Carlos was already waiting for him there.

Michael knew Carlos for many years. They were both members of the Brotherhood of Freemasons, both antique book collectors and shared common interests in various esoteric teachings. Carlos respected Michael for his knowledge in esoteric sciences, and was one of the few friends who never judged any of Michael's mischiefs. But, there was a big difference between these two men. Contrary to Michael, who completed none of the goals in his life, Carlos was a well-established medical doctor, a professor at a university, and a writer.

"Olá Michael! Welcome to Portugal," Carlos said and hugged his friend when Michael walked out of customs control at the airport.

Like Michael, Carlos was in his fifties. He was a medium height, slightly overweight, strong black hair with almost no gray, big blue eyes, tan skin, clean shaved, and with almost perfect facial lines. Carlos was a handsome man. He always dressed in fitted designer suits, with his routine straight posture, giving off the impression of an authoritative, wealthy man.

"Hi, Carlos. I'm happy to see you. At last, I got to Lisbon. We have been talking for years that I should come and visit."

"Yes, but I know that you would not come if you were not going to Faro. Anyway, good to see you even for one hour. I was wondering what happened to you after you broke your affiliation with the Grand Lodge of Freemasons back in New York. You never called, never wrote. I heard many bad things, but I never paid attention to those rumors."

"Oh well," Michael said, "People like to talk about others when they have nothing smart to say about themselves."

Carlos drove Michael to the Lisbon Oriente train station. There was still about two hours before the train to Faro, so they sat in the café and spoke about the times they spent together searching for rare medieval manuscripts or how they discussed arcane books in the Grolier Club. Carlos knew about the conflicts that Michael had with several Freemasons in New York. He also knew about the bad investments that Michael made in publishing and the debt he had accumulated over the years, thanks to his failing publishing endeavors, but he mentioned none of it.

Finally, he asked, "So, Michael, what brings you to Portugal? You mention this book by a Portuguese author that you want to publish, but that doesn't seem too convincing to me. What are you up to, my old friend?"

"It is about the book. But you are right, that is not the main reason. It is also about the author. I want to meet her in person. We met online a few months ago and communicated. She is a very interesting person. Not only does she have an exquisite mind, but she is also good looking. I don't know why and how it happened, but we became attracted to each other. Everything happened so fast over distance, online. I know it sounds crazy and childish, but I need to see her in person, to spend time with her, and to figure it out."

Michael didn't want to tell Carlos about his dream and his mission. He didn't want to tell him he was for years a captive of his own dreams; chasing after something he couldn't know if he would ever find or if it even exists at all. That 'something' made him leave his family and friends, destroy his marriage and his business, and it almost cost him his life. It was an obsession he couldn't control. Sometimes, he would have the urge to get up and search for it. He didn't know where to search, but for the last couple months, a strange voice was echoing in his brain, telling him over and over again, "Go to Portugal. She is the one." So here he was.

On the other side, Carlos and everybody who ever met Michael knew that he was an incurable dreamer. He always aimed for goals and ideals hard to be realized in the material world. Somehow, he always managed to make his dreams a reality. But almost always, once he reached his goal, he lost interest in it and would turn to something else. So, people admired him for his ability to achieve almost anything he put his mind to, but they also perceived him to be an unstable person that doesn't always know what he wants.

"Yes, I suspected it was something like that," Carlos said. "It is so typical of you. I've known you for years and there is only one thing constant in your life. You keep chasing dreams. And I admire you for your persistence, but as your friend, I have to give you a word of caution - for a dream to come true, first you have to wake up and then stay awake. And I give you credit for your ability to turn your dreams into reality, but somehow, you never learned how to maintain them that way—how to stay awake with both feet on the ground. I hope you know what you are doing. You are not a kid anymore. You know that, don't you?"

"Yeah, I know what you mean. My life portfolio is not so commendable. I messed up so many things over the years, but I am on the right track this time. You don't have to be concerned."

Before boarding, the train Michael thanked Carlos for driving him to a train station. Carlos said: "Not to worry Michael. This is the least I could do. Good luck to you and be careful. If you need anything, you have my number." Michael smiled. It was good to know that he still had a friend he could count on.

The train pulled into Faro train station and stopped. Michael walked out looking for the station exit. 'There must be a taxi out there,' he thought. It was early January, but an unusually warm Thursday evening. The weather was in contrast to cold, windy New York which was covered with snow when he left the night before.

The station was full of tourists from England and Germany. Faro, with its mild Mediterranean weather and beautiful beaches, sitting on the southern coast of Portugal is a popular destination for tourists from northern parts of Europe.

"To Hotel Santa Maria," Michael said to cab driver as he got into the taxi.

The hotel was just a few minutes' drive from the train station. It was one of the oldest hotels in Faro, located in the center of town. Michael chose that hotel because of the name. He thought of it to be symbolic. He was going to be in that hotel with a woman he loved whose name was Maria. It was also the ancient name of Faro. Until the ninth century, when Moors conquered that part of Portugal, Faro was known as Santa Maria.

"I booked a room for two," Michael said to the receptionist at the hotel.

"Do you want a room with two single beds or one double bed," the receptionist asked.

"One double bed, please."

The young woman at the reception desk said, "Here it is. Let me print the invoice and get you the keys. And the second person is arriving...?"

"Oh, my friend is arriving tomorrow night," Michael said.

Michael woke up tired on Friday morning in the hotel room. He dreamt about Maria again. She was lying next to him, touching his ears with her fingers, holding his medallion in her hand, pulling his arm to make a comfortable resting place for her head. She placed her leg over his and then she disappeared. It was a beautiful dream. Again.

The phone rang. He picked it up.

"Mr. Nicolau, there is long distance call for you," the voice on the other side said.

"Okay. Put me through," he answered, wondering who was calling.

"Hi, sweetie, how was your flight? Did you find her?" It was the ironic voice of Natasha, Michael's ex-wife.

"What do you want?" he answered. "It's two o'clock in the morning in New York. Are you drunk again?"

"No. As a matter of fact, I was drunk for sixteen years living next to a man who never really loved me, but now I am completely sober. So, did you find her?"

"Listen, I am on a business trip and I don't have time for this nonsense. I suspect you must have told Jeremiah that you have some type of emergency, so he gave you my hotel number, but this trip is not a joke. I am busy," Michael said.

"Come on, sweetie. You know I know you. We've been divorced for five years, but you are still the same. I called your home this morning and your friend told me you are on a business trip to Portugal. You are hardly surviving with your web design and publishing and now you suddenly have money to travel to Portugal. So, what kind of business could you have there? It is about her. Isn't it? It's about your obsession."

"Listen, I'm going to hang up now," Michael was getting really nervous listening to her badgering.

"Oh, go ahead. That is what you always do. It is so you. Wouldn't surprise me. Just make sure you don't hang up on her one day when you find her. She must be human after all. And nobody likes to be hung up on. So, be careful."

"Just tell me what you want," Michael demanded.

"Nothing. Just wondering when you will stop this madness. I don't care about you. I'm only thinking about our kids. You don't call them anyway, but they don't need that embarrassment once everybody realizes how crazy you are. When are you going to get back to reality? Instead of spending money on plane tickets, you could get a good psychiatrist. Why can't you, like all crazy people, go to the psychiatrist and share your nightmares and then act like a normal person. Is that so hard?"

"Listen, please try to understand. I had a long flight, and I am tired. I have an important meeting today. Can't you forget me for a day? What's your problem? Did your boyfriend ditch you and you put that back on me?"

"No, you listen. My boyfriend didn't ditch me. As a matter of fact, he proposed a few weeks ago, and I accepted. I am perfectly happy. I can't wait to get rid of your last name. After all, it was always reserved for her. Wasn't it? I would never keep it anyway if not for children. But you, Michael, need to get help. I don't care if you ruin your life. I don't care about you. But you will ruin our children. They are grown-ups and they still don't understand what happened to you. Get back to reality. When you told me about your dream that day on Brighton Beach, just before you left, I thought it was a mid-life crisis. A man needing to prove his manhood by running after young women. But then I realized it was not that. If you wanted younger women, New York was full of easy women. They would all be happy to please a man like you. It was something worse. It was an obsession. An obsession that ruined all of your business endeavors. You were chasing your dreams. It is still an obsession and you need to get out of it. For your own good. You should accept that you are sick and that you need help."

Michael hung up the phone and turned to another side. He didn't need this wake-up call. 'She must be drunk again,' he thought.

The First Weekend

30

Michael was standing on the platform of the Faro train station waiting for the train from Portimao arriving at 9:04 p.m. She was on that train. At last, they would meet.

It was warm January night, unusual even for Faro. Michael just arrived the day before from New York. For almost three months he was dreaming about the moment he would meet Maria and there he was on the station platform just a few minutes away from seeing her. The train arrived. People were getting off and then Michael saw her.

His heart was pounding. She was tiny. Just about five-foot tall, but proportional. She was the most beautiful woman he had ever seen. He found her curly brown hair, pale skin, her spectacular light blue almost gray eyes, her lips, her nose, her cheeks, her body, her small feet, and her gracious walk so attractive. She was thirty-three years old, but with her baby face, she appeared like she was just twenty. Michael didn't know what to say. He stared at her.

She stopped in front of Michael and said, "Hi," with such a cute Portuguese accent.

Michael hugged her softly. She smiled.

"Hi. How's your trip?" he asked.

"It was good, only hour and a half. I was reading on the train so it went fast."

Michael took the bag she was carrying, and they walked toward the cab outside the station. As they were walking, they kept looking at each other, almost like they were examining each other.

"I was right," Michael said. "You are beautiful. So you can't tell me anymore when I say you are beautiful, that it is only the picture. I see you now in person. And you are beautiful!"

"You are just in love. I am normal, nothing special," she answered and smiled again.

"No, you are beautiful!"

In the cab going towards the hotel, they kept looking at each other. There was a sense of excitement between them that both of them could feel.

Upon arriving in the hotel room, she unpacked her bag, looked around the room, commented on the hotel, and then she stopped in front of Michael.

"At last, we are together. I told you I would come to Portugal and I am here," he said and put his hands through her hair, softly touching her long neck. Her skin was white and baby soft.

"You know, I am shy," she said.

"Yes, I know. We will go slow. You are so precious my love. Don't worry."

Maria and Michael went out to a nearby restaurant to have a dinner, and had a pleasant time. They were talking about the countless hours they spent in front of the computer chatting to each other till late into the night. They were talking about their dreams, the strange way they fell in love with each other online, over a long distance.   In previous months they exchanged so many thoughts and they felt like they had known each other forever. Maria took Michael's hand, looked straight into his eyes and said, "I love you, Michael."

He was the happiest man in the world that night. Michael heard the same words so many times from her online, on Skype, but now it was different. She was there, sitting across from him, holding his hand. They were together. All Michael was thinking was that his dream had come true. That was the woman he wanted to find.

They were walking back to the hotel. She looked so beautiful under the yellowish street lights. He loved the way she moved, smiled, and spoke. Her voice was angelic, but it wasn't only about the way she looked. He adored everything about her. It was what was inside her, everything from her mind and reasoning to her sense of humor. 'I would do anything, just to see that smile and hear that voice forever,' Michael thought. He knew he would want no one else for as long as he lived. 'She is the one. There is no one else.'

For Michael falling in love with that woman was real and deep. He didn't remember ever experiencing anything like that. Everything before Maria seemed so superficial, so fake, like he loved nobody. First, they met online, and then in person, and everything changed. For many years he thought of himself to be a cold, lying, and unfaithful skirt chaser that could never commit to relationships, but at that moment he felt like he had found his destiny. It seemed like she was the woman he wanted all his life.

The answer to everything Michael loved and admired in women was right there with her dreamy eyes and her mystic smile. There was a particular pride in that smile and nobleness in her facial lines and in the set of her small nose. As they were walking, he wanted to hold her hand, but she pulled her hand back. "I am sorry, but I don't like to show my feelings in public. I don't like holding hands or kissing in public," she said.

He then placed his arm softly on her shoulder. She didn't mind that. They arrived at the hotel and walked up to the room. As they entered, without words, she turned towards Michael, pressed her body to his and they kissed. The kiss was long, deep, and passionate with tongues invading their senses. They almost could not breathe anymore, but didn't want to break the kiss. Their hands were stroking over each other's body. They slowly undressed each other, throwing clothing to the side. Once naked, they laid on the bed and kept kissing.

Michael continued gently touching her body. He felt desire racing through his body. He then placed his hands over Maria's breasts, massaging them tenderly. With his fingers he traced soft circles around her nipples, tweaking them, gently at first, then harder, then lowering his head and licking and sucking them. He could hear her heart beating fast and her excited moans. Her skin was pale and smooth. He enjoyed the pleasant and discreet scent of her perfume.

Michael placed his left hand under her tiny but long neck, taking it in a strong grip. He kissed her neck and gave her a gentle love bite. She trembled in excitement. Their lips met again in a passionate kiss with their tongues rousing as wild animals caught in a deep cave. He moved his right hand between her legs. Her pussy was wet and hot and he rubbed her clitoris with his fingers. Maria moved her hand between their bodies and took a hold of his erect penis. She spread her legs and gently pulled his penis towards her pussy. "Get in, I want to feel you," she said. Michael pressed the head of his penis on the opening of her wet pussy. He moved slowly at first, forward and back a few times until his penis was lubricated with the warm juices from her vagina and then in a quick move he slid deep into her. They both sighed in excitement. He pushed even harder as their bodies were rhythmically moving faster and faster towards ecstasy. "Yes, yes my baby," Michael rumbled while exhaling. He grasped her buttocks with his right hand sticking his middle finger into her anus.

She was clutching his back with her arms and pressing her fingers into his skin while kissing his neck and shoulders. Then, she moved her head back and opened her mouth with a passionate moan. She came. As she was gasping for air, her body started trembling and she moaned again. She came again. Michael came at the same time. He pressed his penis deep into her vagina as he was ejaculating. As he was filling her with his sperm he said victoriously, "Yes, baby, yes."

Ejaculating into Maria's vagina was very important for Michael. It was like claiming possession, like leaving a mark, like a completion of the unity.

He was laying on top of Maria. His penis was still inside of her but they were not moving. Just breathing. Enjoying the aftermath of ecstasy. Enjoying the unity of their bodies.

"I love you, Maria. I adore you."

"I love you too, Michael."

For both of them, this was a desired completion of the feelings they were sharing online for months, day after day, chat after chat. They were talking and dreaming about this physical encounter for so long. And it happened. They consummated their love. Their bodies merged. Their souls united into one in absolute completion.

He moved beside her and started stroking her hair softly with his hand.

"So, did you like it?"

"Yes," she said quietly and smiled. "Very much. But you came inside me, didn't you?"

Michael didn't answer. He just smiled with an innocent expression on his face.

"I told you I don't use any protection and I don't want to be pregnant. I am not ready for that. You have to be careful. If I get pregnant, you will never see me again."

"Don't worry, it will not happen. Men of my age don't have a sufficient number of spermatozoids to impregnate a woman. It is rare. It will not happen."

He was lying. That was stupid comment he made. He knew that she could get pregnant, but he didn't mind. He was hopping she would. He wanted to have a son with her. It was a crazy thought. He already had three daughters from previous marriages. They were all adults now. His youngest daughter was almost twenty-two. In his position and with his age, the last thing that one would want was yet another child, but somehow, Michael felt that his child with Maria would be a special child. He didn't know why, but from the beginning of meeting Maria online, the thought of having a son with her became for him almost an obsession. After all, he wanted to spend the rest of his life with Maria, and it was part of his dream. Just as Archangel had told him.

Passionate and full of desire for each other, they were making love all night. In the morning, she fell asleep with her head resting on his chest. He looked at her face for a while thinking how happy he was. It was a dream come true. He hoped it would never stop. Then he fell asleep too.

When they woke up, it was already one in the afternoon. They decided to go out, eat, and explore Faro. Maria lived for the last six months in Portimao, but she had never been in Faro.

Faro is a southernmost city in Portugal. It is the capital of the Algarve region with its origins as a habitat dating back to prehistory. Medieval fortress with an old town within its walls, Faro cathedral from the thirteenth century, many old buildings dating back to medieval times, a marina, beautiful sandy beaches, Ria Formosa lagoon, charming taverns serving local specialties, mild and stable Mediterranean clime, warm people—it all makes Faro a very attractive destination for tourists from all over the world. The tourism and hospitality industry are the main source of income for most of its inhabitants.

Michael and Maria walked out of the hotel and turned left onto Rua de Martinha. It was a street closed to traffic, with the pavement made of traditional Portuguese tiles and cafes, stores, and restaurants lined up on both sides of the street. All the cafes had outdoor seating areas.

It was a sunny Saturday afternoon with temperature in the sixties and they started their day with coffee in an outdoor café.

"In Portugal, you start your day with espresso coffee and pastel de nata," Maria said.   "Pastel de nata is a Portuguese egg tart pastry."

Michael liked pastel de nata. It was a nice vanilla flavored custard inside a flaky pastry shell. He also liked he could smoke in the outdoor café, something he couldn't do anymore in New York. Just after two days, Faro impressed Michael. The pace of life was so much slower than in New York and people seemed warm and friendly. Almost everybody he met spoke English.

"I love this weather!" Michael said. "Do you know that there were two feet of snow and temperatures below zero when I left New York on Thursday."

"Ha, ha, what a difference! So, do you like it here?" Maria asked.

"I do. But the best part is that you are here. That is why I want to move here."

"You are crazy Michael. Are you sure about that? It's a big step. And I can only come to be with you on weekends and still, not even all weekends. I told you already that I enjoy my solitude and sometimes I like to spend weekends alone."

"I know that Maria. And don't want to pressure you into spending time with me when you don't feel like it, but I need to be close to you."

"What about if I move to another part of Portugal at the end of this year? You know that The Ministry of Education is sending me to a different school every year. I never know before August where I will live next school year. What will you do then?"

"I will move too. I don't mind."

"But how will you live? Do you have enough money? You need to have backup money too. You don't know Portuguese. What about your work in New York? How will you do that? Can you do it from here?"

"I did my research already Maria. Life here is much cheaper than in New York. Only with the amount of money I pay for rent back in New York, here I can pay rent, utilities, and all monthly expenses. I think I will be able to cover living costs here. And my work, I can do from anywhere as long as I have the internet. I do everything online anyway."

Everything wasn't that simple. The truth was that Michael's savings could enable him to come to Faro one more time, rent an apartment, and have for two months of living at the most. And that would be it. If he doesn't make more money working from Faro, he would have a big problem. He didn't worry about that part as much. Often in his life, he had been in risky situations and he could always find a way out. All important to him at that moment was to be close to Maria. Nothing else mattered.

"So, what do you say? Should I look for an apartment today?"

"You realize that everything is not that simple, do you? You are a tourist and can stay without a visa only six months. After that, you would have to apply for a resident status or different visa. I don't know how it works, but you would have to take care of all of that."

"I can do all of that when I come next time." Michael answered.

"Okay then. I think you are really crazy. I guess, that's why I love you. We can look today and tomorrow for an apartment. I will help you with that," Maria said and smiled.

They had their lunch in the same café and then spent the afternoon walking around the old fortress and Faro marina. They enjoyed their time together. Michael was almost twenty-two years older than Maria, but in spite of the age difference they had so many things in common. Their characters, habits, and interests seemed to be so similar. Sometimes, Michael would joke that the two of them were just two opposite aspects of the same person. Like one soul divided between two bodies of male and female. All occasional differences were only coming out from their specific gender and age characteristics.

Maria was born in Northern Portugal. Her father had a vineyard in Douro region, and she grew up surrounded with the beauties of the countryside on the hills overlooking

Douro River. She loved walking over the meadows and through the valleys and forests. Living in the secluded stone house surrounded by vineyards, she didn't have many friends as a child or a school playground nearby. Pastures and woods became her playground and small forest animals became her best friends. Maria became devoted to nature, and it was a source of her energy and inspiration. She would spend all of her holidays and vacations back in her parents' home. Never thought of going anywhere else. Once she told Michael that she could see herself, at an old age, living in the same house she grew up. That was the place she felt happiest.

The other reason she would go to her parents' home whenever she could, was her strong attachment to her family. Her parents were simple, but hard-working people and they raised Maria to be a person with a strong sense of family, responsibility, and duty. She started working right out of the school and never quit or changed her job.

From what she told Michael, her father was strict, and remained a strong presence in Maria's life. Early on, she learned to keep her feelings to herself, afraid of her father's disapproval or criticism. Her parents knew little about her private life. She wrote poetry since she was a teenage girl and her parents never knew that. Michael was preparing to publish her first collection of poems and she already told Michael that she didn't want her parents to find out about it.

Almost every year Maria would be transferred to another school, to another town. She would make new friends, start relationships, and then have to do the same thing again next year. Maria learned to live in solitude and enjoy it. She was afraid of commitments knowing that her way of life would clash with any possible commitment.

Besides her family, the only other permanent part of her life was with her friends online. She could be with them at any time, anywhere she was. She could talk to them about anything. It was her own virtual world and her parents could not interfere or comment on it, but she had dreams too. And her dreams included a man—a man she created in her dreams and thought she would never find in the real world. Then Michael showed up claiming to be that man.

"You know, Michael, it will take time for me to get used to the idea you are here. Sometimes I am afraid. It's a big change for me and especially for you and I don't want to feel responsible if this doesn't work for you."

"It will work," Michael said, "because I am not asking anything from you. I am not making any conditions. I feel I need to be close to you. That is all."

They went back to the hotel and looked online for available apartments for rent in Faro. There were many. They decided to keep looking for text two months, and when Michael get back in March, make appointments to go see those he likes. Then they went to dinner at a nearby tavern.

They had a pleasant time with good food and good wine, chatting about her poetry, work, family, and Michael's plans for the future. The waiter serving them looked at them with curiosity. He saw she was Portuguese, and that Michael was a foreigner. The age difference was obvious. Michael and Maria were guessing what his thoughts about them might be.

Back at the hotel, they started kissing while still in the elevator going to their room. They made love all night again, but now even with more passion than the first night. Full of desire and already accustomed to each other's body, they surrendered to the pleasures of their love. She asked him to be careful and not ejaculate in her. He said he would be, but he wasn't. He finished inside of her again. And again. He wanted to have a son with her.

On Monday night Maria went back to Portimao. The first week in Faro passed fast for Michael. During the day, while Maria was working, he would roam through the old town in Faro, enjoy pastries in the garden of the small café near the hotel and watch people passing by. 'Portuguese women are good looking,' he thought. 'There is something so captivating about them. A magic. Something beyond physical beauty. And I have the most beautiful of them all.' He smiled at these thoughts.

Evenings he would spend in the hotel room talking on Skype to Maria till late night. For them, this was already standard practice. Except, this time, they were much closer. Sometimes, he would joke that he would sit on the train for Portimao and come knocking on her doors.

Next Friday evening, Maria was back in Faro. They spent the weekend together again. But this time, they almost didn't come out of the hotel room except for the occasional fast meals. Maria was insisting on paying half of all expenses they made.

"No way Maria! I invited you to eat out. I am paying for this." Michael said.

"If you don't let me pay half, I will not go out with you ever again. You need to save money if you want to move here, and not to spend on me."

Michael wouldn't let her pay anything, but he liked her attitude.

On Monday morning they got up early in the morning. They went to the Faro train station. Maria took the first train back to Portimao to be there on time for work and Michael took the train to Lisbon one hour later. His flight to New York was at two o'clock that afternoon.

The New Beginning

31

After just four hours of sleep, they got up at ten in the morning. They took a shower together, enjoying rubbing each other's body, but they had to rush. Their appointment with the real estate agent was at eleven. They had little time. They had coffee in the hotel and then ran out to the meeting.

The real estate agent was a woman in her forties and she spoke English. She saw nothing anything unusual in an American renting an apartment in Faro. There were quite a few Americans already living in Faro. They all appreciated the benefits of the Mediterranean climate, easy pace of life, and a much lower cost of living than in the US.

Michael told her he was writing a book with the story taking place in Faro and that he wants to be at the location of the events he is writing about. She thought that was quite interesting. Of course, she didn't fail to ask about Michael and Maria's connection. They told her they were friends working for the same publisher. She smiled and didn't inquire further.

She showed them four apartments and one of them seemed like a place Michael could enjoy. It was a one-bedroom apartment within walking distance from downtown Faro and the rent was reasonable. The real estate agent called the landlord, and he agreed to meet Michael on Monday morning.

It was already two in the afternoon when they finished with the real estate agent. Maria had to catch the train back to Portimao at 5:18 that evening, so they decided first to go eat something, go back to the hotel to pick up Maria's stuff and then go to the train station.

They went to the Adega Nova restaurant, just a few blocks from the hotel. The Adega Nova was in an old tile and brick warehouse, yet had the look of a traditional Portuguese bodega. The place was very popular with the local crowd and they served traditional Portuguese dishes. Maria and Michael ordered a cod dish with potatoes and veggies and a bottle of red wine.

"When you left in January, for a while, I was afraid that I'll never see you again. We had two wonderful weekends together. It was like a dream. I wasn't sure if I was dreaming or you were really here. Then talking to you on the Skype for almost two months every day without being able to touch you, to feel you, it was tough. But now, when you are here again, I am so happy."

"You know; I feel the same. Before I came last time, it was hard not being close to you. But then after I was here in January and left, it was much harder. I missed you every day and every night. We won't have that problem anymore now

I am here. Now I live in Faro." Michael smiled while saying that. He was excited about the apartment.

"I can't believe we found an apartment the first day we looked for it!" he said.

"I think Faro was overdeveloped. There are many vacant apartments for rent and the economy in Portugal is not so good. Even tourism is slowing down," Maria answered. Then she said: "And I still can't believe you gave up your apartment in New York just like that. What did you tell your friends?"

"That I am moving to Portugal."

"And? How did they react?"

"They were surprised. But that's not important." Michael said. Then he remembered Grace's reaction after he told her that he was moving to Portugal. In his usual fashion, he was waiting until the last day to tell her that he was going again to Portugal. It was a big blow for her. Even worst when he finally told her he was not coming back. She asked him: 'What if doesn't work for you there? What are you going to do then?' He told her that for him that option doesn't exist.

"What if doesn't work for you here? What are you going to do then?" Maria asked.

"That option doesn't exist for me. I know it will work. Don't you see that everything falls in its place just as it should? We found the apartment. And I will make it look beautiful for my baby and me."

The apartment was furnished, but it still needed a few things. They discussed what he needed for the apartment and where he could get it. Maria told him she would make a few things for his apartment. She liked to crochet, and she would make placemats for the dining room and a rug for the bathroom.

"You know," Maria started, "next weekend I will have to go north to my parents' house. I haven't been back home in a while, but the following weekend I will be back here again. That will give you time to settle into your new place, learn more about Faro and maybe make new friends. Start learning Portuguese. Many people in Portugal speak English, especially here, being a tourist area, but if you want to live here, you have to know the language. It will be easier."

"And," she continued, "while I am in my parents' home, we can talk in the evenings online. So, make sure that the first thing you do when you move into the apartment is to go to the Vodafone store or another internet provider and get a router for the internet. It takes two to three days for them to come and install."

"Yes, that is most important," Michael said. "Having the internet for me is essential. I can't work without it. All of my work I do online."

After they finished dinner and discussing the apartment, they were just sitting, sipping their wine, holding hands over the table and looking at each other. It was again an exciting weekend for both of them. It was beginning of March. For a moment Michael had a flashback about the time in March two years before when he arrived in New York from Bucharest. It was something he wanted to forget. Now he was sitting with a gorgeous young woman having a good time and he didn't want memories like that in his head.

"Did I tell you already that you are beautiful Maria?"

"No, I am not. I am an average person. It's only in your eyes. You are in love and when you are in love, your mind is controlled by your heart. So you see what your heart wants you to see," Maria said and smiled. "But anyway, thank you for telling me I am beautiful. It feels good to hear that. I hope you won't stop telling me."

"This is how I see it - our eyes serve two masters, our soul, and our mind," Michael started. "Our souls see much further than our mind. We often feel what is ahead of us even before it is registered by our physical ability to perceive it. Our soul sees it before our mind. There is this old expression that everybody knows, which says that the eyes are the windows of the soul. I always thought that to be true. But, somehow, whenever I look at your eyes, Maria, I see my soul, not yours. And I don't know what to think about it. It almost feels like my soul was captured by yours and the only way to reconnect to my soul is through you. It is a weird feeling."

Maria leaned forward over the table, touched Michael's cheek and lips with her hand and whispered, "I love you, Michael." Then she said, "All of my life, I've seen you only in dreams. I thought it would stay like that. In few relationships I had before, each time I thought, this man is the man from my dreams. But each time it was a disaster and a disappointment. I always thought I am not a normal person. That there is something different about me. Something not of this world. So, I decided to be alone and to be with my man only in my dreams. And I love my solitude. I enjoy it. And then you showed up. And I love you, but I still have my doubts. I still have my fears if everything that is happening between us is the story from my dreams. Am I still dreaming? Am I going to wake up one day in my regular life and you won't be there? Like you never existed. Like you were just my virtual man from the virtual world."

"It is interesting that you mention that. I often think about the way we met. Life is always full of surprises," Michael said. "Almost everybody has at least one unusual story to tell. Meeting somebody in the virtual world of social media and falling in love without ever seeing each other in person doesn't seem to be unusual anymore. It can happen to many people, but it was unusual when it happened to me. I was struggling with my feelings. How much of it was real. How much of it was just a dream? Is it possible that all of it was just a play between two lonely people? Was this woman the one I love or just the product of my imagination and of my desire to love and be loved? Would I be able to make this dream come true or was I heading into disillusionment and tragedy? But now when I met you, Maria, I know that you are real and you are the one I wanted to find. So, I need to tell you something very important and I want you to remember that forever."

Michael took both of Maria's hands and continued.

"I know that you still have doubts about me and about your love for me. And I know that you love your independence and your solitude. Also, I know that you have issues with your parents. Out of fear of their disapproval, you would never go to them and tell them you are in a relationship with a man twenty-two years older. I am not asking that from you. Just love me as you do. Your love is so pure, so deep, so universal, expressed to the whole of creation, that directing your love to one person often seemed to you like a limitation of your feelings, like the loss of the freedom to be who you are. I understand all that. You were longing for the man that will understand and love you the same way you love, without asking from you what you couldn't give. I think I am that man, Maria. I'm not asking you for any commitments, but I promise you my soul, my heart, and my body. They will be only yours. I promise you, my unconditional love, forever. And I am not asking for anything in return. Just allow me to be close to you. I need to be close to you. I will never stop loving you. And if you stop loving me as a man, allow me to stay your friend, your best friend. I will not press you into living with me or marrying me, but if you ever decide that it is what you desire, I will always be here for you waiting, as long as I live."

"But Michael, don't promise me that. I can't yet promise you anything. It is not fair for you."

"No, it is my promise and it will stay. You don't have to promise anything."

After dinner, they picked up Maria's bag from the hotel and they walked to the train station. Maria left her bag on the seat in the train and then walked out to say goodbye to Michael.

"Call me when you arrive home," Michael said. "I will hook up my laptop to the hotel's Wi-Fi so we can talk on Skype tonight."

"Yes, I would love that. I will call you at seven tonight," Maria answered. They hugged and they said, "I love you" to each other and then she went back to the train. She sat next to the window and sent a kiss to Michael. He sent her a kiss back. The train left.

On Monday morning Michael woke up early. It was 6:00 a.m. He slept only for two hours after talking to Maria online until four o'clock in the morning. 'She must be exhausted,' he thought.

Even though he was excited about the apartment and meeting with the landlord, Michael still worried. He didn't know the procedures of renting in Portugal, but if it was anything like in New York, he would have a problem. His credit was bad, he couldn't provide any references because he was self-employed, and he had money only for the first month of rent and the one-month deposit. His meeting was at nine so he had to get ready.

He put on one of two suits he had brought with him from New York, a nice shirt, and a tie. He wanted to make a good impression as a professional and serious person.

The top-floor apartment was on the Rue Capitáo Jose Veira Branco No. 16, in the center of Faro. It was a large one bedroom, in the well-maintained seven-story building, with a living room which included a dining room area, with a spacious kitchen, and a big terrace facing south with a view of the marina and the sea. Michael liked it was on the seventh floor. It was a number symbolizing God's creation. From the windows in the living room facing north, there was a view of the hills and mountains surrounding Faro.

Michael met the landlord at nine in the apartment. The landlord was an easy-going Portuguese man in his sixties, who didn't speak English but understood a bit. Somehow, they communicated with each other. The landlord asked only for the first month's rent and for a deposit. He didn't ask for any references or documents. Then he showed Michael around, explained to him about electric bills and hot water, gave him keys, took the money and left.

Michael stayed in the apartment. He couldn't believe. It was so easy. He had his apartment in Faro. And he could be with Maria. At that moment Michael was the happiest man in the world. He walked around the apartment looking at bedroom, closets, kitchen cabinets, bathroom, hallway, and terrace. He needed several things like bed sheets, pillows, and towels. But besides those things, toiletries, and food, everything else was there. 'He could manage until the end of the month,' he thought. 'And with some luck, he would do a project or two before the end of the month and be able to subsidize his living.'

He went back to the hotel, packed up his luggage, checked out and came back to the apartment. The whole afternoon he spent shopping. By the evening he had everything he needed.

He wanted to celebrate, so he bought a bottle of wine. In the evening, he was standing on the terrace, looking at the city lights and the reflection of the moon on the sea in the distance. The sky above was huge and full of stars. They seemed so close. He was sipping his wine and thinking how lucky he was. His move to Faro turned out to be easy. If it wasn't meant to be that way, if it wasn't the right thing, it would not happen that easy. God was on his side, he thought. The whole universe was with him.

Michael didn't have the internet yet, so he couldn't be online with Maria, but they spent time talking on the phone. He didn't fall asleep until late because he was excited. He finished the bottle of wine and around two in the morning he went to bed. In his own bed in his own apartment.

The next morning, Michael went to the Vodafone store to get the internet. Signing up for the internet was easy and didn't cost him much. They told him that by the end of the week they would come to install the router.

The next two weeks Michael spent settling in the apartment. The Vodafone people came when they said they would, so now he had internet and house phone.

On March 14th was Michael's fifty-fifth birthday. It was Friday and Maria came. She made a birthday card for him and wrote on it, "Michael—the man with the key—My King. I love you forever." She gave him her notebook with her poems and drawings. He was so happy.

"I will keep this notebook and cherish it all of my life. This is the most valuable thing anybody has ever given me for my birthday."

Following weekend Maria came again. Maria and Michael almost didn't go out. They spent days fixing things in the apartment, cooking, eating, and talking. Nights they spent making love.

Before she left on Sunday afternoon, she cooked soup for Michael to have for a few days, cleaned the bathroom and ironed a few of his shirts. Michael didn't ask her to do that, but she wanted to take care of him. He thought that was sweet. He didn't remember the last time somebody pressed his shirts for him. She also left her clothing and toiletries, so she wouldn't have to carry them with her each time she came to visit. Michael liked that too. 'She was getting comfortable, moving in slowly,' he thought. That was what he was hoping for.

Michael's work was going well. He got a big web design project from New York that would give him enough income to live for the next three months. Time was passing by and Michael spent weekdays working. He rearranged the furniture in the living room to look like an office. He liked to feel like being in a workspace. On evenings, he would take long walks around Faro, down to the seaport, through the Faro fortress, and back to the center of Faro where he would enjoy evenings in the outdoor cafes having coffee and watching people walking up and down the street. People in the local stores and cafes recognized him as a regular customer and greeted him. He befriended two of neighbors in the building and the owner of the local bookstore. Once in a while he would have coffee with them.

Maria visited on weekends. On Friday afternoons, Michael would clean out the house, buy food for the weekend and go to the train station to wait for Maria. He prepared dinner on Friday nights and she cooked on Saturdays. For Michael, being with Maria on weekends was like being in a heaven. Everything was so perfect. Maria felt the same way. They enjoyed each other's company. They enjoyed making love. They enjoyed talking. Every single moment together felt precious. And it seemed like weekends together were not enough. During the week, they continued with their routine of spending hours on the internet talking until late in the evening.

Michael wanted so much to live with Maria. He knew that in her mind she was not ready yet. She lived for too long by herself and she got used to it. She still feared her parents' disapproval and didn't want to face them with actions they may not approve. Michael knew all of that, but he hoped that her desire to be with him would grow as time was passing by and he will wait. He also hoped that she would get pregnant and that something like that would change things, allowing them to go in the direction he wanted. Each time they would make love, he would finish in her. She would always make a comment "Michael, you were not careful again." Michael would just smile and look at her like the boy who just broke the vase and was pretending like it was somebody else.

Shadows From the Past

32

The first three months in Faro passed fast for Michael. The weather was great, people around him were friendly, and Maria was with him every weekend. Everything seemed perfect. Michael and Maria were happy.

The first days of June brought worries. After the web design project, he had just finished, there were no new jobs coming in. Michael called few churches and companies in New York that he was freelancing for, but they had no new work for him. He suspected that the fact he was in Faro and not in New York caused the lack of new jobs. Most of his clients were Pastors of the Churches affiliated with the Bowery Mission. When he was back in New York, he used to go to his clients' offices, picked up a project, worked from home and sent them back. He wouldn't choose or pick the projects. He would accept everything - book formatting, book covers, editing, web design, copywriting. Even after completed projects, he would still go back to the clients to discuss it. Although, all of his work was online, he liked that personal touch, and it worked for him. It was bringing him more work. He knew how to talk to people, but now he couldn't do that. He was in Faro. Was it possible that distance played a role in not getting more projects? Michael depended on his work from New York. He knew that it would be very hard for him to get any work in Portugal. Didn't speak the language, and he didn't put enough time into studying it, anyway. He spoke English with Maria, and almost everybody around him spoke some English. On another hand, the economy in Portugal was in crisis and there were few job opportunities. Besides, he didn't know where he would look for the job if he had to. Also, he was still in Portugal on the tourist visa, without the right to work.

In spite of everything, Michael thought it was just a small setback and that new jobs would come. He had just paid his June rent and bills and held onto some extra cash to put him through two weeks. 'Something would come in the meantime,' he thought.

Three weeks passed. In a week Michael would have to pay his rent and he even didn't have enough money to buy a pack of cigarettes. Maria came that Friday as usual. Michael waited for her at the train station. On the way home he was quiet. He knew he would have to tell Maria about his financial problems, but he didn't know how. Whatever he would say, he knew it would look bad. He wanted to keep with Maria an image of independent well-to-do man, not a struggling freelancer who was just two years ago in the shelter for homeless people.

"Michael, why are you so quiet? Are you tired? Is it something wrong?" Maria asked while they were walking home from the train station.

"Oh, nothing much. It's my work. It is slowing down. I worry about my income. That's all."

"Maybe it's because of summer. Usually, in summer all businesses get slower. It is normal. Don't worry."

"Yeah. I guess it is summer." Michael said.

"But you are okay with money to put you through the summer, aren't you?" Maria asked.

"Hmm, I am not sure..." Michael said, but then add fast: "But don't worry, I'll take care of things. It is not the first time."

Maria stopped walking and looked at Michael with the surprise in her eyes. "What do you mean you are not sure? Do you have money for rent and food for next month?"

"Well, not exactly..."

"Not exactly! Michael, you came to Faro three months ago with the idea to live here. You should have had backup emergency money for at least six months of living, if not for more, and after three months you don't have for a rent. What kind of man would do that?"

"Maria, things don't always work the way we want. But it is not your problem. You don't have to worry. I'll take care of it."

They didn't talk about money problem anymore during that weekend. They had a good time and on Sunday night Michael took her to a train station.

Monday morning Michael looked at his pantry and

fridge. There was almost no food left. 'He would have to do something,' he thought. He thought of selling his camera. Few months before, he purchased Canon digital camera in New York. It was the useful piece of equipment that Michael was using for his graphic design work. If he sold it, he could make at least two, three hundred Euros. That would help. He walked around Faro looking for stores that buy and sell used electronic equipment. He found two; went there, but they were not interested in buying his camera. That was a blow. Michael was sure he could sell it.

Following Friday Maria was in Faro again. Only that time Michael had no food in the house for over the weekend and no money. He was flat out broke. On the way home they stopped by a supermarket. Maria bought everything they needed for weekend and extra food for Michael for next week.

"So what are you going to do about rent?" she asked when they entered the apartment.

"Landlord is coming on Monday to pick up rent money. I was thinking to call him before to ask him to wait for a few days, but I'll wait until he comes on Monday and talk to him in person. I think it's better."

"Few days? So you will have money coming soon?"

"Yes. I think so." Michael answered. He was lying. There was no money coming from anywhere but he didn't want her to know that.

"I still can't understand how you could allow yourself to be in this position. In all my life, I was never late or in default on any of my financial obligation. I hate when people do that. I think it is irresponsible."

"Maria, sometimes in life there are circumstances one can't control. Things happen. They can happen to anybody."

"Yes. But you can project things in life. Make plans. Prepare yourself for any potential problems. You moved to Portugal, left everything in New York, and after three months you run out of money. That is not a good planning."

"The only aim I had before coming here is to be with you as soon as possible Maria. Yes, I could plan my moving more carefully, but that would mean staying in New York longer until I accumulate enough savings. I didn't want that. You can't blame me for wanting to be with you."

"I don't blame you, Michael. Want you to live without problems like all normal people. I am scared that you rushed with all your decisions. If things don't work out for you here, I will feel responsible. And I don't want to be responsible, Michael. I told you that already."

"No, you don't have to feel responsible. I knew all the risks of coming here and I came anyway. In my mind, Maria, being with you is worth risking everything. So don't blame yourself or me for anything. I am not a kid. I knew what was that I was doing when I set on the plane. And again, I have to tell you: Don't get overwhelmed with this. It is a small problem and I will take care of it. I've been in tight corners before in my life and I always got out. It won't be different now."

"What kind of tight corners?" Maria asked.

Michael didn't answer. He turned his head to the side pretending he didn't hear her question.

"You know, we talk for months every day, all day, but you never told me much about your past. Besides the fact that you were married twice and have three girls, I don't know anything else. Is there anything I should know?"

Michael looked at her. He always wanted to be honest with this woman. He was never honest to anybody in his life. But he was already lying to Maria. He didn't like that. 'I should stop with this before it's too late and tell Maria the truth. She deserves that. She is the woman I love,' Michael thought.

"Okay. I think you are right. I haven't told you much about my past. Not because I wanted to hide anything from you, but because I am not very proud of my past. I will tell you. All I am asking you is not to judge me. One day you'll understand that everything I did in my life was connected with you."

"With me? Why with me? We found each other six months ago." Maria said with surprise in her voice.

"Yes. But now when I am thinking about my life, from the distance of over fifty years, I can see the pattern and the connections, cause, and effect of everything that happened. And everything points into one direction: Finding Maria. And finally I have found you. I wish I have found you when I was twenty-five, but it didn't happen then."

"Ha, ha, that was fortunate," Maria said jokingly, "I was three then. You would be accused of pedophilia."

"No, that is not what I meant. I meant I wish that age difference is smaller between us. Anyway, I will tell you everything you should know about your man."

So Michael told Maria everything about his life, including his past business dealings, Bucharest story, conflicts he had with some Freemasons back in New York, and time he spent in Bowery Mission. He thought that the more she knew about his past would help her understand the background of the problems he had. He didn't want her to think that he was a dishonest man or con man, or a thief. In his mind, he saw himself as a victim of the circumstances he couldn't handle. That didn't mean he was not responsible for his problems. His habit of running away whenever he encountered difficulties in his life caught up with him, and he could not understand why people he would leave behind with no explanation were angry and often wanted revenge.

Yet, the more he was telling Maria, the more questions she had. He didn't mind telling her everything. Before Maria, he shared nothing with anybody. Even when he was married, he never shared with his wives any problems he would have, but now he felt he wanted to share everything with Maria. He didn't want to have any secrets. It ended up that what he shared didn't look good.

Maria was concerned. And Michael felt that his life story overwhelmed her.

"You should go back to New York Michael, make money and solve your problems. I love you and I want nothing bad to happen to you. And you don't have to worry about me. I am here and I will wait for you," she said.

Michael didn't want to take this idea into consideration.

"No, Maria. I will not go back. There is nowhere to go back. Faro is my home now. I gave you a promise I will be close to you forever. Whatever happens, I will keep my promise. It is a complicated situation, but I will solve it. I always did. I will do it now."

Michael was concerned as well and furious with himself. Maria was a straightforward and responsible person. She always took care of all of her obligations, never lived above her means, and never borrowed money from anybody. Michael knew that it would be hard for her to understand all of his circumstances, regardless of how much time he spent explaining it to her. He worried that she would see him as an irresponsible and dishonest man and the worst of it was that Michael knew that, throughout his life, he was.

Sometimes, he thought of himself as an elephant walking through the china store, breaking everything in his path and still expecting people not to be angry with the damage he made, but rather to admire his strength and his endurance.

The truth of the matter was that Michael was arrogant and selfish. He never had a respect for anything or anybody. Whatever he was doing in his life, he was never happy. There was always something that he missed, that would make him leave everything and disappear and he didn't know why. Somehow, he always had a strange feeling that everything he went through had to happen like it was predestined; like he was paying for his mistakes from the previous life. He didn't think of himself as a bad man. He was an intelligent man with many talents. Everything he ever did in his life, he did with good intentions. He never thought of hurting, deceiving, or cheating anybody, but somehow, it would always turn out that way. Even the smallest mistakes he would make would turn into big problems just because he was ignoring them.

Since he had his strange dream, he knew that there must have been a reason for everything that happened to him. He regretted nothing until he met Maria. He thought he had found the purpose of his life. He didn't know what it was, but everything about Maria just seemed right. He became a different man. A man with a soul.

Now he was angry that his past spilled over into their relationship. It was baggage he didn't want to bring to Maria. He wanted for Maria to feel his pure love and commitment, what he was for her, and not what he had been for other people. 'The timing of the events cannot be worse,' he thought.

Yet, he expected that she would understand. She loved him. They shared unique dreams. Their love for each other was above and beyond any material matters. That whole weekend Maria looked unhappy. Michael knew that she was preoccupied with the thoughts about his past. But he hoped it would pass. Before she left on Sunday night, she gave him forty Euros in cash: "You may need this for cigarettes until your money comes." She said. Michael didn't refuse it.

On Monday, the landlord came to pick up the rent. Michael invented a story about money being stuck in the money transfer from the US and asked landlord to wait a week or two until he solves this issue. Landlord agreed.

The whole week Michael spent trying to come up with the solution. But nothing was coming to his mind. On

Thursday, Michael had a morning coffee with his neighbor Francisco. Francisco loved photography and had a real passion for cameras.

"Francisco, would you be interested in buying my Canon. It's sitting around, and I don't use it much, so I'm thinking of selling it? I could give you a good price." Michael said.

"No. Not interested. I have three cameras. Thanks. But why are you selling it? Do you need money?" Francisco asked.

"I am short on cash. My money is stuck in the bank transfer so I am waiting for it."

"How much do you need? Maybe I could help you."

This offer from his neighbor surprised Michael.

"I don't know. Maybe four hundred Euros?" Michael said, "To get me through until my money comes."

"No problem Michael. Here." Francisco put his hand in his shirt pocket, pulled out a bunch of money, took out eight fifty Euro bills, and handed over to Michael. "I always like to have cash on me. Don't believe much in multi banco machines."

Michael called at once his landlord to come to pick up the rent. With this loan, he bought time to solve his problem. 'God is helping me again. Maybe a new project will come soon,' He thought.

Michael would not tell Maria about rent until she comes on Friday. And he would not tell her that he borrowed money. At the end he had fifty Euros left for food and he would prepare nice weekend for two of them.

He spent Friday afternoon shopping for food and cleaning the house as usual before her arrival. Then, around five o'clock she called him.

"Michael, I cannot come this weekend. I have work to do around the house and do my laundry. I have a big pile. But we will be together online, anyway. I hope you don't mind."

Michael remembered that Maria told him she could not come every weekend and not to expect that, but for the last three months since he came to Faro, she was with him every weekend. Somehow, he felt that her decision not to come had something to do with the problems he had. He thought that maybe he made a mistake by telling her everything, but again, he wanted, to be honest with her and not have any secrets. She was the woman he loved deeply and he believed that her love for him was the same.

Michael was right about his assumptions. The following days Maria spent searching online for references to everything that had anything to do with Michael. She was good in Google search and she knew where to look with the information that Michael gave her. Soon, she came across comments that some Masons wrote on various Masonic blogs and websites. They were all similar, referring to Michael as a charlatan and swindler. She knew that everything wasn't so black and white and that there was much more to the whole story, but she didn't like what she found. Even the reviews of Michael's books had bad overtones. It was obvious they were written by the people who didn't want to write about Michael's book, and only wanted to slander him. She found two reviews by the same man about one of Michael's books that were completely opposite. In the first review, this man wrote all accolades for the book and the author. In the second review, written a couple years later, he claimed that Michael knew nothing about the subject he was writing. It was obvious that the review was written with the intention to hurt Michael. She didn't know what to think anymore. Suddenly, everything about Michael was so disturbing. Each time, she would find something, she would call Michael to hear his explanation. Each time, he would talk about bad circumstances and destiny accepting no blame. She couldn't understand that.

In her dream, the man she was in love with was of pure heart and soul, honest, strong, responsible, and without a blemish. A man who loved everybody and anything around him and Michael seemed to be like that. She could not believe that she made a mistake. But everything about his past was full of lies, deceit, and conflicts with others. He was tainted. Was it possible he was deceiving her as well? Was this the same Michael that she was spending weekends with and hours on end online?

She always wanted to have a complete life with a sense of purpose, but the one she lived so far, made her feel repulsive and detached. Rejecting uniformity and compromise, she was watching this, for her, a strange phenomenon, of people molding each other in forms suitable for their togetherness. It was the worst kind of degradation and manipulation of one's soul, she thought. It was a twisted picture of warmth and unity like an uncertain experiment in happiness. So, she wanted no part of this so typical life experience. It was just a spectacle, so distant and unattainable. She didn't know if she would ever be ready for it.

So, for years, she kept running away from her true needs. To her, they were just mindless and frantic echoes of anxiety and adversity. She denied and rejected them like monstrous apparitions, jolting the image of herself. To discard them meant to awaken the spark of desire for change. Constant change. It was the only thing that made her feel herself.

After a long mind quest, she had found peace in being with herself. She learned to enjoy her solitude. Some unclear energy, irrational hallucinations, and dreams were accompanying her even when she was satisfied. She already felt an intimacy with them and seemed to be seeking the comfort of mind in these dream creations. With them, she was never alone, and they were almost always serving her desires and kept her on the right course. They were sending an unquestionable message to everyone that this was her own world. Or at least, it was like that until she met Michael.

Then, an unexpected multitude of thoughts from Michael spilled over to her. Who was he? What gives him the right to disturb her dreams? His thoughts were like an army of invincible outlaws and the enemies of her common sense. Armed with deception and cunning, artists of fraud and undisputed rulers of manipulation, reinforced with the desire to enter her dreams, and place himself there as the only solution for her destiny. How did he ever get so far?

It seemed like he knew all of her ways. He was almost like the mirror image or the male version of herself. Yet, she wasn't ready to accept him as her counterpart. Her world of dreams was just that—dreams. And he wanted to pull them out and materialize them in time and space. What nerve! What lunacy! He was a bigger dreamer than herself or a reckless player in the game of life. He made her feel happy and complete, but achieving that in reality was too scary and too dangerous a thought. She already felt the loss of herself, the collapse of the power of her imagination. She was being suffocated by her own love for this uncommon man.

Even if this conversion of dreams into reality was possible, her everyday life was far too common to fit such glorious dreams, she thought. One or the other would collapse. In many ways, she even liked her life. It was nothing like her dreams, but it made her feel secure and in control. She never cut the cord with her childhood and that connection with her family was a big portion of feeling part of the whole circle of existence. She didn't want to lose that connection. Not for anything.

Michael knew all of that. Yet, he was determined in his ambition. He knew all the obstacles they were facing, but he believed in his dream. It was her dream too, he thought. She kept him in this dream all of her life. She allowed him to find her. He loved her for it. He loved her forever, but he thought that the world we lived in would never get this far without dreams. It was made of dreams and dreams turned into reality.

Another weekend passed and Maria didn't come to Faro.

She kept talking to Michael online for long hours all weekend, but this time, she didn't say why she wasn't coming. Michael didn't ask.

One more week passed. Michael noticed that during that week Maria was avoiding him online. They spoke just twice for a few minutes. She would just ask him, "How are you?" and then she would stay quiet. Michael would ask her, "Is everything okay? What is bothering you, Maria?"

Her answer would be short, "Nothing." Then she would get quiet again. He knew that she was thinking about their relationship and he wanted to give her time. He didn't want to bother her. The following Friday she didn't talk to Michael at all, so he thought she would not come again, but then around seven o'clock in the evening a phone rang.

"I am at the train station in Portimao, just getting on the train. I will be in Faro at the usual time. Wait for me at the station, please."

The Last Weekend

33

Michael was at the train station just at the moment the train arrived. Maria walked out of the train. She didn't look happy. They walked back to the apartment and on the way she didn't say a word. When they arrived, she left her bag in the bedroom and went to the terrace. Michael brought two glasses of wine and set them next to her.

"Michael. I came to pick up my stuff I have here. I don't think this will work. It was mistake. It was mistake you came to Faro. I was alone all of my life; used to being alone. I love you, but for me being in a dream with you is enough. And I am not even sure if you are the man from my dream. You are tainted Michael. You already have a mark. I cannot live with it."

Michael expected she would say something like that.

"Maria, I came to Faro to be close to you and I gave you a promise of eternal love. That will never change. I am not asking anything in return. Never was. But I feel that my soul is with you and I need to stay close to my soul. If you don't want to be in a relationship with me, it is your choice. But don't break the connection between us. Allow me to stay close. If not as your man, then as your friend. I can be your best friend. I am your best friend already and want to always stay close to you and for you whenever you need me. With no conditions Maria."

She looked at Michael, sighed deeply and said, "Oh, I am not sure that we can even be friends. You are just saying that. You will always want a relationship. I don't know if that would work."

"Yes, it would. I love you Maria, always will and I know how to be a faithful friend."

Michael walked into the living room and came back with a few sheets of paper in his hand. "Look, I wrote short story last week. I haven't written in a long time and then it came to me last week. I would like it if you would read this and tell me what you think." He handed her papers, and she read.

"Amo's Gorge - A Story About the Last Unicorn"

The unicorn is a legendary animal that has been described since antiquity as a horse-like animal with a large, pointed, spiraling horn sticking out from its forehead. It was described as a wild forest creature, a symbol of purity, grace, and independence, which could only be captured by a virgin. It was believed in the old times that its horn had the power to turn poisoned water drinkable and to heal sickness. According to the legend, there were many unicorns inhabiting the earth centuries ago, but, under the advance and pressure of the human civilization, they disappeared.

In the mountains of Southern Portugal, in the region of Alentejo, is a ravine called "Amo's gorge." I was there some time ago and heard from the locals the story about the last unicorn called Amo. According to the story, there were two unicorns. Male Amo and female Ama, but nobody could tell me what happened to Ama. Some believe that she is still somewhere around running through forests and over the meadows. At least, that is what the legend says.

This is how the story goes. Some three hundred years ago, there were two last unicorns left in the world. Male called Amo and female called Ama. They didn't know each other because they inhabited different lands, but they felt each other's existence. Often, they would dream of each other and felt some strange longing, like they belonged together. But, life was going on and they lived their lives never expecting they would ever meet.

Ama was a young unicorn, happy with her being, proud of her independence and freedom. She often looked at other animals wondering why they allowed humans to tame them and use them. Couldn't understand them. Ama enjoyed every bit of nature that surrounded her. She loved wildflowers, cold streams, deep and mysterious woods, sounds of the wind in the trees, and the music of birds. Ama could only be complete feeling the land, roaming over mountains and through valleys. She felt the wholeness of creation. And knew that she was one of the most majestic living creatures still around and she was proud of it.

Once in a while, humans would see her running over lands and they admired her beauty and grace. They wanted to catch her and tame her, but she would never allow that. She enjoyed their admiration and liked to play with them. She enjoyed the attention they were giving her. So, sometimes, Ama would even let humans come close and touch her, manipulating their senses, just so they could feel she was real and not a dream. Then she would run away, leaving them wondering what happened, and often, leaving them sad for the missed opportunity to catch such a precious animal.

She wasn't sure what she felt about people, but she was sure she never wanted to give up her freedom and the wholeness and happiness she felt while running through the wilderness. It was who she was, and she didn't want to change, not for anything in the world.

On the other side, in other part of the world, lived Amo. He was a different story. Like Ama, being a unicorn, he loved all the same things and was proud of his independence and freedom.

He was quite older than Ama, but still a very strong male unicorn. But being male, he always needed to prove his strength and superiority over other animals. He always needed a recognition for who he was. Especially from humans.

Once in a while, he would allow them to catch him and make them believe that they tamed him. For a while he would work on their fields, pull their carriages, run in the horse races, and do everything they asked him, just to show his superiority and strength and to enjoy admiration by humans. But then, he would get bored by it and run away always leaving damage behind him. He would knock down barns, break fences, run over crops he was working on, pull out vines; always wanting to show to humans he can't be used; wanting them to pay for the belief he could be tamed. Then he would run free over lands until the next time he would allow humans to catch him.

Over time the word spread around among humans of Amo and many furious humans were trying to catch him and punish him for the damage he was always leaving behind him. Some were even claiming that he was not a real unicorn, but just a wild horse who deserved to be put down. For them, unicorns were gracious beings, who would never have acted like him. Amo didn't care about their opinion. He knew who he was and continued running through life the same way.

After many years, he became tired of the game he played, and settled somewhere where nobody knew him, in different part of the world, so he could avoid humans forever. He came to the mountains of Alentejo, not knowing that he moved to the lands Ama was inhabiting.

One morning, he was standing on a high ridge, enjoying the warmth of the early morning sun, when in the distance he saw Ama running over the fields. He couldn't believe his eyes. She was the most beautiful creature he ever saw. She was the one from his dreams. His heart pounded fast. She saw him too. Ama was equally excited, but cautious. On one side, she was happy to see another unicorn. He was old, but still appeared strong and handsome. Ama was asking herself if it were possible he was the one whose existence she sensed all her life. She wasn't sure if she should come closer. Always afraid of being disappointed.

Amo ran to her direction. He was running fast, trying to impress her and show his strength. For a while, they were running parallel, but in the distance examining each other. By each mile, Amo was coming closer and closer. Ama was still afraid, but she was allowing him to shorten their distance. In t he evening they came to the same meadow. They were drinking water from the same spring and observing each other.

Then, Amo came to Ama. She wasn't moving. She just looked at him. They could hear each other's heart. He touched her. They laid next to each other with their bodies touching. It was a glorious feeling for both of them. A sense of completion. Of dreams come true.

In the morning, they woke up and continued running and walking through the woods enjoying the surroundings and more than anything, enjoying each other. Ama was happy. At last, a real unicorn was next to her, somebody that could understand her. Some- body that would not try to tame her. Somebody to share in the joy of freedom and of creation without limits and without conditions. Somebody of the same kind. She couldn't believe that it would ever have happened, but it was right here, in front of her eyes. She still had her doubts, being all her life by herself, the only unicorn. But he was here, strong and true.

Amo was also happy. He promised never to leave her side. He thought he would always be there for her, but Ama didn't want him to be there for her, but with her. She never felt she needed any protection or help. Ama was strong enough and wise enough to care for herself. She wanted to be with Amo as two equal independent beings, respecting and enjoying each other's freedom. Ama wanted to share the greatness of her pure love, the experiences of nature. She wanted to be enriched by the same soul, not restricted or slowed down by it; wanted to share the affection for the things they both cherished.

Well, Amo knew what Ama wanted. He wanted the same thing, but the time he spent around humans changed him a little. On one hand, he wanted to run with Ama to the end of time and enjoy their togetherness in the freedom of open fields, forests, and mountains. He also wanted to have a place that would be their home. Somewhere, where they could settle and feel the warmth of their togetherness.

The home he was thinking about was a human category. For unicorns, home was the whole of universe. Space without boundaries. That was what Ama called home. Anyway, Amo was persistent. He took her to the ridge he discovered. He wanted to make a garden for her, full of different fruits and plants. She looked at him thinking he was playing a childish game. Why would unicorns ever want a small garden to work in when the world was a huge garden ready to be explored. For a while, she enjoyed in planning, even helping him make the garden.

Yes, she was thinking, maybe once in a while, they could stop there and rest, but for her settling somewhere was an impossible thing — something she thought she would never enjoy. Amo failed to realize that she wanted an equally independent and free unicorn. Somebody she can admire for his freedom. She wanted to give him her love, but she didn't want to sacrifice her liberty. It was not the nature of unicorns. She would be unhappy forever and she didn't want him to sacrifice anything for their love and togetherness either.

Amo was of a different mind. He thought if he settled down, and built a home, that she would join him. Too many years spent with the humans had blurred his mind. He was thinking like the humans. So, he sacrificed his freedom and settled on the ridge. He wanted to show Ama that he would sacrifice anything for her love, even the freedom of a unicorn. He was waiting for her.

Ama would come once in a while and spend time with Amo. She loved him and she hoped that he would realize his true nature and continue to run around with her as unicorns should, and forget those ideas of home.

But Amo was persistent and kept remaining on the ridge. She was getting less and less excited to go there. It was just a ridge, one of many ridges in the mountains of Alentejo. She was losing her patience with Amo. Ama couldn't understand how a true unicorn could act like a human. A true unicorn would never sacrifice his freedom, not even for love. Freedom is a part of true love. For unicorns, love was an unconditional category. She saw his sacrifice as a weakness, something that made him lose her respect and not gain her love. She heard stories that humans were spreading around about Amo, and sometimes, she was asking herself, 'What kind of unicorn would ever act like that?' Maybe he is a wild horse pretending to be a unicorn. Is it possible she made a mistake about him? One day, she couldn't look at him like that anymore. He didn't appear as the unicorn from her dreams. She almost felt sorry for him. That was not Amo that she first met—the fast and strong unicorn running with her shoulder to shoulder. She told him she would not come back anymore to the ridge and that everything was a mistake. And she left. She was disappointed and hurt, but she knew that nothing would lower her spirits once she was back running over open fields and through deep woods. It was the open air of the high mountains that made her feel alive. For her, it was better if Amo remained as he was, just in her dreams.

Amo stayed on the ridge feeling sorry for himself and for the lost love of Ama. He couldn't believe that she left him. Amo neglected his garden and soon he had no food left. He didn't eat for days. Amo didn't want to eat. He didn't want to live; didn't care about anything anymore. All he was thinking was how he needed Ama. He realized what a big mistake he made. All she wanted from him was to be who he was, a true unicorn. He was angry with himself for acting like a human. How could he be so stupid?

As he was laying for days on the ridge, humans from the valley trying to find him and punish him, noticed him there. They advanced up the hill, getting more and more eager to make him pay for his bad deeds. He looked at them approaching. He wasn't sure if he wanted to run or stay there and wait for his destiny, but something inside him told him he should jump and run. That he should try to be a true unicorn. Maybe one day, it didn't matter when, Ama would meet him again. Amo will show her that he is the one: a true unicorn. He was the unicorn from her dreams.

Amo stood up. He couldn't go down the hill. Humans were closing in on his escape route. The only way was to jump from the ridge to another ridge over the deep ravine. He looked at the distance. Amo used to jump further than that before. He would make it, he thought. Then he jumped. But his muscles were weak and his body wasn't what it used to be. Days spent laying down without food and water took their toll on him. He didn't make it to the next ridge. He fell into a deep ravine and died there.

Humans came to the edge of the ridge looking down at his

motionless and bloody body. One of them said, "Well, they were right. He was not a unicorn, just a wild horse who met his deserved destiny. A real unicorn would jump this distance."
Years later, at the place he fell, a spring broke out from the rock with an abundance of pure and fresh water. Local people were talking about the magical properties of the water that was healing many illnesses. Some local people remembered that a unicorn fell and died there and connected those two things, so they named the spring, "Amo's Spring" and they named the gorge, "Amo's Gorge." Some say, it was just as he would want it. He always craved human recognition. Now, he had it forever. Once in a while, people swore that they saw Ama coming down to the gorge to drink water from Amo's spring. But those were only stories. People like fairytales.

Maria finished reading Michael's short story, raised her eyes, looked at him and said with sadness in her voice, "Yeah, this is us, this story is about us."

"I don't want that to be our story," Michael said. "I respect your independence. I respect the way you strive for your freedom and I will never try to constrain you in any way, but I will never stop loving you, Maria. No matter what you say or what you do, I will always keep my promise."

Maria stood up and then sat in Michael's lap. She hugged him, looked at his face for a few seconds and then said, "You are my Romanian rascal and I love you, Michael." They kissed.

Their kiss was long and passionate. Then they went to the

bedroom and made love into the morning.

During that weekend, everything seemed as normal as before. They took long walks around Faro, cooked together, watched movies and made love. On Sunday morning she cleaned the bathroom, did laundry and ironed Michael's shirts. They never spoke about Michael's problems. Michael thought that she had changed her mind and that everything would be as it was before.

In the afternoon, she started packing the clothing that she kept in the apartment. Michael looked at her.

"Why are you taking all of your clothing?"

"Oh, I just have too many things over here. I want to wash them at home. I will bring some when I come next time.

Michael didn't like that. But he didn't want to comment anymore.

Mercy and Grace

34

Five weeks passed since Maria's last visit. Weekend after weekend Michael hoped that she would come, but she didn't. They would speak online once in a while, but most of the time, she would be online and she would see that Michael was there, but she wouldn't say anything. Michael was hurting, but he didn't want to press her. He never wanted to start the conversation. He was waiting for her.

The apartment felt empty without Maria and her things. Michael's financial situation was still bad. Except for two small projects, work was not coming from New York and he had none motivation to call people and ask for more work. He felt like he was losing his strength and his will to live. He didn't have money to pay his rent again and his landlord was upset, but he agreed to wait.

Michael borrowed small amounts of money from Francisco again. His neighbor felt that Michael was in trouble and he didn't even bother asking him when was he going to repay his debt. Michael still owed him first four hundred.

The last week in July, just as Michael was thinking about what to do to get work and continue living in Faro, Maria sent him a message on Skype:

"You are a deceiver and liar Michael. All of your life, you were deceiving people. You deceived me too. How could I be so stupid not to see that? You are just like a sick old dog in heat chasing after young women. I hate you."

That was all. Michael looked at the message and he couldn't believe it. He tried to call her on Skype and on the phone, but she wouldn't answer. The next day, Maria deleted herself as a friend and contact from all Michael's accounts online—Facebook, Goodreads, Skype, Google mail, and iMessage.

A few days later, Carlos came from Lisbon on business to Faro and he met Michael in a café near Michael's apartment.

"Bom Dia," Carlos said. "How are you today?"

"Bom Dia, Carlos," Michael answered. "I don't know. Just having a coffee and feeling sorry for myself."

"Why? That is not a useful thing. Solves nothing," Carlos said.

Michael told him about the happy times he spent with Maria and about the way everything ended after she learned about his past.

"I kept asking myself where I made a mistake. For years I was searching for her, until I had found her. That first weekend I thought I was at the last door and all I had to do was knock and it would be open. The King with the key. But the doors didn't open. I remained in front of it, hoping it would, week after week, but nothing happened. If I don't have hope, I don't know how I would live and go on day after day."

"You say, you can't live without hope? My friend, hope is our biggest enemy. It does not bring realization. It prolongs suffering." Carlos kept talking. "You know, when Pandora opened her box and released all the evils of mankind, the only one remaining in the box was hope. And since then, hope keeps flirting and deceiving human souls. People say that hope is an emotional state opposite of despair. But in reality, hope triggers despair. You are now in despair, my friend, and you wouldn't be if all you were doing, wasn't just hoping."

"But for me, Carlos," Michael said, "hope is essential in searching for the higher meaning of life when one is on the path often covered with a mist of the unknown before him. Faith in the unseen and hope of finding it, moved pilgrims for centuries in their discoveries, with no expectation of reward other than to understand our inner nature and the creation."

Carlos smiled and kept talking. "The concept called positive thinking people often confuse with hope. But they are different. Positive thinking is a state of mind while hope is a useless state of the heart. Positive thinking is about doing and hope is about feeling. So, positive thinking is what you need."

"Yes, but what should I do?" Michael asked. "For three

months everything seemed flawless. It felt like a completion of an alchemical process with all the right elements coming together in perfect harmony and then after that, nothing."

"So, you mentioned the answer yourself. Positive thinking, in your case, would mean trying to recreate the same conditions you had during that time. Think about the elements that were there, about the conditions. Think about what brought the feeling of perfect completion. Work on those elements. Strengthen them. Work on those conditions. Make them permanent. Chemical processes are a sensitive matter. Keep all the tools and vessels you are using clean at all times. Even if you have the right elements and conditions, the dirt of the vessels would corrupt the process, without you ever noticing. And the way I see you, you are sitting and hoping, and the dirt in your alchemical laboratory is piling up and it will be harder and harder for you to get anywhere like that."

"But I don't know how to recreate that process. It took years of work, going through different phases to come to this point. I know I am at the right place, yet nothing is working right."

"You know when I was a kid I wasn't good in math." Carlos continued like he didn't hear Michael's comment at all. "And I had a good teacher. She was maybe in her thirties, but she looked much younger. All the boys in school were in love with her, including me. Sometimes I was even happy that I wasn't doing things right because she would spend time with me trying to explain the right way and how to get to the correct result of a math problem. But most often, I wouldn't listen, I would just stare at her. I remember one thing. If you have a math problem to solve and you fill up pages and pages with different calculations and at the end, you come up with a wrong result, the only way to find a mistake is to go back to the beginning and re-check your calculations. She used to tell me, Carlos, you showed that you were working hard, but the result is wrong. You made a mistake. Go back to the beginning. So, I have the same advice for you. You claim you had the perfect result, but you don't know how you got there. To find if it was the right result, how you came to the point of perfection you are mentioning, you have to go back to your beginning, wherever that was."

Carlos always had smart words of advice. After they finished their coffee, Carlos gave Michael one hundred Euros. "Here, you may need this. You will give it back to me whenever you want." Then, he left. Michael stayed there thinking about his words. He was right.

But, where to go? What to do? Michael didn't know. He felt stuck. He felt stuck within himself. His mind, his soul, his heart, and his body all felt stuck. He knew that we all are our own creations. We are what we think and what we believe. And now all of his thoughts and all of his beliefs remained in that first weekend in Faro. He wanted it to last forever, but it was over and nothing seemed good afterward.

He went home. His home didn't feel warm anymore. He knew why. Before he knew how to be happy anywhere with anybody, at any place, because his true home was always in himself. But at that moment, he felt like he placed his home in somebody else's soul and that soul wasn't there. So, he felt misplaced in the place he lived. He had to do something. He had to regain his home. He lost himself. He had to regain himself.

'Carlos was right,' Michael thought. He had to go back to the beginning. But where was the beginning? He decided that he should go back to New York. He called Carlos and asked him if he would get him a ticket from Lisbon to New York. Carlos agreed. One hour later, Michael received a confirmation email for the flight next day at noon.

Early next morning, he packed in his backpack the laptop and the notebook Maria gave him for birthday. Everything else he left. The apartment keys he placed in the envelope and left in the mailbox for his landlord. He was planning to send him an email from New York. Michael didn't know what was he going to say to his landlord, but he would think about that later. He took the first train to Lisbon and then a cab to the airport, checked in and went straight to the passport control. He spent a few minutes waiting while a border policeman was checking his passport. Then the policeman turned the page and stamped it.

Michael continued walking to the terminal. 'My life is falling apart again,' he thought. 'Mercy and grace.' He felt exhausted.

The Hope of the Rose

35

Michael arrived at the Newark Airport at four o'clock in the afternoon. He walked out of the terminal building looking for a bus to Manhattan. With only fifty dollars in his pocket and no place to go, it was a repetition of his last return to New York.

As the bus was making a turn towards the entrance into Lincoln Tunnel, Michael could see across the Hudson River the panorama of the city. 'Another failure, another fight for survival,' he said to himself. He felt defeated. 'I spent all my life in vain. That is so sad,' he thought.

Once in Manhattan, he walked straight to the Bowery Mission.

At the entrance of the Bowery Mission, he bumped into Keith, the Mission Director. "Good afternoon, Director."

"Hi, Michael. How are you? Haven't seen you in a few months. Is it everything okay?" Director asked and looked at Michael with curiosity.

"Well, no Director, nothing is okay," Michael said with the heaviness in his voice.

"Why? What happened Michael?" Director asked and place his hand on Michael's shoulder, "Tell me."

"I am back. Messed up my life again, Director. So ashamed… I need a place to stay," he said after a deep sigh.

"I am sorry to hear that, Michael, but it happens. You are neither the first nor the last one. Many men come back to the Mission several times before they live on their own. You should not be ashamed. We will find a place for you here. You will regain your strength again. Come with me upstairs to the reception office."

Michael signed up again for a six-month recovery program in the Bowery Mission. Director Keith was his counselor. "I don't know if you knew that, but Pastor Charles transferred to our new facility in Harlem. It is better for him. It's closer to his home, and he will retire soon, anyway. So I will be your counselor."

Director Keith and Michael spent many hours talking about Michael's life. He wasn't a typical homeless man that took part in a program. Most of them were alcoholics or drug addicts and their reasons for becoming homeless were obvious. His reasons were unusual and deeper. And sometimes they were far above and over anything that Director Keith could apprehend, regardless of the rich experience he had with men in the recovery program.

Michael's moods were changing from day to day. Sometimes he was upbeat and full of energy. Other days he would be sad and on the verge of crying. In one session, he spoke about his dreams.

"You know," he started, "the reason I failed in my try to

get close to Maria was not my past. Both of us were dreamers, but she was still asleep and I was dreaming awake. I could not wake her. She was afraid to wake up with somebody who was dreaming awake. Dreaming awake is sometimes a dangerous thing. In trying to get to heaven you may end up in the hell."

"So, why don't you stop dreaming awake? Learn to control your dreams," Director said.

"It is easier to say than to do so. Coming so close to understanding my dreams and trying to turn my dreams into reality without success, left me torn apart between the world of dreams and reality."

"Did you ever think that you are dreaming so much because you are trying to avoid to face reality? Are you afraid of anything? Are you afraid of reality? You told to Pastor Charles once you would like to have a new beginning in life with this new woman you were chasing after in Portugal. Why do you want so much this new beginning? Do you think that the new beginning will postpone the end? Are you afraid of the end? Are you afraid of death Michael?"

"No, Director. For me, death is just another voyage. The natural continuation of things according to God's master plan. By itself, death is not sad or tragic. It is the sense of separation and loss that stay with those who remain behind in the world of living that brings sorrow. It is the same like with the falling tree in the forest. If nobody was there to hear it falling, did it make noise? If one departs this life and nobody was around to feel sorry, does that makes death tragic? No, it's just another voyage in the great adventure called Creation."

One day he came to Director's office with the little black notebook in his hands.

"Once in a while, I look at a little notebook she gave me. I know that everything written is the truth. I also know that I was not the only seeker of the Holy Grail."

"Holy Grail? What is for you the Holy Grail?" Director asked.

"It is the unconditional love thought to us by our Teacher from Nazareth. Red Rose plucked from the Garden in Heavens to be sacrificed for the sake of the ultimate lesson. One day, somebody will be worthy enough to fulfill the mission. Everything left for me are my memories—the weekend in Faro, when I was so close to it and so happy and so in love." – He cried. He slammed his fist into Director's desk, moaned, jumped, and ran out of the office. That was the only time Director saw him cry.

Most of the days, Michael would spend in the Mission Chapel meditating and praying or in the computer room writing. When Director asked him what was he writing about, he said:

"About the eighth door. Many years ago, a friend of mine told me to be careful when going through the eighth door. It is the one before the last and final, ninth door. The Eighth door is a revolving door. I would have to go straight through, not thinking about words. But I made a mistake. I was thinking about words and I kept spinning around. That brought me here. When I was back in Faro, I lived on the seventh floor. It was a sign for me I passed seven doors and that I am in front the eighth door. But I failed. I didn't pay attention. I didn't see that as a sign. But it will not happen again."

Director didn't understand what Michael was talking about, but he didn't want to ask further.

Director Keith read Michael's old file and Pastor Charles' notes; spoke with Pastor Charles on the phone several times after sessions with Michael; consulted with Pastor Paul; spoke with Michael's friend Grace and with his ex-wife Natasha. He tried to understand Michael and help with advice, but after a few sessions he gave up on that idea. Michael already knew what he was after in recovery program. The Bowery Mission was just a break for him. The way to regain his strength back and continue with whatever he was after. Men like him never gave up. So at the regular sessions with Michael, Director would just sit and listen to what Michael wanted to say.

Then one morning, just as Director arrived in his office, Michael ran in all excited. He had his backpack with him.

"Listen, I am leaving. I have to go home. It is time. Please, sign my discharge papers," Michael said.

"Hold on, slow down. Where are you going? Which home? Are you leaving the program? Sit down and tell me what happened?"

"Okay. I will, but I don't have too much time. It is time. The doors will close if I don't rush," he said, he sat down, then continued. "I was up all the last night in the Chapel praying. There was nobody else there but me. And then in the middle of the night, I had a visit. Archangel Michael came again and spoke.He told me that Gods decided that my punishments in this world are over. I paid for my crimes. My soul is restored as a pure soul of a righteous man. I will dream my dream again. I will go to the world of dreams and be with my Love again. Isn't that great?"

"Yes, Michael, that is great. But what about this world? What will you do when you walk out of here? Where will you go?" Director asked.

"That is not important, man. Wherever I go, whatever I do, it will be a success. Nothing can happen anymore. I am under protection."

"Whose protection Michael?" – Director asked.

"The one who taught me to love others as I love myself and to do unto others as I would want them to do unto me. Now I can do that. My punishment is over. I am a free man."

Then, he left. Keith wanted to stop him from leaving, but the Mission counselors don't have that authority. For a while, he worried that Michael did something stupid; like jump off the bridge; or walk off of the roof like his friend Chris; but Keith heard nothing. If something like that happened, he was sure he would hear about it.

It was nine thirty Thursday morning when Michael entered the lobby of the National Library of Portugal in Lisbon. He sat on the sofa opposite of the security desk. 'Carlos should come soon. He is never late,' he thought.

Carlos entered the lobby, approached and sat next to Michael. He was in his office in the Santa Maria hospital all morning and didn't have time to change. He was still in his whites.

"Olá Michael."

"Hi, Carlos. Thank you for coming. You are a real friend."

"Listen Michael. I don't know why I am doing this. Everybody is saying bad things about you. Wherever you go, whatever you do, there is a noise after you. If I tell our Masonic friends in New York that I am helping you, they would say I am crazy. In spite of everything, I respect your courage to go after your ideals, no matter what. Men like you make this world move. I know that the road you went is covered with thorns. But I also know that it must be a road to the stars. So, I brought you money you ask. If you are careful, it will last you for three months. I am sure you can find a room in Lisbon for two hundred a month. So try to manage. It is my gift to you. No need to repay me ever. If you ever get in a position to think about repaying me, give instead a donation to some animal shelter in my name. And please, don't call me soon to get you another ticket to New York," Carlos smiled here, "In last three months I bought you two tickets already. Or maybe, just give me enough notice in advance so I could find a good deal, ha, ha."

"Not to worry Carlos. This time, I have everything figured out."

"I hope so. You are an expensive friend to have Michael. So what did you figure out?"

"I figured out where the key to my purpose is."

"Where?" Carlos asked.

"Right here," Michael said.

"Here? In this Library?" Carlos asked.

"Yes. Or better to say, this is where the key will unlock the door of my purpose."

"I am not sure if I understand you?" Carlos asked.

"I was going after a woman believing that the key is in being with her. But the key is in writing about her. The key is in words and words are in me. Longing for her is just an impulse for words to come out. And the whole purpose is for words to come out. Words are important. Words about love. About life. And they are not my words. They are just channeled through me. Remember, in the beginning, there was the word, and the word was with God, and the word was God, and the word was made flesh. The whole purpose of all my life was to accumulate enough impulse for all the writings that need to be done. That is my mission. That is the Holy Grail I was after. There is so much despair in the world today. People are losing faith in God. Nobody believes in love anymore Carlos. Nobody. Hope, Love, and Kindness are today only empty phrases from the Sunday Bible school. People need love. They need hope. Hope of the Rose. But before they understand what hope of the Rose is, they need to hear the truth. The truth is important."

"Truth according to Michael?" Carlos said.

"Yes, according to Michael. It could be also according to Carlos, according to Maria, according to anybody. The name doesn't matter. But in each of us is a bit of Michael, ha, ha," Michael said, "and many don't like me because they recognize themselves in me. My truth belongs to all."

"And I assume this place is where you will write it?" Carlos asked while pointing at the glass door of the reading room.

"Yes. I love this space. I can sit here in the reading room surrounded by books and write all day. It is so quiet and inspiring. They have wi-fi. And it is free." Michael smiled.

"And young girls from the Lisbon University writing their school papers next to you," Carlos said with irony in his voice while shaking his head.

"Yes, I was thinking about the same thing. Isn't that nice ha, ha, but it won't make a difference. I'll be with my Maria."

"Whoever that is..." Carlos said and smiled.

About a year later, in New York, Director Keith was passing by the Barnes and Noble bookstore on Union Square. He saw a familiar face on a poster in the store window. It was an announcement of the book signing, *Bread of Life* by Michael Nicolau. He smiled and continued walking. 'Yes, Michael was right - he was under protection,' Director was thinking, 'I wonder if Michael ever passed through the eighth door. I'll ask him. I'll go to that book signing and ask him.'

Stevan V. Nikolic

About the Author

Stevan V. Nikolic grew up in Belgrade, Serbia, and moved to New York in 1987. He wrote nine narrative nonfiction books on various esoteric teachings before turning to fiction. Stevan's debut novel *Weekend In Faro*, the first in the *Michael Nicolau Series*, was published in 2014. *Truth According to Michael* is the second book in the same series. The follow-up, *e Diary of the New York Baker*, is due out March 2017. His books have been translated into several languages and published worldwide. To learn more, visit **www.svnikolic.com**.

www.ingramcontent.com/pod-product-compliance
Lightning Source LLC
Chambersburg PA
CBHW051206120726
47905CB00004B/1008